D0842782

# THE LEFT-HANDED POLICEMAN

*Also by Robert Westbrook*
Journey Behind the Iron Curtain
The Magic Garden of Stanley Sweetheart

# THE LEFT-HANDED POLICEMAN

## A NOVEL OF MURDER IN BEVERLY HILLS

*Robert Westbrook*

CROWN PUBLISHERS, INC.
NEW YORK

Published by Crown Publishers, Inc., 225 Park Avenue South, New York,
New York 10003
CROWN is a trademark of Crown Publishers, Inc.
Manufactured in the United States of America


**Library of Congress Cataloging-in-Publication data**

Westbrook, Robert.
    The left-handed policeman.

    I. Title.
PS3573.E827L44   1986        813'.54        85-24310
ISBN 0-517-55953-6


10  9  8  7  6  5  4  3  2  1
First Edition

*This is for Loam, Gabriel, and Torello—all my sons*

Do not go gentle into that good night . . .
Rage, rage against the dying of the light.

Dylan Thomas

Errata: At the bottom of page 305 the following lines
were dropped inadvertently:

---

himself tightly between the walls. His right hand was bloody and he
had scraped his knees. Just as he was catching his breath, he noticed
two cold, reptilian eyes upon him from a crack in the rock. He shivered
and kept going upward, faster than before.

The climb took more than half an hour. At last, battered and panting for breath, he pulled himself up on level ground. The ledge was
much larger than he had imagined from down below. It was a flat plateau, the width of a football field, and several miles long. Nicky
scrambled to his feet and pulled out his gun.

He heard a sound directly to his right.

He spun around.

# PART ONE

*On the First Day of Dying*

# 1

On Thursday afternoon, Lawrence Ferguson learned he was going to die. He was not much to look at: just a frail little man with a pinched face and worried, cavernous eyes. He had been losing weight the past two months, and folds of skin hung from his cheekbones, making him look a bit like a basset hound. He wore a crumpled brown suit that was too large.

In the City of Angels few people had ever given Lawrence Ferguson a second thought. He was not rich, not strong, not good-looking, not sexy, and not young.

Not only that: He did not drive a nice car, or have a great suntan, or hold an important job. Even his vices were few and nondescript, for he did not drink or gamble, or visit the sex shops on Hollywood Boulevard. He had certainly never considered cocaine.

As he sat in the waiting room on the third floor of the Santa Monica Hospital Medical Center, a fantasy was unfolding in his mind. He saw himself as he wished he could be: young and strong, running down the street with a gun in his hand.

*. . . He leveled the gun and took three neat shots at the car that was speeding away. He hit the rear tire, and the car spun crazily out of control, slamming into the side of a building. Still, the two men came out with their guns blazing, the flames from their revolvers lighting up the night. Cordite hung in the air. In the distance, sirens screamed.*

*There was a searing pain in his shoulder. He was hit.*

*A girl ran out of the car toward him, tears streaming down her face. "Larry! Larry! Are you okay?"*

"Lawrence . . . Mr. Lawrence Ferguson? Dr. Golden will see you now."

He returned reluctantly to the third-floor waiting room, where the nurse-receptionist was calling his name. A dread feeling clutched at his stomach, sent ripples through his body. He had come here today because a week earlier a biopsy had been done on a small lump embedded in his groin. Yesterday he had received a phone call saying he should return to the hospital as soon as possible. So he had come, fearfully, taking an extended lunch hour from his job at the Southern California Life Insurance Corporation, where he had worked as an accountant for the last twenty years.

*Something terribly wrong inside.*

He was tempted to stand up, walk away. Tell the receptionist it was all a mistake. He didn't really want to know. . . .

"Mr. Ferguson?" the receptionist called again. She was a cute blond girl with freckles on her nose and a deep tan from the beach. She was the sort of person people noticed in Southern California. Lawrence stood up, feeling very dizzy for a moment. He had to reach out and steady himself against the chair in front of him.

"Yes," he said, "I'm coming."

He moved across the room, a man with a habitual, apologetic stoop and a vague smile. The blond receptionist smiled back impersonally to a place a little above his right shoulder.

# 2

Dr. Golden looked up from his stack of papers and smiled. "Well, Mr. Ferguson, the test is positive," he announced brightly.

"Oh, that's good," Lawrence replied.

Dr. Golden frowned. There had been a slight misunderstanding due to the rather large gap between his cheerful manner and the information he was trying to impart. The doctor was not yet thirty and had worked so hard to arrive at this office that he had developed few social graces.

"Well, actually it's not so good," he said at last. "But perhaps not so bad either."

Now Lawrence was thoroughly lost. "I'm sorry. I don't understand."

"The tumor is malignant," the doctor said too loudly, irritated at his own confusion. "You have cancer, Mr. Ferguson."

"Cancer?" he repeated, in a whisper that was as dry as wind through a dusty canyon.

"Well, a form of cancer," the doctor said, trying to retreat a little. "But don't be frightened by mere words. Actually, at this early stage, the prognosis is far from certain. . . ." He let go a string of big words, ten-letter words. He was quite cheerful again, now that he was back on

4

familiar ground. He spoke as if he were addressing a classroom of interns, with just a smile here and there for punctuation. As if to say, Aren't I clever to know all these things?

Lawrence could not understand a word the doctor was saying. He stopped understanding after the single word that so overshadowed all the others: *cancer.*

He saw the doctor's lips moving, but the young man might just as well have been speaking Japanese. And why the doctor was so cheerful—smiling, in fact—was quite beyond his comprehension. Maybe the doctor was glad he was going to die. Was that it?

They would all be glad. Lawrence's face drained of color. He looked off, past the doctor, to the window and the sprawl of Los Angeles three stories below. The thought that went through his head most clearly was, simply, *It's not fair!* There he was, forty-seven years old, a balding certified public accountant who had worked for twenty years at the Southern California Life Insurance Corporation and had been promoted only twice. None of the good things of life had ever come his way . . . and now he was going to die.

*It was really, without a doubt, not at all fair.*

The doctor was setting up a time for him to check into the hospital. Lawrence nodded and retained nothing. He was no longer distracted or agitated. He drifted . . .

*. . . to the street at night, where the smell of gunfire still hung in the air. Two men lay dead on the pavement by the smashed car. He clutched his shoulder where the hot blood seeped out, and sank back on the sidewalk, while the sirens screamed ever closer.*

*The girl was above him now. She cradled his head in her lap and offered relief.*

*"It's all right, Larry. I love you," she said. "I'm going to take care of you forever. . . ."*

# 3

It was a bland L.A. afternoon in mid-October, unseasonably warm. A shroud of smog covered the city. Lawrence was due back at work. But he did not even consider returning to Southern Cal Life. Driving back along Santa Monica Boulevard he actually ran a red light. Deliberately. A driver in the intersection honked at him angrily, but he did not care. Why should he? He felt too restless to drive directly home, and so he continued to the end of the boulevard, where the gray, insipid sky merged into the greater gray of the ocean. Lawrence parked by the Santa Monica Pier and walked out to the end, where the fishermen stood patiently, their lines cast down into murky waters.

He bought an ice cream cone and licked thoughtfully, staring out at the swelling Pacific. The waters stretched beyond the horizon, farther than he could see. Was death like that? He could see himself floating head down on the waves. Rocked by eternity . . . No, it was impossible to imagine. Not for Lawrence Ferguson, who once had a mother and a father, who had been a child in Bakersfield, California. He would not allow it.

The fisherman beside him on the pier pulled up a small, shimmering perch from the water. The fish wiggled frantically, wide-eyed. The fisherman casually pulled out the hook and tossed the fish into a white plastic bucket.

Lawrence watched the fish slowly die. Its spasms grew further apart, and within a few minutes it lay still.

He was glad he saw this, somehow. Dying made you feel so monstrously alone.

*But if others were to die with you?* Now there was a thought. But he felt weak and his head hurt from so much thinking. Lawrence Ferguson walked back along the pier, accompanied by the sharp cries of sea gulls, found his car, and drove home.

# 4

I t was almost evening by the time he arrived at his studio apartment just a few blocks from the beach in Santa Monica. This area where he lived was called Venice, for its several tired canals, awash with garbage. The neighborhood was inhabited by junkies, gays, old people, and a few straggling romantics, leftovers from the sixties—all refugees from the city at large.

Lawrence's building, the Cresswell Arms, was a solid old stucco affair with narrow windows, built in the early 1940s when Santa Monica was still fashionable. Lawrence did not mind the shabbiness. He had taken his apartment five years earlier because from one window he could actually see the Pacific Ocean shining a wonderful blue on clear days, like a promise.

He took the narrow elevator up to the fifth floor. A light had burned out weeks before in the hallway and had not been replaced. The gloom was so thick that Lawrence could barely see the lock to his front door—but his hand knew the way, guided by the years.

He threw open the front door, switched on the TV, and went to the kitchenette to take out a frozen dinner and pop it into the oven. Salisbury steak.

A long arduous sigh escaped his lips as he waited for his dinner to heat. His body seemed to deflate like an old tire. His eyes fell wearily upon the room that contained his life: a Formica table, a narrow single bed, an armchair purchased from the Salvation Army, a color TV. On the walls were a number of posters and cards from the desert southeast of Los Angeles, scenes of cactus and desert sunsets. But most were of television personalities, cut out from magazines and *TV Guide,* and thumbtacked all over the walls. He preferred the cop shows to the soaps and melodramas.

He had arrived home just in time for a six o'clock rerun of his favorite series, "Cassie and the Cop," about a beautiful young woman—Cassie—who is married to a policeman and decides to outsmart her husband by doing a little detecting on her own. Everyone on the show was good-looking and did interesting things all the time. Even the villains were always rich, with a stable of mistresses, fancy servants, and elegant houses.

He tried to line up his television viewing a week in advance. A good night was one where "Cassie and the Cop" was followed by reruns of "Charlie's Angels," "Magnum, P.I.," "The Rookies," and an eleven-thirty showing of "Columbo."

But it was Cassie herself who appealed to him the most. She was fresh and all-American, yet naughty and sexy as well. Once he had tried to masturbate, imagining Cassie and himself together. But he did not get very far. Not even in his most farfetched fantasies could he imagine a girl like that in bed with a man like him.

Still, five nights a week, from six to seven, he could join her and live in her world, which seemed so much more vivid than his own.

Tonight, however, he was still too restless to follow the plot—something about heroin being smuggled into the country in the racket of an international tennis star. Some racket! There were all kinds of characters Lawrence couldn't quite sort out.

It was during the second commercial that he got up, went to his closet, and pulled out a small .22 caliber pistol from the back of the top shelf. From a drawer he got a box of shells, which he brought with him back in front of the TV.

Cassie was flirting with the tennis star–dope fiend, trying to get to his racket.

Lawrence fingered the cold hard steel of the gun. It was not much of a gun. He had bought it two years before, at a time when the TV news was full of a homosexual killer who had raped and mutilated nine young boys before police gunned him down in the bushes at Roxbury Park.

Lawrence always followed such crimes on the news with grim satisfaction.

He felt it was his civic duty, really, at such a time to own a gun. Owning a gun thrilled him. For a few months he had carried himself with a new degree of self-importance. He sometimes brought out the gun and held it in his lap while watching the detective shows on television.

He had never actually fired the gun, or even put a bullet in the magazine. But today, on this most unusual Thursday, he opened the box of shells and took out one small bullet. He rolled the bullet between his fingers: It felt good. Powerful.

It was death. He opened the magazine and placed the small metallic piece of death inside.

On TV, the tennis star had Cassie in his bedroom. She was being terribly seductive, without actually letting him kiss her. Because she was a good girl, after all. Good girls did not kiss villains.

Lawrence Ferguson opened his mouth and placed the barrel so it was pointing upward toward his brain. He had seen this done on a show once. He stayed with the pistol in his mouth for many long minutes, while the images flickered across the screen. Finally, he sighed and lowered his arm and the gun back to his side.

It wouldn't do to kill yourself when there were still fifteen minutes left to go of "Cassie and the Cop." The ending was terrific; he put the gun down on the floor. Cassie was on the bad guy's yacht. The scene allowed her to wear a bikini that showed off her beautiful legs and figure. . . . Lawrence had not made love with many women. And none of them, certainly, had ever looked like *that*.

He followed the climactic scene with rapt attention. The tennis star covered Cassie with his gun. The image of the hard, potent gun pointing at Cassie's sweet, flat stomach caused an uncomfortable stirring in his pants ... but she knocked the gun away with a swift karate kick. They wrestled in the crowded interior of the expensive boat, crashing into lamps and glasses, and throwing bottles of champagne at each other. The music behind them was swift and terse. Cassie ran out of the cabin on to the deck. The villain grabbed his gun and ran after her.

She was on the deck. He aimed the gun, was about to shoot her dead ... when a shot rang out, and the villain clutched himself in agony and took a long, slow fall off the deck into the water.

On the dock stood Cassie's husband, the cop, pistol smoking in his hand. He had arrived, as always, in the nick of time to save scatter-brained Cassie.

The husband and wife had a really cute little argument about a woman's place ... and the show was over.

Lawrence watched the coming attractions. Then he did the most unusual thing he had done in years. He walked over to the TV and turned off a rerun of "The Rockford Files."

He paced restlessly. He sat down in his armchair and got up again three separate times. Then, decisively, he rose one last time, took out an overly large sports jacket from his closet, stuffed the small pistol and the box of shells carefully into different pockets, and took his car keys from the dresser top.

Armed, and very dangerous, Lawrence Ferguson stepped out into the night.

# 5

The evening was warm and close. Though it was mid-October, the gray mist that had been upon them all day long now held in the city heat like the lid on a pot.

Lawrence wound down all the car windows, turned on the radio to his favorite light rock station, and drove for hours in no particular direction. He had no plan. Motion itself seemed to offer some relief. But he found himself drawn eventually to Beverly Hills, where quite often a Rolls-Royce would drift past, or a long black limo with opaque windows so that you could only imagine which famous person might be inside.

Maybe Cassie herself might be in one of those long cars.

Lawrence drove a 1982 Ford Galaxie that was a vague brownish gold. He drove into Hollywood along Sunset Boulevard, part of an endless river of traffic. In Hollywood, all things competed for attention: neon signs flashed in vivid colors, radios blared, hairstyles beckoned, sex called like a wolf. There were prostitutes and break dancers, con artists and cops. A girl in a gold bikini drifted by on skates. In all this glitter, the little man in the brown-gold Ford caught no one's eye. He drove and watched. The pistol lay ready next to him on the seat.

And because it was a warm night, and the car windows were open and convertible tops were down, Lawrence came within inches of the other worlds that were people. He caught little pieces of conversations. He was curious about all these cars and people; he turned off his car radio so that he could listen in more effectively. It became a game he played with the traffic—to pick out a certain interesting car and try to stay alongside, or directly behind, for as long as he could. The goal was to come to a stoplight at the same time as the other car, and for a few moments to be right there, alongside, just inches away from the other people.

A red Corvette convertible caught his eye. There was a good-looking man behind the wheel and a very attractive young woman next to him. How carefree they seemed! Lawrence followed them for half a dozen blocks, weaving in and out of traffic so that he could be near them.

At the corner of Sunset and Vermont he succeeded in coming to a red light beside the Corvette. He was on the right-hand side of them, and since his car was higher off the ground, he could look right down on them.

The girl was young and really pretty. She couldn't have been more than nineteen. The man was older, maybe thirty-five, but ruggedly handsome, tanned.

The radio was playing. They were laughing. Lawrence could smell the girl's perfume: something fresh and flowery. But close as he was, the couple didn't notice him at all, staring out his open window at them.

Suddenly the girl reached down to the man's crotch, pulled down his zipper, and took his cock in her mouth.

They laughed mischievously.

The girl said, "Mmmm . . ."

Then the light turned green, and the Corvette hurried forward. Lawrence was so stunned that he simply sat there watching the car drive away. His left hand clutched the steering wheel. His right hand held the gun.

Absently, he made a right turn on Vermont Avenue and kept making right turns around the block until he was back on Sunset again, heading toward Beverly Hills.

For Lawrence this was beyond imagining: to be rich and good-looking, and have a beautiful young girl do such intimate things, as you drove along in your fancy sports car!

Why hadn't anything like that ever happened to him? It was so goddamned unfair!

He continued driving west on Sunset Boulevard, but he wasn't just vague and aimless now. It had all crystallized, and Lawrence knew exactly what he was doing.

He was hunting.

# 6

It was cat and mouse for many hours, up and down Sunset. He felt wonderfully calm and in control. The workers in the accounting department at Southern California Life would not have recognized the deft, decisive way Lawrence moved through traffic, stalking, waiting, jockeying into position.

There were a few near hits, aborted at the last moment. He did not mind. He was more patient than stone.

A brand-new white Rolls-Royce joined the river of traffic two cars ahead. Lawrence ruthlessly cut in front of an old MG so he could come up on the Rolls from the left lane. At the next stoplight, on Sunset and La Cienega, he was able to glide up directly alongside his intended victim.

The driver of the Rolls was a hippie. From the rear he had thought he was following a woman, but now he saw he was a man with long, curly hair that fell below his shoulders. Maybe a rock star. The young man, whoever he was, had dark circles beneath his eyes and seemed totally preoccupied. Music played loudly in his car.

At the light, without warning, the long-haired young man glanced up to the car next to him and found Lawrence's eyes hotly upon him. He snorted contemptuously and darted forward with the changing light.

Lawrence was furious. "You think I'm admiring your car?" he shouted. "Maybe I want your autograph?"

He kept up with the Rolls for another block. The next light was green and both cars sailed through at thirty-five miles per hour. The driver of the expensive car seemed to have forgotten him. He did not glance in his direction again.

The next light was amber. The two cars arrived at the corner of Doheny side by side, just as the light turned red.

Lawrence took a deep breath and raised the gun to the open window at the passenger's side.

What caught his eye? He wasn't certain. Somewhere in the corner of his vision, a familiar shape. There was a cop car standing in the gas station across the street. Lawrence quickly dropped his gun hand out of the window to the seat.

When the light changed, the Rolls-Royce, unconcerned with the nearness of death, turned up Doheny toward the expensive homes above. Lawrence, his heart pounding very fast, continued straight along Sunset.

# 7

It was after one o'clock in the morning when Lawrence came to a red light at the western edge of the Sunset Strip that led toward the residential streets of Beverly Hills. He was drowsy, for it was long past his regular bedtime, and he didn't see the light change to green. The car behind him honked impatiently. It seemed to Lawrence a very rude and abrasive noise. He looked in his rearview mirror and saw a silver Mercedes-Benz sports convertible, top down, with a man at the wheel.

The Mercedes driver honked again, ordering him out of the way. As soon as they cleared the intersection, the expensive sports car swooshed into the left lane and passed him with casual arrogance. To Lawrence, this was like saying, *You don't count in your Ford Galaxie . . . move over, for these streets are not for you.*

Up ahead, the Mercedes crossed back into the right lane, slowed down, and seemed to forget all about him. The insult was complete. He had been merely something in the way, to be passed and forgotten by some high-powered businessman in a hurry to be someplace else.

Lawrence sped up to come alongside the Mercedes and have a better look. With a mystical certainty, he knew this was the moment he had been waiting for all night long. His lips were pressed together, bloodless and thin. Within a block, he had narrowed the distance between the two cars, so that he was trailing just a few feet behind on the left. He could see the other driver clearly now—a distinguished-looking man of early middle age, with hair that was starting to gray. He was wearing a well-cut and obviously expensive suit. Lawrence came up alongside, but the man in the sports car still did not look his way.

They sat out one red light together near the Beverly Hills Hotel. Lawrence could smell the rich leather of the Mercedes's seats. He was in no hurry now, just savoring everything. He felt larger than life, as if he were in a movie.

The man exuded wealth and power. But Lawrence had the power of life and death, and wealth was nothing compared to that.

They drove another half mile, almost side by side, until they came to another red light. Lawrence was still in the left lane, and there was not another car around.

"Excuse me," he called out his right-hand window. "Can you tell me how to get to Roxbury Drive?"

"What?"

"Roxbury Drive!"

The man in the Mercedes looked over to the nondescript car and the rumpled little man inside. At the last second of his life he saw the gun pointing rigidly out the window, inches away. It was too late.

The gun made a little pop. Not a big sound at all. But the man in the Mercedes had a hole in his forehead, and he slumped over to the passenger's side, staring emptily at the night sky.

Lawrence made a left turn, drove carefully through the quiet streets of Beverly Hills until he came to Santa Monica Boulevard. Which took him home.

# PART TWO

*The Left-Handed Policeman*

# 1

**L**ate Thursday night, Lt. Nicholas Rachmaninoff, chief investigator of the Beverly Hills homicide department, sat at home playing an old Steinway upright piano.

Growing up in California with a long Russian name, he had received a plethora of nicknames: Nick, Nico, Nicky, even Rocky, and most recently—among a growing number of colleagues at work—the Rock Man. Occasionally, someone would go all the way and call him Nicholas. Generally, these were ladies on a romantic quest.

He didn't particularly care. He answered to all his names, without prejudice. But he thought of himself as Nicky, which was the oldest name of all, what his mother had called him.

Nick-y. A childish name, perhaps. But he was a childlike man, who had somehow managed to arrive at middle age without ever having completely grown up.

Nicky lived high in the Hollywood Hills, in the last house on a road called Sunshine Terrace, which veered up at crazy angles from Laurel Canyon. It was a country cabin standing on a quarter-acre of land, among manzanita and oak trees and long grass, perched at the very top of the ridge overlooking the city below. His father had bought this place back in the late forties when Sunshine Terrace was still a dirt road and few people wanted to live here, besides starving actors and eccentric policemen.

Almost everything had changed since that time. The starving actors of the forties became the establishment of a later age. The quaint canyons and beaches where they lived were now fashionable, expensive, and overcrowded. The hills around Sunshine Terrace had become covered with houses, many on long stilts, hanging over the cliffs at ridiculous angles in order to utilize every last inch of ground.

Today, much of the music industry lived here, as well as screenwriters, directors, actors, and photographers, who had not quite made it to the dizzy heights that would allow them residence in Beverly Hills or Bel Air.

Only the house at the very end of Sunshine Terrace had not changed; it seemed to defy change. Nicholas Rachmaninoff had grown up in this cabin. He had seen his mother die, his father die; he had been a young married man here, a father himself, and now he was a bachelor again, once more on his own. Everything, in fact, had changed except for this little cabin, which seemed to exist out of time, perpetually in need of a new coat of paint. It was still visited by families of raccoons that managed to pass on from generation to generation the secrets of how to get into his garbage, and still surrounded by the same long grass, manzanita, and gnarled oak trees that whispered in the wind.

Nicky had often wondered why he had not sold this house and left. All the people he had ever loved here were gone. Recently, he had begun to leave out little bits of food for the raccoons, afraid they might be the last raccoons left in Hollywood.

Tonight he had been drinking both beer and wine, which was a dangerous and emotional combination, and led to thoughts like this. He sat at his piano with a can of beer within easy reach on the floor, playing a slow gospel blues, going back and forth from a big fat G chord to a C, and holding it together with a shuffled, syncopated bass.

Nicky was left-handed, which probably had no bearing whatsoever on his performance as a cop. But as a blues piano player, being left-handed was a definite advantage. He could keep a figured bass pattern going for hours, leaving his right hand free to wander and doodle independently up and down the ivories.

This was not music so much as a form of meditation. His mind would drift and float about on all kinds of matters. Quite a few of his cases had been solved right here, worked out on the Steinway.

This morning, an ancient Beverly Hills matron—eighty-nine years old with a face like a Sun Maid raisin—had heard a commotion on her doorstep. Convinced it was a robber-rapist-murderer she put down her knitting, took one of her dead husband's many handguns, and flung open the front door. It was the mailman, and she shot him dead.

The old lady had lived in a crumbling old mansion on North Rodeo Drive, with only a nurse and a television set for company. She had hardly left her house in the last ten years, and her only image of the outside world came from television. Judging from what she saw, it was clearly prudent to remain barricaded at home with a gun in easy reach. She was still convinced she had saved herself from great harm.

This Beverly Hills matron was so old and senile that Nicky was trying to avoid putting her in jail even for a few hours. At this moment, she was under something that resembled house arrest. A police-

18

woman—as a favor to him—was staying with her and the nurse, while he tried to track down any living relative who might take her off his hands. So far, nobody wanted to claim the old woman at all. Tomorrow he would have to book her. She had, of course, killed somebody, and couldn't be left free to do it again. The whole thing was a shame. The mailman had a wife and two kids who weren't thrilled about the situation either.

He stopped playing long enough to get another beer from the refrigerator. When he returned to the piano, he discovered that the progression from G to C was no longer really making it for him. He changed the pattern to a G major 9th moving to an A minor 9th, and back again. This had the effect of changing decades and styles, from the thirties blues to a more modern sadness.

Nicky was not quite forty years old. A few weeks before he had awakened in the night and come up with this idea that he was going through a midlife crisis. Ordinarily, he tried to avoid these labels of pop psychology. But midlife crisis had a certain appealing concreteness about it. Also, he had to admit, it corresponded fairly accurately to what he had seen in others, as they approached that significant age of forty: usually arriving at a first or second divorce, with a child or two, and pressures of all kinds.

It was when you asked yourself: What am I doing all this for? Who am I? And whither am I going? Questions that you asked when you were seventeen and going through your teenage crisis. Except now you were older and less resilient, and more afraid of the answers.

Well, Nicholas Rachmaninoff was a fighter. As soon as he had given it a name, he tried to strike back. Tonight, as a part of a deliberate effort to expand his horizons, get out of the house more and meet new people, he had accepted an invitation to a party that he normally would have shunned. Two attractive young women, models from New York, had moved in four houses away. A few days earlier, as he had been driving home from work, they had been outside their new house, struggling with an impossibly heavy sofa. Nicky had stopped to lend a neighborly hand; the girls were grateful and delighted when he told them no, he was not an actor, he was a police lieutenant.

He had taken a bottle of Pinot Noir and walked down Sunshine Terrace in an optimistic mood to spend some time with his new neighbors. His first shock came when he saw that he was more than a decade older than anyone else in the room. This was a gathering of young Hollywood hopefuls. Linda, one of the long-legged models, seemed to like him. Nicky ended up drinking too much, flirting with her, and feeling ridiculous and out of place.

This just wasn't his scene. Music blared. Small talk went on a rampage. There was lots of talk of auditions and opportunities and important people who really liked your work and were going to call *next week.*

Linda had a very lovely figure, but her face was a little too long and horsey. She posed seductively, asking questions about his gun, if he had ever shot anybody. Nicky knew the type too well. He grew more and more depressed. When she rejoined the rest of her guests, telling him with a significant look that she would get back to him *later,* he quietly slipped away and walked home.

The piano was a better friend. And yet . . . maybe he should have stayed. God knew he could use getting laid. It was unfortunate to be too much of a romantic to enjoy casual sex.

Well, fuck it all!

He hit a truly nasty chord: a D dominant 7th, with a flat 9, sharp 13, and the third finger falling at random. A chord like two garbage trucks colliding, dissonance upon dissonance.

He got up from the piano and began walking toward the kitchen to get yet another beer. The phone rang.

He glanced at the kitchen clock. It was almost one-thirty in the morning.

"Hello?"

"Hey, Rock Man" came the familiar voice of Sgt. Kim Lee from the station. "I got a hot one for you, pardner. We have a stiff in a Mercedes-Benz on Sunset and Edgeworth Road. The guy's been shot in the head."

"Do we know who he is yet?"

"Only that the car is registered to a Gerald Eastman. The CHP is there. They got the first call from someone passing by. Our lab guys are on the way. And I've called you. That's all that's been done so far."

"Okay, Kim. I'll be there in ten minutes. Give a call to Charlie Cat, will you?"

"Sure thing, Rock Man. Hasta la pasta."

*Hasta la pasta?* Kim had been born in Korea, had learned his English from American Westerns, and came out with the strangest malapropisms. Maybe he was only joking. With Kim, you could never tell.

Nicky reached in a drawer for his small, snub-nosed .38 revolver and slipped it into the holster on his belt. It was more a prop than a weapon. In his somewhat cushy assignment in Beverly Hills he did not have to use his gun very often.

Which was just as well. Lieutenant Rachmaninoff had been one of the worst shots ever to graduate from the Los Angeles Police Academy.

He gave one more look in the mirror. His eyes looked puffy. Too much beer and abuse. He yawned deeply to try to get the oxygen going in his body. An hour before he had almost smoked a joint, but decided he'd better lay off.

Thank God for that. He was fairly hardened to the grisly sights that sometimes came his way. But murder, when you were stoned, was no fun.

# 2

Nicky owned an aging Austin-Healey sports car that loved these narrow canyon roads. On this early Friday morning, he fairly glided down out of the hills onto Sunset like a bird swooping down on the city.

He could tell from the flares on the side of the road, the bright lights, the ambulance, many cop cars, that he was the last to arrive. The CHP had the entire area blocked off. A young highway patrolman with a flashlight was controlling traffic, urging on the ambulance chasers.

Nicky had to show his shield to get past the police barricade. Because he looked more like an assistant professor of literature than a lieutenant in homicide, he was used to showing his shield. He parked in a driveway and made his way to the body.

Surrounded by a ring of police and lab specialists, bathed in white, unreal light, the body lay in the Mercedes convertible, slumped over onto the passenger side. The bullet hole in the forehead had not bled very much. It gave the body a mystical, Indian look. Tim Mathews from the police lab nodded in his direction and held up five fingers: five minutes and the body would be his. Until then, the deceased belonged entirely to the fact finders and specimen gatherers, who might be called on months from now to stand in some courtroom and testify that yes, the body's left foot was resting three and a half inches from the brake pedal.

Outside the circle of specialists, Det. Sgt. Charles Katz stood by himself looking grumpy. This was Charlie Cat. Appropriately, he *did* look vaguely catlike; with his moonish face, comfortable stomach, and his generally satisfied expression, he looked about to purr.

Charlie was Nicky's partner—his subordinate really, though neither man thought in terms of rank. Together, they were the homicide department of the Beverly Hills police station. *Rock Man and the Cat.*

Charlie was a gourmet chef, read classical Chinese, and was a champion chess player. But none of the qualities were apparent on the street, where he aspired to be only a cool dude. Barely literate.

"Hey, Rock Man. How's it, buddy?"

They shook hands absently. Nicky saw right away that his partner was not purring tonight. He shook his head. "Fuck, what a time for some asshole murder!"

"What's the matter?"

"What'sa matter?" he echoed. "The man wants to know what'sa matter? I'll tell you, for chrissake! I just spent $150 wining and dining the most gorgeous nineteen-year-old girl you could hope to imagine. We had just got back to my apartment and were getting into the good stuff when that idiot Korean calls from the station with all this hey, pardner shit, telling me to get my ass down here. Christ! She was licking my balls when the goddamn phone rang!"

Charlie was always telling him the graphic details of his widely varied sex life, expecting the same in return from Nicky, in which he was always disappointed.

"Have you looked at the corpse yet?" Nicky asked sarcastically.

Charlie shrugged, as though getting murdered on Sunset Boulevard was nothing compared to what he had gone through tonight. "Looks like a small-caliber pistol, one shot to the head. Very close range."

Nicky looked back to the Mercedes. The police photographers were having their turn now. Flashbulbs exploded in the night.

"I'll tell you what, Charlie. Why don't you go on back to your little nineteen-year-old, and I'll take care of the business here tonight."

He didn't add his unfinished thought: I might as well be the one to stay. No one is waiting in *my* bed.

The Cat was uncharacteristically quiet and made no move to go home.

"Well, what's the matter now?"

"I kicked her out. Sent her home," he said defensively. And then, under Nicky's continuing, speculative gaze, "I mean, I hardly knew the chick. I'm not going to leave her alone in my apartment with my stereo and all my records, for chrissake!"

Nicky burst out laughing. It was the first real laugh he had had in weeks. Sometimes it seemed a man like Nicky needed a man like Charlie around him, to keep a sense of the ridiculous.

The circle of men around the Mercedes opened up, and Tim Mathews and Dave Wahlburg of the coroner's office came out to greet the two detectives.

"How long has he been dead?" Nicky asked.

"Less than forty-five minutes," Dave replied. "The body's still warm."

"You didn't find a gun in the car?"

"No way." Tim laughed.

A gun inside the car would have indicated a probable suicide, which would have saved everyone a great deal of work. Nicky walked over to the body, with Tim and Charlie Cat behind him. When he reached the car, he simply stared at the dead man for several minutes, taking in the expensive clothes, the gold wristwatch, the well-shined shoes, and small diamond cuff links protruding from the jacket sleeves. This was one urbane gentleman. The bullet had not disfigured the man's face. He looked like someone you would see at a table in one of the more expensive restaurants around town. He was well shaved, and still smelled vaguely of cologne, though this was mixed with the smell of death-loosened bowels.

"Charlie, why don't you take someone and go around to some of the houses nearby? Maybe someone noticed something." Nicky glanced up at the castles that lined this quiet stretch of Sunset Boulevard. Would anyone inside be aware of anything so commonplace as what was happening outside their gates? "Also take a good look in the bushes, on both sides of the street," he added.

"Now *there's* a fun job," Charlie grumbled. But he tapped a uniformed cop nearby, and the two of them walked off to do as they were told.

The dead man looked as if he'd just spent a comfortable and elegant evening with friends and was perhaps returning home, when this ultimate interruption occurred. Nicky explored the interior of the car, front seat and back, opening the ashtrays and various side pockets. The car was immaculate. In the glove compartment were neatly folded road maps and an owner's manual for this particular Mercedes-Benz model.

He had been putting off examining the body itself. "Anyone find a wallet?" he asked the men behind him.

"It's in the inside breast pocket of the sports jacket."

"May I?"

"Go right ahead."

Nicky reached gingerly into the jacket and pulled out the man's leather billfold. Inside he found several hundred dollars cash, a driver's license and car registration slip, an assortment of credit cards, photographs, and a small address book. Whatever the motive was for this crime, it wasn't robbery. Nicky took his find back to his Austin-Healey, where he could sit down and examine it at leisure. He opened his glove compartment for his police radio.

"Hey, Rock Man," came the voice of Sergeant Lee. "How's it going out there, pardner?"

"I'm not sure yet, Kim. I got a name for you. Gerald Eastman, 1440 Lomimar Drive, Beverly Hills. Can you run it through the computer?"

"Sure can. Be back to you in five minutes."

Nicky sat in his car with the dead man's billfold. There was a photograph of a very pretty girl wearing a tiny bikini. She smiled at the camera. Pretty nice smile, Nicky thought. Not posed or phony. The address book would bear some careful scrutiny, but at first glance the billfold and its contents appeared just what you would expect from a man who drove around town late at night in a $40,000 car.

The radio squawked out his number.

"I'm here, Kim."

"Okay. Gerald Eastman. No criminal record, just the usual traffic offenses, and one drunk driving charge five years ago. The man's a big-shot movie lawyer. We know about him because he was involved in working out some liability stuff with us a few years ago. They wanted to film inside the old Hollywood station, and he was the spokesman from M.G.M. We have him down as married . . . and that's about it."

"Listen, I want to go see the wife. It's just a few blocks away, if she's home. Will you give her a call for me? Say it's about her husband, but leave it vague. Tell her that sexy Lieutenant Rachmaninoff is on his way and will explain everything in due course. Okay? Otherwise she probably won't let me in this hour of the night."

"A woman not let you in? My God, what's this city come to?"

"Not safe for sex fiends," he said. "See you later."

24

"Alligator" was the rejoinder, and the radio went dead.

Nicky stared out moodily at the scene of the crime. The bright work lights made it look like a movie set. The lead actor in the expensive silver sports car had only one expression, but that was true of quite a few actors Nicky could think of. It was a peculiar spot for a murder. If the gun had been fired from outside the car, as it appeared, then somebody had been waiting, either in another car or on foot. But who had known that Gerald Eastman would be passing this way at one o'clock in the morning?

Nicky began to sketch out possible scenarios . . . a jealous wife? Surely, a man like this must have had a complex love life. An angry business rival? A greedy relative? Nicky, in his fifteen years on the force, had seen them all.

"Jesus, buddy," he said aloud. "Maybe someone just didn't like the color of your car."

# 3

Lomimar Drive lay in the flats of Beverly Hills, between Sunset and Santa Monica boulevards. Nicky pulled up to a large, Spanish-style house set well back from the road. A light was on in an upstairs bedroom and in a room on the ground floor.

He walked up to an elaborate front door—a portico of heavy carved oak and wrought-iron grillwork—pulled out his police shield and rang the bell. Footsteps sounded from inside, and then a heavily guarded grille opened before him. The inhabitants of Beverly Hills did not fling their doors wide to strangers.

"Yes?" came an equally guarded, feminine voice.

Nicky held up his shield to the open grille for inspection. "Lieutenant Rachmaninoff of the Beverly Hills Police Department, ma'am. I asked Sergeant Lee to call and say I was on my way over. . . . It's about Gerald Eastman."

A series of locks and bolts was thrown open, and then the door itself, revealing a very pretty woman who was clutching her robe and looking at him anxiously. It was the blond woman in the photograph from the dead man's wallet. He had imagined her as not a wife but a girlfriend.

25

She was older now than in the photo, possibly in her early thirties, but the years had treated her well, the clinging robe suggesting a very provocative body.

"What's this about Gerald?" she asked.

"You're Mrs. Eastman?"

"Yes, yes! Now please tell me before I lose my mind."

Their eyes locked together. Hers were hazel. Specks of gold and blue and green. Intelligent eyes, opened very wide.

"Your husband is dead. I'm sorry."

The eyes seemed to get wider still. "Dead?"

"He's been murdered, Mrs. Eastman. Shot while he was driving home."

The blood drained from her face. Her eyes broke away from his and she stepped back blindly.

Nicky closed the door behind him. The foyer opened into a large, comfortable room with deep sofas, thick carpets, and an old brick fireplace. One entire wall consisted of sliding glass doors looking out to a swimming pool and patio. Spanish-Hollywood-Modern. Pretty Mrs. Eastman sat down limply on a sofa. "Shot?" she repeated softly.

"I'm sorry."

She covered her face with her hands. But a moment later she stood up. "I want to see him. Where is he?" she demanded.

"Well, actually, just a few blocks away. The shooting happened on the corner of Sunset and Edgeworth."

"Take me there. *Please.* I want to see him."

"Okay, Mrs. Eastman. If you want."

She was about to walk out the front door. Nicky said, "Umm, hadn't you better put something more on?"

She looked down dumbly at the light robe she was wearing. "Oh . . . yes, I'll be right back."

She disappeared up a curved red-tile staircase to the second floor. "I'm going to use your phone, to tell them we're coming," he called after her. By dialing the communications room at the station, he was able to get patched through to Sergeant Katz's patrol car at the scene of the crime.

"How's it going, Charlie?"

"The lab boys are finished, Rock Man. The coroner is about to take the body away."

"Okay. Tell them to wait another ten minutes. I'm bringing the dead man's wife over to get a peek. She might have something useful to tell us."

"Okay. They won't like waiting, but I'll manage."

"Thanks, Charlie. I'll see you in a few."

Mrs. Eastman came down the stairs wearing jeans and a cotton shirt. Even with her hair messed up, no makeup on, and in a state of near shock, she was an eye-catching woman. Gerald Eastman had lived his life surrounded by nice-looking things.

They walked to his ancient Austin-Healey without speaking.

"I used to have an old Austin like this," she said numbly. "It seems like ten lifetimes ago."

Driving back to Sunset, Nicky stole a few glances at his passenger. She had high cheekbones, a touch of the Slavic in her. Her skin was smooth and perfect, with just a few wrinkles about the eyes: crow's-feet. Although her blond hair was feathered in a fashionable way, there was something about her that suggested an unconcern with styles.

An intriguing, handsome woman. Yet something spoke of secret sorrows. Nicky guessed that there had been pain and suffering in Mrs. Eastman's life, long before tonight.

# 4

They arrived at Sunset and Edgeworth a few minutes later. Nothing had changed. The silver Mercedes with its dead driver was unmoved, still lit by the glaring white work lights. The cops and technicians were lounging around now, smoking, talking. The shiny ambulance stood waiting to take Gerald Eastman to the morgue, and a tow truck waited to haul the Mercedes to the police lab for a more detailed examination. Everything was in limbo.

Nicky helped Mrs. Eastman through the roped-off area, and found himself holding her arm protectively. When they got near the car, she broke free and ran up to the body, gripping the dead man's hand in her own. Tears ran down her cheeks.

"You fucker!" she shouted to the corpse. Nicky raised an eyebrow. "Just look where it all brought you!" she cried.

She stood still for another moment, and Nicky thought she was going to continue her shouting match with the dead, but she wheeled around suddenly and stomped briskly away from the car.

As she passed Nicky, she said without looking at him, "Please take me home now. Please. I can't stand any more of this."

"Uh, sure . . . Charlie, will you please finish up here? I'll look at all the reports tomorrow."

Sergeant Katz was leering at him. One of the boys from the lab gave him a wink. But Nicky ignored them all and joined Mrs. Eastman in his car.

She was staring straight ahead. Her face was immobile, almost rigid. He drove slowly.

"What was all that shouting about, Mrs. Eastman?" He tried to sound like an old friend of the family.

She turned and looked at him, as if surprised he was still there. She just shook her head sadly and sighed.

"I know this has been a shock, and you're upset," he continued. "But anything you can tell me about your husband will help me find his killer. . . . Do you know who might have killed him, Mrs. Eastman?"

Again, the same sad shake of the head.

She mumbled something that was lost in the wind of the open car. "I'm sorry?"

"I said, my husband was his own worst enemy," she said crisply.

"Oh . . . I mean, I'm looking for something a bit more *concrete,* if you know what I mean. Was there anything going on in your husband's life, some business rivalry, something that might have led to what happened tonight?"

"Listen, I know you're trying to do your job, Lieutenant, but can't your questions wait? I mean, I really don't know if I can take any more tonight." Her voice was rising, her fists clenched tightly in her lap. But Nicky was not sympathetic. This was a spoiled though beautiful Beverly Hills lady, who lived in a million-dollar home and was used to getting her own way.

The ride was all too short for him to really work on her. But as they pulled up to her house, he couldn't resist one more little jab.

"Mrs. Eastman, I hope you're not going to be offended by what I'm going to ask you, but this is something I really have to know. Was your husband seeing any other woman?"

She was halfway out of his car. She turned to him, speechless with indignation. When she did find her voice, she was shouting—extremely loud in the deathly stillness of the sleeping neighborhood.

"You want to know if my husband was screwing around? He's been dead for an hour and you want to know . . . Don't you guys have any sensitivity at all? How can you ask me, when just an hour ago . . ."

"Mrs. Eastman, please . . . "

"I mean, *Christ!*" she shouted. "Where do they find guys like you?"

Lights were beginning to go on in the houses nearby. If you fire a pistol at night, no one wakes up. No one wants to get involved. But a fight between a man and a woman: That's good entertainment.

"Mrs. Eastman, can't we . . . "

"Fuck you, asshole!" she shouted with operatic resonance. Then the angry and most attractive Mrs. Eastman spun on her heels and marched to her front door. Nicky waited as she fumbled with her keys, got herself inside, and slammed the door. A less solid house would have shook to its foundations. But this house was as sturdy as a Rolls-Royce. A most passionate woman, this Mrs. Eastman.

Nicky sat in his car for a few minutes without moving. He was exhausted and depressed. It was almost four-thirty in the morning.

Where *did* they get guys like him, anyway? That was either a fairly long story, or ridiculously short. Basically, he was just following the well-worn path laid down by his father, Sgt. Samuel Rachmaninoff, who had been one of the more popular cops ever to be on the L.A.P.D. until a bullet brought him down. A bullet fired by a sixteen-year-old junkie, who was robbing his first liquor store, and who almost got away with $36, when Sergeant Rachmaninoff's patrol car came screaming up, answering the silent alarm.

Nicky sighed wearily and drove back to Sunset and then up Laurel Canyon to Sunshine Terrace. Maybe he should have gone easier on the woman who had just lost her husband. He, more than most, could understand how many dreams a single bullet could end.

Dawn was just breaking when Nicky got home. He flicked open a can of beer and walked out to his front lawn. The city was spread out below him like a magic carpet. He lay down on the sweet grass.

The only good thing about the polluted atmosphere that hung over Los Angeles was the terrific sunrises it provided.

Nicky watched the eastern sky explode into vivid reds and orange. It was as if a million gallons of gasoline had been suddenly set on fire by a torch.

Thus began another day.

# 5

**N**icky didn't get to his office in the basement of the old Beverly Hills City Hall until well after ten that morning. His eyes burned from lack of sleep. He and Charlie Katz had an office together at the end of a long corridor, past the many-roomed labyrinth of the robbery division. In Beverly Hills, robbery was the crime that the citizens spent their tax dollars to prevent. That and traffic control. In those areas, the small town excelled. Beverly Hills had one of the most efficient robbery divisions west of Palm Beach, Florida. And God help the person trying to make an illegal right turn on to Rodeo Drive.

Homicide, on the other hand, rarely showed its ugly head here. When it did, nine times out of ten it was certain to involve robbery in some way. A hungry Chicano might be shot climbing over a fence: those who *had* protected themselves from those who *had not*. The hordes from East L.A. looked westward to Beverly Hills, like children regarding an ice cream cone on a summer day. So tempting. It was inevitable that someone might try to take a bite.

So nearly everyone in Beverly Hills owned a gun.

Doors were very solid.

Most people subscribed to private electronic security systems, which guaranteed to deliver armed guards within two minutes of any break-in. Some celebrities went so far as to wear bullet-resistant clothing, expensively tailored by a shop on Rodeo Drive. With paranoia running at such a high level, it was inevitable there would be a few careless shootings. But out-and-out murder was not very common, though when it happened it was often a spectacular case involving much publicity. Nicky Rachmaninoff had been chosen head of the Beverly Hills homicide department partly because he could handle himself with the media. Girlfriends had told him he looked great on television.

Today when he arrived at his office, Charlie was there, typing up the reports from last night. He looked as unrested as Nicky.

"Morning, Charlie. When did you get here?"

"Half an hour ago."

One bonus of a two-man department was that they could keep very loose hours.

"Nick, the captain called a few minutes ago. He wanted to see you as soon as you got in."

He made a face. "Okay, I'd better get that over with."

"By the way, I was worried about you last night. Thought I should send some reinforcements to protect you from Mrs. Eastman."

Nicky grinned. "I survived. Barely."

Charlie clearly wanted to discuss the lady's anatomy, but Nicky was already out the door and down the maze of corridors that led to the office of Capt. David Molinari, chief of the Beverly Hills Police Department.

# 6

Nicky had known Dave Molinari all his life. Had called him Uncle Davey when he was a kid, though now he was careful only to call him Captain. Sir.

Dave Molinari and his father, Sam Rachmaninoff, had once been friends and partners. They were rookies together, and together they had worked their way up through the ranks. When Nicky's mother died of leukemia when he was eight years old, Dave and Sarah Molinari half adopted him, taking him along on many of their family outings, treating him almost as they did their own two children.

There were some who claimed Nicky had risen so quickly to the rank of lieutenant due to connections like this, passed on to him by his father. There was a bit of truth to it, of course. Police work, like other businesses, depended on people knowing each other and doing favors for friends. Sam Rachmaninoff had been an exceptionally popular cop and had left behind many friends eager to help his orphaned son along. But Nicky, waging his own private competition with his father's memory, had worked twice as hard as most of the other cops of his generation. As a lieutenant, he had already risen higher in the system than his father had; this gave him a subtle satisfaction.

Actually, at the time Sam Rachmaninoff died, in the summer of 1967, Nicky and his father could not have been further apart. They had not spoken or written to each other in months.

Nicky, in those days, had hair down to his shoulders, smoked dope with almost religious fervor, and belonged to the peace and love generation. This was a time when the nation had been divided against itself; father against son, generation against generation. Nicky and his father were a perfect symbol of this split. They could not agree on a single thing. The Vietnam war was the focus of most of their disagreements, and from that point their views on drugs, music, sex, and length of hair passionately diverged.

Nicky had left home as soon as possible. After high school in Hollywood, he went to college in New York City, partly because it was as far as he could get from Southern California and his policeman father. He rented a cheap railroad flat on the Lower East Side and soon frequented the galleries and cafés seething with youth and revolution.

In the spring of 1967, he was graduated with honors from NYU and had been accepted in a postgraduate program at Columbia. He was going to study English literature and become a teacher and a writer. But on the morning of August 24th, Dave Molinari telephoned from California to tell him his father was dead.

That was the end of his youthful rebellion, the end of his youth, in fact. The shoulder-length hair was left on the barber's floor, and within two months he had married his high school sweetheart and was attending the police academy in Los Angeles—hoping to be even half the cop his father had been. It was only in the last year or so that he sometimes asked himself what would have happened if he had stayed in New York and become a professor. What would his life have been like then?

But you made your choices, and you had to live with them. Nicky hadn't done too badly. He knew he was a better detective than his father had been, though certainly not as good a cop.

Today he came into the captain's outer office, guarded by Sgt. Nora Wolfolk, a large matronly woman who had been the captain's secretary for years. She had always taken a motherly interest in Nicky, constantly asking about his health and bad habits. Nicky waved at her quickly, hoping to avoid a lecture on nutrition, and walked on through to the inner sanctum. Dave Molinari, a very big man, had been increasing in size since becoming a desk-bound policeman. He liked to eat, and there had been perhaps too many Lions Club luncheons and various official banquets that arose from the ceremonial part of his job. Probably his old partner, Sam Rachmaninoff, would not have recognized this man at all. With his white hair and ruddy complexion, he was beginning to look like a beardless Santa Claus.

32

The captain was seated behind a very large oak desk, talking on the phone. He gestured for Nicky to sit down. Said "Yeah . . . yeah . . . yeah. Well, I'll get back to you" into the receiver. Then hung up and swiveled around to face him.

"Well, Nicholas, I hear you got yourself a new case last night. I got a phone call this morning from the head of M.G.M. *and* the production chief at Universal, asking if we've caught the killer yet. . . . You've got him by now, I presume, Lieutenant?" he added with only a slight twinkle in his eye.

"Yes, sir," Nicky answered. "I have him handcuffed to the urinal in the men's bathroom. I'm just waiting for the Channel 7 news team to arrive."

Both men laughed.

"You look exhausted, Nick. You should get more rest."

"I was up most of the night dealing with a man who had a hole in his forehead. And with a very wild widow."

The twinkle faded from the captain's eyes. "Hmm . . . you'd better tell me about this."

Nicky began with the phone call from Kim Lee, and covered the ground from there. Ending with waking up the neighbors on Lomimar Drive at four in the morning. It wasn't a lot of information.

"How about the wife as a suspect?" the captain asked when he was through.

"I don't think so. It doesn't look like a crime of passion to me. Whoever did this had to have the whole thing pretty well planned out, to intercept him like that late at night on Sunset. I would think it's a professional job, except for the small-caliber gun. But I'm going to have to learn a lot more about Gerald Eastman before I can tell you why he died."

"Okay, Nick. If you need more manpower, let me know."

"The only other thought I have, Captain, is this: If it wasn't a well-planned hit—someone who knew that Gerald Eastman would be driving past exactly that spot at one o'clock in the morning—then perhaps it was just . . . arbitrary. A nut."

Captain Molinari sighed deeply. They both knew that psychopathic, motiveless crimes were almost impossible to solve.

To be a good Sherlock, you had to proceed deductively from point A to point B. Unfortunately, this was not a particularly rational period of human history. There were an increasing number of violent crimes that had no rational motive, between people who had never met each other.

Without a motive, you just had to get lucky. Maybe your killer would conveniently leave his wallet behind with his address inside.

"Let's hope it's not a nut case, my friend. Keep working on the professional-hit angle. But . . . just to be safe, let's put out a computer alert to see if there have been any similar killings in the last year."

"All right, Captain. I'll get on it."

"Keep me informed."

It was a dismissal. Nicky went down to the station's main computer room to begin punching in the little information he had. He hoped nothing would link up.

A psychopathic killer was just about the worst thing you could run into as a cop. But a serial killer, a repeater like the Hillside Strangler or the Trailside Killer up north, was even worse. Then you were no longer talking about an isolated police action. What you had was something that had the power to paralyze the entire proud city of Los Angeles.

# 7

Julie Eastman's line was busy, so Nicky phoned a friend of his, Andrew Long, a gay press agent at Universal. Andrew was a great lover of gossip and knew almost everything going on about town. In Hollywood, information often meant real power and was a thing to be bartered back and forth.

"Andrew, I was wondering if you could give me a few minutes. I'm trying to get information on Gerald Eastman, who was murdered last night."

"Oh, yes, that's all people are talking about this morning!" he said in a low, excited voice. Andrew thrived on this sort of thing. "Was he really *murdered?*"

This was Nicky's cue. To get, you had to give—and he quickly recounted the few known facts concerning the shooting on Sunset Boulevard. It wasn't much, but Andrew would have an inside edge the next few days at lunch and over cocktails, whenever the conversation chanced upon the unfortunate Gerald Eastman.

"Well, I can't say I'm surprised," he said when Nicky was done. "A real bastard, that one. Married a pretty girl, though. Julie Darnell. We had her signed at Universal briefly, but the old man didn't want her to act."

"Tell me about Gerald," Nicky insisted. Andrew possessed such a formidable storehouse of information and trivia that one had to be constantly on guard against endless digressions.

"Okay. Gerald Eastman. Real sharp lawyer. He arrived from the East Coast about seven years ago, representing a Broadway playwright who was suing M.G.M. He managed to make a bundle for everybody. The playwright. Himself. Even M.G.M., who got so much publicity from the lawsuit that everybody went to see the picture. So he figured Hollywood was his kind of town, and he's been fucking people over and making tons of money ever since. Jack Warner once told me an amusing story about lawyers ... "

"Tell me who he's been fucking over," Nicky interrupted ruthlessly.

"Do you have a few hours?"

"It's that bad?"

"Well, let's start with one of the biggest fuck overs of all time. I bet you didn't know that *The Enchanter* was originally owned by Sy Perkoff?"

"No, I didn't."

Andrew told him the story. *The Enchanter,* a film about a lovable little creature from outer space, had been the second largest box office hit in the history of the movies. And like many of the greatest hits, no studio in Hollywood had wanted to underwrite it. The story was too original.

Kenneth Schramburg, the writer-director, who was eventually hailed as a genius, took *The Enchanter* script all around Hollywood. Eventually Astor Productions, an independent operation run by Sy Perkoff, was interested enough to buy the story at very favorable terms. But they had trouble raising money, so the project was put on the shelf, where it remained for two years.

Meanwhile, Schramburg made two other films for another studio. These films became fairly big hits. Sy Perkoff remembered the script he had bought a few years earlier, and he got very excited. Since Schramburg was hot, Sy would be able to get the financial package together.

But Schramburg, now that he was a success, wanted his story back for himself. *He* had always known that this was the big one—the film that would make his name a household word. And he had given it away for $5,000.

This is where Gerald Eastman came in. Schramburg hired Eastman to get his script back from Astor Productions. Any way he could.

Nicky, who had been listening idly, tapping his pencil on the desk, began to get interested. He had read that *The Enchanter* had grossed over $200 million within the first year. This was money you could murder for.

Andrew paused for dramatic effect, making Nicky ask, "So how did Eastman actually get the film back from Sy Perkoff?"

"It was pretty smooth," Andrew said with genuine admiration. "The story I heard was this: Gerald put pressure on a group of financial backers who were personally in his debt, to lend Astor Productions the money for the film. Gerald worked out the contract so that the backers actually assumed ownership of the project. Sy Perkoff signed the deal, ecstatically pleased with himself, and woke up the next morning to find out he had been fired from the picture by his own people. They just turned around and hired Schramburg to produce and direct his own story. The rest, as they say, is history."

"Sy was angry, huh?"

*"Angry?* He had a small stroke and was hospitalized for a month. I heard him say once that he would like to cut off Gerald Eastman's balls with a dull, rusty fork. And he was serious, my boy. Very serious."

"Okay, thanks for the lead. Can you tell me something else? Were there any women in Eastman's life besides his wife?"

*"Women?"* Andrew was delighted. "My dear Nicholas, have you seen his personal secretary? She wasn't hired for her typing abilities, I can tell you that. And then there was the starlet, Sandra Cummings. And God knows how many more. I mean, who can keep count?"

"Okay. I get the picture. Thanks for the information. I may get back to you if I think of any more questions."

"Anytime. How's *your* ex-wife, by the way? *She's* certainly done well for herself, I must say. Have you heard . . ."

"Gotta go now, Andrew. Thanks." He hung up in the middle of a sentence and looked out the window, visualizing Susan Merril, blond and perfectly lovely. She had been the first girl he had slept with in high school. Later she had been his wife.

Nicky forced her image from his mind.

He picked up the phone and called Sy Perkoff's office at Astor Productions. A secretary told him that Mr. Perkoff was in London and would not be back until Monday.

Next, he telephoned Julie Eastman. A man with an elegant voice answered the phone.

"This is Lieutenant Rachmaninoff of the Beverly Hills Police Department. I would like to speak with Mrs. Eastman, please."

"I'm sorry, but Mrs. Eastman is unavailable."

"Who is this, please?"

"My name is John Fitzpatrick. I'm Mrs. Eastman's attorney."

"Okay, now why is she unavailable?"

"I'm sure you can appreciate what a shock this has been for her, Lieutenant. She is under sedation, and it may be several days before she is able to deal with practical considerations."

Nicky decided the best way to play this was to get angry.

"All right, now listen to me, John Fitzpatrick. I am investigating a murder and I don't have a couple of days. I am going to be at her house in one hour's time—"

"But—"

"—and if she is not there, ready to talk, I'm going to pick her up, throw her in jail, and hold her as a material witness. Got that?"

"You can't do that!"

"Wanna make a bet?" He slammed down the phone so hard that Charlie Cat looked up from his work.

"You think you can get away with throwing somebody like Julie Eastman in the slammer?" Charlie asked.

"Probably not. But it sure felt good to shout. Now let's see what the lab boys have to tell us."

# 8

The bullet had been extracted from the dead man and was identified. A small .22 caliber slug.

There was no indication that there had been another person in the car that night.

Gerald Eastman had been killed no earlier than 1:00 A.M. Friday morning and no later than one-thirty. He had had sexual intercourse within four hours of his death.

Various diagrams analyzed the bullet's path and velocity, placing the killer about three feet away from the victim, directly to the left of the victim's car door.

A search of the immediate area had revealed nothing of interest. No footprints, tire marks, and, most important of all, no gun. A door-to-door survey of the immediate neighborhood also brought no results. No one had seen or heard a thing. It was not wildly encouraging.

Nicky took an official police vehicle over to Lomimar Drive. He much preferred to drive his little two-seater for most of his work, but he needed all the props of his trade to help him with Julie Eastman.

By daylight, the large Spanish house looked drowsy and serene. Several expensive cars were in the driveway: a Rolls, a Jaguar, and a mere Lincoln Continental. They were all well polished, perfect, without a scratch. Even the lawn, which sloped gently up to the house, was perfectly green and well manicured.

Once again, Nicky found himself before the ornate, carved wooden door, showing his identification to unseen eyes behind the wrought-iron grille. The door swung open to reveal a tall, well-dressed man, who looked to Nicky like an aging Ivy League schoolboy.

"Hello, Lieutenant, I'm John Fitzpatrick. Won't you come this way."

Nicky was led past the comfortable living room into an oak-lined library with a fireplace at one end. Julie Eastman was sitting in a green leather armchair, wearing a dark green suit, with a strand of pearls around her neck. She was perfectly color coordinated. The green of her suit and armchair matched the green specks of her hazel eyes.

"Mrs. Eastman, I'm sorry to disturb you, but I really must ask you a few questions."

"Do you always bully your way into a house by threatening to throw people in jail if they don't talk to you?"

"Not always. I've made an exception in your case."

She looked at him gravely. And then suddenly—wonder of wonders—she smiled. It quite changed her entire face from something severe and petulant to something that was soft and warm and feminine.

"You don't look very much like my idea of a policeman, Lieutenant Rachmaninoff . . . that is your name, isn't it? Like the composer?"

"Yes, ma'am. He was supposedly a great-great-great-uncle or something. My grandparents fled Russia in 1914."

"So, do you compose music in your spare time? When you're not busy throwing people in jail who won't talk to you?"

"Well, actually, ma'am, I do. Though classical music is a little beyond my scope. I play the piano and write a little jazz."

John Fitzpatrick cleared his throat in an elegant little manner. "Really, I must insist you come to the point, Lieutenant. Mrs. Eastman is in no shape for a conversation about music."

"It's all right, John. Why don't you leave us alone? I'll talk to the lieutenant."

"I really think it's best, Julie, if I stay."

"*John!*" Her voice took on some of its former petulance. "You can close the door on your way out."

"All right. But I'll be outside if you need me." He gave Nicky a very dirty look. But he did leave and close the door behind him.

"Well, now, Mrs. Eastman, to begin with, can you tell me what your husband was doing last night?"

"He went to a screening of a new film over at Kenneth Schramburg's house."

"What time did he leave here yesterday?"

"He didn't. He called me from the studio in the afternoon to say he had a business dinner at the Bistro, and then he was going over to the Schramburgs' to see the rough cut of his new film."

"Really? Kenneth Schramburg has a new movie? What's it called?"

"It's called *The Return of the Enchanter.*"

Nicky laughed. "Amazing how you can just keep making the same movie over and over again."

"If it's successful."

"Hollywood sure is some place."

"All right, Lieutenant. You don't have to act like a hick for my benefit. I've been asking about you, and I happen to know you were married to Susan Merril."

Nicky's smile froze abruptly.

"Sorry. Sore subject?"

"Not really. Actually, Susan didn't become a star until after she left me. With me she was just a housewife. But we keep getting off the subject. When was the last time you saw your husband?"

"Wednesday morning."

"*Wednesday* morning? Where was he?"

She was quiet for a moment. "Lieutenant Rachmaninoff, were you faithful to your wife?"

He was about to tell her that it was none of her business. But Julie was looking at him in a serious way. Nicky decided to answer her. "Yes," he said, "I was faithful to my wife."

"Was she faithful to you?"

"I think so. At least until the very end, when I got the piano."

"*Piano?*"

"Well . . . I didn't spend very much time with her in the first place. Buying a piano and taking lessons was sort of the last straw. But we are definitely straying from the subject again, Mrs. Eastman."

"Maybe you should call me Julie, since we seem to be talking about such personal things." Nicky wasn't certain if she was being facetious. "Anyway," she continued, "my husband was not faithful to me. He spent Wednesday night with a very young model who calls herself Yum Yum Frankenstein. I gather she was hoping Gerald would help her become an actress."

"You know all this? Your husband told you?"

"We were honest. That at least. There was not much left to our marriage besides a comfortable arrangement."

"So you also . . . saw other people?"

She smiled at his slight hesitation. "When I was lonely enough, and horny enough, I went for the first man in sight. Once even John Fitzpatrick out there. So you can imagine how desperate I was."

The image of Julie Eastman naked in bed made Nicky a little uncomfortable. He changed the subject. "Can you tell me anything about your husband's relationship to Kenneth Schramburg? I was told your husband helped him steal the original *Enchanter* script away from Sy Perkoff."

"That's quite true. Gerald and Kenneth were thick as thieves. Getting the script back from Sy was one of his greatest triumphs. Gerald literally danced around the living room, kicking his heels in the air. I mean, we were wealthy before *The Enchanter*. But after that, we were *rich.*"

"I understand Sy Perkoff was very angry."

"He was livid. I hear he actually had a stroke over it. But if you're thinking that Sy might have shot Gerald for revenge, I'd say you're on the wrong track. Sy would have been the first one to know it wasn't personal. I mean, that's just the way big shots behave in Hollywood. It's all smiles and hugs and slaps on the back, but underneath everybody is ruthlessly fucking over everybody else. I'm sure Sy would have pulled a deal like that himself. *If* he had thought of it. Gerald was just a little smarter and trickier."

"So you don't think Gerald's trickiness got him killed?"

"*I* don't think so, Lieutenant. Maybe I'm wrong. In the last year or so I haven't been following his deals as closely as before. But my feeling is they don't shoot you for being tricky in Hollywood. They give you an Academy Award."

"Mrs. Eastman . . . Julie, last night when I took you to see your husband's body, you looked at him and shouted, 'You fucker, just look where it all brought you.' What was that all about?"

Julie Eastman rose from the green armchair, walked to a panel of books. The entire panel opened softly to reveal a bar.

"I don't usually drink in the daytime, but I think this is going to be an exception," she said, pouring herself a shot of Courvoisier. "Want one?"

"Have any beer?"

She took a Heineken from the miniature refrigerator and handed it to him.

"I thought a cop was supposed to say, 'No thanks, I don't drink when I'm on duty.' "

"Well, yes, but you see I'm a detective and this is a well-concealed psychological ploy to get you talking more freely." He took a long swallow from the bottle.

"You're a funny man," she said absently, looking out the library window to the street. Julie Eastman didn't look as if anything were particularly funny this Friday afternoon. "Anyway, to answer your question . . . you have to understand that it was not always so bad between Gerald and me. When we lived back east, it was different. We had a *real* house in Westport, and *real* friends, and five days a week Gerald commuted to a *real* job in New York City. I mean, it was never the hottest marriage in the world, but it was nice. When I was in college, I was pretty wild. I ran around with a fast crowd. Artists and musicians and actors. I fell in love a few times . . . but Gerald was a lawyer, and he seemed so stable, and he said he loved me. And for a couple of years in Westport, I thought I was very happy."

She stared out the window.

"And then?" Nicky prodded.

"And then . . . this!" She opened her arms and gestured to the expensive house all around her. "Unreal friends, an unreal job, unreal money coming in like water. An unreal marriage."

"You want a lot, don't you? Lots of people would be satisfied with a mansion in Beverly Hills and a husband who didn't bother them too much."

"You think so?" she asked, as if this had not occurred to her before. "They should try it. I think I'm really quite a simple person, Lieutenant. The things I really wanted are ... not this."

Nicky closed his notebook and stood up. He had not made a single note. "Thanks for the beer," he said. "I'm sorry if I've disturbed you." He pulled out a card from his wallet and began writing on the back. "This is my office number, in case you think of anything else. And also I've written my home number on the back. If you need anything."

He gave her the card. For a moment their eyes met. The "anything" hung between them.

It was hard to walk away from a beautiful woman who was so nice to talk to.

"Well, goodbye. And thanks."

"Goodbye, Lieutenant."


# 9

In his gut, Nicky believed that Gerald Eastman, lucky most of his life, had simply been in the wrong place at the wrong time.

But he had to follow out all the leads. There was a detective on the payroll, Ethan Wright, who specialized in white-collar crimes. Nicky arranged to subpoena all of Eastman's business papers, bank accounts, and IRS returns. Ethan and his team of experts would go through to see if they could spot any fraud or irregularities. Nicky was glad *he* didn't have to do it. He hated that kind of paperwork.

This done, he telephoned Kenneth Schramburg's office and tried to get an appointment with the boy genius who had already made more money than Louis B. Mayer and Sam Goldwyn combined.

He was told by a well-groomed male voice, "I'm sorry, but Mr. Schramburg just left on a business trip to Rio de Janeiro for three days. He won't be back till Monday."

Rio de Janeiro for three days?

Oh, jet age! Oh, Hollywood!

Nicky tapped his pencil against the desk. At the next desk, the Cat was still organizing the stacks of lab reports into a synopsis that would be sent to the captain.

"Charlie, my friend, whad'ya say we knock off for the day and go have a few drinks?"

Charlie threw down his ballpoint pen and grinned.

"Twist my arm, why don't you?"

# 10

The dawn was gray and cold.

Nicholas Rachmaninoff woke to find himself lying at the edge of the small meadow in front of his house—his favorite spot, with a view of the vast city below.

His head ached. His mouth was dry. He was soaking wet, covered with dew. He groaned.

The morning was overcast, and the city of Los Angeles, spread out at his feet, looked dull, flat, and uninviting.

He really should have stayed with beer. Sometime during the night, he and Charlie had switched to margaritas. Was it at the Mexican restaurant on La Brea? No, the margaritas had started earlier than that, probably at Barney's Beanery on Santa Monica.

"Oh, no!" He remembered now getting home at three in the morning and trying to telephone Julie Eastman. There had been no answer. Probably the phone was turned off. Thank God for that.

Afterward, he had come out into the meadow, rolled in the long grass, looked up at the stars, and cried. Somewhere in this little orgy he had fallen asleep.

And today was Saturday. He groaned again, remembering that this was his weekend with Tanya, his eight-year-old daughter.

What time was it? Susan was an early riser and would be over soon. Nicky got himself up and made his way into the shower. His house was a mess, and he picked up socks, underwear, and beer cans as he went through the living room.

In the shower a small tree frog jumped out of the soap dish and hopped around by his feet. He was shaving when there was a knock at the door.

"Come in!" he shouted. "I'll be right out."

His daughter couldn't wait. She came running into the bathroom, squealing with delight, and gave him a big hug so that she got shaving cream all over herself. "I've missed you, Daddy."

"Me too, Munchkin."

These weekend visits always started off so well.

Nicky wiped the lather off his face, wrapped himself in a towel, and went out to say hello to his ex-wife.

"Hi, Susan. How's it going?"

"I'm fine, Nicky. How about you?"

She was dressed casually, in white jeans and a sleeveless T-shirt. But he was struck, as always, at how beautiful she had become.

When he first knew Susan Merril, back in the days of Hollywood High, she had been pretty, cute, the cheerleader type. But money, so-phistication, the years—all this had changed her from cute and pretty to a great beauty. Though she was thirty-six years old, this morning she looked more like twenty-six. And on her TV show, she hardly looked old enough to buy a drink.

"Nicky, your house is an absolute mess! One of these days I'm going to send my maid over to clean it for you."

"You know this house hasn't really been clean since you were here, Susan."

They laughed. But this was a little jab, with undertones. The ques-tion of whether or not Susan was willing to be a housewife had been the superficial reason for their separation. Actually, Nicky would have been supportive of almost any other career than the one she chose. He had always been wary of the Hollywood scene. He didn't like actresses particularly and had always told her so.

So she left him and became a big star. Perfect revenge.

Their relationship was still complex. Two months earlier, Susan had arrived on Saturday morning and come into the house by herself. Tanya had fallen asleep in the back seat of her car. They had stood for just a moment, at both sides of the living room. And then they came together, drawn by the old force. They kissed, pulled at each other's clothing, and made love urgently on the big pillow on the living room floor. Hoping Tanya wouldn't wake up too soon.

Sex was the one area where there were no problems between them.

After making love that Saturday morning, neither of them referred to it again. If anything, they were more polite and a little more awk-ward with each other than before.

"How's Frank?" he asked, as Tanya ran around, delighted to be together with her real parents. Frank Fee, Susan's new husband, was a famous movie star of the action variety, who now had his own TV show. He played a fairly bloodthirsty cop. Frank, in person, was actually a very nice guy. Nicky referred to him secretly as "The Moronic Man."

"Frank's fine. He wants to invite you to a barbecue on the twenty-sixth. He thinks you should come over more."

Nicky shrugged his shoulders. "I don't know, Susan, it sounds a little too sophisticated to me." He was not referring to the social atmosphere.

Tanya meanwhile was running circles around him. "You gotta come to the barbecue, Daddy. You gotta come!" She was making him dizzy.

"Stop running in circles, darling."

"Well, I'll leave you two to your own devices," Susan said. She smiled strangely and left. Nicky walked her out to the carport and waved as she drove away in a very vintage, dark green Bentley.

He thought, There's no one quite so familiar nor quite so foreign as an ex-wife.

He really liked her, though. Susan had been a good friend and a very sexy lover. Sometimes he wondered why he had let her slip away. After some years of thought, he decided finally it was just their basic outlooks. Susan, simply, did not have an ironic point of view. She was a straight arrow. Not roundabout, like himself. It was like this: If Susan looked in the mirror and decided she was gaining weight, she would go on a good, healthy diet and start jogging every day.

And Nicky? He would just drink more beer and sit on his meadow and think about the strange passing of time. People like that clearly couldn't live together. When they tried, they only got on each other's nerves.

"Daddy, Daddy! What are we going to do this weekend? Let's do something fun!"

"Well, I thought we might go out on the meadow for a while, and just look at the city and talk."

"Look at the city and talk? What kind of thing is that to do? . . . Hey, I got an idea. Let's go to Disneyland!"

"Now, honey, we went to Disneyland last time you were here."

"But it was great, Daddy! Disneyland, Disneyland . . . let's go to Disneyland!"

"How about the beach?"

"Ugh! The beach! What's there to do at the beach?"

"Well, I tell you what, honey. Let me have a cup of coffee and I'll think about it. I haven't really had a chance to wake up yet."

Hell, maybe he'd take her to Disneyland.

# 11

Tanya fell asleep on the way to Anaheim, but woke up with boundless enthusiasm when they arrived at the Magic Kingdom.

Nicky was not a great fan of Disneyland. He preferred the older, funkier amusement parks. Where you could smell that nostalgic aroma of popcorn and hot dogs and mustard, and it was all mixed up together with the sounds of the calliope and whooshing roller coasters and barkers trying to get you to pitch a dime. The old amusement parks took you back to an older America, where every day was the Fourth of July. When Nicky was a kid, Pacific Ocean Park, on a pier in Santa Monica, had been a place like that. But all the old amusement parks were gone.

For Nicky, Disneyland had about as much personality as a Howard Johnson's restaurant. There were no nostalgic smells or swirls of color and sound. There wasn't even any beer. Now *that* was a low blow to weekend fathers who needed all the help they could get.

But Tanya loved it, and he could enjoy it from her eyes. It was wonderful to feel her childish animation, and as they went from Adventureland to Tomorrowland, Fantasyland to Frontierland, he gradually got into the spirit of the day.

Later they laughed their way down a nonalcoholic, drug-free Main Street, U.S.A. Then it was back to Tomorrowland, where he had to hold her very tight through the indoor roller-coaster ride of Space Mountain.

It was only later, driving back to Los Angeles, that he allowed himself to wonder about a place like Disneyland—how very strange it was to spend millions and millions of dollars on a land of escape, and draw visitors from all over the world. What was the difference, he wondered, between a junkie shooting up with heroin, to find *his* little Magic Kingdom, and an average American family going to Disneyland for the day?

46

They were almost back to West L.A. when Tanya said drowsily, "I wish you had a TV in your car like Frank does."

"Isn't it a little hard to drive when you're watching TV?"

"It's in the back seat, silly! Of Frank's new Rolls-Royce. Mommy gave it to him for his birthday last week."

"The TV?"

"The *Rolls,* Daddy . . . and it's so neat! The TV has a video recorder, so you can watch any movie you want. We went up to Santa Barbara for dinner, and I saw *The Enchanter* on the way up and *Fantasia* on the way back."

"Hmm . . ." Now you could be driving on the freeway, but not actually be there at all. Nicky was enough of a moralist to feel there was something basically wrong here.

"Daddy, why don't you get a Rolls-Royce, like Mommy and Frank?"

"Well, honey . . . I'm just a cop and I don't make nearly the kind of money they do."

"But Frank's a cop."

"Frank's a *TV* cop, honey. I'm a *real* cop," he told her wearily. "It's a big difference, my dear."

# 12

They ate pizza at a little restaurant on La Cienega, and when they got home, Nicky let her watch television until she fell asleep.

Tanya tried mightily to stay awake for "Saturday Night Live," but she conked out somewhere during the ten o'clock news, which Nicky had wanted to watch.

There was no more mention of the unfortunate demise of Gerald Eastman. The story had received much coverage all day Friday, but now was already buried, thanks partly to renewed fighting in Nicaragua and the suicide of a famous writer. Nicky was just as glad not to have the public eye upon him.

He carried Tanya to bed. When she came for these weekends, twice a month, she stayed in the same bedroom Nicky had when he was a kid. He liked the sense of continuity.

She was so adorable when she was asleep. Awake: That was another matter. Nicky felt he did not have the patience for children. He got irritated so easily. He kissed her sleeping forehead and felt a stab of love and guilt.

I'm a shitty father, he told himself.

He went to the fridge for a beer and took it out to his meadow above the city. But he was too restless to stay there long.

He came inside and tried to play an easy Bach fugue on the piano. Halfway through, the fugue turned into boogie-woogie and then just drifted off into silence.

He stared at the telephone. Maybe she would call. No . . . she hated him. It made him smile to think of her shouting at him in the street. Well, now they had talked and she probably didn't hate him anymore. Now in her mind he was just nothing, a big zero.

Maybe he could call her up. "Mrs. Eastman, I'm afraid I've got to make a thorough search of your body, to see what formidable weapons you may possess."

But the phone still did not ring.

# 13

Tanya snuggled against him as he drove her home on Sunday afternoon to Bel Air.

Being a weekend father was not easy. He always seemed to be getting the hang of it just as it was ending. They would begin again in two weeks' time, once more as strangers.

Nicky drove up the gentle, tree-lined streets that whispered wealth. Bel Air made Beverly Hills look like a slum. The houses, protected behind great walls, were old and aristocratic. They came at last to a huge iron gate. Nicky pressed the button on the talk box.

"Yes?" It was the voice of Anna the maid.

"It's Nicky and Tanya."

The gate swooshed open, and he drove up the long curving road to what appeared to be a great English Tudor manor. Outside the wall was California; here they could be in Sussex.

Frank was in front of the house to greet them. Frank's famous face looked older and tired. Doing a TV series was hard work. "And here you are! Did you have a good weekend, guys? How ya doing, Nicky?"

Great . . . fine. All was wonderful in the best of all possible worlds.

"Hey, Nicky, why don'cha stay for dinner?"

A nice man. If someone was going to marry your ex-wife and be stepfather to your kid, it should be someone like Frank.

"Thanks, Frank. Maybe another time. I got to check in with the station. Got a murder case going that I've been putting off all weekend."

"Crime never sleeps, eh?"

"You should know, Frank."

He gave Tanya a big hug and waved goodbye to Frank. Turning around in the driveway, he saw the shiny new burgundy Rolls-Royce convertible that Susan had bought Frank for his birthday.

It was a beautiful car. Despite himself, Nicky was impressed. It was amazing to him that someone might spend $100,000 for a car.

And what was even more amazing to Nicky was that all the money had come from what had to be one of the worst shows ever on television, worse now in its fifth season even than it had been in the beginning.

Nicky's ex-wife, the girl he knew as Susan, was better known to millions of American families as Cassie O'Day. Of "Cassie and the Cop." A killer of a show.

# PART THREE

*The Car Killer*

# 1

**P**aul Hovarth was the head of the accounting department at the Southern California Life Insurance Corporation. Unlike Lawrence Ferguson, he had been with the company only five years, promoted rapidly until he was the head of his department. And he was only thirty-five years old.

Paul was concerned. In five years he had never known Lawrence to be late. The strange little man was as punctual as the clock. Paul could imagine him working for Ebenezer Scrooge, bent over a great ledger with a feather quill.

He was the only one in the department who had given Lawrence more than a passing thought. Paul was an intelligent man, not without some imagination, and it horrified him to consider how lonely a man like Lawrence must be.

Once, when they had been working late, Paul had invited him across the street for a drink. Lawrence had been hesitant—clearly he just wanted to go home. But Paul, with rough good humor, had insisted. And Paul, of course, was the boss.

Sitting in a vinyl booth at Pete's Glow Worm Bar and Grill, Paul had struggled at conversation. Where did you grow up? Were you in the army? Ever married? Who do you think's going to the Super Bowl this year? He really wanted to ask: What makes you tick, Lawrence? But Lawrence answered his questions so briefly, so monosyllabically, that he closed the door to further inquiry.

After the third drink that Paul had pressed on him, Lawrence looked as if he were about to burst into tears. With wounded dignity, he rose from the booth, tottered drunkenly, and said good night.

Poor little guy. In the last six months he had looked more like a scarecrow than a person. Thursday afternoon he had asked for an hour after lunch to keep a doctor's appointment. Paul tried to encourage him to take the entire afternoon off. But Lawrence insisted he had too much work on his desk. Still he had not come back after lunch. And he had not come to work Friday morning.

Paul searched through the employee phone directory and dialed Lawrence's home number. He let the phone ring many times, but there was no answer.

# 2

Lawrence had risen that morning with an amazing new strength and confidence. He touched the lump deeply embedded in his groin and he was convinced it had grown smaller in the night. Cancer was for losers and had no reality for a man like him.

He stayed home from work.

At ten o'clock he turned on the local TV news. There was a teachers' strike, a fire . . . and then, finally, *his* story. His heart pounded. There it was, on the screen, the silver Mercedes convertible. No body in it, of course. They couldn't show that on TV. But a serious-looking young man stood holding a microphone, with the Mercedes in the background, telling the viewers how Gerald Eastman had been shot in the forehead at this intersection on Sunset Boulevard. The police were releasing no other information so far.

Lawrence laughed delightedly. As if they had any other information! But it ended too soon. The next story was about a cold spell threatening the citrus crop in Florida. Lawrence paced about his small room excitedly.

It was really very nice to be on TV. But he shuddered to remember how he had almost taken a shot at the guy in the Rolls-Royce, with the cop car right across the street. From now on, everything would be meticulously planned, scientifically *executed*. He was smiling at his witty little pun when the telephone rang.

The office must be wondering where he was. The phone rang many times. Probably it was Paul Hovarth. A wave of cold anger swept over him. Lawrence never before realized how shocking, how criminal it was, really, that Paul had been named head of the department after only five years with the company, when *he* had been there twenty years.

Then there was the cruel memory of that time more than a year ago when Paul made him go to the bar. Forced him to drink, when the taste of alcohol sickened him. Asking questions, prying into his life, probably to tell the others in the office, so they could laugh at him, because he was different.

Well, he *was* different. He had known that ever since grade school,

54

growing up in the harsh town of Bakersfield with a brutal, beer-guzzling father and a mother who talked constantly about the exact date of the coming end of the world. He had been a sickly, frightened child who had learned to make himself invisible so people would leave him alone. All his life he had thought he was inferior. But now he discovered it was quite the opposite. He was a chosen soul.

Lawrence had to sit down. For a moment he felt very weak.

But he began to make his plans. First he needed money, then a better weapon. Many wonderful new ideas were beginning to form in his mind. When he was on TV again, he would be the first story. Not the third.

He looked over at the wall to his favorite picture, taken from the cover of *TV Guide.*

"Well, what do you think of me now, Cassie?"

# 3

An hour later he stepped into the glass and steel lobby of his neighborhood Bank of America. He waited in line, briefcase in hand, smiling to himself, humming the McDonald's theme song.

A window became available, and he stepped up to the teller, a young Japanese girl.

"I want to close out my savings account." He smiled and tried to wiggle his eyebrows the way Magnum did.

The teller looked at him strangely, but she gave him a little yellow card to fill out, while she began typing information into the computer.

Lawrence had been working for Southern Cal Life for twenty years. The only expense he ever allowed himself was a brand-new color TV every three years. And so, unpromoted and passed over as he was, there was currently just under $40,000 in his savings account. He had managed to save an average of $2,000 for each of the twenty years.

The Japanese teller returned to the window with new respect in her voice. "I imagine you want us to transfer these funds into another bank, Mr. Ferguson?"

"No, I want cash."

She hesitated. "Wouldn't you prefer a cashier's check? Or perhaps a letter of credit?"

"I want cash."

"Ah . . . just one minute."

The girl fluttered away and returned in a few moments with the branch manager, Mr. Winkleman, who wore a sports jacket and tried to project an image that California banks were not stuffy. He was a pink, overfed man whose stomach arrived several inches before the rest of his body.

"Mr. Ferguson!" he called out in his friendliest manner, "I hear you're leaving us?"

Lawrence nodded tightly.

Irwin Winkleman, who was shrewder than he looked, and had been sizing up people all his life, thought, Jesus, this guy looks *sick*. There is definitely something wrong here. "If I could make a recommendation," he said, lowering his voice to his most effective confidential manner, "I'd really suggest taking this money in a cashier's check. Good as cash, but a lot safer. You'd be the only person able to negotiate it, so you wouldn't have to worry about being robbed."

"Thanks, but I can handle myself," he said with a bizarre, twisted little smile. "I'll take the cash."

Mr. Winkleman studied Lawrence's banking records for a moment, trying to gain time. Should he call *his* boss downtown? Shit, did they have $40,000 in the vault? Probably . . . Brinks had not arrived yet. It all seemed in order.

"Well, it's your decision, Mr. Ferguson. Why don't you step inside my office? We'll bring the money to you there. Hundreds all right?"

"Hundreds will be just fine."

Later, when Lawrence left the bank with his briefcase stuffed with money, Irwin Winkleman could only shake his head. Imagine a little guy like that walking around L.A. with almost forty grand in a briefcase.

Well, it was Fergie's funeral.

# 4

**T**wenty years in a briefcase!

Lawrence threw it negligently into the back seat of the Ford. He felt a little dizzy with liberation. He wanted to jump up in the air and click his heels. He wanted to shout for joy. But, momentarily, he felt so weak that he had to sit in his car and breathe deeply for ten minutes, before starting up the ignition.

When he was strong enough, he headed up Santa Monica Boulevard toward the sporting goods store where a couple of years before he had bought the small .22 target pistol. Halfway there, he suddenly pulled over.

Across the street he had seen a vision of beauty: a shiny red Corvette convertible, standing in a used car lot. It was almost exactly like the car he had tailed last night, the one where he had seen that pretty young girl do such intimate things to the man at the red light.

Lawrence stared at the car and found himself actually getting an erection. It was a little bit like Magnum's red Ferrari. He drove his anonymous brown-gold Ford into the car lot. An hour later, he emerged happily onto Santa Monica Boulevard behind the wheel of the red Corvette.

It cost him approximately seven years of his savings: $13,000 cash and the Ford in trade.

Lawrence had some trouble at first with it. The center of gravity was much lower than in his Ford, and it had been some years since he had handled a standard transmission. He turned on the radio and let his arm rest casually on the window.

At a red light, a teenager looked over at the car appreciatively. Lawrence half smiled in acknowledgment.

S'all right, kid. Maybe you'll have a Corvette one day.

He gunned the car jerkily and hurried along to his next destination.

At Goody's Sports and Surplus he bought a mean-looking .38 clip-loading automatic, a double-barreled 12-gauge shotgun, and a very wicked army bayonet. He also purchased several hundred rounds of ammunition and an expensive pair of sunglasses.

The clerk, like the bank teller and the car salesman, felt there was something amiss with this odd customer. But Lawrence was able to show the proper I.D., he filled out the forms correctly, and he had a gun permit from when he had purchased the .22 at the store two years earlier. The clerk was still uneasy. He had specific instructions to call a police hot line if anyone suspicious attempted to buy a pistol. But this was quite a big sale, and he worked for a minimal salary plus commission. So he decided it was probably all right. You couldn't worry about every paranoid freak who walked around Los Angeles armed to the teeth.

He shrugged his shoulders. No skin off his ass.

# 5

By the time he got back to his apartment, Lawrence was drained, exhausted, but satisfied. With a flourish, he dumped out the money from the briefcase onto his bed. He ran his hands through the stacks of hundred-dollar bills.

He was a rich man! *Why had he never realized this before?*

He thought he might take a nap. But first he looked through the West Los Angeles directory and telephoned the Beverly Hills Hotel. This was a phone call he had been fantasizing all day.

A soft-spoken woman gave him the reservations clerk.

"Heya, Larry Ferguson here. Listen, guy, I'm in town from New York for a couple of weeks, working on a script at Paramount. Do you got a room I can have, starting tonight?"

"This is a single room?"

"That's right."

"And going two weeks, to the thirty-first?"

"Yeah."

"Hold on, sir, and I'll check."

The phone was dead for a moment. Then the polite male voice returned. "Yes, Mr. Ferguson. We can give you a single room with a king-size bed that runs two hundred sixty-five dollars a night. Is that all right?"

"Sounds terrific."

"All right, sir. May I have your address and phone number, please."

Lawrence had a bad moment. He had never been to New York, and the only streets he had heard of were Fifth Avenue, Park Avenue, and Broadway. He gave his address as 5074 Park Avenue, hoping it was a reasonable number. The reservations clerk at the Beverly Hills Hotel had never been to New York either, so it passed. And his phone number? The first numbers out of his head: 555–4567.

"And your zip code, sir?"

"Hey, gee, fellow, gimme a break! I can never remember my zip. I'll give it to you when I arrive. Okay?"

"Certainly, sir. We'll look forward to your arrival, Mr. Ferguson."

Lawrence hung up and lay down on his bed, pushing thousands of dollars aside. The Beverly Hills Hotel! All his life he had wanted to stay there. But he never imagined he would. He fell asleep thinking of the wonderful things he would do there. But he was not asleep long when the buzzer from downstairs began to ring.

He woke up, not quite certain where he was or what was waking him.

The downstairs buzzer rang again. Insistently.

Lawrence sat up wearily and rubbed his eyes. He did not press the answering bell in his apartment that would have opened the downstairs door. Let them go away!

But five minutes later there was an actual knocking on his front door. He stood up cautiously. All the money was out, scattered over the bed where he had been sleeping. The shotgun and automatic pistol were on the kitchen table. He tiptoed to his front door and looked through the small peephole, to see Paul Hovarth standing in the hall.

Lawrence was completely awake now, wondering what he might do. A slow and wicked smile came to his lips.

"One minute!" he called at last through the door in a sugary and dangerous voice. "I'll just put something on. . . . What a nice surprise," he added, more to himself.

He walked softly to the kitchen, stuffed the pistol and the shotgun and the ammunition into a small utility closet. Then he propped the bayonet out of sight behind the half-wall that tried to make a separate room out of the kitchenette.

At last he walked back to the front door.

"Come in!" he said expansively. "Welcome to my little lair."

# 6

aul noticed the difference right away. Lawrence was not standing with his usual apologetic slump, but held himself fully erect. His eyes were strangely bright, and he was smiling in an altogether charming way that Paul had never seen before. He walked hesitantly into the small studio apartment. Something seemed wrong to him. Glancing nervously about the room, past the many photographs of Susan Merril, his eyes stopped in amazement on the bed and the piles of hundred-dollar bills there.

Lawrence laughed. "Come in, come in," he insisted, leading Paul into the room and closing the door behind him. "I bet you're wondering where I've been. It's really terrible I didn't call, but I came into an inheritance rather suddenly," he said, nodding at the money on the bed, "and I've been just awfully busy today. I'm afraid I won't be working at Southern Cal Life anymore."

"Well, congratulations," Paul said uncertainly. It all seemed a bit farfetched. "I hope you didn't lose anyone too close and dear."

"Not at all. How about a cup of coffee? I'll just put some on."

"No thanks, Lawrence. I got to dash. I only wanted to make sure you were all right. Actually, I was a little worried when you didn't show up today."

"*No!* I could just kick myself for not calling . . . but now I *insist* you stay for a cup of coffee. I absolutely do. It's the least I can offer after you drove all this way to see me."

"Well . . ." Paul had a great desire to leave, but he didn't like to be rude. "I guess a cup would be nice."

"Oh, goody." Lawrence went to the kitchen alcove, where there was a small Pyrex coffee maker. Paul glanced absently around at the shabbiness.

"Have you lived here a long time?"

"Oh, yes, a long . . . long time. Go ahead and sit down," he said from the kitchen. "I won't be a moment."

"Naw. I got a sore ass from sitting all day. One of the occupational hazards of being an accountant."

Lawrence laughed appreciatively at the little joke. "Well put," he said.

60

"You're certainly a lucky dog, not to have to do it anymore."

"Yes, it is going to be wonderful," Lawrence replied, "but I'll sure miss the warm and friendly faces of . . . the old gang."

Paul raised his eyebrows, trying to decide if he was being sarcastic. Lawrence had certainly never behaved as if he had any affection for what he was now calling the old gang.

Lawrence finished in the kitchen and was coming toward him, smiling, holding a steaming cup of coffee out to his guest with one hand. He held the other hand behind his back.

He seemed to be breathing a little too hard.

"You know, Paul, I'm really glad you could come over. I've always wanted to thank you for that night at the Glow Worm Bar."

"Well, honestly, I've always felt a little bad about that. Perhaps I shouldn't have insisted."

"Oh, no! It was a very sincere gesture. I can see that it is that little bit of extra thoughtfulness that makes a guy like you so popular and successful. Do you want any cream?"

Paul took the steaming cup with both hands. He was about to say no thanks to the cream, when he saw the long army bayonet flash out from behind Lawrence's back.

Triumphantly, Lawrence rammed the bayonet into Paul's stomach, and then pulled it out again.

"There's a little thank-you for the first drink, Paul," he said, breathing hard.

Paul's mouth was open with surprise. All the strength had left his body and he was sinking slowly to the floor. He wanted to scream: *No! No!* But no sound would come.

The bayonet struck him again, with irresistible force, deep into his breast.

*"That's* for the second drink."

But Paul Hovarth was dead by now, sprawled out on the floor. He never knew that as repayment for the third round of drinks, more than a year before at the Glow Worm Bar and Grill, his head was severed from his body.

# 7

When it was over, and the studio floor was sticky with blood, Lawrence felt satisfied.

"That'll teach you," he said again and again, as he continued hacking at the body with the bayonet. "You won't mess with me again."

Finally he took a shower to wash the blood off. Underneath the stream of hot water, he began to giggle. "Oh boy!" he said. "Imagine that."

Later, when he was out of the shower, he stood over the dismembered corpse. "Paul, my boy, you've made a big mess of your life." And he laughed so hard he had to sit down on his bed, on all the money.

It was some time before he was dressed and ready to leave his apartment in Santa Monica forever. He was reaching in the utility closet for his newly purchased weapons when he stopped cold.

Oh, what a fool he was!

He couldn't just walk into the Beverly Hills Hotel with an arsenal of weapons under his arm. He didn't even own a proper suitcase.

He kept catching himself in stupid moves. Lawrence did not know very much about crime: Everything he knew, he had learned over the years by watching crime shows on TV. But he promised himself he would get better.

Now it was just a matter of a slight detour in his plans. He went out and drove his new Corvette to a nearby shopping center, where he bought a three-piece set of matching luggage at the Emporium, and also several hundred dollars' worth of new clothes. Finally, he came back one more time to his old apartment. He said goodbye to Paul Hovarth, goodbye to the long, lonely years at Southern California Life. Goodbye to the many evenings by himself watching television.

As he drove toward Beverly Hills, he felt for the first time in his life like a truly happy man.

# 8

The Beverly Hills Hotel on Sunset Boulevard, a great pink stucco building with distinctive green awnings, is a combination of various styles: imitative of the resort hotels in the South of France, vaguely Caribbean. A touch of Spanish architecture, and all glossed over with what could be described as pretelevision Hollywood. Despite this mesh of styles, the hotel remains a last vestige of a once elegant and glamorous world.

Lawrence drove his Corvette up the long curving driveway, where a uniformed attendant waited to take his luggage and park the car. He gave the parking attendant a twenty-dollar bill.

"Thank you, sir."

The entranceway to the Beverly Hills Hotel is a long flat ramp, covered by an awning. In the late thirties, movie theaters on Hollywood Boulevard were built with entrances like this—designed for the great premieres, so that celebrities could parade up the long ramps and be photographed on every side. On the long entrance to the Beverly Hills Hotel, Lawrence could imagine Clark Gable, Marilyn Monroe . . . the old great stars moving magically up this path *where now he himself walked!*

He fairly floated into the hotel, with the bellboy behind him, pushing his luggage on a cart. Lawrence Ferguson had become one of the beautiful people.

The lobby looked a bit like an old, ornate Loew's theater. Where the candy stand might have been, there was the main desk, where an elegant young man waited with a deferential smile.

"Good evening, sir."

"Hi. I'm Larry Ferguson. I called earlier for a reservation."

The young man, who was an assistant manager, looked in his book. "Certainly, Mr. Ferguson. Here's the card to fill out. You are going to be with us for two weeks?"

"Yes, possibly longer. You never know, when you're working on a script, do you?"

"Well, if you wish to stay on past the thirty-first, you should let us know as soon as possible. I don't imagine it will be a problem. We are not completely booked this time of year. . . . By the way, we do require that you establish credit with us when checking in."

"Huh? Oh, yeah!" Lawrence reached in his pocket and pulled out a huge wad of hundred-dollar bills. He peeled off $2,000, one year's savings. "Will this be enough?"

The assistant manager made a little bow. "Certainly, sir."

"Incidentally, are there any messages from Paramount for me?"

The young man looked in a box that had the messages for arriving guests. "No, sir."

"Gee . . . well, I don't want to talk to them tonight. The only person I want you to put through is Susan Merril, if she calls."

"I'll inform the switchboard, sir."

The bellboy was given a room key, and he led Lawrence down the hall to the elevator.

Ironically, of all the places Lawrence had been today, the Beverly Hills Hotel was the only one where no one gave him a second glance. They were quite used to strange-looking people whose pockets were stuffed with money.


# 9

It was a golden weekend, even though Saturday was overcast. Lawrence never imagined he would experience anything quite like it.

On the outside of the hotel, you were on your own, adrift in the ruthless world. But inside, you were at safe harbor. Pampered.

He spent much of Saturday and Sunday by the pool, behind dark glasses, listening for hours to children playing in the water . . . such a happy and vaguely nostalgic sound. How Lawrence envied these children, whose mothers or nursemaids would eventually scold them for being in too long, and take them away back to the safety of their rooms.

Sometimes beautiful young women would swim languorous laps, back and forth, to emerge dripping and happy, their perfect figures glistening in the sun. And sometimes important-looking men, usually fully dressed, would sit down with other important-looking men, order drinks from the uniformed waiter, and talk in low voices. Lawrence imagined that the destiny of millions of dollars was decided in these little meetings.

Sunday afternoon, he went to the Polo Lounge for lunch. With a thrill, he recognized Tony Randall and Bill Cosby, and a woman who was in a TV series, whose name he couldn't quite recall. There were others who looked as if they might be famous, or were trying to be famous. And others, like himself, who were simply there to watch.

In the evening, he returned to his comfortable room, which had soft green carpeting and large French windows looking out upon a palm tree and a patch of well-manicured lawn. He had room service bring him dinner. The linen-covered table even had a small vase and a single rose just for him. He ate contentedly in front of the TV set, lining up the cop shows back to back.

That night he said to himself, This is the best time of my entire life.

On Monday morning he woke up feeling very sick. When he went to the bathroom, there was blood in his stool, which sickened him further. He turned on the television, hoping to forget himself, but he accidentally tuned into "The Today Show," where a doctor was talking about cancer.

Horrified, he turned off the TV at once.

Cancer . . .

Later, he went to the pool and tried to recapture his earlier bliss. But it was ruined now. There was a shadow upon him. And he could only look at the children and the beautiful young women and the important men and feel bitter. *They* did not have cancer. *They* would be able to enjoy this when he was dead and forgotten.

At the pool, he found himself shaking with rage.

That night, after dinner, Lawrence went hunting again.

# PART
# FOUR

*While the City Burns*

# 1

Lt. Nicholas Rachmaninoff began a quiet Monday in his office with Sergeant Katz, reviewing all the notes and reports that they had made so far. There were already almost thirty pages of typewritten and hand-written material, prepared by Nicky, the Cat, and the various forensic experts. Nicky optimistically began a new notebook, to correlate all the divergent threads. If only killers knew how much paperwork they caused they might have mercy and desist.

Yet the bulk of paperwork was still to come. Ethan Wright, the white-collar crime expert, was just beginning to examine Gerald East-man's business dealings. Kenneth Schramburg, the Golden Boy of Hollywood, was still to be seen, as well as Sy Perkoff, of Astor Productions, Yum Yum Frankenstein—Gerald's last mistress—Miss June Taramac, his sexy secretary, and a score of other relationships left to investigate.

After Nicky and Charlie reviewed what they had, they worked out a plan of attack for the next two days, dividing up the work between them. Nicky was not too happy about the progress of the case. There were too many leads and no real suspects. It was a basic rule of homicide investigations that you either solved the case quickly—you found somebody standing over a corpse with a smoking revolver—or it dragged on for months. Maybe forever.

He stared at the telephone and tried to compose himself for his first call of the day. Finally, he dialed Julie Eastman.

He got an answering machine. Everyone in town seemed to have them.

"Hello," it said flatly. "This is Julie Eastman. I cannot get to the phone right now, but if you leave a message and the approximate time of your call, I'll get back to you as soon as I can."

"Hi, this is Lieutenant Rachmaninoff . . ."

Then came the *beep*. He had started speaking too soon. Awkwardly, he began again in a stilted voice: "Hello, this is Lieutenant Rachman-inoff . . ."

"Hello, Lieutenant" came the voice of another Julie, the real one this time. "I'm here. I just put the machine on to screen calls. I haven't felt like talking to a lot of people."

"Mrs. Eastman, I was hoping to see you this afternoon and ask you some more questions about your husband. We've been following through a number of leads, but I'm hoping that if I can get you talking, some little thing may come up that might be of great value."

There was silence on the other end. "If I say no, are you going to throw me in jail?"

"I'll never live that one down, will I? No, Mrs. Eastman, I'm not going to throw you in jail. I would *appreciate* talking with you, though."

"I would appreciate talking to you, too, Lieutenant. Actually, I almost telephoned you yesterday, but I didn't want to disturb your Sunday."

"What did you want to talk about?"

She was silent. Then: "Yesterday I was feeling pretty silly. My first Sunday as a widow. It was a hard day to get through. I just . . . wanted to talk."

Nicky was biting his lip, trying to think of the right thing to say. Finally, "It would have been all right. You should have called me."

They were both silent now.

"Well, then, do you want to come over now?"

"Yeah, I'll see you in half an hour."

He put down the phone.

Damn it. There should be a law against cops who are horny and lonely. Better cool it, he told himself. This is murder.

# 2

He pulled up to Lomimar Drive in his Austin-Healey with that pleasantly painful sense of lust and anticipation he had known so long ago, when he was back in high school, driving over to see Susan.

Julie opened the front door while he was getting out of his car. She had been watching out the window. She was wearing jeans and a man's white shirt. Not all that fashionable for a Beverly Hills lady, but Nicky thought she was lovely . . . lovely in quite a different way from his ex-wife. Susan was the eternal, dewy-eyed girl. Julie Eastman, watching him with her cool and appraising eyes, was most definitely a woman. There was nothing innocent or girl-like in her gaze.

"Mrs. Eastman, thank you for seeing me. I imagine you've been having a tough time."

"It hasn't been exactly great. By the way, do you think we could dispense with the nineteenth-century formality? I mean, you *can* call me Julie."

"All right, Julie. My name's Nicholas. . . . My friends generally call me Nicky."

She studied him a moment. "I think I'll stick with Nicholas, if you don't mind. I've always had a thing about romantic Russian names . . . hmm, Nicholas Rachmaninoff, the piano-playing policeman."

"At your service." He performed a little bow. Her lips were pouting and voluptuous. Even in jeans and a man's shirt, she looked expensive. Too expensive for him.

"How about taking me for a drive, Nicholas Rachmaninoff?" she asked. "This house is driving me crazy. I'd love to feel the wind on my face."

"Okay."

Julie went for her handbag. She locked up the house and in a few minutes was sitting next to him in the open car. She wore large sunglasses that effectively hid her expressive eyes. She smoked a cigarette thoughtfully.

Nicky didn't try to speak at first. He drove her, pointedly, the short distance to the corner of Edgeworth and Sunset, and pulled over into a driveway. She looked at first as though she didn't understand why they had stopped. Then she recognized the spot.

"Oh," she said, "you believe in getting right to the heart of the matter."

"Thus my success as a cop." He smiled. She didn't smile back, just sucked deeply on her cigarette, hidden behind her glasses. The afternoon traffic whooshed past along Sunset.

"I'm not trying to be cruel, bringing you back here where your husband was killed, Julie. Really. I'm sorry about the whole thing. But it just bugs me that whoever shot Gerald is still out there. I thought coming here might put us both in the right mood to work together."

Julie exhaled cigarette smoke. There was nothing left to mark this intersection as different from any of the others, yet Nicky and Julie could both vividly see the silver Mercedes-Benz, with the dead man inside, and the ambulance and the police all around.

"Poor Gerald," she said at last. "What a way for it all to end."

"Who killed him, Julie? Can you help me?"

She shook her head. "You know, I've thought about it all weekend. But of all the creeps we knew, I just can't imagine any one of them actually risking their skin enough to commit murder. This may sound strange, Nicholas, but I came to the conclusion that all of our so-called friends were basically too selfish even to kill. I mean, if they got caught, they might not be able to go to Bali for Christmas. Do you know what I mean?"

"Sort of. But you got to remember that I'm a homicide investigator, and I've known killers. Except for the pros, I can't think of a single killer who actually looked like one, whom you could pick out in a crowd and say, 'Hey, there's a person who's actually capable of taking a human life.'"

"What are killers like, then?"

"They're just like you and me, Julie. Only a little more driven to the edge. And more self-indulgent."

"*Self-indulgent,*" she repeated speculatively, and then lapsed into silence.

They sat in the driveway without speaking, gazing over to Gerald Eastman's intersection with death. Julie looked pale behind her dark glasses.

"So what do you want me to do?" she asked finally.

"Just talk," he said. "Tell me about yourself and Gerald, and your friends and acquaintances. Anything and everything. Let me put it all together."

She laughed. "Do you have all afternoon?"

"As a matter of fact, yes. I do."

# 3

Nicky drove down Sunset to the beach. He should have called in to the station on his radio in the glove compartment. But he kept the radio off. He wanted her all to himself this afternoon.

He drove and she talked. Hesitantly at first. But by the time they hit the Pacific Coast Highway, she was talking freely, the ocean wind blowing through her feathery blond hair. Nicky tried to interrupt as little as possible.

He heard about her childhood in New York City, where her father was a diplomat for the U.N. And then college at Sarah Lawrence, and the crazy sixties, and how she had been a hippie for several years and had taken acid and smoked pot, and then had met Gerald and settled down.

Gerald was very funny in those days. He used to leave her ridiculous little notes all over the house, which she would have to find, one after the other, like a treasure hunt. He had been involved in civil rights. As a young lawyer, Gerald had wanted to protect the poor and fight injustice.

And then . . . at what point came corruption? She was inclined to say it was when they moved to Hollywood. Although, looking back, it had begun before then. Back in Westport, when Gerald's salary began inching over $40,000 a year. When he found he was a mover and a shaker, and there was no ceiling for a man like him.

Gradually, the humorous little notes around the house ceased. There was no more talk about civil rights or the poor. Gerald had swallowed the hook that was going to land him in a big fat house in Beverly Hills, and his wicked humor turned bitterly sarcastic at the very mention of the old ideals he had shared in the sixties.

The traffic along the Pacific Coast Highway was stop and go until after Malibu. Then the road opened up. Nicky put his Austin-Healey into fifth gear and glided along the contours of the rolling Pacific hills. Past Malibu, even the traces of Los Angeles smog disappeared, swept clean by the ocean. The sky was perfectly clear and fresh. The sun was to the west, warming them in the little open car as they sped along.

Nicky drove and listened, and learned about a Beverly Hills life. Was this really the way to conduct a murder investigation? Was he wasting the taxpayers' money? Well . . . it was unorthodox, but you had to put the flesh on the facts. Nicky had learned as much about crime detection from Maigret as he had at the police academy and the many courses he had taken at U.C.L.A. He believed you had to get into the psychic space of all the people involved in a crime. You had to know what made them laugh and cry, what they liked for breakfast, and what made them angry. Then gradually, almost mystically, the crime became transparent—because you were on the inside of it, looking out. Nicky had once described this process to Charlie as the Stanislavski method of murder investigation. For Nicky, at least, it worked. Most of the time. He had solved some very oblique murders in his time by following his imagination more than the established facts.

Would it work now, in the case of Gerald Eastman? Nicky had a foreboding that nothing was going to work. This case was the exception. Still, you couldn't quite say that in the beginning. And, meanwhile, it was decidedly pleasant to be driving with Julie Eastman on a sunny afternoon up the Pacific Coast Highway, with the wind and the sun and the sparkling blue sea.

# 4

Some miles up the coast, he pulled into Skipper's Bar and Restaurant, a very nautical-looking place on a cliff overlooking the ocean, with ship's bells, foghorns, nets and coral, starfish and seashells—all in a great clutter throughout the old wooden restaurant. The man behind the bar had a long white beard and red boozy face. He looked like an old ship's captain, but probably was just a failed actor, a reject from "Gilligan's Island." The majority of waiters and bartenders in Los Angeles were really on the ascending or descending side of a career in show business.

They sat at a table by the window, where they could look down at the ocean breaking against the rocks below. Appropriately, Julie was talking about her marriage being on the rocks. Nicky was reminded of the Jungian term: *synchronicity.* There were no accidents. Everything that happened was a psychic parable, designed for our instruction.

He watched a wave swell up past the kelp bed, rise as it approached the beach, arch its back, and strike with great force against the rocks.

They ordered margaritas and touched glasses.

"When did you first become aware that Gerald was seeing other women?"

She grimaced. "I think I always knew, even back in Connecticut. Though you don't like to admit it to yourself. You see, Gerald *liked* to lie, he enjoyed manipulating people and living on the edge. I never really knew what he'd been doing when he came home late. But when we moved to California, he stopped even pretending. With him it was a matter of power. Actually, he was never all that great in bed. I don't think he even really liked sex all that much. What he liked was having a beautiful woman surrender to him. *Lots* of beautiful women surrender to him. I think he felt that the more women he had, the more powerful he would seem."

"Why didn't you leave him?"

She shook her head and took another sip of her drink. "I don't know. I've asked myself that. Maybe I was weak. I was definitely hooked into a way of life."

Nicky kept his eyes on the distant waves. "When did you start seeing other men?" he asked.

She looked directly at him. "That wasn't until California. Not until Gerald was away from home so much, wheeling and dealing and fucking around. I guess I was the proverbial lonely housewife." She laughed bitterly. "The first one was actually the tennis pro at the Bel Air Hotel. Can you believe that? When I was in college I thought I was going to spend my life meditating on some mountaintop and reading Hermann Hesse. And then I find myself living in Beverly Hills and fucking the tennis pro in the sauna . . . but a woman really *needs* sex. You probably don't understand that. It's not just the mental bullshit that men go through. A woman needs it *physically,* to feel grounded and sane."

Nicky risked meeting her eyes for a second. She was regarding him a little humorously. He looked back to the turbulent ocean.

"Who came after the tennis pro?"

There was a famous actor, a lawyer friend of Gerald's, a screenwriter, John Fitzpatrick, and more. Julie candidly recounted her affairs, laughing often at the absurdity of it all.

As she talked, the sun gradually lowered in the western sky, until it lit brilliantly red the fluffy clouds at the edge of the ocean. They drank several more rounds of margaritas to welcome the approaching night.

Julie talked like a dam breaking free. "You know," she said at one point, "I used to have conversations like this in college. I had friends who I could talk and talk to. . . . We'd tell each other every little detail of what we were feeling and doing. But out here, where everybody has so much money . . . we all just live in our own little castles, and no one has any real friends at all. I never even realized how much I miss just having someone to talk with."

Nicky nodded in a noncommittal way and guided the conversation to Gerald's most recent affairs. Perhaps there was some motive there for murder.

The sun sank completely into the ocean. There was a brief explosion of color and then a deepening twilight. The bartender came over to light the candle on their table, and they ordered two steaks and a Caesar salad to share. Nicky switched to beer—he was feeling lightheaded from the tequila—and Julie ordered a glass of red wine.

When the bartender walked away, Julie whispered to him, "I bet he would never guess that you're a cop working on a murder. He probably thinks we're lovers."

Nicky laughed. Their eyes met briefly in an unspoken connection, but then he had to look away. Was this an official police interrogation, or was he on a date? In the last few hours, the dividing line had grown very faint. It made him a little uncomfortable.

"Okay, now you know everything about me," she said. "It's your turn. I want to know everything about you."

"Hey, wait a second," he protested. "I'm not sure that's in the game plan. Anyway, with me, there's not that much to tell."

"Oh, I don't know about that. Frankly, I find you rather intriguing, Lieutenant Rachmaninoff. You don't seem at all to fit my idea of a cop."

"Listen, I'm a good cop," he said defensively. "I take it very seriously. And you're wrong if you have some stereotype of cops as a lot of crude guys going around bashing people over the head with their nightsticks."

"*I* didn't say that." She laughed and continued to look at him in a very penetrating way. Her hazel eyes were both beautiful and intelligent; for Nicky this was a powerful combination. He really did want to open up and talk with her. And more; much more.

She waited. She *knew*.

"Well, it's all very strange, isn't it?" he said at last. "You know, I grew up here in California, but I was in New York in the mid-sixties, probably about the same time as you. Maybe we passed each other on Bleecker Street. I had this really crummy railroad flat on Avenue B and Tenth Street that cost thirty-five dollars a month. I was going to NYU and I thought I was going to be a great intellectual. I no more planned to be a cop than you thought you'd end up in a big house in Beverly Hills."

"So what happened?"

He shrugged. "My father was a cop. A very good, very dedicated cop, although he only made sergeant. One night in 1967 he was killed in a liquor store hold-up."

Nicky was surprised, after all these years, that hot tears momentarily threatened to engulf him, sitting at the table with Julie. Now he had to gulp back the tears and take refuge in a rather elaborate sip of beer. Julie was watching him closely. He had an uncomfortable feeling that she could look right in on his soul.

"You see, at that time in New York," he went on, when he could, "I had a lot of friends who had big ideas about changing the world. Pretty radical ideas. But my father was just a simple man. I mean, he fought in World War II and afterward he joined the L.A. police. He saw the world as a battlefield between good and evil. My father was just fighting all the way for the good.

"Anyway, when I was in college, I smoked pot and I thought I was clever, and I was pretty sure there was no good or evil. Just lots of shades of gray. My father seemed very ridiculous to me.

"But when he was shot . . . it all changed. I looked around at my friends who were talking about peace and nirvana and civil rights, and you know, Julie, I just suddenly saw it was all a lot of bullshit. I *knew* they would all end up making lots of money and live in Westchester or Beverly Hills. It doesn't really surprise me about what happened to Gerald. I could see it coming back in '67, what was happening to our whole generation. Hell, it's no big thing really. We were just like every other generation of prosperous times. Maybe a little more pretentious. That's all.

"But my father was different. You see, for him this whole fight between good and evil was *real,* and he put his life on the line for it, again and again. And he finally died for it, too. *He* was the idealist, not my friends who were talking about planetary consciousness and went on to become stockbrokers. I guess I decided that it was better to be like my father. So, *voilà,* I'm a cop."

The dinner came. They ate slowly and ordered yet another round of drinks.

"Okay, now I know why you're a cop," she said. "Now I want to know about your marriage to Susan Merril."

Nicky laughed. "You want the whole works, don't you?"

"Don't you?" she asked.

"Okay . . . Susan Merril. The prettiest girl in Hollywood High. I spent my whole junior year trying to work up enough courage to ask her out. Finally, the end of the year, *she* asked me if I would take her to the spring dance. I'll never forget it. She was only a freshman; she came up to me in the hallway between classes, and just asked me. I think my mouth opened all the way to the floor. I mean, we were so different. She hung out with all the clean-living, popular cheerleader types. And I was Mr. Young Hipster, trying to be as cool and sexy as I could."

"She probably thought you *were* sexy," Julie interrupted.

"Yeah." He grinned. "I guess she did. Anyway, we went out all that summer, and she was the first girl I ever went to bed with. We were so hot for each other and so young, our entire relationship consisted of just trying to get off alone together as fast as we could.

"So, we went together for most of that year, and then I suppose we just wore it out. By spring term senior year, I started seeing a long-haired girl named Beth, whom I could discuss Lawrence Ferlinghetti with. And smoke dope with. Susan found out, eventually, and that was it."

"You couldn't discuss poetry and get stoned with Susan?"

"No. Never. You see, that's the point. We were opposites, and we were really attracted to each other for a while. But it's hard to build a relationship with someone you can never really talk with. Sex can hold you together for a while, but not forever. . . . Anyway, we broke up. I went my way, and she went hers. After high school, I went back east, and Susan stayed and eventually studied acting at U.C.L.A. Everybody told her how pretty she was, and that she would be a big star.

"I didn't see her for four years, until my father was killed and I came back to California. She read about my father in the newspaper and called me up to say how bad she felt. I was feeling pretty wide open, and we fell in love all over again. I think it was partly that we were so familiar to each other. Being with her again was like coming home.

"So . . . we got married. I went to the police academy and then became a uniformed cop riding around in a patrol car. Our relationship really wasn't much better than in high school. She spent her days auditioning for parts in TV shows and trying to find just the *right* agent. I spent my days seeing the absolute pissiest parts of Los Angeles. Arresting hookers and junkies, and seeing dead people and suicides and losers of all kinds. We didn't exactly have a lot to talk about at the dinner table. When she would tell me about her auditions, it was hard for me to take them seriously. She got her first speaking part on the same day I had to bust into a place where an out-of-work black man had just killed his entire family. After what I was going through as a rookie cop in L.A., it was hard to get excited about a sit-com.

"So that's about it. We had a child, hoping she would bring us together. But all it did was make Susan resent me more. She was completely housebound with Tanya. She couldn't even audition anymore. So as soon as our daughter was old enough, Susan just packed and got out. I gotta admit, I admire her for it. We're both better off."

"Is it strange for you that she became such a big star?"

"A little. I don't watch television very much. I did go to see her two movies. I thought they were pretty bad. But I'm glad for Susan that she got what she wanted. She's a nice lady. And we're friends now. Sort of."

The twilight had faded to a dark, moonless night. The ocean was not visible out the restaurant window, but the roar of the waves seemed louder. Nicky paid the bill and they walked out into the cool wet night. She helped him put up the canvas top of the Austin-Healey, and he warmed up the car and let the heater run.

Julie sat quietly. The lights from the restaurant set her head in profile. In the distance, the waves broke. . . . He knew that if ever there was a moment to kiss her, this was it. He moved toward her as the car still idled. And she came toward him.

They kissed, gently at first, until their mouths opened and their tongues touched and explored. Nicky thought she tasted very good. His hand moved from her shoulder to a breast. Outside the shirt at first, then, opening a button, he reached inside her bra and touched a hard nipple. It seemed to take her breath away. The bulge in his pants was so hard it hurt.

They broke free from each other, laughing.

"Is this part of the investigation?" she asked.

"There's really a great deal about you, Mrs. Eastman, that I would like to investigate."

He put the car into gear and entered the highway, driving back toward town.

# 5

They did not get far. In the enclosed car, sex screamed unspoken louder than the sound of the engine. When Julie let her hand rest on his leg, it was more than he could bear. The touch of her hand seemed to burn through the thin cotton of his pants. He pulled over into the deserted parking lot at Zuma and turned off the ignition. In the dark, the attraction pulled them together instantaneously. Magnetically. They kissed and pawed at each other's body, and broke away panting for breath.

She laughed. "You'd have to be a contortionist to make love in this car."

"Let's go out on the beach."

Light from a passing car illuminated her face for a moment. She was looking at him a little humorously.

"You wish to fuck me on the sand, kind sir?"

"The sand, the parking lot, the ladies' bathroom over there . . . any place at all."

She laughed, slipped off her shoes, and ran out of the car, down the expanse of dark beach toward the edge of the water. Nicky ran after her. She stood with the phosphorescent waves hissing up the sand to her toes. A wave caught her by surprise, and she was standing knee-deep in the water.

"Ah! It's freezing!" she cried.

Nicky splashed in after her, not worrying about his pants or his shoes, though he did have some vague thoughts for the service revolver in his shoulder holster. He held her against him and kissed her hard on the lips. Another wave came in well above their knees.

"Come on." He took her hand and led her out of the cold water, and walked with her down to the southernmost edge of Zuma Beach. It was a spot he had found before, exploring the beach with his daughter. At the very end there was a protrusion of rock that hid a secret cove. He took her there now and led the way up a narrow crevice between two great boulders, and then down the other side into the small cove. The beach there was no more than twenty feet wide and an equal distance across.

He just had time to take off his gun and holster and wrap it carefully in his shirt, when she was upon him. All over him. The rest of their clothes were soon strewn all over the cove: a bra hanging on a rock, a pair of pants near the waterline, soft lace panties on a bed of dry seaweed.

When he entered her, Nicky felt as if they were two prehistoric forms of life, washed up from the ocean to mate on the sand. Some atavistic racial memory found sex by the sea particularly *right*. . . .

The light, when it came, was blinding and sudden. Nicky broke free from Julie and crouched in a naturally protective position. The two flashlights were pointing down from the trail where they had just come. Julie curled up in a little ball, like a snail.

"Well, well . . . what do we have here?" came a voice from the trail.

"Turn the goddamn lights off!" Nicky shouted furiously. He held up a hand against the glare. As the lights came closer, he could make out the unmistakable, heavy-laden profile of uniformed cops.

"Oh, shit!"

"Okay, kids, let's see some I.D." came a second voice, out of the darkness.

"All right, but we're not kids and you can turn off the goddamn flashlights so we can get dressed."

The two cops chuckled, hugely enjoying the vicarious situation. The beams of light played especially on Julie's naked form.

"Turn the fucking lights off, you cocksuckers!" Nicky screamed.

"Hey, buddy, you'd better mind your manners or we're going to haul your naked ass off to jail so fast you won't know what hit you" hissed one of the voices. But the beams of light veered off to the ocean.

After the glare of light, Nicky had trouble seeing where his clothes were. He closed his eyes and counted slowly to fifteen, then opened them again. His pants were lying a dozen feet away. The two cops were chuckling and talking in low voices, but they did not put the beam of light back on Nicky until he had stepped in his pants—not worrying about the underwear. He opened his wallet and handed it to them.

One of the men took it under his light. It took him a second to register that he was looking at the shield of an L.A.P.D. lieutenant. When he did, he gasped and almost dropped the wallet in the sand.

"Oh, shit!"

"What are your names?" Nicky demanded, buckling up his belt and trying to regain some dignity. He was afraid to look over at Julie.

"I'm Deputy Juan Riviera and this is Steve Jesstraub. Sheriff's Office, Malibu. . . . I'm really sorry, sir, but this is a popular spot for teenage drinking parties and it is definitely part of our beat."

"Okay, okay. Now get lost, will you?"

There were a few more mumbled apologies, and the two cops, flashlights on, disappeared up the trail to the other side of the rocks.

Nicky finally dared look over at Julie. She slowly uncoiled from her protective position, still naked, and looked at him in a very strange way. He was afraid she was in a state of shock. She lay back on the sand and a deep, strangled sound rose up from the back of her throat. Was she having a fit? It took him a moment to realize that she was laughing. Almost uncontrollably at first. A deep, freeing, unselfconscious laugh that spilled out into the night. She was laughing so hard she clutched her sides in pain.

Nicky was burning with humiliation. He stumbled around the cove searching for the rest of their clothing, while her laughter rang in his ears, gradually subsiding into a few isolated giggles.

"Come on, Nicholas," she said at last. "This is *funny.*"

He looked at her angrily. "Yeah . . . *ha-ha.* Let's get out of here, okay?"

# 6

They walked back to the parking lot without a word between them. When Nicky was twelve, he had come upon the Latin phrase *coitus interruptus* in a Krafft-Ebing study of abnormal sexual behavior which his father kept.

*Coitus interruptus.* A horrible condition, leaving Lieutenant Rachmaninoff limp, irritated, angry, speedy, exhausted, and furious, all at the same time. He didn't know what Julie was feeling, now that she had stopped laughing. At this point, he did not care.

In the parking lot, he could see the Malibu sheriff's car standing next to his Austin-Healey. He let out an unintelligible string of profanity.

When he got closer, Deputy Riviera called to him. "Sorry, sir, we just ran a make on your car. Didn't know it was yours. We get a lot of abandoned vehicles here."

Sure, Nicky thought. You bastards just wanted to make sure you got my name right so you could tell all your friends exactly which lieutenant you caught romping naked in the sand. The police grapevine worked very fast, and Nicky had a horrible feeling that he was going to be the joke of the department.

"Anyway," the deputy was saying, "when I got your name, I remembered hearing it on the air just now. Your captain has been trying to raise you for the last hour. Want to use our radio?"

There was something gloating and sarcastic in the deputy's manner.

"I've got my own," he growled.

The deputy glanced dubiously at the small antenna coming from the back of Nicky's car. "Ours will put you through all the way to Beverly Hills, sir."

"Okay."

He grabbed the microphone, pressed the send button—which cut off the ceaseless squawking of police routine—and called out the code letters for the Beverly Hills station. A familiar female voice at the other end came on the air. "I'll patch you through to the captain's car, Rock Man. He's at the scene of a shooting." There was a pause, and then the gruff voice of Capt. David Molinari.

"Goddamn it, where have you been, Nick? No one has seen you since early this afternoon."

"I've been, ah, gathering information, Captain," he replied, avoiding the smirking looks of the two Malibu cops. Avoiding looking at Julie. "I'll tell you about it when I see you. What's up?"

"We have another dead body in a car!" he exploded. "That's what's up. This stiff is famous. I don't want to say his name on the air. How soon can you get to the intersection of Carmelita and North Palm Drive?"

Nicky looked at the two deputies. He hated asking them for anything. "Can you guys give me an escort to Beverly Hills?"

"Can do."

"Fifteen minutes, Captain. I'll get there as soon as I can."

Nicky hung up the microphone. "Let's make some time, okay? I want to go past Lomimar Drive to drop the lady off first—it's on the way."

Julie was already in his car. He reached over her, unlocked the glove compartment, and pulled out a small red light at the end of a wire, which he clamped onto the metal frame of the car roof. He jumped into his seat, started up the car, and turned on his own police radio.

"I'm all set. Let's hit it," he said to the sheriff's car on his radio. Both cars, red lights flashing, sped out of the parking lot on to the Coast Highway. From Zuma to Malibu there was a good road, almost a freeway, and the sheriff's car cruised effortlessly at ninety-five. Nicky accelerated his gear shifting as fast as he could, and managed to get up to ninety-five in fifth gear, with his foot all the way down on the gas. The small car shuddered with the effort. Julie was silently clutching her seat.

At Malibu they entered heavier traffic and an older road. The lead car turned on its siren, and they slowed to a hair-raising eighty, weaving from lane to lane as the traffic pulled over to let them pass. The boys from Malibu seemed intent on showing what great drivers they were. Nicky had to struggle to keep up.

They veered through a red light and turned on to Sunset, speeding toward town. At Pacific Palisades, some late shoppers and kids in a drive-in food joint watched them pass without great interest. Screaming sirens were a mundane reality of modern times. Nicky was so intent on his driving that he barely thought of the woman in the seat next to him. It was only as they approached the Beverly Hills town limits that he stole a glance at her. She was sitting, rigid and pale, staring straight ahead without expression.

"I'm sorry," he said. "I was enjoying being with you."

"Sorry? Forget it. . . . It's my mistake. You're just like Gerald, all wrapped up in your bullshit. I thought you were different, but I was wrong."

Nicky groaned. He was going to respond with something—anything—but a car ahead of him was slow moving out of an intersection, and he had to use both hands and all his skill to keep from crashing into it. They came into Beverly Hills and Nicky got on his radio to the sheriff's car, to tell him where to turn. In a few moments they were in front of the Eastman house.

He looked at her while she was getting out. "I'll call you," he said.

She closed the door behind her, and then bent down, her face in the window.

"Goodbye, Lieutenant." She turned and was gone.

He felt like a horse had kicked him in the stomach. Nicky hit both his fists savagely against the steering wheel in frustration.

"Shit! Shit! Shit!"

But this wouldn't do. He had work ahead of him. He radioed to the sheriff's car behind him to say they'd better get the fuck on their way.

He sped through the sleeping streets of Beverly Hills for his rendez-vous with a corpse.

Why couldn't she understand that this was important?

# 7

The intersection of Carmelita and North Palm Drive was a replay of the scene Thursday night on Sunset: only larger, much larger. There were a dozen black-and-white patrol cars, flares, unmarked police vehicles, an ambulance, and the press. Houses half a block away reflected the crazy patterns of flashing red and blue lights, and even in blasé Beverly Hills, curious spectators were leaning out their windows or standing on their lawns to get a better glimpse of what was happening.

Nicky had to park on Maple Drive, a block away. It was only as he was getting out of his car that he realized how inappropriately he was dressed. His pants were still wet below the knee and caked with sand. He wasn't wearing any socks and his shoes made a little slurpy wet sound when he walked. Also, as a psychological disadvantage, he was not wearing underpants: those had been washed away by the ocean.

The uniformed cop was definitely about to send him on his way as he approached the brightly lit scene of death when Nicky flashed his shield and was let through the police line. Crowded all along the outside of the ropes were dozens of newspaper photographers and a few TV cameras. Dressed as he was, Nicky went unnoticed by the press, which was a blessing.

He made his way through the confusion of activity and throngs of officials to the center of all this attention: an elegant vintage Rolls-Royce Silver Cloud, perhaps twenty-five years old, but perfectly preserved. Inside this gorgeous car an arm reached up lifelessly out the window. Nicky peered in the driver's window and grimaced. This person was not shot by a delicate .22 caliber gun, but by something with much more power. He had been wearing a white linen suit, which was now mostly red. The face was a bloody pulp, completely unrecognizable. More like meat than a person. Nicky felt a little sick.

He turned away to find himself standing before Captain Molinari.

The large, red-faced man put a big hand on Nicky's shoulder. He seemed too upset to notice Nicky's disheveled appearance.

"Glad you're here, Nick. This one's bad and is going to get worse."

"Who is he?"

"Brian Stewart."

Nicky whistled. Brian Stewart was a famous English rock star of the sixties, who now managed to get something on the charts every three years or so. He was mostly in evidence as an emcee at Grammy time, and on the cover of *People,* where his various romantic exploits commanded more attention than his music. He was married to an oil heiress, who received almost equal attention from the tabloids for her string of husbands, polo ponies, and excesses of every kind.

"Do they know yet?" Nicky asked, glancing over to the hovering photographers and TV cameras.

"Hell, no . . . these guys haven't even gotten on to the fact that this is the second Beverly Hills car killing in four days. When they do, we are tomorrow's headlines. *And* the day after. Believe me, we are in for it."

Nicky looked back at the Rolls. There were bird-shot indentations on the metal frame all around the driver's window. The glass on the passenger's side was completely shattered. This guy had been blasted away.

"Shotgun?"

"Without a doubt. It looks like someone in a car pulled up next to the Rolls at the stop sign and just let him have it. Real cute. We got a call almost immediately afterward at nine-seventeen by the neighbors in the house over there."

The captain indicated a ranch-style house across the street, where an elderly man and woman were standing in their open front door, taking in the spectacle.

"They've been questioned?"

"Charlie's talked to them. We've got one more thing. We know where Stewart was coming from. He had been visiting a lady friend four houses down the street. Apparently, he had just driven away when she heard a shot. Thought it was maybe just a car backfire until she heard the police sirens. Then she looked down the street, saw his Rolls, and came running down here hysterical and half-dressed. Charlie's with her now."

Nicky looked gloomily back to the Silver Cloud. "Captain, I want to question every household in one block's radius of this intersection.

Maybe someone actually looked out of their window and saw something. Can I have four men tonight for that job?"

"Yeah. I'll spring some guys from robbery for you. Anything else?"

"I'm going to start with the woman whose house he was at. I'll send Charlie over to Stewart's wife. I've had enough of Beverly Hills widows for a time."

Captain Molinari raised an eyebrow. "What about the other killing, Nick? Any suspects yet?"

"Well, we've been investigating it as if it were a conventional murder and we're getting nowhere. There's just no material evidence of any kind. It's still early, but I'd say the killer got away clean on that one.... Now *this* one, maybe we'll get lucky. He was a lot messier here, letting off a shotgun in the middle of town. I'm betting we will get a solid lead out of this."

The captain hesitated painfully. "Nick ... I know you think this is the work of the same person as Thursday night, and you may be right. But for the time being I want you to treat this as a separate crime. Okay?"

"Captain, we have a psychopath out there, I'm sure of it, who just doesn't like people who drive expensive cars. He's cruising around, killing people at random. That's what I think."

"Now wait a second, Nick. You don't know that yet. That's just one of many possibilities ... and we don't want the press to get too carried away on some imaginary psychopath we're not even sure exists. We could have some serious panic in this town if people felt they couldn't get in their cars to drive to the store without some nut taking a shot at them."

"I hear you, Captain. You know I'll do my best with the press. Though in this case, a six-year-old could put tonight's shooting together with last Thursday's."

"You might play on that, Nick. That the simple explanation is not always the correct one. You should mention that the murder weapon in this case is completely different from last Thursday's. Give 'em any double talk you want, but for God's sake play down the psychopath angle."

Nicky looked at Dave Molinari critically, with narrowed eyes. This was a man he had looked up to since childhood. It was only in the last few years that he had begun to sense shortcomings, weakness; maybe the captain had had too many comfortable years as the head of the

Beverly Hills station. Whatever: He seemed to be running scared, backing away from uncomfortable truths. It gave Nicky a hollow feeling.

"Okay," he agreed, "I'll give it a try. Actually, I'm hoping to avoid the press entirely tonight, but I'll give a news conference tomorrow if it seems necessary. Meanwhile, I'll look for conventional motives here. But for my money, we got a loony out there, and there's no way we're going to hide it for long."

The captain turned away and sighed. He looked back to Lieutenant Rachmaninoff—the son of his best friend—as if seeking support. He seemed to notice for the first time how strangely Nicky was dressed.

"Jesus, you just crawl out of the ocean, Nick?"

Nicky felt his ears grow red. "Something like that. It's a long story, Captain. I'll tell you some time."

icky walked up the street to the house Captain Molinari said the victim had been visiting. Charlie, looking exhausted, was walking down the steps of a renovated Victorian house.

"Hey, Rock Man! You look like you've been swimming."

"Christ . . . what do we have here, Charlie?"

"An *extremely* good-looking lady named Samantha Winters. She lives here alone with her eleven-year-old daughter. It seems Brian Stewart was an old friend. He came by in the afternoon, had dinner with them, and had just driven away to go home to Bel Air."

"Was she a girlfriend?"

"She denies it, but I would imagine so. This lady oozes sex."

"Okay. I want to ask her a few questions. Listen, Charlie, I've asked the captain to send a team of men around the neighborhood to see if anyone saw something. Start on the houses at the end of the block and work your way back to Carmelita. What I'm hoping is that someone heard the shot and went over to their window in time to see the killer. I'll work my way up from the other direction as soon as I'm finished here. Christ, you'd think you couldn't blast someone away with a shotgun in the middle of Beverly Hills without *someone* seeing it."

"I don't know, Nick. To live in the twentieth century, you gotta have selective vision. Most people seem to be able to block out all the unpleasant things they don't want to see."

"Let's hope not."

Charlie waved and headed off up the street, while Nicky walked to the front door of the Victorian and rang the bell. In a moment a very fashionable woman opened the door. Nicky imagined she was somewhere in her late twenties—tall and long-legged, with perfect golden skin and sculptured features. Not-so-innocent blue eyes measured him as he stood in the doorway. Nicky was so caught with looking at her that he momentarily forgot to show his shield and introduce himself.

"Oh," she said, "I was expecting my friends." She had a cultured accent, not quite British, not quite American. It was the speech of the rich and well traveled.

Nicky managed to get his shield out. "Samantha Winters? I'm Lieutenant Rachmaninoff of the police. I'm investigating the shooting down the street, and I was wondering if I could ask you some questions."

"Bloody hell! Do you have to? I've been telling Sergeant What's-his-name everything I know, and I'm really *rather* freaked out by all this. If you know what I mean."

"Yes, I can imagine. But you see, anything you can tell us can be of great value, especially when it's fresh in your mind. There may be some things you know and saw that you are not quite aware you know and saw. If you see what *I* mean."

"Oh, well, come in then," she said ungraciously.

"Won't take long."

Nicky entered a very feminine, Victorian world. Delicate antique furniture. Potted palms and ferns. Art Nouveau vases with fresh red roses. But on the walls, where there might have been landscapes of the countryside, were framed posters announcing old rock concerts. Some of them were signed by famous names. "To Samantha . . . love your cherry pie. XXX, Mick." As Nicky sat down on an uncomfortable love seat, a trickle of sand spilled out of his pants pocket. He tried to brush it off unobtrusively, hoping no one had noticed.

The woman's daughter was sitting across from him on a sofa, watching him curiously. She was a younger replica of her mother: quite beautiful, with long blond hair and delicate features. Though she was not yet a teenager, the promise of sensuality lay barely concealed beneath the frilly lace nightgown she wore. She seemed not so much a child as a miniature adult.

Samantha settled in a rocking chair.

"First of all, how well did you know Brian Stewart?"

"I've known Brian for years and years. We were close friends."

"I see. Are you married, Samantha?"

"Not at present."

"What time did Brian come over today?"

"Let's see . . . he called me about noon to say he was at loose ends. He had had a recording session all lined up for the afternoon, but the bass player got the flu. Since they were laying down the rhythm tracks, they decided to postpone. I suggested he come over for lunch. I just happened to have some cold lobster in the fridge."

"I see. So he came over at . . . ?"

"About one. And he left a little after nine."

"Did he seem worried about anything? Preoccupied?"

"Not really. Though he was really into his new album and was frustrated to have a delay."

"When he left here, how soon did you hear the shot?"

"Just a minute or two. I didn't know it was a shot. It was just this terribly loud explosion. Actually, my first thought was that it was an earthquake—I don't know why. Then maybe a gas main. I didn't really think to look outside until I heard the sirens. Then I saw Brian's car just sitting in the intersection. . . . I . . . I ran down there . . . it was *horrible.*"

Samantha finished speaking in a little whisper.

"You and Brian were lovers, I presume?" Nicky asked blandly.

"We were . . . friends."

The doorbell rang before he could ask anything else about this friendship. Samantha rose to let in two long-haired young men, whom she ushered into another room, presumably to spare them the unpleasant necessity of meeting the police.

Nicky was left alone with the young daughter, who was continuing to eye him curiously with her mother's large blue eyes.

"You're not wearing any socks," she announced.

"You're right. You're very observant." He smiled. "I was at the beach just before I got the call telling me about Brian."

"You went swimming with your *clothes on?*"

"Well . . . not quite. Tell me, what's your name?"

"Christina."

"How old are you, Christina?"

"Eleven."

Nicky's eyes narrowed with concentration, and he gazed off into space. It was something Charlie Katz had noticed long ago—the look he had when his mind got into gear and started making intuitive connections.

"Was Brian your friend, too?" he asked.

"Uh-huh. We were all friends."

"What did you do this afternoon?"

"Oh, I don't know. We swam in the pool. We ate lunch. After a while, we came in the house and took some pictures."

"Pictures? What kind of pictures?"

"Just sort of silly pictures. It's a game we play."

"I see. Can you show me these pictures, Christina?"

The young girl glanced toward the next room, where there was the sound of *oohs* and *ahs* of consolation.

"It's all right," Nicky said. "I'm a policeman and I'm here to find out just what happened. Your mother won't mind if you show me the pictures."

"They're in her bedroom," she said.

"Well, why don't we go there and have a look."

"Okay."

Nicky hoped his luck would hold and the mother would remain in the next room for about five more minutes. Christina led him down a hallway, opened a door, and brought him into a large, airy bedroom that had a canopied double bed against one wall and windows looking out onto the swimming pool. The girl reached in a dresser drawer and brought out a stack of square prints.

They were what Nicky had suspected: Christina, Samantha, and Brian Stewart, all very naked and in a variety of pornographic positions. The first few were of Christina and Brian engaged in oral sex. Then the mother had joined them. There must have been some kind of timing device on the camera. All three naked bodies were intertwined together.

Nicky flipped through the photos, trying to maintain as neutral an expression as possible. As if the child were showing him a 4-H project. But she was regarding him in a nonchildlike way, her large blue eyes appraising him in a very sexual manner. Quite deliberately, she let her robe fall halfway open, to reveal more of her already well-shaped legs.

Nicky sighed, feeling very depressed. Wearing clothes, Christina looked very much older than eleven. But naked, in the pictures, she was just a child. Hardly older than Tanya. A small, vulnerable child thrown headlong into the adult world.

"Did you take pictures like this with some of your mommy's other friends?"

She shrugged her shoulders. "Sometimes. When they wanted. It was sort of fun at first, but now I think it's boring."

The mother came bursting into the room at just this point. "So here you are," she shouted. "What the fuck are you doing in my bedroom?" Then she saw the photographs in Nicky's hand. "Oh . . ." She looked at him apprehensively, and then tried to make a grab for the pictures. Nicky held her off with his one free hand. "You don't have a search warrant! You don't have any right to those pictures."

"Sit down!" he commanded. When she still grabbed for the photographs, he pushed her roughly onto the bed. "Look," he said, "in one more second I'm going to arrest you for assaulting a police officer. So sit still and shut up!"

Samantha went limp on the bed. The little girl was watching both of them unfazed, as if she had seen all these kinky scenes before. "Christina, would you please wait for us in the living room? I want to talk to your mother alone for a moment." The little girl left the room without a word.

"What do you want from me?" Samantha asked, a subtle, erotic promise in her voice.

"In many ways you are extremely lucky, Miss Winters. I don't particularly want to make Christina a ward of L.A. County, and I don't want to complicate my murder case with lurid newspaper accounts of the victim's last hours. But I don't like you, and I don't like the way you are exploiting your daughter. So I think I'm just going to hang on to these photographs for the time being, until I can think of some way to make sure that this kind of thing never happens again."

"You are very moral, aren't you?" she said sarcastically. Her elegant, international accent had reverted to something that had a tinge of Cockney in it.

"I just try to be a human being in this pisshole."

"Fuck you, asshole," she retorted, without a great deal of energy.

In the living room, the little girl was rocking back and forth in an elaborate Victorian rocker. The large, unfathomable eyes were turned upon Nicky as he emerged from the hall. He came up to her and knelt by the rocker, so he could be on eye level with the child.

"Christina, I told your mother I don't want you taking any more pictures without your clothes on. And I don't want you doing those sex things anymore with your mother's friends. Do you understand me? Those are grown-up things to do. They aren't right for children."

He had absolutely no right to be telling this child what was right or wrong, but he did so with such conviction and authority that she nodded. Nicky took a card out of his wallet and handed it to her. "This is my telephone number, Christina. I want you to put it away where your mother won't find it. And I want you to give me a call right away if she ever tries to make you do these things again. Do you hear me?"

"Yes" came a little voice.

Nicky strode out the front door back to North Palm Drive. He felt ridiculous. Like the little Dutch boy sticking his finger in the dike to hold off the entire ocean.

But you had to try.

# 9

The ambulance had departed with the body, and under the bright lights a tow truck was hooking up to the Rolls-Royce, to pull it downtown to the police lab for further tests.

With a young uniformed cop, Nicky drove up North Palm Drive the two blocks to Sunset, and they laboriously worked their way down the street back to Carmelita. House by house. Nicky left the red light flashing on the patrol car so that people would open their doors. Still, a good half of the houses he tried did not answer. Either the residents were not at home, away visiting the glamorous spots of the world, or they just chose not to answer—to remain cloistered behind their great walls of wealth.

Only one household had any information worth writing down, and even that was doubtful. A Dr. Showalter, who lived a dozen houses up from where the shooting occurred, said he heard a loud explosion shortly after 9:00 P.M. He had been reading a book in an armchair by a window overlooking the street. Out of curiosity, he pulled back the curtain in time to see a sports car drive by at a fast speed toward Sunset. The doctor assumed the sound he heard was the backfire of a souped-up car, driven too fast by some spoiled child.

And what kind of car was it?

The doctor was fairly sure it was a Corvette. An older model with the top down. He didn't really notice the driver, but seemed to remember that there was just one person in the car. At night, with the blue-yellow streetlights, the color of the car was impossible to tell—perhaps a light color. As to the license number, he had not a clue.

A speeding, older model, light-colored Corvette with the top down. Such a sight was not exactly uncommon in Beverly Hills. Probably it had nothing to do with the shooting at all.

Also, Nicky was beginning to make a few tentative suppositions about the killer. He was imagining an outsider, someone who was jealous of those who had wealth and power and expensive cars. It didn't seem likely that such a person would drive a Corvette. But you never knew.

Maybe the killer wasn't an outsider at all. Perhaps it was an angry Beverly Hills adolescent who was furious with his parents for being given a Corvette for his sixteenth birthday instead of a Mercedes or a Rolls.

There were endless possibilities, and Nicky went to bed finally in the early hours of the morning exhausted, but no closer to any solution.

It was only as he was on the verge of drifting off to sleep that he thought briefly of Julie, and how sweet it had been with her. Just for a little while. Talking in the restaurant. Naked on the sand.

Well, she wouldn't see him again. Nicky didn't blame her really. He had probably been pretty uncouth. In the department, it was proverbial that no woman except a complete masochist would be crazy enough to go out with a cop.

# 10

Unfortunately, war had not been declared in any foreign country. No world leaders had been assassinated, and no nation had declared bankruptcy. As a result, the apparently senseless killing of a famous rock and roll star in the middle of Beverly Hills made the front-page headlines in every newspaper in America, as well as most of the more Westernized countries abroad.

The Europeans, in particular, loved stories of senseless American violence, and since Brian Stewart was British, that nation was especially interested in all the grisly details.

Even worse, as far as Nicky was concerned, the L.A. morning paper had giant letters: CAR KILLER STRIKES AGAIN.

The connection had been made, as he knew it would. A psychotic killer was on the loose, striking the citizens of Los Angeles in the most sacred of places: the automobile. Anyone driving to work or to the corner supermarket now had to face the added peril of being gunned down by some maniac.

Beverly Hills City Hall was surrounded by a ring of national and international reporters, waiting like vultures for scraps of information. Nicky tried to drive unobtrusively down the ramp into the garage, but a reporter from the L.A. *Times* recognized him, and in seconds the press swarmed around his car.

"Lieutenant, can you tell us if any progress has been made . . ."

"Is there any way the people of the city might protect themselves?"

"Can you tell us the motive for this shooting . . . ?"

Flashbulbs were exploding in his face. Nicky smiled gamely in his best imitation of General Eisenhower Meeting-the-Troops. "Ladies! Gentlemen . . . I can't make any comment right now on our investigation. Perhaps a little later in the day."

His car was completely surrounded, and he might have been trapped for some time if the guard at the entrance to the station had not noticed what was happening. In a moment, six large uniformed cops came out of the building to clear a path for him.

"Shit! What a way to start the day . . . thanks, guys."

Inside the station, it was almost as chaotic as outside. The poor tend to suffer their misfortunes in silence. But the rich . . . It seemed that every Beverly Hills tycoon who had once met the mayor at a $500-a-plate fund-raiser, or had sent money to the Policemen's Ball, now was telephoning the mayor, the police chief, senators, anyone in power, to complain indignantly that their expensive streets were not safe for their expensive cars to travel. By later in the day, it was becoming obvious that the car lots on Santa Monica Boulevard and Melrose were doing a brisk business selling unostentatious Fords and Chevrolets to people whose first cars were a Mercedes or a Rolls.

It amazed Nicky how greatly one person could disrupt the flow of everyday life. He was only glad the press had not learned of Brian

Stewart's final incestuous ménage à trois. When that happened, the weekly tabloids would have a field day. It would be impossible to get any work done.

Nicky went directly to Captain Molinari's office. It seemed that everyone he passed was talking furiously on the telephone, and when he got to the captain's inner sanctum he, too, was shouting on the phone. He looked up, saw Nicky, and slammed down the receiver.

"Jesus, what a madhouse," he lamented. *"This* is where we should be looking for psychotic killers!" The captain opened the door to the next room and told Sergeant Wolfolk not to let any more calls through for fifteen minutes. The formidable matron folded her arms protectively. She looked as if she would be pleased to personally massacre anyone who might disturb her babies.

But the captain had no sooner sat down back at his desk when the phone rang again. It was the mayor.

# 11

After the captain had soothed the mayor's political jitters, he put down the phone, leaned back in his swivel chair, and put his large feet up on the desk. The older man's shrewd light blue eyes rested on Lieutenant Rachmaninoff.

"I gotta tell you, Nick, there's a feeling downtown that maybe you are too young and inexperienced to head a murder case of this dimension."

Nicky narrowed his eyes and stared past the captain out the window. "Whose decision is it going to be?" he asked.

"Mine. At least for the time being. If I fuck up and make the wrong decision, I could be replaced here, too. . . . Look, Nick, we both could really bust our asses on this one. The chief has suggested the possibility of a joint Beverly Hills–West Hollywood task force under Captain Discher. We would still be involved, just not in charge."

"I don't like it," Nicky said adamantly. "These killings are happening in Beverly Hills. It's our turf. We've been involved since the beginning and I'm getting a sense of who this guy is and how we are going to get him."

"Okay, lay it on me. How are we going to get him? Or her, as the case may be?"

"First of all, I do want a special task force. But under me. There's too much ground to cover for Charlie and me alone."

"That could be arranged," the captain assented.

"Okay, now let's discuss our killer. We have someone who is striking out against the rich and the famous. That implies, to me, someone who is neither rich nor famous. Someone who is bitter about not making it to the top. Someone who does not live in Beverly Hills, but is driving in from someplace else."

"Possibly," the captain said. "Of course, if you just started shooting at random in Beverly Hills, the chances are you'd hit someone rich and famous."

"Well, I don't think these shootings are *completely* random. Granted, the killer probably actually did not know his victims, but he had to set up the situation pretty carefully. He had to choose someone, follow him, find a place where there was no other traffic, a place where he would be able to pull up alongside. Now you would have to do a lot of cruising before you could come up with all those conditions."

"Possibly," the captain conceded.

"Okay, so the first part of my plan is preventative. Our second shooting came only four days after the first—our guy is hot to trot, and I think he's going to try again within a couple of days. He may be out there cruising right now. . . so the first thing I want to do is double our nightly patrol of the whole area, up in the hills and canyons, too. We should start pulling over *everybody* who is out driving at night. I also want to place permanent patrol positions on all the major arteries in and out of Beverly Hills—on both sides of Sunset, on Santa Monica, on all the canyon roads that go over to the valley. If there is another shooting, I want to be able to close off Beverly Hills completely from the rest of the world in a matter of minutes."

"Uh-huh . . . you're talking about a lot of manpower, Nick. What if he leaves Beverly Hills for Bel Air, or Holmby Hills, or even Malibu?"

"Hey, I think all those areas should be well patrolled, too. But right now, the action seems to be here. For some reason or other, our killer *likes* Beverly Hills."

"How nice."

"At least it limits the area. . . . Anyway, that's the preventative part. Next, I want to start looking for a person who has a gripe against Hollywood. I want to go to every studio and record company and find out who's been fired recently, who has not had a contract renewed. I want to start feeding these names into our computer and checking out alibis.

"Also, I want a list of every Corvette registered in West L.A. Last night, the only real lead I could come up with going door to door was a doctor who saw a Corvette coming from the scene of the crime just after the shooting. It may not be the killer, but whoever was in that car must have seen something, and I want to talk with him."

"Jesus, Nick, there are probably ten thousand Corvettes registered in West L.A. How are you going to check out every one?"

"The first thing would be to run all the names into the computer and see if they connect with any people on our crazy list, or against the list we're going to make of all the people who might have a grudge against Hollywood. It's a matter of making cross-references. Maybe we'll find a deranged screenwriter who owns a Corvette and can't make payments anymore 'cause he hasn't sold a story in five years—that's the kind of person I'm looking for."

Captain Molinari pushed his great bulk farther back in the swivel chair. "Okay, Nick. You seem to have a grasp on this case. For the time being, you're still in charge. But that could change—you understand? We're going to have to take this one day by day, and I don't want you to get out of radio communication as you were yesterday. Okay? Plus, I want you to keep investigating the Eastman killing and the Stewart killing as if they were nice old-fashioned homicides, with nice old-fashioned motives like greed, lust, and envy. Maybe we'll get real lucky and find that we don't have a psycho on our hands after all.

"And last of all, you got to take care of the press outside. We've got to give them something reassuring. I think you should hold a press conference this afternoon."

"Okay, Captain. You'll get me my task force?"

"I'll put it together today, if the mayor will give me more men."

"Thanks . . . listen, there's one more thing. I'd like the city to borrow a Rolls-Royce for a couple of weeks. I want to place a decoy on the streets at night."

"Jesus, Nick, I can't ask anyone to volunteer for that."

"It's all right. I'm going to do it, Captain."

"Nick!"

"I can do it, really. I'll put a radio in the car and have two unmarked cars within a block of me at all times. No one is going to sneak up alongside of me unawares."

"Well . . . I don't know if I can get a Rolls. Since the Jarvis-Gann tax cut, the police department hasn't had a Rolls-Royce budget, you know."

Nicky smiled. "Why don't you leave that one to me, Captain? I think I know where I can borrow the shiniest, most ostentatious Rolls you've ever seen. Shit, your tongue will be hanging out!"

# 12

He set up the press conference for one o'clock outside on the front steps of the City Hall. The producer for ABC News wanted to put some makeup on him, but Nicky refused. At the proper time, he walked out on the steps wearing a well-cut suit and tie (his only suit and tie), flanked by four uniformed cops, as well as Charlie Cat. Nicky stepped up to a podium that was a tangle of microphones and wires. TV and still cameras faced him in an impenetrable wall of high technology. Nicky tried to look like he knew what he was doing.

The first question came from the New York *Daily News:* Could he describe the circumstances of Brian Stewart's death?

No problem. . . .

The next question from a scandal sheet in London: Who had Brian Stewart been visiting in Beverly Hills?

Nicky smiled blandly. "We're not releasing that information just now."

The next question from a TV journalist: What connection did this shooting have to the car killing of Gerald Eastman last Thursday night?

"There may be no connection," Nicky said firmly. "Gerald Eastman was shot with a small target pistol, Stewart with a shotgun. At this point, we are investigating quite a few possibilities. All this talk about a so-called Car Killer is really quite speculative."

The questions turned into a melee, a jumble of voices shouting at him, hungry for information. Nicky sensed that the press *wanted* there to be a Car Killer. It was good copy. The phrase had a catchy, ominous ring: Car Killer. Nicky fielded the barrage as best he could, suppressing the gory details and trying to reassure the public at large. The situation—he lied—was well in hand.

The press, of course, had different ideas. They did not want the situation to be well in hand. They wanted it to be as volatile and sensational as possible. It was a game of tug-of-war between him and them, and it seemed to Nicky that he was on the losing side.

It was after nearly twenty minutes of questions that a woman raised her hand. "Tamara Green, *Women's Wear Daily.* Lieutenant Rachmaninoff, you were once married to Susan Merril, who is known to millions of Americans in her title role in 'Cassie and the Cop.' Do you think you could tell us how Cassie would deal with these murders?"

Nicky's TV mask—the grim though good-natured detective—threatened to dissolve for a moment. He was furious. A verbal assault upon this stupid woman who could ask a question like that rose almost uncontrollably to his lips. It was only with great effort, and knowing that his entire career was at stake in this investigation, that he was able to master his anger. He simply looked in another direction.

"Next question?" he snapped.

There was general laughter among the reporters. Then the questions began again, a rehash of what had gone before. It always amazed him how TV newsmen could go over and over the same ground, and still behave as if they were asking something new.

It was only when he was back inside the safety of the station that he let go of the string of profanity that he had been holding back. Charlie, standing next to him, got the brunt of his anger.

"Can you imagine that bitch! Connecting this to a fucking TV show, for God's sake. . . . It's people like her who are creating all this madness, Charlie, I swear to God!"

# 13

By Tuesday afternoon, Nicky was in charge of a special thirty-man task force that had been put together with officers from all over L.A. County. They were given office space in the robbery division, which now took second place to death.

It was easier to head a two-man homicide department. Nicky found most of his time was spent in setting his various plans in motion, monitoring the activities of thirty men and women, and correlating the volumes of mostly useless information that were coming in.

He was desk-bound, frustrated, feeling the close contact with the killer ebb away.

On Tuesday night Nicky was so frustrated that he crisscrossed the streets for four hours as a passenger in an unmarked patrol car. Fewer cars than usual were on the streets. People would accelerate sharply from intersections whenever another car approached. He passed Julie Eastman's house three times that night. There were lights on and cars in the driveway. He felt a little lonelier each time he drove by.

After four uneventful hours, he was driven back to the station where his own car was parked. He went home to sleep in a house that felt lonely, cold, and unlived in. He sat at his piano and played through the opening bars of "Cast Your Fate to the Wind"—so *misterioso* and far away, with the A flat drone in the left hand. But tonight it wouldn't come alive. He simply didn't have the heart for music.

He was back in the station by eight Wednesday morning. There was a list waiting on his desk of 11,213 people who had Corvettes registered in West Los Angeles. The computerized readout was thirty-seven pages long. Nicky felt like crying.

As for the failures in Hollywood—those who might have cause to feel bitter against the system—the numbers were uncountable, staggering. Potentially much larger even than those who owned Corvettes.

So many came; so few conquered. Out of all those who came to Hollywood, searching for their place in the sun, Nicky estimated that only about four percent even eked out a meager, uncertain living from the entertainment industry. The numbers of disappointed souls living in cheap furnished rooms around the city were so large and depressing that Nicky decided to concentrate on people who had been fired or had their contracts terminated within the last month. By Thursday morning he had a list of 184 Hollywood rejects to consider. That day, he gave each of his thirty investigators a list of six names to check out. When these reports came back, he and Charlie would personally check out the most depressed and bitter of the lot—not in itself a very cheerful task.

By Thursday morning, the car killings had slipped off the front page of the newspaper and were no longer all one heard on the staccato, hyperactive news breaks on the radio. That evening, the local TV news brought the case up-to-date right before breaking for the weather. The public, fortunately, had a short memory, and Beverly Hills traffic was returning to a just slightly more paranoid normal.

On Thursday afternoon, Nicky telephoned Frank Fee and asked to borrow the Rolls-Royce. He also mentioned that despite the way he played it down in his news conference, as far as he was concerned there really *was* a danger in driving around West L.A. in an expensive car.

"Rent a Chevy, Frank," he told him. "You'll find it's the new chic."

Frank laughed. "Okay, Nicky, you can have the Rolls, though I'm not sure I like this idea of you setting yourself up as a decoy. You can pick it up after five this afternoon, on one condition: You got to stay for dinner. Look, we're having a small barbecue in the yard for our friends the Silversteins, from Italy. He was the production manager of the picture I made in Rome last year. Real nice guy. Funny as hell. I know Tanya would love to see you. She watched you on TV Tuesday night and has been talking about you ever since. So what ya say, buddy?"

Nicky rolled his eyes to the ceiling in helpless frustration and guilt. "Okay, Frank. It's a deal."

# 14

In the late afternoon, Nicky was ready to knock off. He was tired and hungry. He hadn't eaten a decent meal since Monday night with Julie.

The sun was sinking low as he snaked his way up the narrow hillside roads of Bel Air and came to the gate of Frank and Susan's Tudor mansion. A late tour van ("See the Homes of the Stars!") was ahead of him, off the road in front of the gate. As Nicky drove up to the intercom, he could hear the driver of the van speaking over the loudspeaker: "And here, folks, is the beautiful Tudor-style home of Frank Fee and his gorgeous bride, Susan Merril. The house has almost three acres of prime Bel Air soil and reputedly was purchased for *$5 million.* There is, of course, a tennis court, an Olympic-size swimming pool, and—what else?—a separate cottage for the gardener and maid!"

Nicky pressed the intercom and waited in front of the closed gate. He had a funny feeling in the pit of his stomach—aware that the envious eyes of the van passengers were upon him, as someone who had legitimate entry to this $5 million home. He glanced up to the van while he waited, curious about the kind of people who would thrill to see the gates and fences of the famous.

He found—hotly upon him—two eyes set in a cavernous, unhealthy face. The eyes looked at him with such an intensity that Nicky held his breath. The man was wearing a sports shirt that seemed several sizes too large for him. There was something cadaverous about the face.

Nicky felt a shiver creep up his spine.

The metal intercom came to life. "Hello?" It was the maid's voice.

He tore himself loose from the unsettling eyes. "Hi, Anna. This is Nicky."

With a whirring sound, the gate pulled slowly open. Nicky drove inside, and the great iron gate immediately swung back into place.

On impulse, he stopped his car and looked back at the van, which was just beginning to drive away.

Nicky had a very strong and unsettling feeling that this encounter was important for him. Some key words came to his consciousness as he watched the van turn a corner and disappear: *Fame . . . envy . . . fortune . . . fury . . . sickness . . . death.*

This was exactly what his case was all about. He was certain of it, and sitting in the middle of Frank and Susan's driveway he reached for some great conclusion, not just about Hollywood, but the American way of life.

Suddenly, he wanted to follow the van and find out a lot more about the frightening little man who had been watching him so intently. But the gate was locked in place; he was a virtual prisoner.

# 15

Anna showed him through the house and out the other side, where Frank, Tanya and another man and woman—evidently the Silversteins—were seated on a comfortable patio by the lawn.

Tanya ran up to him. "Daddy, Daddy!" He caught her as she flew into his arms. He swung her up into the air.

"How's my girl?"

"Hi, Daddy. I saw you on TV. You see, you *are* a TV cop."

"And a better one than me," Frank added gallantly, rising to give Nicky a big, outdoor handshake.

"I don't know about that, Frank. I wish I could solve my cases in sixty minutes like you do."

"Fifty minutes. Don't forget the commercials. You just need a better scriptwriter, my friend."

"That's for sure," he agreed.

"Nicky, I want you to meet my dear friends, Ed and Norma Silverstein."

He shook hands all around.

"Susan's not home yet. They've been working her like a dog. But *I* got the day off. Wonder of wonders. We had night shooting on Wednesday, and they can't work us for thirty-six hours after that. Union rules. . . . Whad'ya wanna drink, Nicholas? You're way behind us, lad, and you'd better catch up!"

Nicky was amazed, especially after the tour van scene outside, how *normal* it felt here, on the inside. He had noticed before in Hollywood how the almost famous went to great lengths to appear glamorous and exotic. But the really famous, like Frank, did just the opposite. They wanted you to think they were just ordinary folk. Just your everyday, down-home movie star.

Frank poured drinks and set the barbecue going. He put on an apron, and had a variety of tongs and long forks to aid him with his work. This was clearly a man who took backyard recreation seriously. Nicky went through two vodka martinis and had a great desire to swim in the seductive Olympic-size pool. He really wanted to skinny-dip, but it seemed so down-home, all-American in this backyard, that he thought it would be best to borrow some trunks from Frank.

Tanya said she would swim, too. They went into the house to change, and then raced across the lawn and jumped into the water. After the tension of the last few days, the pool felt almost unbearably good. He was washed clean, almost purified by the cool, delicious water. He groaned with delight and would have just floated and stretched in the water, except that Tanya wanted to climb all over him and do acrobatics.

Susan arrived home to find Tanya doing dives off Nicky's shoulders. She came out to the pool still in her TV makeup, looking more like Cassie than Susan. Nicky thought she seemed older, too, and more tired than when he had seen her last. Even with the makeup, he could see new lines around her eyes.

"Look who I dragged home for dinner," Frank said.

"Hi, Nicky . . . *Tanya,* go easy on your father!"

"Look at me, Mommy! Whee . . ."

Susan laughed and went inside the house to take off her makeup. Nicky and Tanya swam for another few minutes, until both decided they were cold. They ran dripping wet into the house, up the stairs, back to Tanya's bedroom to change.

It had been some time since he had seen his daughter's room. Last time he was here, there were *Star Wars* posters on the walls and pictures of various furry little munchkins. Now there were androgynous young men, rock stars he presumed, though they were all quite unknown to him and seemed very strangely dressed.

"Do you like Boy George?" she asked, pointing to a poster above her bed of a particularly strange-looking individual, with lipstick and painted eyes. "Boy George is *awesome.*"

"Hmm . . ."

Well, *his* father had found Bob Dylan as strange a looking creature as he found Boy George. Life goes around in circles.

# 16

With the swim and the martinis, Nicky felt almost human for the first time in days. He was walking down the upstairs hallway to go back to the barbecue, when he heard the sound of crying through a half-opened door.

He hesitated, knocked lightly, and opened the door. Susan was slumped over a dressing table, crying into her arms. The bedroom was enormous—a fantasy bedroom really, almost fifty feet across, and Susan in her bathrobe seemed dwarfed by the size of it all.

"Are you all right?"

She looked up and brushed away her tears. "Oh . . . come in, Nicky. I'm all right, really. Just exhausted." And she started crying again.

Nicky sat down on the edge of her enormous double bed.

"I guess being an actress is even harder than being a cop," he said sympathetically.

"God, I'm so sick of it I could scream," she exploded. "I never thought I would say that. But, *Christ!* I'm up at five-thirty in the morning six days a week, and sometimes I'm not home until ten or eleven at night. And I've been doing this show for *five years!* Some glamorous life, I tell you. I've been so tired recently that a few times I found myself falling asleep standing up. Now *that's* not easy!"

"Well . . . you've done very well for yourself, Susan. You could always quit."

"Quit?" she repeated. "You can't quit this business. Eventually they just haul you offstage with a hook."

"What about more films?" he asked. "You don't have to do TV."

Susan sighed. "I'd like to, believe me. But it takes a different kind of talent than what I've got. I mean, I've done two movies now, and they both bombed. The critics murdered me, and even my agent is saying that if I do another bad movie it is going to start hurting my TV career. I'm . . . I'm just not good enough, Nicky. I'm a shitty actress. I didn't used to think that. But it's true. I mean, in 'Cassie' all I have to do is stand there and look sort of cute and say cute things and occasionally wave a fake gun around. The only hard part of the show is the stunts, and my double does all of those."

Susan began to cry again. Nicky went up to her, put a hand on her back, and rubbed her gently.

She turned and was in his arms. They hugged tightly and then broke free. It was a little dangerous for them to hug like that.

"You're just tired," he told her. "You'll feel better about this tomorrow."

"Nicky, tell me, it's a terrible show, isn't it?"

"It *is* pretty terrible," he admitted. "But that doesn't mean you're terrible, Susan. Just watching you move around is the one good thing the show has. *You're* the reason it's a hit."

"Oh, Nicky," she said very wearily, "it's all such bullshit." She laughed suddenly, out of nowhere. "One of the writers was on the set today. You wouldn't believe it. This guy was strutting around like he was *Shakespeare,* for chrissake."

"What's wrong, Susan? This isn't really like you to carry on and complain."

"Ha! My ex-husband, the detective!" She looked down at her feet, and her voice changed, grew very bitter. "Frank is having an affair. . . .

It seems he's been fucking Carol for years. I was the only one in Hollywood who didn't know."

Carol was the co-star of Frank's current series. On television, they played a husband and wife.

Nicky sighed. "When did you find out?"

"Last week. He came home pretty late one night. Drunk. I asked him where he was, and he just . . . told me."

"You know, I think Frank really does love you. Sleeping with Carol is probably no big thing."

"Yeah . . . Frank loves everybody. Everybody loves Frank. No big thing. I'm not really jealous. Who cares if they screw? I don't, really."

She looked at him meaningfully and let her robe fall open. She was wearing nothing underneath.

"Do you think I'm still attractive, Nicky?"

"You're beautiful, you know that. As you always will be."

"You know, I was faithful to Frank. Always. Except that one time with you, Nicky. That crazy Saturday morning on your floor." She laughed mischievously. "But that didn't really seem like being unfaithful to Frank. It's funny . . . afterward, when I was with Frank, it felt more like I was being unfaithful to you."

She came up to him closer, her robe still open. She reached and touched his hair." "I *liked* making love with you again," she said. "Why didn't you call me afterward? I could still feel you inside of me for days."

Nicky fidgeted and backed away. He was both aroused and distressed, and he suddenly felt very uncomfortable being in her bedroom in Frank's house.

"A lot of years have gone by, Susan."

"You still want me, Nicky. I know you do. I *know* you."

"It never really worked out between us. You know that."

But she only laughed and seemed far away. The years flew from her face. "God, I remember high school. I remember the songs on the radio, and how you looked in your old blue jeans and that denim work shirt you always wore, trying to look so tough. All my friends thought you were terrible. But I thought you were very . . . sensitive. And sexy."

"Stop it, Susan. I'm not so sensitive anymore."

"Nicky . . ." She came up to him, closer, and let her hand trace a line from the front of his shirt down slowly, tantalizingly, until she touched his cock.

He took her wandering hand firmly in his own and kissed her lightly on the lips—pulling back when she tried to make the kiss linger.

"Christ, Susan, you're my oldest friend in this town. My life hasn't been all that easy lately either. I *need* an old friend. So let's not do anything stupid now, and have Frank and Tanya walk in on us like this. We would regret it later."

"Okay . . . okay. I'll wait. But *you'd* better wait for me downstairs while I change. Or I'm liable to lose my self-control."

Nicky returned to the folksy barbecue on the lawn and the aroma of filet mignons sizzling on the grill. Frank was opening bottles of Dom Perignon, letting the champagne corks fly off merrily like rockets across the lawn.

# 17

He drank too much, ate too much. In a while Susan joined them, vivacious and charming, without a hint of the intimacy that had passed between them in her bedroom. Nicky felt too much of a sense of duplicity, too much underlying sadness, to enjoy the evening all that much. He left as early as he could, claiming he had to get back to the station.

Frank walked him to the Rolls and showed him how to adjust the seats and put the top up and down, and where the button was to open the electronic front gate. Frank seemed to think it was nothing, lending him a $100,000 car. What's a Rolls between us good buddies?

As Nicky drove away, in a soft cloud of luxury, it occurred to him that while many in Hollywood owed their success to manipulation, Frank owed his to being such a goddamn nice person that everybody liked him, studio bosses as well as Mr. and Mrs. Average Public. So what if he was screwing his co-star? He was just such a nice guy he had probably been unable to say no.

At the end of the driveway, Nicky touched the button near the ignition switch, and the front gate magically swung open. He drifted out into Bel Air and down out of the hills on to Sunset. He had never driven a Rolls before. It was a rather pleasant luxury. The car seemed to drive itself.

He thought, *Well, all this luxury sure hasn't made Susan too happy.* But perhaps that was just wishful thinking from a man who couldn't afford a Rolls himself. Anyway, who was happy?

He cruised into Beverly Hills, absorbed by his thoughts, thinking about high school and Susan, Tanya and Frank. It was a few blocks after crossing the Beverly Hills line that he came out of the past with a jolt. If he was not careful, there would be no future. For in this car, driving through Beverly Hills, he was a prime target for the maniac who was shooting people.

Nicky took his revolver from his holster and held it in his lap. On impulse, he took off from Sunset and began zigzagging slowly up and down the flatland part of town.

He was a big, fat, sexy Rolls-Royce target. With his revolver safety off, ready in his lap. Danger was intoxicating and brought him fully into the present.

He drove and listened, and watched. Ready to respond instantly if another car drove alongside him.

But most of the cars he saw were police vehicles, marked and unmarked, on their patrols. Some of the patrols, not recognizing him, followed at a discreet distance. Finally, after driving up and down in a clearly aimless pattern, a red light went on behind him. A police bullhorn ordered him to pull over and walk out of the car with his hands up in the air.

He did as he was told, recognizing Officers Sammy DeWolfe and Don Ewing before they recognized him. They were both new recruits, on the force for less than a year, and green as they could be. Right now, they were rigidly pointing their pistols in his direction. Fear had made them forget everything they had ever learned in the police academy.

Nicky smiled wryly. They looked like children to him, pretending to be cops. He knew he must be getting old if those in their twenties seemed so young. "At this point, you're supposed to have me turn and spread my legs and put my hands on the car," he said gently.

"That's right," Sammy replied. "Turn around and spread 'em!"

"You asshole," Don Ewing hissed at his partner. "It's Lieutenant Rachmaninoff."

Officer DeWolfe stared at him numbly. "Oh-my-God!" he said in an inadvertent Valley Girl imitation, and immediately holstered his gun. Both officers, in their short stay in Beverly Hills, had earned reputations as clowns and fuck-ups—the sort of recruit older cops liked to point to when illustrating the decline of police competence. The young cops were looking at him glumly, waiting for a reprimand.

"It's all right, guys. Not your fault. Glad you're on the ball. We're going to do this for real starting tomorrow night. I just borrowed this car and couldn't resist a little trial run."

"Boy, you'd better be careful, Lieutenant," DeWolfe told him seriously. "Believe me, you've got the only fancy car cruising these streets tonight. All the expensive cars of Beverly Hills have magically disappeared."

"Okay. I guess I'm going to call it a night. See you tomorrow."

Nicky drove back to Sunset. He drifted up Laurel Canyon, up Sunshine Terrace to his little cabin above the city. He changed into old blue jeans and a sweatshirt, throwing his work clothes on a chair, and went out on the meadow.

It was a clear night and the stars sparkled overhead almost as brightly as the city lights at his feet. He lay down in the grass. Did he want to see Julie again? Well, yes, actually. Did he want to make love to his ex-wife? Again yes. Or a qualified sort-of. It all spun around in his head, chaotically. He didn't really know what he wanted.

Nicky began to do sit-ups, slowly and rhythmically. It had been a long time since he had worked out. He counted up to twenty and kept going.

Tomorrow he was going to get up early and do a full round of exercises. He had been letting himself go too long. This fucking laziness and self-pity had to stop.

. . . 21 . . . 22 . . . 23 . . . 24 . . .

Lt. Nicholas Rachmaninoff was ready for a big change in his life.

. . . 25 . . . 26 . . . 27 . . .

He was ready to get out of this crazy town. Like Susan, he could quit.

. . . 28 . . . 29 . . . 30 . . . 31 . . .

But first he was going to catch that son of a bitch who was knocking off all these sad and beautiful people.

# PART
# FIVE

*The Cancer*

# 1

She woke before dawn, before the alarm. The enormous, soft bedroom was clothed in darkness. Frank was snoring flamboyantly by her side, blowing out clouds of vaporized Scotch into the room.

She hadn't heard him come in last night. She had fallen asleep by eleven, still waiting for him to return home.

Susan Merril, by great effort of will, began another working day. She rose alone in the predawn darkness and padded barefoot over the thick carpet to her bathroom. There were certain symbols of success in Hollywood: the bathroom was perhaps the most intimate. The greater the success, the larger the bathroom. Susan entered a complex of interlocking rooms—a dressing room that had one door opening into a huge walk-in closet, and another opening to the bathroom itself, which contained an enormous sunken tub, fit for any orgy, a separate shower, Jacuzzi, bidet, two sinks, toilet, mirrors, lights, and dressing tables. This bathroom was hers alone. Frank had another, even larger, on the opposite side of the master bedroom.

Susan had long ago stopped noticing the glory of her bathroom. This morning she had a strange feeling that everything was slipping away:

Frank, who could disappear any moment into the sunset, smiling his famous smile, his arms around another woman.

Her career. Two short years ago she had been absolutely on top. Now "Cassie and the Cop" was beginning to slide in the ratings.

Even the mansion in Bel Air. All slipping away. Most of the great houses of Beverly Hills and Bel Air changed owners very quickly, inhabited briefly by those who had just a few seasons of success. They were dream castles. You could turn around one day, and they would be gone.

Standing in her dressing room, putting on a comfortable gym suit, Susan admitted the truth. She was already on the edge of obscurity. Her public did not know yet. But Frank knew. And her agent knew. And she knew.

However, Susan was strong. Today, she forced herself through her morning ritual, making her way downstairs through the sleeping household to the sun room, which she and Frank had converted to an

113

exercise studio. The room had three walls of tinted glass, looking out on to the lawn and the small forest of the estate. She put on a tape of Vivaldi's *Four Seasons* and began her daily torture of sit-ups and stretches and aerobics. Then it was out into the early morning mist, for a run along the gravel paths that twisted through the estate, up and down through the lawns and forests.

After her shower, drying herself in front of the full-length mirror, she examined her naked body with a critical, professional eye. Had she gained any weight in the past twenty-four hours? Beauty was the source of all the good things that had ever come her way; but beauty was also a tenuous thing, changing from day to day.

Today, at least, she was satisfied. She smiled at herself seductively, puckering up her lips. . . . She had lied to Nicky about his being the only other man she had slept with, besides Frank, while she was married. There *had* been others—not many—and they were always very discreet.

It was just a little white lie, really. The others were safe and married and older. Susan liked to indulge her taste for older men who treated her like their favorite little girl. Nicky was the only one who didn't fit into the mold, and never had. He was the only one who was dangerous to her.

And so, her life on shaky ground, her future most uncertain, Susan Merril began another day. She was due in makeup at eight sharp, at the Paramount Studios in downtown Hollywood. The old days, where stars could be late getting to the set, were long past. She left the house at seven-fifteen exactly, as caught up in her routine as any factory worker answering the summons of the morning whistle. For the last five mornings, she had been driving Nicky's old Austin-Healey to work, which he had left when he took the Rolls. She told Frank it was to keep a low profile during this time of danger on the streets. But there was more to it than that.

The Austin-Healey had Nicky's warm, musky scent clinging to the upholstery. She had still been married to him when he bought the sports car, so many years ago. With everything changing so fast, Susan liked it that here, at least, was one thing that had not changed.

She eased the car into gear. Years ago, she had actually learned to drive a standard transmission in this very car; she could almost hear Nicky shouting at her not to rev the rpm's too high. She still didn't have it quite down. She lurched unevenly down the gentle sloping driveway to the closed front gate. It was awkward not having the built-in remote control. Susan had to park, get out of the car, and activate the gage by inserting the key into the lock.

The gate swung open. Susan drove through, parked once again, and put the key in another lock outside. The gate swung closed.

She was pulling the key out of the lock when she was startled by a sound behind her.

She turned and screamed.

# 2

He stepped out of the shadows and moved toward her. "Oh, please don't be afraid. . . . I didn't mean to scare you."

The man was ghostly in the early morning light. His pale face was mostly skull, from which two penetrating eyes were fastened upon her. Susan bit her lip fearfully, trying to decide if the Austin-Healey was too far away to make a run for it. The engine was idling in neutral, with the emergency brake on.

"Oh, I did scare you. I'm terribly sorry. *Please. . .*" The little man gestured helplessly. "It's just that I've run out of gas. It's the most unbelievably stupid thing! I'm out of gas," he said again, pointing to a red Corvette across the street.

Susan's heartbeat began to return to normal. She laughed nervously. "That's all right," she said at last. "You just startled me. I wasn't expecting to see anyone this time of morning."

"I live just up the road." He gestured vaguely up the street. "I can't believe I forgot to buy gas yesterday. I was wondering if I could ask you . . . I know this is a terrible imposition . . . but do you think you could give me a ride down to the gas station on Sunset? I wouldn't ask, but you see . . . you see, I'm not really very well."

Susan didn't know what to do. Natural caution told her she shouldn't pick up strangers, particularly one who looked so bizarre. But it was morning, after all. The man was certainly strange, but not really threatening. He was very fragile and polite. Susan, fresh from her morning workout, felt she could pick him up and throw him ten feet down the road if she needed to. His body seemed as insubstantial as a stalk of wheat in the wind.

"I'd be glad to pay you for your time," he said hopefully, actually reaching for his wallet. This seemed so ridiculous that she had to laugh.

"It's okay. Hop in."

"Thank you! You really are extremely kind."

They both got into the car, and she began to drive down the twisted hillside roads to Sunset. "I just didn't know what to do," he said, now that he was comfortably in the car. "I was going to try to walk to Sunset when I saw you come out of your driveway. But actually, you see . . . I'm not very well. I . . . have cancer."

This last statement came out breathlessly, in the manner of a terrible confession. Susan glanced sideways to her passenger. She could see it now, death in the man's face. She guiltily tried to suppress the fear of the healthy toward the unhealthy.

She didn't know what to say.

"I'm not bothering you, am I?"

"No," she lied, wondering how long it would take her to get to the gas station. She was beginning to regret giving him a lift. She sped up somewhat.

"I imagine a healthy and beautiful young lady like yourself wouldn't want to think about something horrible like cancer. But you should, you know. *It's all around us.* Oh, it's so strange—it was only when I learned I had cancer that I really began to live. I mean, for the first time in my life, I realized that time was running out so very fast, and I should grab hold of the moment! Take it, and do the things I wanted while I still could. My only regret is that I didn't understand this earlier. . . . I just wish I could go on television or something and tell everybody that *we are all dying.* It could happen at any moment. Right now, for instance! A car could be coming around that curve on the wrong side, and we could both die, just like that. *This could be our last moment on earth.* . . . I'm bothering you, aren't I?"

Susan laughed darkly. "Well, it *is* a little early in the morning to think about dying. But I do see what you mean."

"You do? I thought you would." The little man seemed very excited. "It's just I've had this incredible revelation that *dying is freedom!* When you know you're going to die, all your priorities turn around. Everything you've been taking seriously just isn't serious anymore. Do you see that? And other things that you never thought about, suddenly are everything."

The man was breathing hard, rubbing his hands together with furi-

116

ous energy. At a stop sign, Susan looked at him, and her heart melted just a little. Her own troubles seemed suddenly very petty.

"I'm sorry," she said. "I don't know what to say. I can hardly imagine what it would be like to have . . . cancer. You see, I can hardly say it." She laughed. "You must be very brave."

"I'm not really. It's just that I'm having a marvelous time. Like right now, talking to you. I would never have talked like this to a stranger before. But, you see, now I don't have anything to lose, and it's quite wonderful. Can you understand that?"

She laughed. "Yes, I can."

"Really? You *are* wonderful!"

"No, not really."

"You are . . . but I can tell that you worry too much. I can see it in your face. And a girl like you, you should have a marvelous time before they . . . carry you away."

She laughed. This really was one of the strangest encounters she had ever had. Already, she could imagine turning this into an interesting anecdote . . . and the strangest part of all was that this funny, nervous little man was perfectly right. It was all so sad and pathetic how seriously we took our troubles when we should seize the moment and enjoy ourselves.

She needed to remember this more. "You know something? I'm glad I picked you up this morning."

"Really? . . . *Really?*"

"Yes." She smiled. "Really. I think I was due for a little hit of reality. I guess, like most people, I get caught up in my own little bubble and forget what's really important."

"Gee, I'm glad I ran out of gas!" He said this so emphatically that Susan laughed again. The dying man's zest for life was contagious. "I have to tell you," he said, "that ever since you picked me up I've had this strange feeling that I've seen you someplace. Like I know you."

"Well, I'm an actress . . . maybe you've seen me on TV."

"You're . . . aren't you . . . my God! You're Cassie O'Day!" he screamed.

"*Susan,*" she corrected. "Susan Merril."

"Ah . . ." He squealed with delight and was so excited that Susan was worried for him. Perhaps he would have a fit and die right here in her car. "I just can't believe it! I *love* your show. You are without doubt the most beautiful woman on earth. And here I am sitting next to you!"

"Well . . . thank you." Susan never quite knew how to deal with the effusive praise of fans. She was blushing. "Thank you," she said again.

"God, I can't believe it!" he said. "I must be dreaming!"

She had reached Sunset and made a left turn toward the gas station a half-mile away.

"But this isn't *your* car?" he asked incredulously.

She laughed. "Oh, no, a friend lent it to me. With these horrible car killings going on, it seemed best not to drive around in anything too expensive."

"Oh, yes!" he agreed somberly. "It's a horrible, horrible thing, these senseless killings."

"L.A. is a violent city."

"It's everywhere, you know. Violence and craziness." He shook his head in dismay.

They reached the gas station. Susan pulled in off Sunset and put the car in neutral.

"Well, thank you, dear lady! I can't tell you what a pleasure it's been to meet such a wonderful and beautiful young lady. I feel somehow complete now."

"Now, it's nothing."

"No, it is! It is! Not many famous television stars would just stop and pick up some stranger who's run out of gas. I've got to tell you that you are as kind as you are beautiful, and I thank you from the bottom of my heart."

Susan was feeling a little uncomfortable. She wondered how she could ease him out of the car.

"Could I impose on you for one more thing? Could I have your autograph? I know it must be boring—I'm sure people ask for your autograph all the time. But it would mean so very much to me."

"Of course. Do you have a piece of paper? No? Well, I have paper in my bag. . . . What's your name?"

"Larry . . . you can just make it out to Larry."

Susan tore a page from a small notebook. She wrote: "To Larry, with much admiration to a truly courageous man. Love, Susan Merril."

He took the piece of paper, read it, and hugged it incredulously to his breast.

On a sudden impulse, Susan leaned over and kissed him briefly on the cheek. His skin felt to her like the very thinnest onionskin paper.

He sat stunned, touching his cheek where she had kissed him. He was unable to move.

118

"Well, I *do* have to go to work now."

"Oh, yes . . . yes . . ." He stumbled awkwardly out of the car, almost tripping over his feet. Susan waved and drove away.

# 3

On the sidewalk by the gas station, Lawrence Ferguson watched Susan until the car merged into the early morning traffic. He still was touching the spot on his cheek where she had kissed him.

"I love you, Cassie," he said softly. "I love you madly."

It was a long time before he could move. Finally, he telephoned a taxi from the pay phone by the gas station. In twenty minutes he was back in front of Susan and Frank's Bel Air mansion, where his Corvette was waiting for him, the tank full of gas.

He had to smile. Susan, to his mind, was certainly a great actress. But he wasn't so bad at make-believe himself.

He was exhausted by the time he got back to the Beverly Hills Hotel—not from "his condition," as he thought of it, but from the sheer excitement of the past week.

Lawrence lay down on his soft bed and looked out the French windows to the hypnotically moving palm tree outside. The maid had already done the room. It was nice to have a maid. Life had changed greatly for Lawrence since he had moved from his studio room in Santa Monica to the hotel. Occasionally—quite often in fact—he had seen famous TV and film personalities downstairs or by the pool, but Lawrence was no longer so impressed. *He* was a celebrity now. After he shot Brian Stewart, the newspapers and TV news had been full of *his* exploits. None of these glamorous show people who glided in and out of the hotel had made the front page of every newspaper across the country as *he* had.

He was more famous than all of them put together.

It was his secret, of course. But that made it more fun. In fact, when Lawrence saw a famous film star in the hotel now, he would smile condescendingly, as a greater luminary to a lesser.

And then there had been the excitement of discovering that his opponent—this Lieutenant Rachmaninoff—had been married to Cassie herself! Lawrence had come across this information in a newspaper article the second day after the Brian Stewart killing. All afternoon he had been too excited to sit down, but paced his hotel room talking to himself and sometimes laughing. Once he had cried, sobbing into his pillow with sheer relief and joy.

And she had kissed him!

Lying on his bed in the luxurious hotel room, he relived the kiss again and again. From a little peck on the cheek it gradually became a passionate, heartful kiss of love. She had wanted him. Desire had glistened in her eyes.

One day he would show her how to live. And how to love.

# 4

Lawrence was hardly aware that he rarely watched television anymore. Life was no longer something to be experienced secondhand. He watched the news, of course—but that was for his work. And he watched "Cassie." But his spare hours were taken up with quite another project.

Lawrence was writing a book about cancer.

What he had told Cassie was nonsense, of course, part of his carefully prepared act. He did not have cancer anymore. He was not going to die. In fact, it was quite the opposite. He was going to live, because he had discovered the cure to the century's most dreaded disease.

Cancer was only a state of mind. He had found that by changing his basic attitude and way of life the disease was slowly ebbing away out of his system. There were moments, of course, when he was still sick. It was impossible to correct forty-seven years in a few glorious weeks of life.

He wrote sitting around the hotel pool, occasionally summoning Guido, his favorite waiter, to bring him his usual treat—a chocolate malt made with chocolate ice cream.

The first chapter was called "I AM." It was a declaration of positive thinking. Cancer, he said, was simply a matter of negative thinking. In the second chapter, on which he was now engaged, he felt it necessary to list all the negative, life-threatening situations that would lead inevi-

120

tably to cancer. This second chapter was twenty-seven pages long and still growing.

On the afternoon after meeting Cassie, he sat down beneath his favorite umbrella by the pool and began the list where he had left off:

Waiting in line at a crowded supermarket is death.
Waiting in line at the bank is death.
Stoplights are death.
(Important note: Stop signs, if you do not come to a complete halt, are only a little bit of death.)
Commercials are death.
Office buildings are death.
Muzak in elevators is death.
Muzak over the phone is double death.
Waiting in line at the post office is death.
Paying taxes is death.
Saving money is death.
Working for goals is death.
Waiting for coffee water to boil is death.
Fear is death.
Envy is death.
(Important note: Lust and Anger are not death, if they are dealt with in the right way. This will be covered in a later chapter.)

The list went on and on. With infinite patience, Lawrence had spent days covering every conceivable situation and human emotion. Writing this book—for Lawrence—was *life*. It was part of his own self-affirmation. It would be published one day, after he was dead, and in this way his name would live on.

Of course, the main part of his own anticancer program he did not divulge. Perhaps one day ... but he knew others would not understand. It was hard to understand. Even he could not explain it fully.

Later in the afternoon, Lawrence walked from the pool to the elevator and then back to his room, deep in thought. It was time to go hunting again. This time he wanted to do something truly amazing. Something he could dedicate to his love. . . . Cassie was going to be so proud of him!

# 5

At exactly 9:00 P.M. on a Thursday night—two weeks after murdering Gerald Eastman—Lawrence Ferguson stepped out of the elevator and walked through the hotel lobby toward the carport.

There were some colorful people out tonight. In the past weeks he had become fairly used to an occasional glimpse of some young person with orange hair and bizarre clothing. He thought nothing of it. He was sophisticated now. Tonight he merely smiled to see an elderly gentleman dressed like Count Dracula, walking with a woman who looked very much like Marie Antoinette. At the curb in front of the hotel, waiting for the uniformed parking attendant to fetch his car, he watched Tarzan and Jane emerge from a stretch limousine. They were both dressed in scanty fur and looked terrifically healthy. The car behind them disgorged the Lone Ranger and Tonto, who likewise strolled into the hotel without attracting much notice.

Lawrence rolled his eyes with tolerant amusement. The people of Beverly Hills were certainly more flamboyant than those back in Santa Monica! He rather liked it, though he himself was conservatively dressed, with his oversized tan raincoat concealing the snub-nosed .38 automatic underneath. It was a misty evening. Rain had fallen earlier in the day, but now it had stopped.

Joey, the young blond parking attendant, brought the Corvette to the curb with a big grin. Even in his red valet jacket, Joey always looked as if he had just stepped out of the surf at Malibu. Lawrence enjoyed knowing the first names of the hotel employees. He slipped Joey a few dollars.

"Thanks, Mr. Ferguson. Have a good night."

"Thank you, Joey. I plan to."

Joey gave a little salute as the Corvette pulled away. "Weird dude, huh?" he said out of the side of his mouth to the other attendant, the happy smile never faltering.

"How much he give you this time?"

"Two fucking bucks."

"Hey, man, don't knock it. Like maybe that was a big tip in 1932."

The two kids chortled to themselves, as Lawrence blissfully crossed

122

Sunset. He made his first pass through Beverly Hills down Beverly Drive straight to the commercial section of town south of Santa Monica Boulevard. He had the convertible top up because of the weather, and it reduced his visibility. Still, he had the distinct impression of *cops everywhere.* In the one pass down Beverly Drive, he saw two patrol cars and at least one big anonymous car—like the Ford he used to have—that positively smacked of the police.

Even worse: There were groups of people, strangely dressed, walking on the sidewalks. This was unheard of in Beverly Hills. Something very peculiar indeed was going on tonight, and Lawrence could not figure out what. Hunting was clearly going to be more difficult than he imagined. He continued along Beverly Drive all the way to Wilshire, where he parked in front of a drugstore to figure out his next move.

A suspicion finally dawned on him. Probably it should have occurred to him earlier, but it was a long time since he had been a child, and as an adult he had lived a mostly solitary and antisocial life. Also, since quitting a regular job, he had begun to lose track of the date and the days of the week.

In front of the drugstore there was a newspaper rack. Lawrence hurried over, put change into the slot, and bought a copy of the *Herald-Examiner.* He took one look at the front page and tossed the paper in a nearby garbage can.

Lawrence sat back down in the Corvette. A subtle smile played at the corner of his mouth. At first he thought he should just go back to the hotel and wait for a better time. But this could work out yet. The more he thought about it, the happier he became.

It was October thirty-first. Halloween night. And he was the scariest goblin in town.

# 6

Halloween was a mute affair in Beverly Hills that year. There was a chill in the air, a sense of impending rain. The two car murders in the short period of two weeks had left their mark upon every aspect of day-to-day life. Even in ordinary years, Halloween had become a dangerous event, an occasion of great paranoia for parents and homeowners. Enough razor blades had been found in apples, and enough windows had been smashed, to bring out extra police patrols and private security guards. Tonight, Beverly Hills felt like an armed camp.

It was surprising, then, how many children still went optimistically from door to door, their bags opened wide, ringing doorbells and saying "Trick or Treat!" The kids of Beverly Hills, of course, were like kids everywhere else: They liked to get dressed up, and walk around at night, and have grown-ups give them lots of candy.

By the time Lawrence began cruising the streets, almost all the very small children were safely home in bed. By nine o'clock, only the sub-teens were left on the streets—those who were not quite old enough to drive and go to parties. This year, even the majority of eleven- and twelve-year-olds had adults with them, parents or butlers, or even—in some cases—bodyguards. Lawrence passed small groups of witches and goblins and creatures from outer space, guided from house to house by worried-looking adults carrying flashlights.

He returned to the residential part of Beverly Hills along Foothill Drive and cruised three long blocks toward Sunset. He drove at exactly thirty miles per hour, his every sense alert and fully alive. After he had gotten over the shock of its being Halloween, he had decided that there might be safety in numbers. Still, some of the blocks were very quiet, especially as he approached the great mansions near Sunset. His heart pounded, and there was a strange taste in his mouth. This was the true anticancer: the hunting, when time and experience seemed to compress itself into an intense, omniscient reality. All around him, Lawrence could almost feel the heat of hostile bodies that were trying to track him down.

At the corner of Foothill and Carmelita, he glimpsed a patrol car coming at him at a right angle. He kept going, at exactly thirty, putting about him an aura of invisibility. In the rearview mirror, he saw the lights of the patrol car continue past Foothill along Carmelita.

He reached Sunset without incident, made a left turn on to Alpine, and headed south again toward Santa Monica. He knew that every pass through the streets of Beverly Hills increased his risk of getting caught. Sunset and Santa Monica boulevards represented safety. Lawrence could visualize the gridiron pattern of Beverly Hills as a game board, upon which he moved at great peril between the two crowded boulevards.

In this manner, he drove up and down at random for the next half-hour. By ten o'clock, there were only a few isolated groups of Trick or

Treaters left on the streets. His car engine reverberated in the quiet canyon of houses.

He came to Rexford Drive. Near Elevado, he passed two small ghosts who were hurrying home, lugging great bags of candy. The rest of the block was very still. On the left-hand side was a public school, dark for the night, stretching all the way to the next block. On the right-hand side, the only sign of life was a police patrol car parked against the curb.

This was the exact situation for which he had been patiently searching. Lawrence reached over and opened his right-hand window, slowing down imperceptibly to twenty-five. He held the .38 underneath the raincoat as he came up next to the patrol car. Two officers were inside, lit by the ceiling light, examining a clipboard of papers. The radio squawked on senselessly, an endless river of code numbers and half-phrases.

He stopped parallel to the police vehicle and leaned over to his right-hand window as far as he could.

"Excuse me," he called. "I'm a bit lost. I was wondering if you could tell me where Doheny Drive is?"

The officer behind the steering wheel looked up. "Doheny?" he repeated. Lawrence opened fire out his right-hand window at point-blank range. The officer's face seemed to implode and disintegrate.

Meanwhile the second officer was reaching for his gun. But he was too stunned to move fast. Lawrence kept firing round after round into the patrol car. The first two bullets killed the man behind the wheel. The third shot hit the passenger in the chest, the fourth a killing shot to his brain. Still, Lawrence fired two more rounds into the dead policemen, until all the bullets were gone, and his wrist ached from the sharp kickback of the pistol. Smoke hung in the air and drifted away up the street. After the six shots, the silence was deafening and seemed to ring in his ears.

He waited, listening. Not too far away, a siren began to wail. And then from another direction, a second and a third siren joined the chorus.

Lawrence accelerated sharply down the street. As he came to the corner of Carmelita, he had a glimpse of a flashing red light several blocks away. He squealed a right-hand turn, ran halfway up the next block, and then made another right turn into an alley. At the last second before turning, he glanced into his rearview mirror. The street was empty—perhaps the police car had not seen him. He turned into the alley not knowing if it was going to mean safety or if he would be trapped in a bottleneck from the other side.

He drove as fast as he dared down the narrow lane, past garbage cans and bins full of leaves and branches. In the flats of Beverly Hills, the alleys run parallel to the streets, servicing the rear of every house. Lawrence had explored these back roads in the daytime, a week earlier. It had occurred to him then that the real life of Beverly Hills was more apparent here in the rear than in the front. You actually saw children playing and had glimpses into the protected backyards.

Lawrence raced along at forty. He had a claustrophobic feeling of being in a tunnel. Halfway to the next cross street, he hit a bag of leaves and a garbage can that someone had left too far from the side wall. Leaves, grass, and garbage flew in all directions. Lawrence cursed and slowed down just a little.

A hundred feet before the alley spilled out into Elevado, Lawrence braked to a stop and turned off his headlights, letting the engine idle.

In every direction now, far and near, came the awful wail of sirens, rising and falling in the night. Everywhere there was menace and danger. Lawrence stared at Elevado just a hundred feet away, and he wondered what danger was waiting for him there.

He remembered that his .38 was empty. He turned on the small map light by the ashtray and groped on the floor for the spent cartridges. He found four shells and tossed them out the window toward a plastic garbage bag. The other two must have flown out the window as he was firing; he could not find them in his car.

Then he took out a box of shells from his raincoat pocket and began to reload the clip. He had four bullets pressed down into the spring of the clip when a siren screamed by very close.

Lawrence slammed the clip into the handle of the gun: Four bullets would have to do.

Ahead of him, at the end of the alley, a police car raced past on Elevado, just a blur of flashing red and blue lights. The siren soon grew fainter; fortunately no one had considered the maze of alleys yet. But Lawrence was certain this would not last for long.

He drove almost to the end of the alley and listened one last time. As far as he could tell, there were no cars with sirens nearby, but he was very nervous. He found his hands were slippery with sweat: the left hand on the steering wheel, the right holding both the .38 and the stick shift. He was ready to drive, or to shoot—whichever came first.

Lawrence flicked on his headlights, and froze.

126

At the top of the alley, two ghosts stood paralyzed in the beams of light. The bigger ghost held the smaller ghost's hand. They both faced the Corvette, unable to move, clutching their bags of candy. They had frightened no one tonight except Lawrence, who screamed with the shock of their sudden appearance.

For one insane moment, he thought he was looking at the spirits of the policemen he had just murdered.

Lawrence revved his engine. The car lurched forward and mowed the children down. Tootsie Rolls and lollipops, Candy Corn and Hershey bars: all were sent flying in every direction and lay at last broken on the pavement among small pools of blood.

# PART SIX

# SIX

*The Politics of Death*

# 1

This was Lieutenant Rachmaninoff's fifth consecutive night as a decoy. By day he had interviewed all the members of Brian Stewart's band, as well as his various producers, friends, lovers, and favorite recording engineers. He had also talked with dozens of psychopaths and losers, failed actors and writers—those who had been beaten by Hollywood's harsh game. And still there was nothing. Not a clue. Not a glimmer.

And at night, he cruised in Frank's Rolls, with a large support team of marked and unmarked cars spread out in a great circle around him. This had all seemed very promising at first, but after five nights everyone was discouraged and bored.

Right before the pistol shots, Nicky had been in a familiar late-night limbo of fast-changing images from his interior landscape. He talked with his dead father. He apologized to Julie Eastman for acting like an asshole . . . better yet, he lived out the evening the way it should have gone, uninterrupted by the harsh flashlights of the Malibu deputies. Uninterrupted by death . . . Nicky was driving, but he was half asleep. Working both day and night was becoming a bad habit he could easily break.

Then: six explosions, one right after the other, fired almost rhythmically in perfect six-eight time.

By the second shot, Nicky was fully awake, out of his stupor. By the fourth shot, he had pulled over to the curb and turned off his engine and police radio so he could hear better. He almost had a fix on the direction when the last shot was fired. The silence that followed was more ominous than what had come before.

Nicky waited.

In the distance, the first siren began to wail. And then another. He flicked on his radio and called Charlie, who was in a mobile command center a few blocks away. They had their own task force frequency so they could talk to each other directly, undisturbed by regular police routine. This was supposed to be a well-organized operation.

"Did you hear it, Charlie? Where did the shots come from?"

"Don't know yet, Rock Man . . . wait a moment. Everyone's calling in at once. I'll get back to you."

The next five minutes were utter chaos. Almost every cop in Beverly Hills was on duty Halloween night, pulling in overtime. Besides the regular patrol cars, there were fifteen special task force vehicles on the street tonight, as well as the Rolls and the mobile communications van. As if on cue, each officer turned on his siren, got on the radio, and began speeding about Beverly Hills in crazy circles. Everyone went on the radio at the same time, and no one could tell where the shots had come from.

Over the din of radio voices, Charlie was taking charge. Nicky heard him shout at everybody to get off the air. When there was silence, he began checking in with each vehicle, one by one, asking first for their position, and then if they had some idea of the origin of the gunfire.

Nicky didn't wait. He kept his radio up loud and drove toward the center of Beverly Hills. Sound at night was confusing; the shots had seemed to ricochet and come from several different directions at once. But Nicky let his instincts take over. He raced down to Carmelita and turned west, looking up and down each passing street. All he saw were other police vehicles in blind motion like himself. No one even knew what he was looking for.

Meanwhile, on the radio, all of the fifteen patrol cars had reported in, except for car 257, which was manned by Officers Don Ewing and Sammy DeWolfe.

Charlie was trying to raise them on the radio. "Car 257, report your status . . . 257, come in, you guys . . . Don? Sammy? Where the hell are you?"

Nicky raced along Carmelita with a sickening dread.

Suddenly, on the radio, came a hysterical voice: "No! Oh, holy shit! Oh, no! Sergeant, I found 'em . . . oh, Lord!"

Nicky pulled over to the curb, stopped his car, and listened. Charlie was making a noble and futile effort to restore order. "Attention *everybody!* Pull over to the curb, turn off your goddamn sirens, and await further instructions!"

The quadraphonic din of police sirens, which was beginning to sound like the end of the world, quickly subsided.

"All right, now who's found them? Who's reporting what?"

"This is Officer Adams, sir" came a shaky voice on the radio. "I've found car 257 on Rexford, about two hundred feet north of Carmelita. Ewing and DeWolfe are inside the car and they're dead, sir. They're shot to fucking pieces!"

Nicky could feel the hysteria rising in the policeman's voice. His own feelings were too shattered even to allow out of their carefully closed box for examination. He picked up his microphone and pressed the send button.

"Okay, Adams, this is Lieutenant Rachmaninoff. I want you to stay right there. Everybody else fan out and approach Rexford with your eyes open. Pay attention to the alleys. I want every car and person you find stopped and screened. We're going to get this sucker *tonight!* Now, Charlie, I want you to call the station and have them implement 'Close Beverly.' Also, you'd better have them wake the captain and send out the M.E. and the lab boys. When you're finished, rendezvous with me at the scene of the shooting."

"Will do."

Nicky sped toward Rexford, squealing around the final corner in an undignified manner the makers of Rolls-Royces had never intended. The unlucky car 257 stood by the curb, looking unusually still. The windshield was milky with spiderweb cracks and bullet holes. Nicky parked the Rolls and walked around to the side of the car. Officer Adams stood near the car, choking down his tears; his face was a ghastly shade of white. Nicky himself felt as if someone had shot Novocain into his soul. Hollowness reached out from his center and seemed to engulf his arms and legs, his heart and brain. He really did not want to look inside the patrol car.

There was broken glass. Pools of blood. A sticky, sweet smell of death. The two policemen had met death with great surprise and fear. Don Ewing had been taken out without a struggle. Sammy DeWolfe, in the passenger's seat, had his revolver halfway out of his holster. The gun lay precariously balanced, held by dead and bloodless fingers. This was the only visible sign of resistance.

Nicky had a cruel image of these young officers, very much alive, rousting him from the Rolls-Royce last week. Now, even in death, they still looked to him like children.

"You know, I've never lost any men before," he said finally, in a strangely calm and hollow voice. "No one in my command has ever been killed, while they were under my orders."

Officer Adams looked at Nicky as if he were mad.

It didn't matter. In the distance sirens screamed again, closing in on Beverly Hills from all sides. Nicky felt as if he were in the eye of a hurricane. In a moment or two, this little spot on Rexford Drive would be the center of furious activity. But now the scene belonged only to Adams and himself. And the two dead men in the car.

A siren, coming ever closer, pulled at him. It was the scream he wished would come from his lips.

Without warning, he raised his fists and brought them down as hard as he could upon the hood of the dead patrol car.

"Goddamn it!" he shouted at the top of his lungs.

What a stupid thing to do! For good measure, he pounded the unresisting metal one more time.

# 2

So far, roadblocks had been established all around the perimeter of Beverly Hills. Everyone leaving the town limits was being stopped and questioned and asked to show identification. All these names and addresses were being recorded. There was heavier than normal traffic tonight due to Halloween, and already there were massive traffic jams on both ends of Sunset, Santa Monica, Melrose, Beverly Boulevard, Wilshire, Coldwater, and Benedict Canyon roads. The highway patrol had its hands full. Nicky's hope was first to isolate Beverly Hills from the outside world, and then examine every street and alley, inch by inch, for the monster who had killed his men. The majority of the cars were placed in a rectangle around the outer perimeter of Beverly Hills. They formed a dragnet, moving slowly in toward the center on Rexford Drive.

There was a knock on the door of the communications van, where Nicky and Charlie sat before an array of high-tech radio gear and maps of Beverly Hills. Sergeant Bramley, on loan to the task force from downtown, stuck his beefy face inside. The sergeant was an older man, who always treated Nicky with a certain amount of sarcasm. "Hey, Lieutenant, I took it upon myself to question some of the neighbors. I've got a guy across the street who saw the shooting. Says the killer was driving a light-colored Corvette."

"Did he get a look at the killer's face?"

"You kidding? He was looking down from a second-story window. As soon as he realized there were bullets flying, he ducked the hell down and didn't look up again till the Corvette was gone."

"All right. Thanks, Sergeant. Charlie, put that on the radio, will you? At least we know what we're looking for now."

A new face appeared in the rear window: Captain Molinari, who looked dazed, like a sleepwalker or a ghost. Nicky pushed open the van's back door, and the captain loomed very large before them.

"How did this happen, Nick?" he asked quietly. "How did we lose two good men?" Near hysteria on the radio interrupted his thoughts. Almost simultaneously, three different Corvettes—in various parts of Beverly Hills—had been stopped and the drivers pulled out of their cars at gunpoint by very nervous policemen.

Nicky took the radio away from Charlie. "Hold them," he ordered. "Take them down to the station and make them prove where they were the last hour. Have the lab go over the cars."

"Nick, for chrissake, you can't arrest everyone in Beverly Hills who's driving a Corvette!" the captain said.

He shrugged his shoulders. "Well, with all shit breaking loose, a few irate citizens won't make much difference."

The next radio message came from a twenty-year veteran, on loan to the task force from Hollywood. In a flat voice, empty of emotion, he announced the discovery of two unconscious children found at the head of an alley, near Beverly Drive and Elevado. The children appeared to be victims of a hit-and-run. They were more or less alive.

Nicky and the captain exchanged dark looks, while Charlie radioed for an ambulance.

"Maybe this is related?" the captain asked.

"Jesus!" was all Nicky could say. He was busy finding the alley on the map of Beverly Hills. He noticed it was in the path of a reasonable line of flight from where they were on Rexford to Sunset Boulevard. "Charlie, radio all the CHP units on Sunset. Tell 'em there's a good possibility the killer is headed their way. Captain, why don't you and I go and take a look at that alley?"

Nicky climbed out of the rear of the van. The scene surrounding the two dead policemen was growing in size and intensity. Two new arrivals came screeching up: a police car, followed by a long black limousine. Out of the limo stepped the mayor of Los Angeles and the chief of police.

Captain Molinari spoke out of the side of his mouth. "Holy shit! You ready for this, my friend?"

"No," he answered bluntly.

It was moments like these when Nicky wondered again why the hell he hadn't stayed in New York and become a professor of English literature.

# 3

The mayor was an elegant black man, with a round, bowling-ball face. He had been a policeman for a number of years before going into politics, and there was a no-nonsense air about him. Chief of Police McWilliams, walking two paces behind, was a big, tough cop of the old school, who looked as if he might be the leader of the local Ku Klux Klan. The black mayor and the redneck police chief made an unusual duo.

Nicky had known both men over the years. Without a word, he took the two dignitaries over to the dead men in the car. The mayor winced only slightly, while the chief betrayed no emotion at all. They looked into the car seeing headlines and politics, not men.

"I don't understand how this happened," the mayor said at last. "Can you explain this, Lieutenant? Were they asleep, or what?"

Nicky found this irritating, and unfair to the dead. He only shook his head.

"Well, what exactly is the status of your investigation?" the police chief asked. "What we need now is an arrest."

The mayor, the chief of police, even Captain Molinari—all regarded him solemnly, as if this bit of mayhem on Halloween night somehow were his fault. Nicky had a childish feeling that they were all playing a game of tag, and he was *it*. He spoke very quietly. "We have a new problem, I'm afraid. Two children have been run down on Elevado. The captain and I were on our way over there, when you two gentlemen arrived."

The mayor continued to study him carefully, with narrowed eyes. "Well then, we'd better get over there, hadn't we? You can ride with us."

The three older men climbed into the back of the limousine and settled into the plush rear seat. Nicky was offered the fold-out jump seat. He rode the short distance to the alley without a word, staring bleakly out the car window at the passing houses. All the Trick or Treaters had long since disappeared, but Halloween was not completely over in Beverly Hills. Entire families stood in their doorways, watching the passing parade of emergency vehicles with ghoulish interest. Captain Molinari was talking nonstop, trying to make up for Nicky's silence.

He described the roadblocks out of Beverly Hills, and the fact that the perp's car had been definitely identified as a Corvette. He said that, with any luck, they would have the killer in custody within the hour. It sounded good, but no one was paying any attention to the captain.

The ride was mercifully brief. The limousine arrived at the end of the alley at the same time as the ambulance. Three police cars were blocking off traffic, their red and blue lights flashing patterns along the street.

Two small forms, the children, were lying where they had been scattered, at both sides of the alley entrance. They were half hidden beneath shrubbery, which is why they had escaped notice for almost half an hour.

Nicky rushed out of the mayor's limousine as soon as it stopped. He squashed a Tootsie Roll beneath his foot. There was candy everywhere. Paramedics were busy examining the kids. Their ghost costumes had been cut away, revealing two blond faces. The older was a girl, perhaps eleven. The younger was a boy, eight or nine. Nicky knelt by one of the paramedics. "How are they?" he asked.

The man flashed him a brief look of *Leave me alone, asshole, so I can do my work!* Nicky was sympathetic: It was just the way moments before he had been looking at the mayor. "They're alive," the medic answered. "Barely."

The ambulance attendants were bringing up the stretchers.

"Hold on a second," Police Chief McWilliams said loudly, before the children could be moved. "Where's the fucking photographer? Where's the lab?"

Nicky looked up at the bull-like chief. "They're not here yet. Everyone's still around car 257 on Rexford."

"Well, get them here, for God's sake. You gotta get a fucking picture of these kids before you move 'em."

Nicky glared at the man. This was quite correct. The position in which the kids had been thrown would reveal countless things to the various experts. A photograph was definitely in order. Only it didn't take into account the fact that the children were in need of urgent medical care.

Nicky stood up and turned directly to the ambulance attendants. "Get these children to the hospital," he shouted. *"Now!"*

He looked over to the mayor for confirmation. The city's leader was standing nearby, his hands on his hips, watching in silence. The mayor nodded briefly. The attendants carried the children away, while Chief

McWilliams regarded Nicky with cold and predatory eyes. Nicky realized he had just made a very serious enemy, but for the moment he gave not a shit.

The ambulance pulled out just as the police photographer and the lab unit arrived.

"Nicky? Come over here for a second."

He looked up, surprised, to see the mayor gesturing to him. The politician put a hand on Nicky's shoulder. He had a quiet and intellectual public image, but the hand on Nicky's shoulder felt as hard as steel.

"Look, I can see there's a lot of pressure on you right now, Lieutenant," he said softly, so that no one else could hear. "You're the man in the hot seat, but you just gotta be cool, and it'll turn out okay. You dig?"

Nicky looked into the shrewd brown eyes and felt some of the strength and determination of this black man who had managed to become the mayor of the city of Los Angeles. Nicky had never before heard him speak quite as casually as this, either in public or in private. The steel hand, which seemed as though it could break his neck as easily as swat a fly, patted him affectionately on the shoulder. "I like you, Nicky. You got a little growing up to do, but you're a good cop."

The mayor winked, and the moment was over. He moved away and walked with Chief McWilliams to say some words to the press, on the other side of the ropes.

Nicky was stunned. *A good cop?* He certainly didn't feel like one, not tonight. But the words had their effect. He was ready to carry on.

"Lieutenant, excuse me." A plainclothes cop, carrying a walkie-talkie, came hurrying up to him. "We've found something down the alley. Some bullet shells and garbage all over the place."

"Bullets and garbage, huh? Well, shit . . . let's take a look."

# 4

Jason Whittle, an elderly, professorial-looking man who reminded Nicky just a little of photographs he had seen of Albert Einstein, was standing down the alley, waiting for him. A photographer and a uniformed cop were also nearby.

"So what do you have for me, Jason?"

A craggy finger pointed toward the alley wall. "We got four empty thirty-eight cartridges scattered near that garbage can. I would say they were tossed out of a car."

The policeman obligingly shone his light on each of the four shells. To Nicky they looked like the droppings of some monstrous animal.

"There are two more empty shells someplace," he said. "I counted six shots."

Jason Whittle shrugged. "We were lucky to find these in the dark. . . . Come on, there's more."

They walked together, with the photographer trailing several feet behind. The sound of their footsteps was loud in the night. From the backs of the houses, Nicky could see lights in second-story windows, warm and beckoning from the desolation of the alley.

A hundred yards farther along, a policeman was standing by himself with a flashlight. The cop seemed spooked, all by himself in the night. He was relieved to see the approaching men.

*"Voilà! le garbage!"* Jason said grandly, indicating the strewn leaves, dog-food cans, and unsavory bits of refuse scattered along a twenty-foot path. "I think our killer was going too fast and had himself a little accident."

"I see. Did he leave anything for us?"

Jason smiled thinly. "Naturally. We all leave traces behind wherever we go—our little spent offerings of good and evil. We'll find something."

Nicky raised an eyebrow. This had been a very intriguing way of saying "Nothing yet." No wonder the man was head of his department.

Nicky looked up the alley and tried to imagine the killer: murdering two policemen, rushing through this alley to get away—a little too fast, it turns out, for he has a small collision with a pile of garbage. He keeps on, slower, until he reaches the end of the alley. He stops, listens, gets rid of as many empty bullet shells as he can find, and then makes his leap out of the alley for safety . . . only two small ghosts, on their way home from Trick or Treating, happen to be at the wrong place at the very worst of times. The killer runs them down. . . .

It was fairly straightforward. Except, where the hell was the guy? How could the Corvette vanish into thin air?

# 5

I wonder whatever happened to the Age of Aquarius?"

"The *what?*"

"The Age of Aquarius," Nicky insisted. "Don't you remember? There was supposed to be enlightenment and love and peace on earth. . . . Whatever happened to all that?"

Charlie Cat snorted his contempt. "It was all kaka bullshit, that's what happened," he said. "Just a lot of self-serving nonsense. You and I are not fools, Rock Man. We know that people are bad. They are greedy, lustful, envious, and insecure. And there would be a hell of a lot more murder in this world, except for the likes of us, strutting around with our guns and billy clubs, keeping people in line."

Nicky and his partner sat in the submarine gloom of the communications van. It was after two o'clock in the morning, and most of the task force had been sent home.

Officers Sammy DeWolfe and Don Ewing were at the L.A. County Morgue. The two children were in intensive care at Cedars Sinai Hospital. They had been identified: Carrie Provlaska, aged twelve, and her brother Alyosha, who was nine. Their father was a well-known composer, Alexander Provlaska, who had fled the Soviet Union a decade earlier and had been doing well in Hollywood ever since, writing rousing orchestral scores for big-budget adventure movies. The kids lived with their mother. She had gone to a Halloween party, leaving the children on their own, and had returned—very drunk—at one in the morning with two young men in tow. The police had been waiting on her doorstep to drive her to the hospital. But the woman could not stand up unaided and seemed not to be able to understand what they told her. The cops decided to let her go to bed and sleep it off. Tomorrow she would have the worst hangover of her life.

As for the children, they were in critical but stable condition. Neither one had yet regained consciousness. Nicky put an officer in the corridor outside intensive care. His job was to let Nicky know the moment the kids' condition changed for better or worse.

And the investigation itself: Examination of the physical evidence

140

had revealed surprisingly little. Nothing, in fact, had been left behind around car 257. Everything they had, so far, was in the alley—the garbage, the bullet shells, and also a clear impression of a tire mark in a chocolate bar found near the children. A plaster mold of the chocolate bar had already been made, and tomorrow—perhaps—the type of tire would be identified. This, of course, could be useful one day in a courtroom, but had no immediate value.

Most important of all, what they did not find was the killer. He had apparently gotten on a broomstick and flown away.

By one o'clock, new disasters had begun to pop up around West Los Angeles, draining off the high concentration of policemen in Beverly Hills. A hostage had been taken by a gunman in a liquor store hold-up on La Cienega . . . an elementary school had been set on fire by teenage vandals in posh Brentwood . . . a prostitute had been stabbed to death on Hollywood Boulevard. Squad cars rushed off, their sirens screaming, to the new disasters. It was all in a night's work. By two o'clock, Nicky and Charlie had lost all but six patrol cars. It seemed pretty hopeless.

Not long after two, Nicky sent Charlie home, and half of the remaining patrol cars. He sat by himself in the communications van, before the banks of high-tech electronic equipment, and tried to get his thoughts in order.

The question he asked himself was, Why had two policemen been killed?

It did not fit the pattern of these murders up to now: single, successful Hollywood men gunned down as they drove through Beverly Hills in expensive cars. Patrol car 257 was certainly no Rolls or Mercedes-Benz. The men inside were neither rich nor successful.

A few days earlier, Nicky and Charlie had spent an afternoon with a criminal psychologist from U.C.L.A., Dr. Dorothy Anglund, trying to work up a psychological portrait of the killer. Dr. Anglund had made two points in particular that had intrigued Nicky and had been circling about in his mind ever since.

The first: Crazy people believe they have a logical motivation for what they do. You simply have a different starting point—a different bias, as it were, from which the logic springs.

And second: With mass murderers, the motive can change over the course of the crimes. If killing has become in itself an enjoyable release, then it might be sought simply for its own sake, regardless of the original motive of the first crime.

Maybe gunning down the policemen was just an "enjoyable release."

Christ!

Maybe it was a personal challenge to Nicky himself.

Maybe it was totally arbitrary. Gerald Eastman, Brian Stewart, and now the men of car 257 had simply been the first targets available for some unhappy person who wanted to see blood of any kind, no matter whose.

If you knew the motive, you could generally find the killer. That was basic. But in this case, there were too many maybes. That had been the problem from the beginning—too many possibilities and no real information.

Sitting in the semidarkness of the van, Nicky began to imagine various characters who might be the person he sought.

First, there was the failed screenwriter, whom he had thought about before and who was almost becoming a real person in his imagination. Nicky called him Peter, to give him a little more flesh and blood. Peter had once been good-looking, though now his face was decadent and cruel. He had not sold anything for ten years, and the Corvette was the last remaining possession of more successful days. Perhaps he had once imagined being a serious writer, a novelist. But he had sold his soul to Hollywood, which did not even want him anymore.

Then there was Ridgely, sixteen years old, living in one of the mansions nearby. Ridgely was a real sicko. He made life hell for Mommy and Daddy, just as Mommy and Daddy made life hell for him. They gave him every material thing his rotten little heart desired, including a vintage Corvette for his sixteenth birthday. But it still wasn't enough. Ridgely's favorite pastime was to kill people.

The last character in Nicky's little menagerie was not a man but a woman. Nicky, as a matter of fact, had brought up the possibility of the killer's being a woman with Dr. Anglund, who had been almost violently opposed to the very thought. Impossible, she said: *There has never been a female serial killer.*

Women killed people they knew, usually for very specific reasons of the heart. Only men could kill total strangers for no apparent reason at all.

But Nicky was not so sure. He called his imaginary woman Lady Macbeth. She was quite sexy in a dark and witchy way. Perhaps she had been raped as a young woman, and killing strange men was her form of revenge. In operational terms, she had a great advantage over Peter and Ridgely. Driving up alongside of men, late at night, in her little open Corvette, the victims would not be on guard. Perhaps she would smile at them seductively, before blowing them away.

It was a lot easier to imagine these various killers, Peter and Ridgely and Lady Macbeth, than to find the real killer.

Meanwhile, the night passed slowly by, minute by minute. Several times he thought to end the search for the evening, but something held him there. Perhaps it was just self-indulgence. He could tell from the tired, discouraged voices on the other end of the radio that his officers had lost hope. It was only when the gray light of dawn began inching in upon the night that he admitted temporary defeat. He called the remaining men on patrol and sent them home. He could feel the relief in their voices over the air.

He had one of his men return the communications van to the station while he reclaimed the burgundy Rolls-Royce, feeling ridiculous behind the wheel of the luxurious car. Some decoy he was! Guilt kept him going. He drove to the station instead of returning home. He wanted, at least, to plan out the course of the next day before going to sleep.

His office seemed stark and barren by dawn's early light. He picked up the telephone and tried the hospital again. A weary nurse told him that the two children were hanging on, but there was no change in their condition. He put down the phone and began to write a note for Charlie: *Let's get some media help. Call major TV and radio networks. Set up a hot line for anyone in Beverly Hills who might have seen something.*

What else? Surely there was something more he could do. He brought out the two thick files that covered the deaths of Gerald Eastman and Brian Stewart. There were many words here, and in all these words maybe he was missing something . . . but his brain was soggy with fatigue and couldn't seem to bring it all together.

He laid his head down on his desk for just a moment . . . and jerked himself awake an hour later. It was definitely time to go home. He forced his bones to carry him downstairs to the waiting Rolls.

It was a little past eight in the morning. The streets were full of freshly risen faces beginning another day. Nicky pulled out of the police parking lot and began driving home. It was on Rodeo Drive, halfway to Sunset, that he got an interesting new idea—one that had nothing to do with his multiple murder case. He was too exhausted to resist such an interesting idea.

He made a left turn on Elevado and headed over to Lomimar Drive to see if Julie Eastman was at home.

# 6

Standing in front of the ornate wooden door, he had some second thoughts about the wisdom of this move. Too late now. He rang the doorbell, and a Mexican maid he had not seen before opened the door.

*"Buenos diás,"* she said.

*"Buenos diás* to you, too. Is Mrs. Eastman in?"

The maid looked at him blankly.

"Señora Eastman, *por favor?"*

"Ah . . . *momento."* The girl disappeared indoors. The fact that most servants no longer spoke English was creating monumental communication problems in certain parts of town. Nicky had heard many rich house owners mourn quietly for the days when blacks took care of them. The good old days, before blacks decided that one of their number could be mayor of the city, or multimillion-dollar entertainers.

In a moment, Julie appeared in her open doorway. She wore a robe of white silk. She looked ready for karate or Tai Chi, but not for Nicky. Her face registered a quick succession of emotions upon recognizing him: surprise, relief, and irritation. She blocked the front door with her body.

"Hello," she said coldly. "What do *you* want?"

"I . . . uh, wanted to speak with you."

"Is this an official visit, Lieutenant?"

"No."

"Then I don't know what we have to talk about."

"Listen, I realize I acted pretty badly the last time I saw you. I've been wanting to come by and see if we could work something out."

"There's nothing to work out."

"Julie . . . for just a little while, there was something pretty strong between us. I've been thinking about that—and you know, these things don't happen so often that you can afford to throw them away."

She regarded him quietly, her expression cold and unchanged. Finally: "Yeah, there was something between us for a few hours. It was the world's fastest love affair, and then you turned into some zombie policeman driving ninety miles an hour back to town. *I thought I was going to die in that fucking car!* By the way, you look horrible."

"I was up all night. Haven't been to bed yet."

"Well, why don't you go home and go to bed, Nicholas?"

"Because this is important!" he shouted, and then immediately lowered his voice. "I'm sorry ... but can't you understand how lousy it was for me to get caught with my pants down, literally. By colleagues! If you can call those jerks policemen."

Julie smiled, just a little, at the memory. But the smile was replaced quickly by severe frost. However, she stood on the doorstep waiting for more.

"And then I found out there was another killing. . . . Christ, it was my case! I felt guilty that I was making love with you at Zuma when I should have been in Beverly Hills. I was on duty, for chrissake."

"Isn't it the duty of every officer to help a woman in distress?" she asked bitterly.

"Julie!"

"Okay, I hear you. I've thought about it, too, believe me. I know you're an honest, hardworking policeman just trying to do his job and all that. But you have to see it from my point of view. I really don't want to have another workaholic, success freak in my life. One time around was enough! I just want a man who knows how to love, and to feel, and values those things at least as much as his work. I don't think it's too much to ask."

"No, it's not too much to ask," he said, very much aware that he had not made it past the doorway, and beginning to doubt if he would. "Don't you think I feel things? I'm actually a pretty emotional guy, if you haven't noticed ... but I'm a cop, it's true. And I do get into some life-and-death situations that *are* more important than my feelings or my personal life."

Julie laughed bitterly. "Jesus! Don't you think Gerald thought he had life-and-death situations when some $20 million deal was hanging in the balance? I'm sick of all that bullshit, I tell you! I don't want it anymore. . . . You should go find yourself a nice young girl who hasn't been through all that shit before."

Nicky felt as if bullets had gone through his body. "I don't want to find some nice young girl," he said quietly. "I want to find you."

She glared at him, as if challenging him to say more. Their eyes met. Hers were deep green today, with swimming flecks of brown and gold; they were always different every time he looked into them. Suddenly, her expression softened and her body relaxed.

"You really do look exhausted, Nicholas. You should take care of yourself."

He snorted contemptuously at the idea of taking care of himself. "I lost two of my men last night. Two policemen shot. Dead. *Finis.*" The words brought it all back, and for a second tears wanted to gush out. This was ridiculous. He looked off down the street and tried to force his emotions back in line. "I'm sorry. I guess that's why I came over this morning. I sure wasn't wild about the idea of going home. But I'm all right now. . . . Listen, Julie, just think about what I said, okay? And I'll get back to you sometime when I've had a little more sleep."

He turned and began walking down the steps toward the Rolls.

"Nicholas, come back here," she called. "Come on inside."

He turned and faced her again. "You sure?"

"I'm sure."

She took him by the arm and led him into the living room. Nicky was too tired to resist. She put him on a deep, white sofa and sat down beside him. "I saw it on the news this morning. I'm really sorry about the two policemen. Is it the same person who killed Gerald?"

"I think so," he answered wearily. "But maybe I'm wrong. There could be a copy cat killer. As soon as someone is successful in Hollywood, everyone tries to imitate him. At this rate, we could have a Car Killer Five, Six, and Seven in no time at all."

She watched him steadily, not amused. "How about the two children? Are they going to make it?"

Nicky shrugged his shoulders bleakly.

Julie was suddenly angry. "Well, why don't you cry, Nicholas? What kind of asshole are you, anyway, to sit there shrugging your shoulders when two of your men are dead and two little children have been half killed in some alley? You almost cried out there on the steps, I saw you. You think I'm going to call you a sissy? You jerk, *cry!*"

Faced with such compelling logic, Nicky realized he should probably do as she said. He cried. It had been coming for some time. Julie was neither embarrassed nor cloying, but simply waited for him to be through.

He wiped away the last tears with the back of his hand. He felt miserable, but cleansed somehow. "Shit," he said, "I bet Sam Spade never cried."

"Who cares? Fuck Sam Spade."

"Yeah? Actually, I was hoping you'd fuck *me.*"

She looked at him a moment before replying. "Okay. But first I'm going to get you in my bathtub and feed you some breakfast. As a general rule, I don't like to have unwashed policemen starving to death in my bed."

# 7

Julie's bathtub was almost the size of a small indoor swimming pool. Nicky groaned with delight. He wallowed in the jet spray of the Jacuzzi. Julie came in after a while with a mug of hot coffee, which she put on the side of the sunken marble tub.

"Join me," he said. "The water's fine."

She laughed. It was amazing to him how different she looked when she was cold and angry and when she was happy and laughing. Her face grew animated and childlike. Years slipped away. She bent over the tub and kissed him on the lips. But when his hands began to stray beneath her robe, she pulled away.

"You're going to make me burn your crab omelet."

"Oh, no! I can't stand women who burn my crab omelet."

She left him to return to the kitchen, and Nicky resumed his game of playing otter in the hot water. Far away, another part of his mind whispered: *Car Killer, Car Killer, where are you?* But no answer came, not even an echo of a half-thought. Not a glimmer.

The coffee that Julie left on the side of the tub was heavily laced with Cognac. Nicky felt like a sultan. Although he had always vaguely disapproved of the excesses of the Beverly Hills rich, on this particular morning self-indulgence didn't seem too bad. Halfway through the coffee, Julie stuck her head in the door. She tossed a white terry-cloth robe onto a chair. "Breakfast is served," she announced. "In the bedroom. Clothing is optional."

He stepped out of the tub, toweled himself down, and put on the

147

thick, soft robe. His gun and holster were draped around a chair in the bathroom, along with the rest of his clothes. What to do with your gun always presented an occupational hazard with policemen when visiting strange ladies. He made a ball out of his clothing, with the revolver tucked away in the middle, and carried it and the cup of coffee into the adjoining bedroom. Julie was struggling with a bottle of champagne. His breakfast waited for him, covered on a wicker tray sitting on the great king-size bed that dominated Julie's bedroom. He offered to help her with the champagne cork, but she gestured him into bed.

Nicky slipped between satin sheets, while she held the breakfast tray for him, setting it down gently on his lap when he was settled. Then she brought over two tulip-shaped wineglasses, filled halfway with fresh orange juice, the other half with Mumm's. They touched glasses and she sat down on the side of the bed to watch him eat.

"You would be a very good person to have in a harem," he said. She laughed, but Nicky considered for a moment that it was the independent women, like Julie, who could be the most feminine and serving. The weak, insecure women were the ones who always demanded to be served by the man.

"What are you thinking?" she asked.

"That you're wonderful." He set to work on his crab omelet, which had a light cream sauce inside the fold of the egg. He washed down a few bites with a swallow of champagne and orange juice. Julie watched him in a very catlike and satisfied manner. Nicky felt like purring.

"You make it look fun to be rich," he said.

"Only if you have someone to share it with."

"I would think that part would be easy."

"Not if you have discerning tastes," she said. "Would you like to be rich?"

"I don't know. I never thought so before. It's funny; most of the kids I grew up with have lots of money now. Or they're dead. I'm the only person I know who hasn't made it to either place. Anyway, I'm not really into owning a big home or a fancy car, or any of that stuff. But I wouldn't mind having money to travel. I have a fantasy of spending a few years traveling around the world. I'd do a lot of walking."

Julie spread out on the bed, propping herself up on one elbow. She continued to regard Nicky curiously with her large hazel eyes.

"Have you traveled outside the States?" she asked him.

"Well, Mexico, of course. A few years ago I spent a month in Europe. What I want, if I ever get the chance, is to go to Peru."

148

"*Peru?* Why there?"

Nicky shrugged. "I like llamas."

"You like llamas," she repeated, moving closer. "I thought they spit at people and are very grouchy."

"That's what I like about them," he replied. "I'm nuts about llamas."

"I think you're nuts, period." She was very close now. Her lips brushed his, for just a moment.

"Are you finished eating, sir?" she whispered.

"Not . . . completely," he whispered back wickedly.

Julie giggled and took the breakfast tray and placed it on the floor. She began to lie down on top of him, but Nicky held her back. "There's just one little thing I've got to do before I can completely relax."

"Yes?" she said dreamily.

"Actually, it's a *big* little thing."

"What is it, Nicholas?" The dreaminess was gone.

"I've got to call the station and leave your telephone number with them, just in case they need to get in touch with me."

Julie moved away as though she had been slapped. "Goddamn it!" she shouted. "I must be nuts."

"Julie . . . "

"I just don't believe it. Are you *ever* off-duty?"

"Julie, look . . . I can't help it. I can't just disappear in the middle of the biggest murder case since the Hillside Strangler. You've got to accept me for what I am. If I wasn't a cop, we'd never even have met."

"Okay," she shouted. "You can call your bloody station. *Only* because I'm beginning to fall in love with you. But if the station calls while we're making love, and you answer it—I'm never going to speak to you again! Do you hear me? This is your second chance, Lieutenant Rachmaninoff, and you'd better not blow it!"

Nicky looked at her in disbelief. She was kneeling over him, her robe opening, looking down upon him with her intense eyes.

He laughed, explosively. She glared at him for just another second, and then she laughed as well, falling down on top of him. They wrestled with each other on the bed, still laughing. Tickling. Nicky ended up on top. His robe had fallen open. Sitting on top of her, pinning her down, he attempted to telephone the station from her bedside phone. But Julie did not make it easy; in fact, she made it very hard. Just as Nicky was about to give her number to the communications officer,

Julie took him deeply in her mouth. He had to repeat the number twice, before he could be understood.

When he put the phone down on its cradle, she lay back on her pillow, grinning at him, holding onto his cock with both hands. Nicky wanted to say something clever, but no words would come. Julie's robe was halfway up her thigh; he pulled it up above her triangle of golden hair, above her flat stomach and round breasts. She sat up enough to let him pull the robe off her shoulders and throw it on the floor. The last time they had tried this, on the beach at Zuma, it had been too dark for him to see how beautiful her body really was—long and graceful and deliciously curved. Nicky wanted to kiss her all over, head to foot, but she pulled him down on top of her.

"I can't wait another moment," she said breathlessly. "I've waited too long as it is."

She guided him inside. Her eyes closed halfway as he entered her, and she let out a small gasp. Nicky moved all the way inside; then she pulled her legs back so that he could go farther still. The muscles of her vagina closed about him, caressed him. He glided back and forth while their tongues met and her arms encircled his back. His last really conscious thought was, I could die now, at this moment, and it would be all right. From that point on, it was sheer dancing.

Later, he could not consciously remember how they got turned around on the bed, or when Julie got on top of him. One thing flowed into another, with a logic of its own. Nicky was too exhausted and burned from the night before to censure himself anyway. At some point they tumbled off the bed onto the floor. Nicky mounted her from the rear, and Julie screamed and cried and had one orgasm after another. But they were back on the bed when Nicky finally came himself.

"Holy Mother of God," she whispered.

It was at this point that Julie heard the front door slam downstairs. She giggled. "Oh, dear, I bet that's the last I ever see of my Mexican housekeeper . . . but you were worth it, Nicholas. You were definitely worth it."

Nicky had just received the ultimate compliment. For in Beverly Hills, it was a truism, known to one and all, that while lovers were always easy to find, a good maid was something you could kill for.

**8**

It was almost noon when Lieutenant Rachmaninoff returned to his office at the Beverly Hills police station. There were dark circles underneath his eyes, but his step was jaunty. He felt relaxed and supple. Muscles in his legs, rarely used before, now were pulled uncomfortably tight.

"Christ, you look cheerful," Charlie said disgustedly, looking up from the mountains of paper on his desk.

Nicky smiled. "It's amazing how just getting away from this place can improve your frame of mind."

The sergeant looked at him with a critical eye. "Hmph . . . well, I'll spare you my great powers of deduction. Won't even mention that you look like a man who's just gotten laid, while your poor overworked subordinate . . . "

"You mean my poor overworked *in*subordinate."

"That's right. Your poor overworked *in*subordinate has been slaving away with a most thankless case."

"Okay, Charlie. You'd better fill me in on what's been happening today."

"Well, Nicholas . . ." Charlie smiled strangely, not really a smile at all, but a gesture of embarrassment. Nicky was duly warned. The sergeant never called him by his full name. "The little girl died forty-five minutes ago."

Nicky felt the wind knocked out of him. He eased down into his swivel chair in front of his desk. He nodded several times. "All right . . . all right. What about the boy? What's his name? Alyosha?"

"Yeah. He seems to be doing a little better. They're hoping he'll make it."

"Nice name, Alyosha," Nicky said distractedly. "Where have I heard that before?"

*"The Brothers Karamazov.* You read that, Rock Man?"

"Yeah, back in the days before I became illiterate."

"Me, too."

The two partners looked at each other without a smile. It was one thing to cry in front of Julie Eastman; here, in the station, all the blocks had to be put back in place.

"Well," Nicky said at last, "what other wonderful things have happened today?"

"Oh, not much. Just a lot of noise and confusion from the big shots and the press. Much smoke and no fire, if you know what I mean."

"Anything new from the lab?"

"A little. They've confirmed that the shells found in the alley were indeed from the bullets that killed Ewing and DeWolfe."

"Were they able to find the other two shells?"

"No . . . though they looked through a lot of garbage in a lot of alleys. The boys *did* express some hope that the next murder would take them to a more exotic location. One other thing. Going door to door on Rexford, I found another person—a woman—who looked out her window when she heard the shots. She also saw the Corvette."

"Yeah? Did she get the license number by any chance?"

"You kidding? Couldn't even tell us the color."

"How about the approximate year of the car?"

"No, we were unlucky there as well. The lady didn't know a thing about sports cars, so she wasn't much help. The man who saw the shooting said just that it was an older model. He didn't know for certain. Only that it was not quite like the ones they're putting out today."

"Was it a convertible?"

"Again, he couldn't say. If it was a convertible, the top was up. He didn't look very long."

Nicky sat thoughtfully in his swivel chair, chewing on the end of a ballpoint pen. "Hmm . . . so all we really have is this Corvette. It's something, but not much."

"Maybe the car got smashed up a little doing the Grand Prix over the garbage in the alley. We might check with auto body shops."

"Yeah . . . maybe." Nicky picked up the phone on his desk and dialed Jason Whittle at the lab downtown. It took a few minutes to get through.

"Jason? This is Nicky Rachmaninoff. Look, we were wondering if you found any sign that the murder vehicle was damaged when it hit the garbage or the children. Incidentally, we're certain now that what we're looking for is an older model Corvette."

"Yeah. Glad you called, Nicky. We're just finishing our examination of the alley, and we have two things—a few scraps of red automobile paint on the garbage can that was hit and some pieces of orange

152

plastic from a lens cover—the sort that might have come from the side running lights of a car."

"That's it? Nothing by the children?"

"I'm afraid not. Apparently the children were too small to cause any damage to the car."

Nicky winced from the image this last statement gave him. "Okay, thanks, Jason." He put down the phone and turned to Charlie. "It's a red Corvette. There's at least some damage to the paint job, and a broken running light . . . big deal. I wish the guy had wrapped himself around a fucking telephone pole."

He tossed Charlie one of the numerous volumes of the L.A. Yellow Pages. "So I guess we start telephoning auto body shops. I'll start with the valley. You can have Inglewood."

Charlie looked at the size of the phone book in dismay. "Great," he mumbled. "Inglewood . . . just where I never wanted to be."

# 9

Nicky drove home to his cabin above the city a little after ten that Friday evening. The phone was ringing as he pulled into his driveway. He fumbled with the key to his front door and stumbled over a variety of clothing and furniture in his mad dash through the darkened living room to the phone.

He was hoping it was Julie.

"Hello?"

"Nicky, my love, this is Rona Barrett," came a well-modulated voice.

"Hi, Rona," he replied, mystified. He knew the gossip columnist, but not well. "What can I do for you?"

"Now, Nicky, I want you to tell me the truth about something . . . remember, you owe me one."

Did he owe her one? Nicky did some fast thinking. He realized there was, in fact, a chance he was in Rona Barrett's debt. She had helped him, very discreetly, on an investigation awhile back.

"Well, of course I'll help you if I can."

"I hope so. Knowing you, you're going to scream when I ask you this—but is there any truth to the rumor that you and Susan Merril are getting back together?"

She was right: he screamed. "That's the craziest thing I've ever heard in my life! Where did you hear such a thing?"

"Is it true?"

"No, absolutely not."

"I've also been told that Susan's marriage to Frank Fee is definitely on the rocks."

Nicky took a deep breath. He felt he was walking a narrow path, with quicksand on every side. Like nearly everyone else in Hollywood, he could not afford to alienate the powerful Rona Barrett (she was too useful to him), and he had to be careful what he said about Susan and Frank.

"Look, Rona, I don't know where you've been hearing all this, but I can assure you, none of it's true. Susan's marriage is a great success. They're very happy together, and I'm just ... thrilled to see them doing so well."

Rona seemed skeptical, but she changed the subject to the Car Killer investigation. Nicky was so relieved that he quite indiscreetly told her about the bullet shells found in the alley, which had not been released to any other member of the press. When he hung up the phone, he had a suspicion that this was what she had really been after all the time. Mata Hari was a Girl Scout compared with the gossip columnists of Hollywood.

Nicky sat in his darkened living room, shaking his head. The phone rang again, almost immediately.

"Hello, Nicky."

It was Susan.

"Christ, you'll never guess who called just now. Rona Barrett! She wanted to know if you and I were getting back together again. Can you imagine *that?*" Nicky laughed loudly at the very thought. When his laughter died, he noticed there was a significant silence on the other end. "Susan? Do you know anything about this?"

"Well, I *did* have lunch with Rona a few days ago at Paramount. I guess I talked about you a lot. . . . I'm *so* sorry. I mean, I didn't want to embarrass you by connecting you in any way with a lowly actress."

"*Susan . . .*"

"Anyway, what I'm calling about is to see if you still want to take Tanya this weekend. I've been watching the news, and I know you must be awfully busy right now."

"Tanya? Oh, yeah . . ." He slapped himself. He had totally forgotten that tomorrow was time again for his weekend visit with her. He sat down angrily. How could he forget his daughter? What kind of father was he?

"Nicky?"

"Yeah. No, this weekend's fine. I'm a little spaced out from working too hard, but it will be great to see Tanya. Just what I need."

"You sure? We could make it next weekend if you're too busy with your case."

"No, it's okay." For all he knew, next weekend there would be even more murders on his hands. Besides that, Julie's words about being a workaholic still echoed in his ears. He was determined to be a better person. Catching the Car Killer was important. But so was being a father.

"Are you okay, Nicky?" There was a new tone in Susan's voice, softer and more intimate.

"Yeah . . . sorry, I'm kind of exhausted tonight. I'll see you in the morning, okay?"

"Are you alone right now?"

"Yeah."

"Me, too. Frank hasn't come home yet, and Tanya's asleep. . . . Nicky, would you like me to come over for a few hours?"

"I don't think so. I think maybe it's better I get some sleep."

"Okay." She sounded like a little girl. Far, far away.

"Hey, Susan, when you come over tomorrow will you bring my Austin-Healey? You can take the Rolls back with you. The decoy bit didn't work out too well."

"Okay . . . the Rolls," she said wearily. It sounded like she was crying.

"Susan? . . . I love you. I'm sorry you're having a tough time."

"I love you, too, Nicky." She was crying in earnest now.

He held on to the plastic receiver and sighed. After a while, he said, "Listen, you can't go backward to the past. You have to go forward to the future."

"Are you sure?" she asked in her smallest little-girl voice. "Not even if you try very, very hard?"

"Not even if you try very, very hard."

"It's okay . . . I'll be all right. I'll see you in the morning with Tanya. Good night."

"Good night."

He put the phone down and sat in the dark. He had no desire for the harsh reality of electric lights. Unfortunately, the phone by his side rang one more time.

"Shit!" he said aloud. "Gimme a break."

He had a strange thought: *Three strikes and you're out.* He let the obtrusive device ring a long time, hoping that whoever it was would go away.

"Yeah?" he said, at last.

"Nicky? Hi, this is Kim. I'm sorry to be calling so late . . ."

Nicky's inner alarm went off immediately. There was no *hey, pardner!* No *hasta la pasta.* Sergeant Lee sounded almost like a policeman.

"I've got a flag against your name that I'm supposed to call you . . ."

"Yeah, yeah! Tell me, for God's sake, Kim!"

Pause.

"The little boy died just now. Alyosha."

"Okay. Thanks for calling."

Nicky put the receiver down slowly. After a moment, he reached under his phone and turned it off. Enough was enough. He stood up, fetched his sleeping bag from the closet, took a can of beer from the fridge, and walked out to his meadow.

The stars were obscured by a layer of clouds. Even the city lights below were barely visible in the mist. Nicky stretched out wearily, but he could not sleep for a very long time.

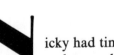

# 10

Nicky had time to do his exercises, shower and shave, and even clean up the house a bit before Susan arrived with Tanya.

In the morning, Susan was once again her vivacious, celebrity self: a very rich young woman, seemingly on top of the world. He was getting used to seeing her moods swing back and forth like a crazy pendulum. Both moods seemed a little unreal to him; overdone. It occurred to Nicky that Susan was really a better actress than she thought. Even the few long, meaningful looks that flashed his way when Tanya wasn't looking had an aura of make-believe about them.

Tanya's presence stopped the possibility of intimate conversation between the two adults, and for this, Nicky was glad. As Susan was leaving, he handed her the key to the Rolls.

"I had a police radio and transmitter put in. I'll have them taken out next week."

"Don't worry about it. Frank will absolutely love it! It will make him feel just like a real cop."

As he watched her drive away in the burgundy Rolls-Royce, Nicky had a sad, nostalgic feeling for the passing of time. He shrugged it off as Tanya came to him, wanting to be picked up and held. Wanting to have her father. He squeezed her tenderly, amazed at the smallness of her bones and the softness of her cheek against his.

"Well, how are you doing, kiddo?"

"Okay, Daddy. How are you?"

"Grrr-eat!" He turned momentarily into a big waltzing bear, dancing about the driveway with Tanya in his arms. Making silly growling sounds and rubbing her tummy with his chin. Tanya's high-pitched laughter almost drowned out the sound of the telephone ringing, which he had turned on (with dire misgivings) after his second cup of coffee. Nicky waltzed her inside the living room, and they both fell down, laughing, next to the insistent phone.

"Hello?" he said, still laughing.

"McWilliams here" came the gruff, unfriendly voice of the chief of police. The laughter seemed to freeze on Nicky's lips.

"Howdy, Chief," he said in a Western drawl, an informality that was certain to irritate the man.

"The mayor has asked me to *invite* you to a meeting in his downtown office at eleven o'clock this morning." The chief managed to sound sarcastic, nasty, and condescending, all at the same time.

"Well, I don't know, Chief. My daughter has just come to stay with me. It's my weekend, you know."

"What the hell are you talking about, Lieutenant? Your *weekend!*"

"Children, Chief. Have you ever heard of children? You know, those little creatures that come out when a sperm gets together with an egg."

"You know, Lieutenant, I'm really beginning to wonder about your competence to deal with serious matters. The meeting's at eleven sharp. Be there!" He slammed down the phone in Nicky's ear.

"What a nice man."

"Who was that, Daddy?"

"Just the nasty ol' head of the Los Angeles police, darling. One of my many bosses."

"Who's your big boss?"

"Well, the mayor, I guess. He wants to see me this morning at eleven. I'm afraid I gotta go, honey. You can come along, too. I'll get you some comics to read while I'm in the meeting. It won't take too long, I hope. Okay?"

"I guess so. . . . It doesn't sound like too much fun."

Nicky nodded somberly in agreement.

# 11

At a few minutes to eleven, Nicky sat at a long wooden table between Police Chief McWilliams and Captain Molinari. He felt like the meat in a sandwich. Others were there as well, waiting for the mayor to arrive—the district attorney, an aide, Professor Dorothy Anglund from the U.C.L.A. School of Criminal Psychology, and the mayor's personal secretary, a tight-lipped young man who was prone to fat and exuded an aura of great prissiness and organization. There were microphones in the center of the long conference table—not for amplification, but for posterity.

Tanya was ensconced in a comfortable chair in the waiting room outside, a large stack of comic books in her lap. Nicky had asked a security guard to keep an eye on her. When he explained that this was his "weekend," the guard knew exactly what he meant. They spent a few moments talking about their various child visitation rights; sometimes it seemed like everyone in Los Angeles over the age of twenty-five was divorced.

The conference room, where Nicky waited, had a somber, old-fashioned feeling to it. A smell of stale cigar smoke lingered in the air. Nicky had always believed that the massive, civic buildings of downtown Los Angeles labored under an identity crisis. They tried to say, to an unbelieving nation, Look, folks, this isn't really Tinseltown. It's not all Disneyland and movie stars. We have a symphony orchestra and the Dorothy Chandler Pavilion, banks and brokerage firms, even a mayor. On one entire wall of the conference room, there was a massive painting, a mural, which depicted great moments in the history of Los

Angeles, from the founding of the small Spanish pueblo, to a science-fiction futurescape of glass and stone that still managed to look—despite its grand stirrings of civic pride—like a fake background to a Saturday morning cartoon.

Abruptly—with a flourish—the mayor walked in, followed by his two aides. His balding head was shined to a black gloss, and he exuded an aura of success and well-being. An expensive cologne wafted into the room from his direction, mixing unpleasantly with the odor of old cigar smoke. Everyone rose.

The mayor nodded curtly and sat down.

"I've called you together this morning, ladies and gentlemen, to ask your advice and come to some decisions . . ."

He spoke in the courtly manner of a black politician. Nicky could almost hear the inflections of a gospel preacher not far beneath the polished surface. "We have a sad and unheard-of calamity in our midst, an *evil* which we must *seek out and destroy.* This cowardly succession of killings strikes out not only against law but against order itself. There is panic in this city. We must act, and we must act fast.

"I would like Lieutenant Rachmaninoff, who has been in charge of this investigation *so far,* to rise now and give us a briefing of the events which have occurred. Lieutenant, will you begin?"

Nicky cleared his throat and stood up. He did not particularly like the sound of his being in charge of this investigation *so far.* All eyes were upon him in a most predatory manner. Higher-echelon civil servants tended to be ruthlessly competitive with one another, and he was the man on the spot.

As precisely as possible, he summarized the events beginning with Gerald Eastman, and ending with the deaths of the two children.

When he was finished, the mayor addressed the group. "Does anyone have any questions for the lieutenant?"

The district attorney raised his hand, as if he were in school. The D.A. was a deceptively soft-spoken man, with slightly dandified airs. His enemies liked to make vicious remarks about his supposed sexual preference.

"It seems to me that the first point we must establish is if we have one killer or several involved here. From what you've told us, Lieutenant, I'm not convinced that we are looking for a single person."

"Well, sir, of course at this point anything is possible," Nicky admitted. "But I believe we are up against a single killer for three reasons. First, the M.O. is the same for all the murders—a quiet street, late at night in Beverly Hills, someone gets knocked off in a car. The two children, naturally, are the exception. But I think it's safe to say that their deaths were an accident of sorts. They were crossing the end of that alley just as the killer was making his escape.

"Second, there's the Corvette. It's a bit circumstantial with Brian Stewart's death, I admit, but a Corvette *was* seen moments after the shots were heard, speeding away from the scene of the crime. With the murders of Officers Ewing and DeWolfe, there's no doubt at all. Two different witnesses saw a Corvette alongside car 257 just as the shots were being fired. And last of all . . . well, I just believe it. I *feel* we are up against a single intelligence, who's taking us for a ride. I feel shooting two policemen was kind of a big, arrogant 'fuck you' from the killer to us."

The D.A. smiled thinly. "As a matter of fact, I was going to suggest that the shooting of two policemen indicates just the opposite," he said. "It's a different type of crime *completely* from the killing of a movie lawyer and a rock star, and suggests a different type of killer. But to my mind, what is most damaging to your single killer theory is the fact that there are three different weapons involved. Gerald Eastman was killed with a twenty-two, Brian Stewart with a shotgun. And your unfortunate colleagues with a thirty-eight." The D.A. shrugged complacently, as if to say, So there you have it, poor boy. How can you argue against my impeccable logic?

Nicky sighed. "Okay, but it's easier to change guns than to change cars. Maybe our killer just has a big arsenal to choose from."

Jesse Bruckner, a sour-looking young man who was the D.A.'s personal assistant, now spoke up. "Lieutenant, it seems to me that all your evidence is *extremely* circumstantial. There must be hundreds of Corvettes in Beverly Hills, if not thousands. So the fact that one was seen soon after Brian Stewart was killed means nothing at all. But let's let that go for a moment and look at the first murder. Gerald Eastman. Here you don't have a Corvette, or much of anything at all. Just a dead body in a car. Now I want to know how this got all hyped up into being the work of some crazed Car Killer who's going around Beverly Hills killing people?"

Nicky started to protest that *he* had nothing to do with any of the Car Killer hype that was coming out of the press.

"Now let me finish, Lieutenant, *please!*" The young man spoke petulantly, in a very self-important manner that Nicky did not like. "What I want to know," he continued, "is why the Gerald Eastman killing can't be a good old-fashioned homicide that has nothing to do with any of this Car Killer crap? I mean, look at it this way: I understand that the victim had some kind of sexpot, nymphomaniac wife who was probably fucking half the guys in town—excuse me, Dr. Anglund," he said hastily, bowing in the direction of the psychologist. Jesse Bruckner did not even notice Nicky become pale and rigid with anger, but continued without a pause. "Now why can't this whole thing be ridiculously straightforward, a simple matter of Julie Eastman and one of her lovers knocking off the husband for the cash inheritance? For that matter, perhaps they went on to kill Brian Stewart and the two policemen and the children, deliberately fostering this Car Killer nonsense to hide their own tracks. Now I'm not saying I'm right," he concluded, with a helpless gesture to the room, "but this is at least equally as plausible as anything Lieutenant Rachmaninoff has managed to come up with."

Nicky sat in his chair, concentrating on breathing in a normal manner.

"Well, Lieutenant? What do you have to say?" the mayor asked, looking at him in a curious way.

Nicky had to restrain himself from a violent impulse to jump across the table and smash the assistant D.A. with his fists. But when he did speak, his words came out with icy control. "If Julie Eastman wanted to kill her husband, there would have been more intimate opportunities than shooting him in the middle of Sunset Boulevard. Actually, it was the *location* of this initial murder that first made me suspect a psychotic killer. Gerald Eastman's movements that night were fairly haphazard. For the murder to have been deliberate, it would have had to be planned with exceptional care. Even so, the killer would have had to wait in the dark at that intersection for some time for Gerald Eastman to drive by, thereby exposing himself to the risk he would appear suspicious and be questioned by a patrol car. . . . No, I'm sorry, it just doesn't make sense to me. *If* Julie Eastman, or any of Gerald's various enemies, had wanted to murder him, they would have found a better spot. I believe it makes much greater sense that our killer is a psychotic who has found a rather simple but effective way to terrorize the streets of Beverly Hills."

"You *believe?*" the assistant D.A. asked sarcastically, and then addressed the room at large: "What we have here is a *mystic,* for crying out loud, not a policeman at all."

"Wait a goddamn second," Nicky argued heatedly. "There are precious few facts in this case so far. Right now, there is not much else to go on except intelligent intuition."

"Can I say one thing?" Captain Molinari interjected, for the first time. "Lieutenant Rachmaninoff's intuition has been very accurate so far. On his instructions, we set up the machinery whereby we were very close to getting the killer last Thursday night. Very close indeed."

The captain meant well, but Nicky wanted to close his eyes and hide. The sour little man from the D.A.'s office rose dramatically from his chair and leaned forward across the table. "Close?" he asked. "Yes, you were close. Only you didn't get him! *He got you!*"

The room erupted with the voices of different factions clamoring to be heard. The mayor had to shout everyone to order, his gospel voice booming through the enclosed chambers.

"Ladies ... gentlemen! This meeting *will* proceed in an orderly manner! ... Now, Lieutenant, do you have anything further to say before we pass on to other voices?"

"Yes, I do. Thank you, Mr. Mayor. With all due regard"—Nicky nodded to the young aide from the D.A.'s office— "there are always a few ... *assholes* who want instant results." Jesse Bruckner blanched; there was a nervous tittering in the room, and the mayor seemed about to object, but Nicky continued forcefully. "This is a complex matter. There is no easy way to catch a psychotic serial murderer. And that's what we have here, whether you believe it or not. Actually, with only two weeks of investigation, we are not doing that badly. Not—may I add—due to my great powers of deduction, but to the killer himself, who really has been very careless. This guy *wants* to get caught, and we are going to oblige him. But he still has one great advantage over us, one great edge. He's crazy."

There was more tittering in the room.

"I'm serious. One crazy person can completely disrupt the regular order of things. Why? Because we guard ourselves against real dangers. We walk cautiously on the streets at night if we're carrying a lot of money, because we understand that everybody wants money, and someone might take it from us. But driving home in your car—you don't look around you for some nut to take a shot at you every time you come to a stop sign or a red light. To do that, *you* would have to be crazy. Right? Definitely paranoid schizophrenia."

There was some laughter in the room, which the mayor cut short. "One more question, Lieutenant," he asked. "If the killer has such a great advantage over us, how do you propose we catch him?"

"Sir . . . what I recommend is time and patience. That's all. Let him make the next move. I realize this is not easy. Naturally, we are going to follow through with our one real lead—the red Corvette—and we are looking for more evidence all the time. But, frankly, I still think our best bet is simply to be out there on the streets, waiting. We must keep our knowledge of the Corvette secret from the media, so the guy doesn't change cars. When he starts to cruise again, we'll grab him."

The mayor shook his head. "Wait for the killer to make the next move? I'm afraid that isn't a solution that will make the people of Beverly Hills very happy. I have decided—and I think it is only fair to tell you this now, Lieutenant—I have decided to restructure this investigation under the direct command of Police Chief McWilliams, creating a city-wide task force that will include each person in this room. I want to thank you for your work, Lieutenant. And I want to make it clear to everybody that this is in no way to be taken as a censure of what you've done. For a fairly young man, you have done a remarkable job here. Remarkable. And I happen to agree with you, as does Chief McWilliams by the way, that we have a single psychotic killer on the loose. This is, in fact, the main reason I'm taking the case away from you. This is no longer a crime that concerns Beverly Hills alone. By naming Police Chief McWilliams as the head of this investigation, I'm hoping to make it clear to the people of Los Angeles—*and* the killer—how seriously we take this situation. We are waging war against this person. It is my hope that he will realize he can no longer get away with these crimes, and will desist from any further mayhem."

Nicky sat with a steadily sinking sensation, trying to maintain a neutral expression.

"And now," the mayor continued, "I want to move on and ask Dorothy Anglund, from the U.C.L.A. School of Criminal Psychology, to give us a portrait of the person we are seeking. Dorothy?"

"Yes, Mr. Mayor . . ."

Nicky was feeling too wounded to pay much attention to her, or to the other various officials and specialists who rose, one after another, to give their view of the situation. Anyway, he did not have much faith in committees to solve crimes. As far as he could tell, nothing new was being said. Police Chief McWilliams, when it was his turn to speak, tried to give the impression that he was beginning an entirely new investigation, but basically he was continuing along the lines Nicky himself had begun. There would be more patrol cars in Beverly Hills.

That was swell. Perhaps if Nicky had had another ten cars on Thursday night, the guy would not have gotten away.

But the changes were all cosmetic. Chief McWilliams would end up waiting—just as Nicky would—for the killer to make the next move. The public would have the illusion that more was being done. It had nothing to do with him. The mayor had to consider public opinion. Cops had to consider politics.

It took considerable effort to sit through the rest of the meeting without betraying his anger. Occasionally he was aware of Captain Molinari, on his left, giving him an anxious glance. For the others in the room, he no longer existed. He was no longer important. Nicky studiously avoided looking at Police Chief McWilliams on his right.

After a very long hour, the mayor adjourned the meeting. He asked them all to keep their places for a few more moments, while several selected photographers from Associated Press, UPI, and the *Los Angeles Times* were allowed to enter the room and record this distinguished gathering.

All the elected officials in the room looked as serious and handsome and concerned as they could. Nicky slunk down into his chair, looking like a rebellious teenager, muttering obscenities beneath his breath. After the pictures were taken, the mayor walked out to give a full press conference in the hall outside, where he would announce the grand restructuring of the investigation.

As Nicky rose to leave, Chief McWilliams turned to him for a moment. "Well, Lieutenant, I'm glad to see you were able to find a baby sitter so you could be here today." He said this in a manner that implied that a baby sitter was the *only* thing he would be able to find.

Nicky faced the man with a thin, neutral smile on his lips. He did not bother to respond that Tanya was outside in the waiting room, but simply said to himself: *You've got to be tough. To be a cop, you've got to be tough.* This was the test. The chief, standing before him, was three or four inches taller, and at least another hundred pounds greater in size. The chief was very tough. He looked down at Nicky with malicious, hooded eyes.

"Lieutenant, I can see that you've been working very hard. Why don't you take the rest of today and tomorrow off. On Monday morning, I would like you to go through our psycho sheets and check out whereabouts and alibis. . . . You know, your problem, Lieutenant, is you like to do all the glamorous things like riding around in a Rolls-

Royce pretending to be some goddamn decoy. But you miss out on the basic routines. So when you've finished with the nut list, gimme a call and I'll find something else for you to do."

Nicky could end his career right there. But he was a model of self-restraint. "All right. Will do, Chief."

McWilliams gave him a withering look and then turned to join the mayor at the press conference.

Nicky walked out of the room before Dave Molinari could say anything to him. In the large anteroom, the press had gathered, but none of them paid any attention to him. Nicky stepped through the throng until he saw Tanya sitting against the wall with her small stack of comic books. The crowd of reporters was moving like a river in the opposite direction, and Nicky had to step aggressively against the tide to reach his daughter.

She put her arms around him. He closed his eyes and held her. He was never so grateful to feel her small body close to his.

# 12

Nicky drove back to Hollywood with an angry ball of tension inside, lodged somewhere just above his solar plexus. He had to concentrate on not driving too fast.

A Cadillac cut too close in front of him, changing lanes.

"Fuck you, you goddamn cocksucking son of a bitch!" he shouted out the window, at the top of his lungs.

*"Daddy!"*

"I'm sorry, honey. This has really been a hell of a morning."

Tanya was in the middle of giving him a blow-by-blow account of a movie she had seen the night before on TV. Nicky tried to listen to the seemingly endless story, but his thoughts kept returning to the conference room and the brilliant and savage put-downs that now occurred to him, too late to be of any use. Now his anger had no release, except to tear away inside and turn against himself. This, he thought gloomily, was what maturity was all about. Ulcers were just a responsible response to modern times.

"... and then, at the very end, there was this really awesome car chase. I mean, there must have been fifteen cars *crashing* together, and the bad guys finally *smashed* into a gas station and a whole city block *blew up!* It was a great movie, Daddy."

"Jesus, it sounds kind of violent, dear."

Tanya shrugged. "It was only PG. They didn't show any sex."

Nicky laughed bitterly. "Personally, I prefer some nice tits and ass to cars crashing into each other," he said.

*"Daddy!* Really!"

They drove off the freeway at Highland Avenue, and Nicky stopped to buy gas. He kept glancing at the phone booth, with a longing to duck inside and call Julie. While the attendant was checking his oil, he decided to give in to this impulse.

After a few rings the maid answered, and in his pidgin Spanish Nicky was able to convince her to put Señora Eastman on the line.

"Hi. How are you?" she asked. Even with a few short phrases, there was a new intimacy—a secret they shared between them.

"I'm okay."

"You sound like something's wrong."

"It's only work that's wrong. How would you like to come over for dinner tonight and meet my daughter, Tanya?"

Julie was silent. Then: "Is that a good idea?"

"Well, why not? Sure, it's a good idea. Anyway, I'm dying to see you."

"Okay, I'd love to come. Is there anything I can bring?"

"Just your toothbrush. I may hold you prisoner overnight."

He gave her the rather complicated directions to his cabin on Sunshine Terrace, and then walked back to his car, where Tanya was waiting very patiently.

"Where are we going now, Daddy?"

"To the store to buy some groceries. And then I thought we'd just go home. I want to clean up the place a bit. . . . This is going to be sort of a quiet weekend, honey. No Disneyland, or anything. I'm feeling pretty wiped out from my job. Okay?"

"Okay," she said, without a great deal of enthusiasm. Nicky started up the car and drove toward Ralph's, a megamarket on Sunset.

"A friend of mine is coming over for dinner tonight," he said after a few blocks.

"A *girl*friend?" she asked immediately, crinkling up her nose.

"You know, you're a pretty sharp cookie. You could be a detective."

"Well, is she?" Tanya insisted, not about to be drawn away from the subject.

Nicky sighed. "Well . . . yes and no. I would say a qualified kind-of, with an unknown future beckoning on the horizon."

"What does *that* mean?"

"It means, mind your own business . . . anyway, you'll like her. She's nice."

This seemed to satisfy Tanya for the time being. They arrived at the supermarket, and Nicky let her push the cart up and down the aisles, as he searched out the ingredients for prawns Veracruz, which was his own concoction: a Mexican-style dish with mushrooms, tomatoes, jalapeño peppers, and cilantro, served over rice. It wasn't exactly a child-oriented dinner, so he gave in and as compensation bought a neon-colored, glow-in-the-dark breakfast cereal which he normally would have never considered. Life was full of little bribes.

Last of all, he picked up a fifth of tequila, a pint of Triple Sec and a dozen fresh limes. The Mexican dinner was a mere excuse to make margaritas. Nicky felt a strong desire to get raving drunk.

At the checkout counter—while he was in the midst of lecturing Tanya for driving the shopping cart too fast and almost running over an aging Korean woman—he looked up and saw the headlines of *The National Star*. On the tabloid's cover, right after SCIENTIST FINDS NEW PROOF OF LIFE AFTER DEATH and I WAS A SEX SLAVE IN A SOVIET CONCENTRATION CAMP, Nicky saw the words: BRIAN STEWART'S LAST SHOCKING MOMENTS: A MOTHER-DAUGHTER MENAGE A TROIS.

His first reaction was, Shit, how did *that* leak out? It was all he needed to make the Car Killer case more impossible than it already was.

Then he remembered . . . it was no longer his case. It was Chief McWilliams's worry now.

Nicky smiled wickedly. When Tanya asked if she could get a pack of chocolate-flavored bubble gum, he said sure.

# 13

After dinner, they played Monopoly on the living room floor. Nicky won, absurdly pleased with himself for cornering the market on all the real estate in faraway Atlantic City. Julie and Tanya, who began the evening in a sort of cautious circling, like two karate partners about to spar, were brought firmly together, united in their common irritation with Nicky, who was gloating over his string of shiny red plastic hotels in a most obnoxious way.

Eventually, Tanya grew sleepy and Nicky tucked her away in her bed.

Julie waited in the living room, looking very elegant—as always— but not completely out of place in his country cabin. Her eyes, which seemed more green than gold tonight, were upon him humorously as he came back into the room.

"I must say, I never would have thought you'd be so competitive."

"I'm *not* competitive," he answered defensively. "I just like to win."

Julie laughed, though he had been quite serious and was now regarding her in a slightly peeved way.

"What's wrong, Nicholas?"

*"Nothing's* wrong. Everything's just *great."*

"Hmm . . ."

They had consumed two rounds of margaritas, which did not seem to affect Julie at all. Nicky, on the other hand, knew he was looking a bit more owlish than usual, and he spoke with exaggerated clarity. He foraged around in a kitchen cabinet and pulled out a bottle of Clos du Val Zinfandel.

"Ah-ha . . . there's the little devil. Can't hide from me!"

"Nicholas, I wish you'd just come over here and sit by me."

"Hold on . . . I'm going to take us on a little expedition to the top of the world."

"The top of the world?" she repeated dubiously.

He opened the bottle of wine and then stuffed the cork back halfway. He gave the bottle and two glasses to Julie to hold, and then rummaged through a hall closet for his two down sleeping bags, unzipping them so they would open up flat. When everything was ready, he led her at last outside to his small meadow overlooking the city.

He could not have asked for a better night. The air was crisp and clear. A million small lights twinkled at their feet, while in the sky an almost full moon rose up behind them, shining through the branches of an oak tree.

"I like your home," she said. "It's like the country up here. I didn't realize there were places like this left in Los Angeles."

Nicky spread the sleeping bags on the grass. They sat down together, and he poured out two glasses of wine. In the distance, giant beams of light pierced the city sky: searchlights far across town, announcing the opening of something or other.

"Are you going to tell me what's bothering you?" she asked.

He sighed. Outside, in the moist and sweet-smelling night air, he felt very sober again, and weary. "I'm sorry. I've probably been acting like a jerk."

"Yes, you have!" she answered without mercy. "And I don't know why you won't just talk with me."

"It's about work. I didn't think you'd want to hear about that."

"Nicholas, I want to hear about how you're feeling about things. Can't you get that through your thick skull? I care about *you.*"

"Well . . . I've been taken off the Car Killer case. I'm still officially on the case, but Chief of Police McWilliams is now personally in charge of the investigation. He doesn't like me too much, so I have a pretty minor role. On Monday, I'm supposed to go through the nut list the city keeps of known psychopaths and sociopaths. It's a job you usually give to a first-year detective, just to cover all your bases. I've never known a crime like this solved by one of those lists."

"I'm sorry," she said softly. "It sounds pretty lousy."

"Well, it's the breaks. I know I shouldn't take it personally. The whole thing's just a public relations job, so the mayor can throw a news conference and give the impression that something is really being done to solve these horrible murders."

"But you do take it personally?"

"Yes and no. I understand the way these things work. Back in the police academy they told us over and over again that to be a good cop, you have to be a team player. I guess, working in a small station like Beverly Hills, I've gotten used to having things my own way. I'm just not sure I *want* to be on the team anymore."

"I'm sure you could do lots of other things," she said.

"Yeah? I could always guard warehouses. Maybe I could become Philip Marlowe, Private Eye."

"You'd make a sexy private eye, at least."

He laughed unhappily. "You know the only work that private eyes really do? They lurk outside houses with cameras that have telephoto lenses, trying to get dirty pictures of people cheating on their spouses."

"You're not a voyeur?"

"I would rather participate, thank you."

He finished off his wine with a gulp and was about to pour himself another. But Julie pushed him down on the sleeping bag. "Well, Lieutenant, I can see you're in a bad way. But you've got a really pretty cabin up here on top of the city, a daughter who obviously needs you a great deal, and a woman who's very horny and is getting very fond of you. . . . Maybe there's something we can do to help you forget your problems. For just a little while."

Nicky looked into her womanly and intelligent eyes, inches away.

"Maybe there is something," he admitted. "Listen, I brought that second sleeping bag to put on top of us, just in case you felt an irresistible urge to take off your clothes."

"I feel an irresistible urge," she said.

"So do I."

# 14

Julie slept beside him on the meadow. They awoke to a fiery dawn and made love once again: fiery love, with the scent of morning dew upon them.

It made other things seem unimportant. Almost.

Later, she took over his kitchen and cooked eggs Benedict. He opened up a bottle of champagne and he almost succeeded in forgetting the Car Killer and the chief of police, and the mayor, and dreamlike visions of ruined cars with dead bodies inside.

He spent Sunday concentrating on human values. Failure was going to make him a better person. He planned all sorts of things.

He was going to *really listen* to Tanya when she spoke.

He made a vow to find himself a good novel to read—Henry James, maybe—and get rid of the crappy escapist fiction he fell asleep with at night.

He was going to take piano lessons again. Get back into Bach and

Mozart and Hanon exercises. He was tired of being a fucking dilettante.

While he was at it, his cabin could really stand a coat of paint.

All these things seemed possible while Julie and Tanya were with him. But Tanya went home late Sunday afternoon, and Julie went home on Monday morning. Five minutes after Julie left, he sank into a dark depression. He dreaded going to work, no longer having an active part in the Car Killer investigation. He felt he was coming down with the flu.

Wearily, he got into his car and drove to the Beverly Hills station. Henry James and Mozart receded. To be a cop, it was better to be ignorant and put a tough shell around you.

He arrived at his office to learn that there had been a homicide over the weekend. It had nothing to do with the Car Killer, and it was not much of a mystery.

Charlie had been on duty Sunday when it happened, and he filled Nicky in on the details: A wealthy Beverly Hills businessman, Bertrand Harrison, went to New York for a week, leaving his much younger wife behind in the big house on North Canon Drive. It was a familiar story: most murders are. The man, suspicious of his wife, returned home three days early, on Sunday, to find his young wife in bed with another man.

The cuckolded husband shot his wife dead while she lay naked in bed. The lover, a teenager from down the street, burst into tears and begged for mercy. The husband made him pose with his legs spread, and proceeded to shoot the young man's balls off. Bertrand Harrison then turned his pistol on himself and committed suicide. The unfortunate lover managed to crawl to a telephone and call the police before he fainted dead away. He was now in the intensive care unit of a Hollywood hospital. He would live, but he would never be anyone's lover again.

"Christ! Shot his balls off?" was all Nicky could say when Charlie was finished. He couldn't help but think: *Jesus, and I thought I was having bad luck.* His next thought: *Hmm . . . now I won't have to go through those goddamn psycho sheets. . . . God, I'm a selfish bastard.* But you had to grab advantage where it lay.

He set to work reading the reports from the medical examiner, studying charts and diagrams that showed the positions of the bodies. His job was to decide if all was as straightforward as it appeared to be, or if any facts had been withheld.

Nicky's mind went into gear as he grappled with this new problem. This was the kind of work that he liked to do.

He was not thinking about the Car Killer.

A little after ten o'clock, the phone on his desk rang. On the other end was an acquaintance, David Hotchkiss, who was the chief homicide investigator at the Santa Monica station.

"Hey, Nicky, I was hoping you could do me a little favor. It has to do with your ex-wife, Susan Merril."

"Susan? What is it that you want?"

"Okay, it's like this. . . . Ten days ago, we discovered a badly mutilated corpse in an old apartment building near the beach in Santa Monica. The guy had been dead an entire week before the neighbors started to complain about a horrible stench in the halls. So we were called, and we broke in and found the guy. He had been stabbed and his head was cut off. Pretty nasty. Well, we assumed the dead man was the resident of the apartment. Right? A Lawrence Ferguson. We thought maybe it was robbery, or some kind of gay pickup involved. But it turns out to be a bit more complicated. The coroner tells us now that the corpse is *not* Lawrence Ferguson, who lived in the apartment, but the guy's boss. A man named Paul Hovarth. Are you getting the picture?"

"It's a little fuzzy. What does this have to do with Susan?"

"I'm getting to that. . . . Let me tell you a bit more about Lawrence Ferguson. He was an accountant for twenty years at this enormous place, the Southern California Life Insurance Corporation. The last time anyone saw him was Thursday, October 17th. Right? He had a doctor's appointment after his lunch hour that day, and just never came back. Going through his desk, we were able to find the name of the doctor he saw—a Dr. Golden, at the Santa Monica Medical Center. We saw Dr. Golden. He remembers Lawrence Ferguson very well. Ferguson had come to him for some tests, and on the seventeenth came back for the results. The doctor had to tell him that he had what was probably a terminal case of cancer. The patient spooked halfway through the office visit and took off before the doctor could put him in the hospital for treatment. He walked away and never came back. The next day, Friday the eighteenth, Paul Hovarth left his office in the late afternoon and was never seen again either. At least not in one piece."

"So let me get this straight," Nicky interrupted. "Lawrence Ferguson learns he has cancer, he kills his boss, and then he disappears?"

"That's right. . . . One more thing. On Friday he closed out his bank account. He took $39,718.35 in cash. Stuffed it into a briefcase."

Nicky whistled. "That's a lot of bread. You figure he's giving himself one last holiday before he dies?"

"Something like that. . . . We have an APB out on the guy, but so far we don't have a clue. He just seemed to vanish. With all that cash, he may be in Paris or Bangkok, for all we know."

"It sounds like this case is going to keep you busy . . . but let's get back to Susan."

"Okay. This is just a long shot. In Lawrence's apartment we found dozens of photographs of your ex-wife. It seems he was a real fan of 'Cassie and the Cop.' Talking to his co-workers at Southern California Life, I have the picture of a lonely, nebbishy sort of person who might have been an aggressive fan of someone like Susan . . . so the favor I want to ask you is if you will just telephone her and ask if she's gotten any particularly strange fan mail recently. It's just a long shot, but frankly, after a week and a half on this case, we're at a dead end."

"Yeah, I know what *that's* like." Nicky agreed. "I'll get back to you."

"Thanks, pal."

Nicky hung up the phone feeling strangely lightheaded. By coincidence, Gerald Eastman had been murdered on Thursday, October 17th, the same day Lawrence Ferguson learned he had cancer and disappeared.

Nicky got up from his desk. He always needed to pace the floor when sudden thoughts were upon him. Charlie gave him an inquiring look, but Nicky ignored him, pretending to walk down the hall to the men's room. Before reaching it, he made a decisive right turn into the central computer center. He had to wait a few minutes for a free terminal: Computers had become a large part of police work, and the room was busy.

He typed in the code that allowed him to enter the enormous memory banks of the Department of Motor Vehicles in Sacramento.

He was very curious about the kind of car Lawrence Ferguson drove.

The answer came back almost immediately. Lawrence had registered a 1982 Ford Galaxie. The original color was listed as rust brown.

Well, it had been an idea. Nicky shook his head and cleared the screen. He walked back to his office and returned to his own present case of murder and suicide and sexual mutilation. The city was full of nasty surprises. But as he worked, the image of Lawrence Ferguson did not completely leave his mind. He felt there was something darkly fascinating about a nebbishy man murdering his boss. Taking all his money out of the bank. Disappearing, freed by cancer to do whatever he liked.

In the afternoon, Nicky drove over to the hospital in Hollywood where the most unlucky teenage lover had regained consciousness. The boy had to be questioned. Nicky was not thrilled at the prospect. But he reminded himself that this was still better than checking out all the registered crazies for Chief McWilliams.

As he walked through the hospital corridor, he had a nagging feeling that there was some angle regarding Lawrence Ferguson that he had not quite brought to light.

The teenager was in a private room, with his two miserable-looking parents standing outside. Nicky introduced himself in grave tones and went inside.

The boy's name was Ronald Walsh. Ronald had been a blond, athletic youth—one of those young California gods of the surf and sun. He lay now with the white sheet up to his neck and a bottle of glucose dripping into his arm. His cheeks were wet with tears, and he did not bother to look toward Nicky as he came into the room. The ceiling apparently absorbed all his attention.

Nicky tried to think of a few words of consolation. But what could he say? *Gee, kid, I bet you always wanted to be a soprano.*

Nicky cleared his throat. "I'm really sorry about what happened, Ronald. My name is Lieutenant Rachmaninoff. I'm a homicide investigator, and I need to ask you a few questions. If you feel strong enough to talk."

Ronald neither looked in his direction nor answered.

"I really am sorry," he repeated. "It's a hell of a tough break."

It was at this moment that Nicky's mind came into focus. It was as if a searchlight had illuminated a hidden recess of his brain. Lawrence Ferguson was suddenly the focus of all his thoughts.

"Ah . . . look, kid. I just remembered something I have to do. I'll let you rest a bit, and I'll . . . uh, come back. Okay?"

The teenager turned slowly in his direction, disbelief entering into the anguish on his face. "Are you for real, man?" he muttered. But Nicky was already stepping briskly from the room.

The parents looked at him quizzically as he came bounding out.

"I'll be right back," he told them. Their troubled eyes followed him as he jogged down the hall. He took the elevator downstairs to the bank of pay phones there.

What Nicky had sought was suddenly clear. With $39,000 and nothing but death to look forward to, the nebbishy accountant might very easily buy for himself the gaudy car of his dreams.

Nicky telephoned the Cat back in the office in Beverly Hills. "Charlie, I want you to do me a favor, okay? When you buy a car at a lot, you get a temporary registration. Sacramento must have these registrations on file someplace. I'm interested in a Lawrence Ferguson—got that name? Go into the computer room and try to find out if he took out a temporary registration on a car either on or after Thursday, October 17th. I'm in a pay phone. I'll give you my number, and I'll just wait here until you call me back."

It was almost ten minutes before Charlie called back. To Nicky it seemed like hours.

Charlie's energy erupted over the phone. "Rock Man, you sly son of a bitch! How the hell did you pull this one?"

"Wait a second, Charlie. Are you alone in the office?"

"Yeah."

"Okay, then lay it on me."

"Here it is . . . Lawrence Ferguson bought a 1972 Corvette convertible on October 18th. The original color is listed as red, you motherfucker. Want the license?"

"Yeah, shoot."

"CSR 545 . . . serial number 4J723349875. Got all that?"

Nicky wrote the numbers quickly in the small notebook he always carried. "Got it. . . . Now, Charlie, I want you to listen to me. I want you to forget about this conversation. Just wipe it from your mind."

"Hey, buddy, this is a pretty big case. . . ."

"*Charlie.* All I want is a little time to figure out how I'm going to use this. Just trust me, okay?"

"Okay," he said reluctantly.

Nicky hung up the phone and stared at his notebook, where he had written the name: Lawrence Ferguson.

He underlined the name three times. A smile came slowly to his face. Suddenly he clapped his hands together and stamped his feet on the floor. Someone in the adjoining phone booth knocked for him to be quiet.

He walked down the corridor out of the hospital. Ronald Walsh would not mind waiting another day.

In the parking lot, Nicky did something he had not done since he was a boy. He let out a loud coyote yell.

People stared at him and hurried out of his way.

Nicky did not care. He was going to get the Car Killer.

# PART
# SEVEN

*The Labyrinth*

# 1

She stood at the top of the stairs, wearing nothing but a diaphanous white slip. He could see her nipples quite clearly, even a hint of golden pubic hair at the apex of her long and lovely legs.

You're sure looking good, Cassie, he said.

She only smiled at him. So naughty. So nice. Her blond hair was longer than he had seen it before and flowed down upon her sculptured shoulders.

She was lovely. Just to see her made him feel like he was walking in sunshine.

But they were in a very strange place: a ruined shell of a building. Lawrence had been there before, though always on his own. There were hallways that led nowhere. Doors that opened into a vertigo of empty space. Closets that concealed hideous secrets. This was a building that had no beginning and no end. It was a Grand Hotel of his imagination.

And now Cassie was here with him. She smiled coyly and stepped back into the shadows of a long hallway. Lawrence bounded up the stairs after her. His heart was beating quickly, the way it did when he was hunting. He took the stairs two at a time and ran after her down the hallway. Darkness closed in around him, thick as tar, and he knew he was lost. He could only move forward blindly, cautiously—feeling ahead with his outstretched hands like a sleepwalker. Putting his feet down very carefully, afraid there might be a gaping hole in the floor.

Or snakes.

His fear grew with each passing moment, until he was too paralyzed to move.

I don't want to die! he said. Please, I don't want to die!

But it was too late. Ahead in the darkness, footsteps were coming toward him. He heard a breathing that was not his own.

Please . . . please *don't!*

With a scream, a figure jumped out of the darkness, a bayonet raised and ready to strike. Lawrence saw the face of the murderer: it was *himself.* Mouth set. Maniac eyes. He screamed as the killer raised the

179

long blade. He tried to protect himself with his hands at the last moment, as the blade came toward him. . . .

Lawrence sat up in bed. He was covered in sweat, and his hands were shaking as he reached for the light.

He screamed and recoiled in horror. Where the bedside lamp should have been, there was now Paul Hovarth's severed head. At four o'clock in the morning there was no safety from his imagination, not even in the Beverly Hills Hotel.

# 2

Then there were the sirens.

The first time this happened, he was lying in bed, sipping a glass of fresh orange juice, relieved that it was ten o'clock in the morning and his hotel room was flooded with warm yellow sunshine.

It sounded like someone screaming in great pain. He knew, without a doubt, that this was *them* looking for him. Like a blind and brutal force, *they* were all around him, seeking him out. His heart began to pound.

Everything changed. The walls of the Beverly Hills Hotel turned to glass, transparent to the eye—so that Lawrence was on the third floor of a glass tower, completely exposed to view.

In terrible fear, he hid beneath the covers of his bed. The day turned to night. He closed his eyes, trying to block it all out. But even with his eyes closed, he could *see* the black-and-white patrol car racing eastward on Sunset Boulevard, with its red and blue emergency lights throwing off a crazy cascade of colors; racing ever closer to the hotel.

Now he could see the men inside the car: a young black policeman, and his partner—an overweight white man with a mustache and a baby face. They slowed down as they approached the hotel. Lawrence's senses were so acute he could actually hear their conversation.

The black cop said: Hey, look at that! They've remodeled the Beverly Hills Hotel.

The white cop answered: Yeah, glass is in this year. Unless you've got something to hide.

And Lawrence was thinking: I'm invisible, I'm invisible, I'm invisible. . . .

The two cops laughed and pointed to something. At first Lawrence thought they had seen him, but then he realized they were looking at the room next to his, where two homosexuals—dressed in black leather—were doing shocking things to each other.

The cops laughed contemptuously and then drove on by. Their siren receded into the distance, and the walls of the hotel once more became solid and opaque.

Lawrence staggered to the bathroom, fell on his knees, and threw up into the toilet.

# 3

He did not understand what was happening to him. After each of his previous adventures, he had been flooded with a sense of victory and well-being. How he had enjoyed racing through the alleys, with the sirens all around him. How clever he had been to get away! How precious his life had seemed to him at that moment.

So why these self-defeating nightmares and hallucinations?

Worse still, why was his health slipping away? Yes, he had to admit it. He was so weak he could hardly rise from his bed. On the day after Halloween he had fainted while trying to make his way across the room from his bed to the bathroom. He could only imagine it was due to lack of sleep caused by the horrid nightmares. It couldn't be cancer, because he had defeated cancer . . . *hadn't he?*

Yet, when he looked at himself in the bathroom mirror, he was terrified by what he saw. There was hardly anything left to his body. His wrists were so thin that a little finger could almost completely encircle them. As to his face, there was nothing but a skull and two deep-set eyes. In some of Lawrence's worst nightmares, he simply looked in the mirror and saw himself.

He had to build up his strength. Though he was never hungry anymore, he forced himself to call room service three times a day and have full meals brought up to his room. He pecked at the food and left most of it untouched. Several times he had vomited immediately after eating, losing most of the meal down the toilet.

It occurred to him that he might die here. There was only one thing that might help him now, and that seemed impossible: to go hunting again.

Was there any way out? Any hope?

Had he come this far from the Southern California Life Insurance Corporation just to die or go crazy, or—worse still—be *arrested,* hauled out of this beautiful hotel in handcuffs, paraded through the lobby like a common criminal?

Every last ounce of Lawrence's remaining strength and imagination cried out against such a fate. *This is all mental,* he told himself. He lay in bed and meditated on anticancerous thoughts: *I am well. I am strong. I am the God of my own life. Hmm . . . I sure am hungry! I think I'll have the kitchen send me up a nice big triple-decker club sandwich and, oh boy, a chocolate malt!*

By the second day, he was walking around the room, trying to get his strength up. He even attempted a few feeble stretches and exercises. That night, hoping to get some uninterrupted sleep, he had room service send him up a cocktail. Lawrence had always detested the taste of alcohol, so he asked the bar to recommend something that would disguise the taste. They gave him a planter's punch, and to his surprise, he rather enjoyed the drink. It tasted mostly like fruit juice and left him pleasantly woozy. That night he actually succeeded in sleeping until dawn, when a fearsome dream brought him awake. But it was more continuous sleep than he had had in days.

The next evening, he had the bar send him up two tall glasses of planter's punch. They sent him, also, a tray of cocktail nuts, thinking perhaps that he was entertaining. For the first time in days, Lawrence actually smiled at the thought.

In a sense he *was* entertaining. And when the waiter left, he touched the two glasses together and proposed a toast. "Here's to you, my dear. Because you are beautiful. And you are pure. And I love you."

For in this time of darkness and fear, Cassie was never very far from his side. She stood before him like a light, a beacon to guide the way. They talked often, and only in her words and gentle tones would Lawrence find a few moments of peace.

And sometimes, with no words at all, she would lean very close and her soft warm lips would touch him on his cheek. At such moments, not even death held any terrors for him. Only Cassie could hold back the darkness.

# 4

By the fourth day, Lawrence had recovered enough strength to begin seriously to consider a way out of his present situation.

Up to now, he had avoided the newspapers and television news. He had not wanted to know how the investigation was going on the outside. It was enough just to hang on. Ostrichlike, he simply wished to bury his head and hide.

But today, on a sunny Monday morning, he opened up the newspaper that arrived with his breakfast cart, and when the waiter left, he went into his closet and brought out the papers from the last three mornings as well, which he had hidden, unread, inside his suitcase—as though the headlines themselves might betray him.

He sat down at the table, picked slowly at his breakfast, and spent the next hour reading about himself: from the blazing headline last Friday morning (CAR KILLER SLAYS TWO COPS IN BEVERLY HILLS), and the next day (DEAD KIDS LINKED TO CAR KILLER), to the more sedate second-page story this morning (BEVERLY HILLS INVESTIGATION CONTINUES). Lawrence soon learned that Lt. Nicholas Rachmaninoff was no longer in charge of the operation against him. This was rather disappointing, since he had enjoyed the indirect connection with Cassie. He stared at a photograph of Police Chief McWilliams for many long minutes. His new adversary reminded him of a bulldog. The man had a brutal and determined face that Lawrence did not like at all.

At last, he threw the newspapers on the floor and munched thoughtfully on a last piece of toast. By Saturday, the papers had begun to mention "undisclosed evidence in the hands of the police." There was a new tone in the articles that implied the police were closer on his trail than before. Closer and more confident of an "imminent arrest."

What did they have? Was it a bluff? Perhaps it was something to do with the Corvette: He had certainly been reckless enough.

He picked up the newspapers from the floor and read them through once more from the beginning. By the time he had finished his second reading, he was feeling better than he had for days. Every time he came across the phrase "the Car Killer," he thrilled just a little bit inside. *That's me they're talking about!* He just couldn't get over it: little Lawrence Ferguson the center of all this attention. He read some of the newspaper accounts a third time. He was now feeling so good he could hardly remember the last three days of sickness and despair. Another day of rest, and he would be in a better shape than ever.

He stood in front of the dresser mirror and examined his appearance. He was certainly gaunt. But it made him look rather distinguished, didn't it? Sort of a gaunt Yul Brynner.

"Hey there, good-looking," he said to his image in the mirror. "How's it going, guy?"

He practiced speaking to himself and studied his reflection from different angles. He was particularly fond of his three-quarter profile. "Well, baby, ready for some more action, huh? Shall we stir up things a little, you killer, you?"

For the rest of the morning, and most of the afternoon, he considered his various options. The Car Killer was impatient to strike again, but he knew it would not be easy. After Halloween, Beverly Hills was in a state of siege. Also, he had an uneasy feeling about his Corvette. The car was hot, red hot. He had used it too often, too openly . . . so what now? How should he proceed?

Eventually, the outlines of a plan began to emerge. He got dressed, went down to the lobby, and made several calls from a public phone booth there. He did not want these calls to be recorded on his hotel bill. When he left the booth, there was a smile on his lips.

He was near the entrance to the Polo Lounge, and with a sudden reckless feeling he decided to walk in and have a drink. Why not! He had never had a cocktail in the afternoon in his entire life. But he was breaking old patterns all the way around.

It wasn't quite five o'clock, but the lounge was already more than half full. Not too much later, it would be impossible to get a table without a reservation. But at this time of the afternoon, Lawrence was shown immediately to a comfortable booth.

"I'll take a planter's punch," he told the waiter easily, and then changed his mind. "No, what the heck, bring me a bottle of champagne."

"Would you care to see the wine list, sir?"

"Naw, I'll leave it up to you." Lawrence remembered a scene almost like this in a movie. "Just bring me something nice."

"Certainly, sir."

He waited pleasantly for his champagne to arrive, one arm draped casually over the back of the booth. He wore his sunglasses, though the lighting in the Polo Lounge was quite dim. He thought it gave him a mysterious, Hollywood aura.

The waiter returned with a napkin over his arm and a silver ice bucket with a cold green bottle inside. The cork was removed and a quarter-inch of champagne poured into the bottom of the glass. Lawrence thought this seemed faintly stingy.

"Would you like to taste it, sir?"

"Oh, yes. Of course."

Lawrence took a swallow and coughed. "Whew! It's a little . . . sour, I think."

"It's brut, sir. Very dry. If you would like something sweeter, we have a nice Asti Spumanti."

"No, no. This is fine, really. I'll just add a little sugar."

The waiter smiled agreeably.

When Lawrence was left to himself, he watched the Polo Lounge fill up for the evening cocktail hour. Beverly Hills had become very formal in the last decade, after a brief flirtation with looser life styles in the late sixties and early seventies. Almost all the men wore dark suits, carefully tailored, while the women's cocktail dresses reflected the more conservative boutiques. Lawrence watched the parade of elegant men and women with great enjoyment. He did not realize that the Polo Lounge was primarily a place of business, however oblique—even if the business was simply to be seen.

To Lawrence it appeared that everyone was having the time of his life. They were all so rich and confident and good-looking. He sat with a vague half-smile on his lips. After the first glass of champagne, he was pleasantly drunk.

At this point, there was a general straining of necks, as a very handsome man with short white hair and a dazzling smile came striding into the Polo Lounge. All eyes turned in his direction.

Lawrence could hardly believe it. It was George Peppard from "The A-Team"! One of his very favorite shows. The actor seemed to know everyone in the room. Arms reached out for him from every booth he passed.

"George!"

"Stephanie, baby . . . I thought you were in Vienna."

"George, have you met my mother?"

"Now come on, that's not your mother, is it? This has got to be your *sister.*"

George Peppard glided from booth to booth, shaking hands with friends, exchanging a word here and there. Smiling all the time. Lawrence watched him with envy and fascination. His heart was pounding in his chest.

"George!" he called out loudly when the actor was near. "How *are* you?"

George Peppard stopped and looked at Lawrence Ferguson, a flicker of uncertainty touching his perfect smile.

"How's it going?" he asked pleasantly.

"Great, George. Hey, listen, I'm glad I ran into you. I got a wonderful script all lined up with Susan Merril over at Paramount. You know, I can really picture you and Susan in a film together. It's got a great part for you."

"Yeah? Well, Susan Merril sure is a doll. You make certain there are plenty of love scenes, and I might be interested," he said humorously.

Lawrence was sweating a little and having trouble catching his breath.

"Oh, it's a very romantic story . . . very romantic . . . Larry Ferguson is the writer. You known Larry Ferguson, don't you?"

George Peppard smiled vaguely. His attention was already on a young woman across the room, who was making eyes at him. He smiled to her and waved.

"Well, you send the script over to my agent, you hear. I'm always interested in new material."

"Yes, that's great, George, great! New material . . . new horizons! You've got to keep expanding, don't you? . . . You can't stand still . . . That's the way you become a great star!"

With an amiable wink, the actor passed on through the room.

"Hey, George, wait a second!" he called after him. What did he mean, send the script to his agent? Who was his agent? Maybe this was just a brush-off.

*"George!"*

But the actor was involved with another table, making his way slowly to the writer from *Time,* who was waiting very patiently for an interview.

Lawrence, who had been sitting up halfway out of his seat, sank back down into the booth. His throat was so dry that he finished off half a glass of champagne in one gulp. He was definitely feeling tipsy. A surge of anger made his face beet red. *You think you're so great, don't you? But I could just kill you if I wanted!* He snorted contemptuously as the waiter hurried over to refill his glass.

Lawrence himself had not gone unnoticed, during his brief conversation with the TV star. At places like the Polo Lounge, where people come to see and be seen, there are always eyes watching from other booths, assessing your importance. Now, from several directions, there was some attention on Lawrence and speculation as to who he was.

"That guy over there, isn't he . . .?"

"That's the new TV critic for the *New York Times,*" one woman whispered confidently to her husband.

And at another booth, not far away, three men were huddled over their martinis, looking in his direction. They decided, after a few minutes of low conversation, that the gaunt-looking man in the booth by himself was the mysterious Brazilian multimillionaire, who—as rumor had it—was about to take over 20th Century-Fox.

As for the subject of all this speculation: Lawrence sat with a faraway smile and a pleasant glow. He had forgotten George Peppard and his anger at being slighted. It wasn't really important. His thoughts were not in the Polo Lounge, not even in Beverly Hills, but were carried ever so sweetly to Bel Air, where destiny was waiting.

# PART
# EIGHT

*The Long Way Home*

# 1

On Tuesday morning Lt. Nicholas Rachmaninoff drove over to Paramount, which was the last movie studio left in the geographic part of Los Angeles that was known to the world as Hollywood.

Paramount stands in the middle of an aging and decrepit neighborhood, surrounded by a high cement wall: a fortress of dreams, among small grocery shops and old Spanish-style apartments.

Nicky had come here often enough as a child. One of his friends had been the son of a famous actor, and every year at birthday time they would come to this studio for a screening of one of Daddy's classic films. After cake and ice cream, they would generally be given leave to explore the fake Western town and have their own mock gunfights in the dusty streets.

His friend had liked imaginary gunfights. Eventually he was killed by a not so imaginary mortar shell in Vietnam. When you grew up in Hollywood, it was easy to forget that in other places the actors might not rise and walk away when the day's shooting was done.

Much had changed since those childhood birthday parties. Paramount had expanded and engulfed the neighboring studio across the street, which had once been known as RKO, and then later as Desilu, and now was just part of a giant conglomerate, a subsidiary of an even larger corporation far away. Few actual movies were made here anymore. Like the other great studios in town, Paramount was devoted to the production of television: sit-coms and cop shows, specials and soaps, fodder for the American consumer, a staple product that had become as necessary to the nation as wheat and steel and cars.

Nicky parked in the visitors' lot outside the new front gate and convinced the guard on duty to let him proceed on foot to soundstage 5, which was the permanent home set for "Cassie and the Cop."

He did not particularly want to be here this morning. Last night he had almost telephoned Susan several times, to ask if she had received any unusual mail from a psychotic killer who happened to be one of her fans. Nicky had actually started to dial her number, and then put the receiver back on its cradle before completing the call. He didn't want to scare her. Susan had once been raped, by two large motorcycle riders. It happened a long time ago, back in the mid-sixties, after she had blithely accepted a ride on the back of a bike while hitchhiking up the Pacific Coast Highway to Big Sur. Although this fact wasn't included on Susan's official studio bio, he knew it to be one of the more important events of her life, leaving its indelible mark. Ever since, she had been more than a little paranoid with strangers and in unguarded situations. Who wouldn't be? Being a beautiful woman in this society was somewhat akin to being a deer in hunting season in Vermont.

Nicky walked through the narrow streets of the inner studio compound, trying to decide on the right attitude to take, so that he could warn her to be careful, without setting her off into a panic. She seemed to be in a precarious enough emotional balance as it was.

Soundstage 5 was a cream-colored, cavernous building, identical to all the other stages. The red warning light was off, so he stepped inside. He should have felt right at home. The main set—surrounded by miles of electric cables, cameras, lights, and equipment of various sizes and complexity—was a mock-up of a police station. The set was crowded with people wandering about aimlessly. Nicky was always amazed, coming onto a soundstage, at this general feeling of nothing much happening. Electricians leaned against ladders, smoked cigarettes, and talked to one another. Various actors, dressed like policemen, lounged around and told stories and laughed, while near the camera, a man in a business suit was having an intense discussion with a casually dressed older man, who Nicky imagined might be the director. The only person who seemed to be doing anything at all that might conceivably concern the making of a television show was a stagehand who was making chalk marks on the floor.

Such were the glamorous inner workings of television.

Outside the studio, much fuss might be made about what these people were doing here. But inside, time seemed to be standing still. The figures who lounged about so casually had an aura of eternally waiting for something to happen, some event that never quite arrived.

No one paid any attention to Nicky, as he stepped around various lights and objects in the musty gloom of the soundstage. The police station interior was intensely lit by a multitude of lights hanging from the ceiling. It all looked two-dimensional and unreal. Outside a fake window there was a backdrop of a fake city; illusion upon illusion. Beyond the brightness of the actual set, the rest of the building lay concealed in semidarkness.

Nicky saw Susan sitting in a canvas chair a few feet from the camera. A man sat next to her, dressed like a cop, in full uniform down to the gun on his belt. They were laughing about something as Nicky approached; waiting as everyone else was waiting, for something to begin.

She did not see him until he was almost right next to her.

"Nicky! Hi! What are *you* doing here?" Susan seemed flustered to see him. Nicky recognized the actor sitting next to her as a regular on the show: Danny Marino, who played the captain of her make-believe husband's make-believe precinct. Danny was in his fifties, with silver hair and lots of personality. Nicky took one look at the way he sat, angled in relationship to Susan's body, and knew that they were sleeping together—despite what Susan had said about his being her only extra marital adventure.

Nicky smiled. "I just wanted to ask you something," he said. "No big deal. I was in the neighborhood, so I thought I'd stop by rather than call you on the phone."

"Great," she replied uncertainly. "Ah, Nicky, have you met Danny Marino? . . . This is Lieutenant Rachmaninoff of the Beverly Hills Police Department, who just happens to be my ex-husband."

The actor stood up in a most friendly way. The two men shook hands warmly and exchanged a little small talk about what he—a real cop—must feel at seeing this mock-up of a police station. Danny seemed to be a warm and earthy guy, which was the image he projected on the show. Nicky went along with a few minutes of good-natured kidding, before indicating to Susan that he really did have something he needed to see her about. In private.

He led her off to a darkened corner of the stage, behind one of the fake walls.

"Look, Susan, your name has come up in an investigation. I wanted to ask you if you'd received any unusual fan mail recently."

"Fan mail? What's this about?"

"Well, there was a crime committed in an apartment in Santa Monica. The place had lots of photographs of you on the walls. We were wondering if anyone named Lawrence Ferguson has ever tried to get in touch with you."

"God, Nicky, I get hundreds of letters every week. I don't even read them anymore. They just go to the publicity department here. . . . I don't remember anyone named Lawrence Ferguson. Is it important?"

"Probably not . . . but look, be extra careful for a while, will you? There's a nut out there somewhere and he seems to be a fan of yours."

"Oh, *great!* That's all I need. Now I *am* getting frightened."

"No need to, really. Just be careful, and call me if anything unusual happens."

But Susan's paranoia was just getting revved up. "*Jesus,* you only investigate homicides, Nicky. Is there some kind of crazy killer looking for me? Is that what you're trying to say?"

Nicky held her firmly by the shoulders. She was in full television makeup, which had the effect of depersonalizing her face. But he could still see a very frightened Susan looking up at him. "Look, baby, this really isn't a big thing. There *was* a murder in an apartment, and there *were* a lot of photos of you on the wall. But then, you're probably on thousands of walls, so it doesn't mean that much. A detective in Santa Monica asked me to look into it, that's all. I decided to come over in person so you wouldn't worry too much. But I don't seem to be doing a good job."

"Shit!" She sighed, and slipped into his arms. "It's so fucking crazy. People see you on TV and they think they own you. It's scary to be famous."

Nicky felt a shiver run up her spine. He held her and rubbed her back gently. He thought to himself, Well, you enter their living rooms, so you have to take the consequences of what goes on there. To Susan, he said, "Don't worry. We're going to have this particular fan of yours behind bars in a day or two. I'm afraid he'll have to watch 'Cassie and the Cop' from prison."

She tried to smile. "You'll take care of me, Nicky?"

"You know I will."

She pressed her thigh against his in a provocative manner and kissed him on the lips. He returned her kiss in what he hoped was a brotherly sort of way, which was not easy with Susan's tongue probing into his mouth.

He broke free, uncomfortably aroused.

"I feel something *growing down there,*" she said demurely, looking up at him like a coy pussycat.

"Jesus, Susan, you're too much." Then he added, trying to break the mood, "So how long have you been sleeping with this Danny Marino character, huh?"

She opened her mouth to protest, but Nicky looked at her in his most knowing-police-officer way.

"Who told you?" she sputtered. And then, realizing she had given herself away to a bluff: "God! I *hate* you!"

194

He laughed. Probably it was unfair to use such a basic police trick on his ex-wife. But, after all, she had been using some rather basic feminine tricks on him.

"Come on, Susan. *I* don't mind. *I'm* not married to you, for chrissake."

She was pouting. "It's your fault, Nicky. . . . If you'd be my lover, I wouldn't have to see other men."

He laughed and shook his head at this strange logic. And he didn't believe it.

"Are you angry that I lied to you?" she asked.

"No. I'm not angry. I'm just a little sad. You know, you don't *have* to lie to me, Susan. You really can tell me the truth."

She regarded him closely, then laughed and hugged him once more. This was different from the hug earlier. It was not provocative or coy. Just the embrace of two people who have known each other, for better and worse, a long, long time.

"Why did I ever leave you?" she asked softly.

"Don't you remember? You wanted to be a star."

He gestured to the bright lights and camera. "Come on, I've got to go back to work," he said, and led her back out of the deep shadows where they had been talking, toward the main part of the set. They walked with their arms around each other's waist, but no one paid them any attention.

In Hollywood, everyone loved one another madly; kissed and hugged and called each other darling all the time. It didn't mean a thing.

Susan's stand-in was in place before the camera, and it appeared that they were finally ready to begin shooting.

"Places everybody!" called an assistant director.

Susan joined Danny Marino in front of the bright lights, on the floor of the fake squad room. Nicky was interested enough to watch for a few moments. The set—with its desks and typewriters, water coolers and computer terminals—did look amazingly like a real police station. At each desk was a policeman (or woman), both in uniform and plainclothes, black and white and Oriental, to represent a fair and typical cross section of the population.

It was all so right, yet totally wrong. It reminded Nicky of Main Street, Disneyland—correct in all the details, yet completely unlike the real thing.

In the scene that Nicky watched, Danny Marino, as the captain, was trying to warn Cassie away from a case.

THE CAPTAIN (*sternly*) Listen here, young lady, this is the Mob you're
       dealing with. Why don't you go on home and take up a new
       hobby. Like cooking, for instance.
CASSIE (*coyly*) Oh, I've got something cooking, all right! Just wait and
       see.
THE CAPTAIN Well, don't let it be your goose!

"*Cut!*" the director screamed. "Can't we do something about this di-
alogue? That's the crappiest exchange I've ever heard. This isn't the
fucking Julia Child show, for God's sake!"

"Now wait a second" came the offended voice of a writer from the
shadows behind the camera. "This is the kind of humor that Aaron
thinks is real cute. . . ."

Nicky smiled and walked away from the artificial world of the
soundstage into the dazzling sunlight outside.

# 2

Up to now, on this Tuesday morning, everything
Nicky had done was quite proper and could be ex-
plained to his superiors. A fellow policeman from Santa Monica asked
a favor, and he had complied. Such things happened all the time.

His next move, however, crossed a subtle but definite line, putting
him out on his own, beyond his authority—disobeying the very highest
echelon orders from the chief of the Los Angeles police and the mayor
of the city.

Instead of returning to his office in Beverly Hills, to proceed with his
assigned task of checking out the various registered psychopaths in the
county of Los Angeles, he drove to the head office of the Southern California Life Insurance Corporation in Santa Monica to learn more
about the dangerous enigma that was Lawrence Ferguson.

Lawrence's last place of employment was located on the twelfth and
fourteenth floors of a vast steel and tinted-glass building on Wilshire
Boulevard, west of the Miracle Mile. Nicky found it somewhat incredible that such a modern building—a product of the most advanced
technology—would omit the thirteenth floor out of superstition. Thir-

196

teen was an unlucky number, and in this case that seemed to be correct. The accounting department of the Southern California Life Insurance Corporation was indeed on that unlucky floor, and the fates had apparently not been impressed by some architect's clever ruse to put the number 14 on the elevator bank.

Nicky was dubious about this building from the moment he walked into the elevator and found himself greeted by Muzak—which he always disliked, but particularly so in elevators and over telephones. An old Bob Dylan tune, rearranged for strings and glockenspiel, accompanied him to the thirteenth/fourteenth floor, where he was deposited in front of a large desk guarded by a fashionably dressed young woman.

Nicky produced his shield and explained the purpose of his visit. The receptionist was both helpful and flirtatious. She suggested Nicky talk with Jack Armstrong, an accountant who had had the desk next to Lawrence Ferguson for the past six years. She directed him through a maze of corridors to a large open room with dozens of desks. Franz Kafka would have enjoyed a room like this. The desks were lined up like an army platoon. High on the far wall a large clock ticked off the passing seconds, marching tediously toward 5:00 P.M.

Jack Armstrong, a man of late middle age, sat behind one of these desks. He was short and round, with stubby fingers and a pink, well-scrubbed face. The man seemed more than glad to stop work for a few moments to talk with a police officer. Nicky was aware that most of the eyes in this room were upon him. Murder had made a big interruption in the monotony of this little world.

"I'm glad to help out any way I can," the man said, when Nicky was seated. "But I don't think there is much I haven't told the police already. Actually, I didn't know Lawrence very well. He was a pretty strange fellow."

"At this point, anything you can tell me would be extremely helpful," Nicky admitted. "For example, what exactly do you mean by 'strange'?"

Jack Armstrong pursed his lips. "Well, it's hard to say. He was just different, that's all. He never joined in the bull sessions, or anything like that. He seemed to live on another planet. You know what I mean? At lunch, he always ate by himself. The guy never even came to the office party once a year. But he was a good worker. A bit prissy, but regular as a clock. Everybody just left him alone."

"When you say prissy, do you mean homosexual?"

"No, I would doubt that. Lawrence struck me mostly as a neuter. He was very . . . rigid in his ways. When anything came up to upset his routine, he would get very irritated."

"So you don't think he ever had a girlfriend?"

"Well now, come to think of it, there was a girl from the typing pool he was dating. This must have been seven, eight years ago . . . the lady was pretty fat, and kind of hairy. There were some snide comments about the relationship, I can tell you. A lot of speculation about whether they were getting it on or not."

Nicky sighed. "Lawrence sounds like a rather depressing fellow."

"Yeah, I guess you could say that."

"Do you remember the girl's name, by any chance?"

"No . . . I'm sorry. She quit years ago. A lot of secretaries come and go in a company this size."

"Do you have any idea if he saw her after she left this company?"

"I don't know . . . but I always had the impression she quit to get away from Lawrence. He was certainly more quiet and depressed for a long time after she was gone."

"I see. Well, how about vacations? Do you have any idea what he did with his time?"

"Sure. He got three weeks off every year. He went to the desert."

"The *desert?* You mean, like Palm Springs?"

"Yeah, somewhere down there. He never said exactly. I doubt if it was any place as swank as Palm Springs."

"How do you know he went to the desert?"

"Well, you gotta understand—I've worked with this guy for *thirteen years.* For six years, I actually had a desk next to him. But all we ever did was exchange a little small talk. You know. 'Rainy day, isn't it?' 'Sure is.' 'Did you have a nice Christmas?' 'Very nice. And you?' That kind of thing. So every year he would take his vacation in April, and he would come back noticeably suntanned. I must have asked him once if he went south to Mexico, and he said no, the desert. So then every year around April, the small talk would be, 'Going to the desert this year?' 'Sure am.' And then afterward, 'Have a good time in the desert?' 'Wonderful time, thank you.' Sometimes in the winter when we would be having really rotten weather, I'd say to him, 'I bet you're looking forward to the desert on a day like this.' "

"And he'd say?"

" 'I sure am.' "

"Sounds like you guys had fascinating conversations."

Jack Armstrong shrugged his shoulders. "Hey, I told you, the guy was not someone you could have a fascinating conversation with."

"Did you ever ask him where exactly he went in the desert?"

"No . . . or if he told me, I forget. Can't stand the desert myself. I've never even been down there, if you want to know the truth. No desire. So if he told me, it went in one ear and out the other. . . . I do remember one year, a month or so before his vacation, he had a catalog on his desk for fishing gear."

"*Fishing* in the desert?"

"I guess it's a little strange. When he got back, I asked him if he caught anything. He said no, all the fish had died. I remember thinking that was pretty strange, too."

"Did you ask him about it?"

"Naw . . . didn't really care, if you want to know the truth."

Nicky stood up to leave. "Thank you very much for your time, Mr. Armstrong. I may get back to you, if I think of anything else."

"Any time, Lieutenant. . . . By the way, the name was Molly."

"Molly?"

"The name of the typist Lawrence was dating. We used to joke about her a lot. I mean, she was ug-*ly!* I don't remember her last name, but they'll have that downstairs in Personnel."

"Thanks."

Nicky made his way back through the labyrinth of corridors, past the receptionist to the banks of elevators. He only had time to listen to a few bars of some dementedly pleasant music, before being deposited on the twelfth floor.

# 3

Mr. Timothy Geer, the director of personnel, rated an office with a tinted floor-to-ceiling window that looked out on a fried chicken franchise. An extremely large, smiling rooster revolved enticingly in the air a few floors below.

The director of personnel was quite a young man, sharply dressed, with small eyes and an aggressive nose. Nicky made himself comfortable in the hot spot—where undoubtedly many nervous job applicants had sweated out their future.

"I am interested," he said, "in any information you can give me about Lawrence Ferguson." He was beginning to feel like a recording.

"Actually, I hardly knew the man. He was hired by one of my predecessors. Twenty years ago, I believe. I was still in elementary school." The director smiled, but it was clear he was all too eager to dissociate himself from the disaster that was Lawrence Ferguson.

"Yes, yes, I understand. . . . What I'd like, first of all, is to see his personal file. Also, I'm curious about a girl named Molly. I don't know her last name, but she was in the typing pool about seven years ago, and I understand she dated Lawrence for a time."

"All right. The file is easy enough. To find a girl named Molly something who used to work here may be more difficult, but we'll give it a try. All our records, you understand, are stored in the central computer." Timothy Geer proudly gestured to the computer terminal and TV screen that was built into one side of his enormous desk.

"I'll show you how it works," he continued. He activated the terminal, typed in a code, and then the name Lawrence Ferguson. The TV screen came to life, magically writing names and words and dates. Timothy Geer watched on with a pleased expression. When the screen was full, he pressed another button. "We'll want a hard copy of this," he explained. With a soft, electronic chatter, a long piece of paper fed out of a slot in the side of the computer. The director tore it off and handed it to Nicky.

"This is Mr. Ferguson's file," he beamed.

"Amazing!" Nicky said, with the right amount of appreciation. Glancing at the paper, he learned that Lawrence had been born in Bakersfield on April 15, 1938. The names of his parents, schools he attended, job history, military information: all this and more followed in the concise fashion of computer talk. Nicky folded the paper for later study.

"Impressed?"

"Yes, I certainly am."

"All right. Now we'll see if we can find your Molly something. She was a typist you said?"

"Jack Armstrong told me she belonged to the typing pool about seven years ago."

"Okay. . . . I'll request the names of everyone in the typing pool for 1978." He sat at the keyboard and deftly typed out his request. Within seconds, the screen wrote out thirty-seven names. Name number twenty-four belonged to Molly Young: This was the only Molly on the list.

"Bingo!" he cried.

"*Very* impressive," Nicky murmured, to keep him going.

"All right. Now we'll get you our file on Molly Young."

Nicky soon had in his possession a long sheet of computer readout similar to the one he had for Lawrence.

"I can't tell you how much you are helping me, Mr. Geer."

"It's pretty amazing, isn't it? Almost science fiction, wouldn't you say?"

"Yes, I would. The science fiction of yesterday becomes the fact of today. . . . Now, if I could trouble you for one more thing, Mr. Geer. Do you, by any chance, have a photograph of Lawrence Ferguson in your files?"

"We do indeed," he said, and then added in a softer, more confidential tone: "A few years ago we became very security conscious and requested that all our employees be photographed and fingerprinted. But, you know, we have already given a copy of these to Lieutenant Hotchkiss."

"Yes, I'm aware of that," Nicky agreed, and then he, too, lowered his voice and moved closer to Timothy Geer in a conspiratorial manner. "Actually, I am not from the same branch of the police as Lieutenant Hotchkiss. Confidentially—just between you and me—I am part of a special task force put together by the mayor to investigate a crime of much vaster significance than the murder of Paul Hovarth."

The young man's mouth opened and fell slack. "Lieutenant Rachmaninoff . . . why, of course. I saw you on television . . . My God! Son of a bitch!"

Nicky simply set his mouth in a grim and knowing way. "So, if you have another copy of the photo and fingerprints . . ."

"Oh, of course! Certainly. The computer can give us that as well."

He returned to the keyboard and began typing out instructions. The hard copy of the photograph flowed effortlessly from the slot in the side, followed immediately by a copy of the prints, taken of all ten fingers.

Nicky took the photograph with a tremulous feeling in the pit of his stomach. A few butterflies were doing daredevil acrobatics inside. The black-and-white computer photograph was made up of many thousands of small dots, yet it was quite realistic. A full-head portrait revealed a gaunt-looking individual with deep-set eyes and thinning hair. Lawrence Ferguson stared into the camera looking both fearful and haunted.

"When was this taken?" he asked, not able to tear his eyes away from the man he had been seeking so intensely these past few weeks.

"Four years ago. That's when we instigated our present computerized I.D. system for all employees. I might say, it's one of the most advanced, nonmilitary systems in the world."

Nicky murmured, "Thanks," shook hands hurriedly, and walked out of the office.

He could not take his eyes off the photograph of Lawrence Ferguson. It was very strange and most unaccountable, but he was certain that somewhere, sometime, he had seen this face before.

# 4

Nicky drove toward Santa Monica, distracted and troubled by his inability to remember exactly where it was he had seen Lawrence Ferguson. Engrossed in his thoughts, he ran a red light on Wilshire, barely missing a city bus.

A siren disturbed his meditation. Nicky glanced in his rearview mirror to see an angry red light flashing for him to pull over. He coasted into the parking lot of a drive-in hamburger joint, while the sleek black-and-white CHP car came up alongside. A young man with a mustache and large stomach ambled up to the side of his Austin-Healey. The highway patrolman's revolver swung importantly in his holster. Nicky sometimes found himself disliking other cops. He wondered if he appeared so obnoxious himself. He imagined he did.

"Okay, let's see your driver's license."

The insolence of the man! Just for running a red light! He brought out his shield.

"Oh, I'm sorry, Lieutenant. . . . You know, you almost had an accident there with that bus."

Nicky narrowed his eyes and gave the young patrolman a withering glance. Theoretically, policemen were supposed to obey traffic laws just like other mortals. One of the perks of the job, however, was that you could pretty much drive any way you pleased. Especially if you were a lieutenant in homicide.

"Well, have a nice day," the patrolman said hopefully, and took his large stomach and protruding pistol back to his car.

Nicky sighed. He knew his behavior was childish and irresponsible, and it frightened him how close he had come to colliding with that bus ... but goddamn it, he had actually met the Car Killer.

He stared out his windshield for five minutes and tried to let his mind roam free to make the right connections. Nothing came. Finally, he got out of his car and went to the public phone at the corner of the parking area.

Nicky's first call was to the Santa Monica station, where he asked to be put through to Lt. David Hotchkiss in the homicide room.

"Dave, this is Nicky. I've talked with my ex-wife and I'm afraid she doesn't remember ever having a letter from Lawrence Ferguson. She doesn't actually get her fan mail, though. It all goes to the publicity department at Paramount. So if you are interested, you should get in touch with them."

"Naw ... it's probably nothing. Thanks for your help though. It seemed like a bright idea at the time. You should have seen the apartment! It was like a shrine to Susan Merril. Pictures of her everywhere."

"Actually, I *would* like to see the apartment, if it's possible. This case has aroused my curiosity."

There was a pause at the other end. Then: "Nicky, is there anything you're not telling me? Why are you so interested in this?"

"Well ... it's just that I'm always very protective about Susan. I want to judge for myself if there is any danger to her in all this."

"I guess that's reasonable. Okay, you can look at the place. Who knows ... if you get any bright ideas, let me know. The case is at a fucking standstill."

"Haven't found him yet, huh?"

"Not a clue. Anyway, we've placed one of our locks on the front door. We're all finished there, but the apartment is still sealed. If you come down to the station, I'll give you the key."

"Is everything intact inside?"

"Just the way we found it, minus the body and the murder weapon, which was an army surplus bayonet we found in the bathroom."

"Okay, thanks. I'll see you in about fifteen minutes."

Nicky hung up, put more money in the phone, and made a call to Charlie Cat, back in Beverly Hills.

"Rock Man, where the fuck have you been?" he exploded. "All kinds of people have been looking for you."

"Like who?"

"Like the captain, for instance. I was able to put him off by saying you were going through the psycho sheets for Chief McWilliams. . . . You *are* doing that, aren't you?"

"Well, actually, that's why I'm calling. My dear friend, I was wondering if you would do me the vast favor of taking over that unpleasant little chore for me. I find myself very busy at the moment."

"Fuck. You're kidding?"

"No-o. I'd be willing to express my gratitude by buying a little Mexican dinner tomorrow night on La Cienega."

"Damn it, Nick. I have my hands full with our teenage *castrato*. Anyway, I'm kind of off Mexican food."

"Look, Charlie Cat, I think I'm really on to something. I just need a little more time. Have you had a good Italian meal recently? What about La Trattoria on Santa Monica?"

"Shit, man, you are going to get us both in a lot of trouble. You know that? For trouble like that, it would have to be something French. You know that new place, Le Coq d'Or, over on the Strip?"

"You have expensive tastes, Charlie. But all right. Le Fucking Coq d'Or it is."

"*With* a good bottle of red wine. Something imported. I'm awfully bored with California plonk. Aren't you, for chrissake?"

"Okay, okay. You got me by the balls. See you later."

"I'll make the reservations for seven . . . think I'll fast tomorrow, so I can build up the old appetite."

"That's just great."

ess than an hour later, Nicky was in the fifth-floor hallway of the Cresswell Arms, outside apartment 5-C. A padlock was affixed to the door, as well as a large sign:

WARNING
THESE PREMISES SEALED BY ORDER OF L.A.P.D.
NO UNAUTHORIZED ENTRY

Nicky used the key he had been given at the Santa Monica station to open the padlocked door. He stepped into Lawrence Ferguson's last-known habitation and closed the door behind him. The stuffy smell of death still clung in the air. On the floor of the studio apartment, chalk marks outlined the positions of various parts of the body that had been scattered throughout the room. Even without these reminders of mutilation, the studio would have been depressing enough.

He wandered carefully through the room, looking at the shabby secondhand furniture, the narrow bed and small table, as well as the obviously expensive, fairly new TV. Above the bed there was indeed a shrine to Susan: a montage of various photographs, mostly from *TV Guide* and *People*. On another wall, above the table, was the official Susan Merril Swimsuit Calendar for 1985. For the month of October, Susan was emerging from a most tropical-looking ocean in a very small, white bikini. Her nipples were just visible through the thin material, and she smiled as if she did not have a thought in the world except to be sexy and adorable.

Nicky shook his head in amazement. He had not actually seen this calendar before, and he spent a moment leafing through the months. These pictures had little to do with the Susan he knew. She was exhibited here as a product, too glossily perfect; some untouchable figment of a press agent's imagination. And although Susan really was a very beautiful woman, it was not in this way. Part of her beauty lay in the fact that she could look, from certain angles—at certain times—almost ugly. It was the fact that she was slightly awkward, vulnerable really, mixed with her all-American good looks, that gave her the unusual fawnlike grace that separated her from the hordes of perfect blondes who roamed the streets and beaches of California. Here she was just a fantasy blonde.

He wandered into the small kitchenette, where there was a hotplate, a toaster oven, and a miniature refrigerator. Nicky opened the door of the refrigerator. There was a bottle of ketchup, a can of half-eaten cocktail sausages, and a few frozen TV dinners in the upper compartment. Lawrence was not exactly a gourmet.

Nicky then opened the utility closet, poked into the various drawers and shelves, and paused for a moment to gaze out the window, where a narrow sliver of the Pacific Ocean was just visible through a slim corridor of apartment buildings. From this angle, even the ocean looked old and exhausted.

His gaze traveled from the window and came to rest on a postcard thumbtacked to the wall. The card showed a desert scene—clusters of bright red flowers coming up, improbably, from the brown, barren earth. Nicky took the card off the wall and turned it over. There was no writing on the other side. Just the printed words: *Spring flowers blooming in the desert. Indio, California.* He tacked the postcard back to the wall and continued his inspection of the other rooms.

There was not much to see. In the main room, he found a small shelf containing a few thrillers, a dictionary, and a Time-Life picture book of the desert. In the bathroom, the desert motif was evident again, in the form of a large poster of an exotic cactus, profiled against a dramatic sunset. Nicky wished he could find some clue where Lawrence went for his annual vacation. Indio was as close as he got—but the postcard, of course, could have been bought while driving through to some other place.

He poked around behind various pieces of furniture, glanced under the bed, and searched through the closet. Among the assortment of shirts and inexpensive suits he found two magazines hidden on a back shelf. The first one was entitled *Dicks and Cunts.* The second: *Girls Who Suck Cock.* The titles were not misleading.

Finally, Nicky sat down dejectedly on the hard narrow bed. This poor studio apartment, which once contained someone's life, was truly dismal.

How many evenings had Lawrence spent here by himself, with his dirty magazines in the closet, his TV set, and TV dinners, and misplaced Susan on the walls looking down?

Nicky took out the photograph of Lawrence that he had folded in his jacket pocket and looked at the picture of the man who was still mysteriously familiar.

"You poor son of a bitch," he muttered.

He was beginning to get a pitifully clear image of Lawrence in his mind. It wasn't a nice image. He had seen the office where he had worked for twenty years, and now the room where he had lived. Nicky couldn't help but think that if he were Lawrence Ferguson, and if he had lived and worked in these places, he might bust out and start killing people, too.

# 6

He drove back to the Santa Monica police station to return the key to David Hotchkiss. His stomach rumbled a reminder that the lunch hour had come and gone without any food passing its way. Stomach would have to wait. There was too much to do.

Driving through the tedious midday traffic on Santa Monica Boulevard, he tried to get his priorities in order. He made a mental list of the people he wanted to see:

Molly Young, the typist Lawrence had dated.

The doctor at Santa Monica Medical Center, who told him he had cancer.

The person who sold Lawrence the Corvette.

And the bank teller who gave him his life savings on that fateful Friday, when Lawrence Ferguson made his extraordinary departure from his drab and constricting routine.

Each of these interviews could be terribly useful or completely useless. They might lead to a dead end, or they might open up a whole new line of inquiry. The problem was Nicky had more concrete leads to follow now that he was on his own than he had when he had a task force of thirty men and women at his disposal to lend a hand.

That was the real issue. As a responsible and mature officer on the payroll of Los Angeles County, he should pull over to the first available telephone and report in to Chief McWilliams with his sensational information that the Car Killer was a sad and sickly ex-accountant named Lawrence Ferguson.

Of course, they wouldn't believe him at first. Nicky would be called into another conference downtown, like the one last Saturday, where he would be grilled and cross-examined as thoroughly as if he were the criminal himself. Nicky could imagine that smug assistant D.A. telling him that no, his evidence was just too circumstantial. . . . The whole case would get bogged down in politics and personalities, and then be taken away from him in the end.

Well, fuck them!

This was definitely not a good attitude for a man in his position to take. But every time he visualized the conference room last Saturday, a cold fury took over his soul. After fifteen years on the force, he felt too old and grouchy to take the bullshit anymore.

Maybe tomorrow he could recant and call in with his information, and become a good team player once again. He knew he should, and that the longer he put it off the harder it would be. But today he did not feel responsible or mature; he felt rebellious as hell.

So fuck 'em. Today, this case belonged to him.

# 7

Lt. David Hotchkiss had been a football player in college and had almost made it to the NFL. He was a powerfully built man, well over six feet tall, with sandy hair and narrow-set eyes. Nicky found him in the homicide squad room, sleeves rolled up, his feet on his desk, taking large bites out of a turkey sandwich. Nicky's stomach once again reminded him that it would be nice, sometime today, to eat.

"Well, what did you think?" Hotchkiss asked him, his mouth full of food.

Nicky shrugged. "Looks like Lawrence Ferguson is a lonely man who lives in his fantasies a lot. I wasn't too happy to see all those pictures of Susan on the wall, but it seems harmless enough."

"Yeah, well, you never know. . . . We're just at a dead end with finding him, but he'll probably turn up. The amateurs always do."

"Yeah, ah, look, Dave . . . I stopped off at the Southern California Life Insurance Corporation this morning, just out of curiosity. The head of personnel gave me this photograph of Lawrence." Nicky handed the detective the computerized photograph.

Lieutenant Hotchkiss took another enormous bite of his sandwich and spoke with his mouth full. "Yeah, we have this picture, too."

"What I was thinking," Nicky continued, "was that you could give this to a police artist and have him go around to some of the people he worked with—maybe even the doctor at the Santa Monica Medical Center—and try to get a mock-up of what Lawrence looks like today. If the guy has cancer, his appearance has probably changed a lot since this photo was taken."

208

"Great idea, Nick. So good I even thought of it myself. The police artist finished yesterday, and we got a great picture. Everybody who knew him says it looks exactly like Lawrence does today."

"Well, that's great." Nicky paused, hoping he would be invited to see this new picture. When the invitation did not come, he handed over the keys to Ferguson's apartment. Hotchkiss took the keys and put them in his desk drawer, and then continued working on the sandwich.

"You know, I would be interested in seeing the new mock-up of Lawrence," Nicky said finally. "Maybe I should show it to Susan and ask her if she's seen the guy."

The Santa Monica detective wiped the mayonnaise off his mouth with the back of his hand and regarded Nicky shrewdly. "How's your case going over there in Beverly Hills? Got any good leads on the Car Killer yet?"

"Actually, it's not my case anymore. Didn't you hear? City Hall did a little cosmetic job for the press and handed over the case to the chief himself."

"Hmm . . . tough break, Nick. I imagine a guy like you would sort of keep poking around anyway. Maybe you hope you might show up the big boys downtown."

"No. It's never a good idea to show up the big boys downtown."

Dave Hotchkiss took his feet off his desk, sat up in his chair, and put the remaining part of his sandwich down. "Then what are you doing nosing around Santa Monica? What's this business of going over to Southern Cal Life and looking through Lawrence's apartment? Why don't you tell me what you're up to, Nick? I'd very much like to know."

Nicky laughed. "You're a suspicious fucker, you know that?"

"Come on, come on. Tell Papa. I just *smell* something going on. Tell you what, Nicholas, my boy. Let's make a little deal. I'll give you the new mock-up of Lawrence that you seem so positively horny to get your hands on if you level with me and tell me your real interest in this case."

Nicky smiled and decided it was in his interest to open up a little. "Put it this way, Dave—I suddenly have quite a lot of time on my hands and I'm curious, very curious, about any apparently motiveless killings going on in town right now."

"Aha! I think we're beginning to get someplace. Keep talking, my boy. I'm beginning to enjoy this conversation."

"You know, Dave, I can really see why everybody tells me you are such an effective policeman. If I stay here another five minutes, you'll probably have me confessing that *I'm* the fucking Car Killer."

"You're changing the subject, friend. So you think that Lawrence baby is the Car Killer, huh?"

"Now hold on, I didn't say that. I'm just interested in failures and psychopaths and weird people running amok. You know? I'd say that Lawrence Ferguson deserves at least an honorary mention on the list of crazies I'm compiling for Chief McWilliams."

Lieutenant Hotchkiss sighed and rubbed his hands together. "You're holding something back, Nicholas. I just know it. Now come on, old buddy. One friend to another. How about sharing the wealth?"

"Hey, man, that's all I got! The rest is just speculation and coincidence. You're not interested in that kind of shit, are you?"

"I'm interested."

Nicky smiled smugly. It was hard to resist the temptation to strut his stuff just a little before this very shrewd colleague. "Well, there are two things, actually. First, the date. On October 17th, Lawrence learned he had cancer and he disappeared. That happens to be the very day of the first car killing—Gerald Eastman, in his Mercedes-Benz on Sunset."

Dave Hotchkiss grunted and seemed to be weighing this back and forth.

"Then, there is the little coincidence that Lawrence is driving a Corvette. We know for a fact that Officers Ewing and DeWolfe were shot by someone who pulled up alongside in a Corvette. That is privileged information, by the way. We're holding it from the press."

"Hmm . . . very interesting, except for the fact that Lawrence drives a Ford Galaxie."

Nicky leaned forward across the desk. "Check *temporary* registrations in Sacramento, my friend. You will find that our Mr. Ferguson traded in his Ford Galaxie on October 18th for a very red and beautiful 1972 Corvette."

"Hmm . . . more and more interesting."

"So now I've done my part, Dave. If you'll kindly give me a copy of the mock-up, I'll be on my way."

Dave Hotchkiss smiled broadly. "Hey, Nicholas, all you had to do was look on the bulletin board of any police station in the state of California. We issued the new picture yesterday along with the APB. So you see, you didn't have to tell me diddley-shit. But I'm glad you did, and to show you my appreciation, I'm going to give you your very own, up-to-date portrait of Lawrence Ferguson. Just so you don't have to lurk in any strange hallways."

"Why are cops always such tricky bastards?" Nicky wondered aloud.

"Nice guys don't last too long in this world." Lieutenant Hotchkiss brought his enormous body up out of the chair, moved over to a metal filing cabinet, and took out a copy of the artist's drawing.

"You let me know if you get a line on this guy, you hear me, Nick? I don't care what the fuck he did in Beverly Hills, he killed someone in Santa Monica. And I don't like that."

"I'll let you know," Nicky murmured, but he was no longer consciously aware of anything except the drawing.

It was a full head portrait, like the computerized photograph. But here, Lawrence was perhaps twenty or thirty pounds thinner. The flesh hung on the bones, and his eyes were hollow and intense. Cancer had eaten away at every ounce of Lawrence's face that was nonessential, leaving a living skull.

Strangely enough, this new picture of Lawrence Ferguson was even more familiar to Nicky than the last.

And still he could not remember where he had seen this man.

8

He succeeded in eating two Jumbo Jacks while maneuvering through the Santa Monica traffic, steering and changing gears with one hand. He managed to drip ketchup on his pants, and in the end the burgers sat like lead at the bottom of his stomach. But he was not hungry anymore. Fast food did deaden your appetite for several hours.

Nicky spent the rest of the afternoon at Jack Long's Super Saver Car Lot, and at the Santa Monica branch of the Bank of America, where Lawrence had had his savings account. At both places, Lawrence Ferguson was remembered. Neither Jack Long nor the bank manager was particularly surprised to have a visit from the police concerning Lawrence's activities on that Friday three weeks before. Both agreed that something was definitely peculiar with the way the man acted—though they also vigorously protested their own innocence in the matter of giving him money and selling him a car.

As far as Nicky was concerned, the afternoon brought him no further information. He had patiently questioned both men, in the hopes that Lawrence had left behind some slight clue as to what he was going to do with his money and where he was going to drive in his new car. But if he had, neither man had noticed.

Nicky was not particularly discouraged.

Every now and then, he brought out the police sketch of Lawrence Ferguson and asked himself where he had seen this face. But no answer came.

It was a little after five-thirty when he hurried along Santa Monica Boulevard toward home. He had a seven o'clock date with Julie at her house. She was going to cook him dinner, and he wanted to go back to Sunshine Terrace to shower and change.

Santa Monica Boulevard brought him into Beverly Hills. At the foot of Rexford Drive, he could not resist turning left to revisit the scene of the Halloween murders one more time. Maybe it would tell him something. He tried to imagine how Lawrence might see this street: how rich and quiet this tree-lined drive must seem after the cheap, seaside squalor of the Cresswell Arms. At the 600 block of Rexford, Nicky slowed down at the place where the two policemen had been killed. At the Hawthorne Elementary School, across the way, children were riding their bicycles in the playground.

He shook his head sadly. "Lawrence, Lawrence, why did you do it?"

Nicky decided to make a U-turn on Rexford and follow the route the killer must have taken that night to get to Sunset. It was just a small detour from his way home. He drove south to Carmelita, and then west the two blocks to the alley where the bullet shells had been found. Nicky turned up the alley and drove toward Sunset, until he came to where two more lives had ended on Elevado.

He had driven this route several times before—but it was quite different now, with an actual person in mind, whose life was becoming increasingly familiar. It occurred to Nicky for the first time that Lawrence must have gone west on Elevado, since he had been going west on Carmelita. He was moving toward a definite location. Nicky made a left turn from the alley and followed the direction that Lawrence would have taken, until he came to the first intersection on Beverly Drive.

He stopped and considered which way to turn. It really was not much of a question. The killer would want to get off the quiet residential streets on to the main, anonymous thoroughfare of Sunset. Nicky turned in that direction.

And it was then that he saw, as if for the first time, the great pink structure of the Beverly Hills Hotel, standing so grandly on the far side of Sunset Boulevard.

It made him catch his breath.

"Son . . . of . . . a . . . bitch!"

# 9

Nicky found he was trembling.

Could this really be the end of the hunt? The Beverly Hills Hotel, which he passed so frequently over the years that he hardly even noticed it anymore?

It made sense in every way, and explained how Lawrence had escaped so easily the other night: He did not have far to go. Not only that, it fit his character; it was very *Lawrence,* as Nicky was beginning to imagine him. Taking out his life savings in cash. Buying a flashy red sports car. And then coming to this famous and luxurious hotel.

In a few minutes, Nicky was able to cross the boulevard and glide up the elegant driveway to the covered entranceway. He flashed his shield to a parking attendant and told him to leave his car right there. Then he walked quickly up the ramp to the lobby and across the thick green carpet to the main desk.

The lobby of the Beverly Hills Hotel seemed to demand discretion. So it was in a most discreet manner that he produced his shield to a rather old-looking young man in a three-piece suit. The young man pursed his lips in a slightly distasteful way at the necessity of dealing with the police.

"Can you tell me, do you have a Lawrence Ferguson staying at the hotel?"

"Lawrence Ferguson? . . . One moment, sir. I'll check for you."

Nicky waited as the young man consulted a list behind the desk. "Ah, yes. Indeed. Mr. Ferguson has been with us for several weeks now. In room 345."

Bull's-eye! Nicky could hardly believe it.

"Shall I call him for you, sir?"

"*No!*" he almost screamed. Nicky didn't know what he wanted to do, but certainly not that. "Thanks," he said at last. "I'll probably get back to you."

The young man made a little gesture, which somehow—politely—made it quite clear that for all he cared the policeman could die in traffic.

Nicky was too much involved in his own thoughts to take offense. He moved slowly, like a sleepwalker, toward the center of the lobby, where he stood with his head half cocked and his hands behind his back, staring out into space.

Charles Bronson, the famous actor, came into Nicky's field of vision and smiled complacently, thinking the man was staring at him and perhaps would ask for his autograph.

Nicky, however, didn't see the actor at all, but simply looked through him. "Hmm," he said aloud, "maybe . . ." And he walked off quickly toward the front door.

Mr. Bronson turned jauntily to his companion. "There's some pretty strange people in Hollywood these days," he said in his throaty way.

"It's music. They're all on drugs. . . ."

However, now that Nicky had decided on a course of action his dreamy expression vanished. He walked back to his car and drove quickly down the driveway to the hotel's garage. Inside the overhang of the building, he came to a glass cubicle where two parking attendants, in their red jackets, regarded him with bored expressions. There was something about their casual pose that reminded him of the stagehands at Paramount that morning: ordinary workers, who found themselves in glamorous places, tended to emphasize their nonchalance. These young attendants in the garage basement looked as if they were the true owners of the hotel.

"Excuse me, sir, you can't drive in here. It's valet parking only."

Nicky got out of his car, produced his shield, and introduced himself. The two young men looked instantly less bored.

"I want to know if there is a Corvette down here that belongs to a Mr. Lawrence Ferguson, who's staying in room 345."

"Yeah. Red '72 Vette? Nice set of wheels."

"May I have the keys, please?"

This was all quite legal; you did not need a search warrant to look inside a car. One of the attendants handed him a set of keys from a large board and gave him directions to the correct aisle. Nicky left his

Austin-Healey in their care and walked through the dank inner world of the garage, almost to the far concrete wall. The red Corvette rested in its stall, wedged in between a Jaguar and a Rolls-Royce. Nicky approached it cautiously, as if it were a sleeping monster that might suddenly awake and run him down.

First, he inspected the right-hand side of the car. And yes: The orange lens cover was broken, just as he expected, exposing the small bulb of the side running light. There were also a few scratches in the paint and a small dent where the Corvette had collided with the garbage or the children.

Nicky felt a strange combination of anger and pity. Behind the front seat, there was a small but gleaming piece of metal that caught his eye. He opened the door and stuck his head inside. The piece of metal was an empty .38 shell, carelessly left behind. He was fairly certain that if he foraged around a little, he would probably find one more empty .38 shell. But it was best not to disturb any of the fingerprints inside.

At the rear of the automobile, Nicky pulled out his shirttail and used it in such a way as to open the trunk with the key, without actually touching the car with his hand. When he managed to get the trunk open in this fairly awkward way, he immediately saw the double-barreled shotgun and several boxes of ammunition. Nicky leaned closer to the weapon and could still smell a hint of cordite that clung to the cold steel.

"Holy shit!" He had a sour feeling inside, confronted as he was with the actual mechanisms of death. He carefully closed the trunk once again upon its dark secret inside and walked back to the office cubicle. He decided he would keep Lawrence's car keys. He knew he had already damaged the integrity of the evidence. Just by examining the car, some lawyer at a future date might claim the police had tampered with the evidence. What concerned Nicky more was that if Lawrence tried to make a run for it, and by some means was able to get to his car, he wanted to deny him access to his shotgun.

At this point, it seemed just about anything could happen.

Nicky, in fact, opened the last button on his sports jacket, so he could reach a little more quickly for his own revolver, if Lawrence should suddenly appear.

The parking attendants told Nicky the shortest way back to the lobby, through the hotel itself. He entered from the garage, showed his shield to a security guard at a desk, and was directed down a maze of corridors. In this part of the hotel there were no thick carpets or crystal chandeliers, just no-nonsense linoleum and clean institutional hallways. He passed by the main office of the housekeeping department and stopped long enough to ascertain a few interesting facts. One: Lawrence's room had not been made up yet today, because there was a DO NOT DISTURB sign on the door, and the staff had strict instructions to take such signs seriously. And two: Room service had been telephoning housekeeping with the same question. There was a breakfast cart still in room 345, and they wanted it back. Nicky phoned room service to make certain this information was true. He told them to leave the breakfast cart right where it was. Under no circumstances were they to disturb the occupant of room 345.

Nicky found his way back into the public part of the hotel. He knew it was definitely time to make the telephone call he had been avoiding the last two days. There was no putting it off any longer.

It was not hard to find a telephone. In the Beverly Hills Hotel, phones were everywhere and could be brought to your table in the Polo Lounge, or to the pool, or even the tennis court. Hollywood hotshots tended to move from phone to phone, like bees passing from flower to flower.

Nicky located an extremely comfortable phone booth, with a door that closed off all outside sound. He sat down on a velvet-covered chair and listened momentarily to the fan that was softly moving the air.

Unlike the wheelers and dealers of Hollywood, Nicky did not care for phones very much—he found them generally obtrusive—and this call he was about to make was harder than most. He dialed the station and asked for Captain Molinari.

He had to wait a moment. And then: "Nick, is that you? There was a rumor that you were still on the payroll, but I wasn't quite sure. Where've you been, for chrissake? From now on I want you to carry a goddamn beeper with you all the time . . ."

"Captain, listen. *I have him.*"

"What?"

"I have the Car Killer. He's a guy named Lawrence Ferguson and he's staying in the Beverly Hills Hotel. I'm in the lobby right now, and I need reinforcements. The guy's in his room, and we should be able to take him without a problem."

"Jee-*sus!* Would you run that by me one more time?"

"Look, I know this is kind of sudden . . ."

*"Sudden* isn't the word. Let's try *crazy."*

"Hey, you gotta believe me, Captain. I've found the Car Killer. He's here at the hotel. His name is Lawrence Ferguson. He's just a little guy who's dying of cancer and living out a few nasty fantasies before he goes. I've just been looking at his Corvette down in the garage. It's banged up in just the right place, there's a goddamn shotgun in the trunk, and there's even an empty .38 shell behind the front seat. . . . I mean, *this is for real.*"

Captain Molinari seemed to be having some trouble absorbing all this. "Does McWilliams know about this?" he asked, at last.

"Not yet," Nicky admitted.

*"Do you mean you've been doing this on your own?"*

"Ah . . . it's a long story, Captain. Mostly, it was all just dropped in my lap. Does it really matter? I mean, I tell you, the guy's right here in room 345. We don't even need a warrant, because there's already one out for him. He hacked up his ex-boss with a bayonet in Santa Monica."

"No shit, Nick? This is on the level?"

"I shit you not."

Nicky could feel the captain getting excited now. This would be a big arrest; a big deal all around.

"Okay, Nick, what do you need?"

Nicky told him his plan, emphasizing the need for everyone to approach the hotel quietly, with no sirens, keeping a very low police profile. If all went well, it would be a smooth and fast operation: the Car Killer would be taken, hardly knowing what had happened.

If it didn't go well . . . there could be a shootout in the Beverly Hills Hotel. Which was unthinkable.

Nicky hung up the phone. There was much to do, beginning with a visit to the manager of the hotel, to inform him of the impending police raid on room 345.

# 10

M r. Richardson, the manager of the hotel, sat behind a large oak desk in his spacious and comfortable office. He was on the telephone, but gestured for Nicky to seat himself on a leather armchair. While he was waiting, Nicky eyed the many photographs throughout the room of famous people who had once stayed here, an assortment of movie stars and heads of state that spanned decades and nationalities, from Marilyn Monroe to Nikita Khrushchev, Elvis Presley to Moshe Dayan.

Mr. Richardson was in quite a few of the photographs, shaking hands with important people. He seemed right at home with all these celebrities; he was an important man in his own right. Nicky thought he looked a bit like a younger Charles Boyer—but he hated to think like that. It was such a Hollywoodism to say someone looked like a younger-older-fatter Richard Gere–Cary Grant–Charles Boyer. As if, in this town, everyone must be compared against the famous and successful.

The manager put down the phone and directed his urbane attention upon the policeman. Nicky was about to introduce himself—the secretary outside had announced him only as a police lieutenant who wished to see him on urgent business—but Mr. Richardson, who clearly had a flair for names and faces, knew exactly who he was. Nicky was impressed.

"Lieutenant Rachmaninoff!" he said exuberantly, as if greeting a long-lost friend. He stood up and offered a hand. "I'm so glad to meet you. I've been following this Car Killer horror along with all the other frightened people of Beverly Hills. I trust you'll get him soon. We've had quite a few cancellations."

Mr. Richardson smiled in a most charming way, as though in this pink paradise of the Beverly Hills Hotel a few murders down the street hardly made much difference. It was just a courtesy to say it did, to make the lieutenant feel more important.

"Would you like a drink?" he asked, when both men were sitting again. "How about some cheese? I've discovered a very nice Brie . . ."

"No . . . ah, Mr. Richardson. Actually, we're *very* close to arresting the Car Killer. I mean, like in about five or ten minutes. He's *here,* right in the hotel, staying in room 345. There are some special tactical forces on the way, and we are about to raid the room."

Mr. Richardson's smile froze on his face. *"Here? Oh, no!"* The manager appeared to be a man who was not often surprised by the twists of fate or human nature. But his mouth hung open, temporarily in shock. *"You're going to make a raid on room 345? Shit!"* he cried, and looked at his watch. "God, you couldn't have picked a worse time. In about an hour and a half, the King of Sweden arrives for a three-day visit to Los Angeles. His plane is probably just about to land."

"An hour and a half, you say? We'll probably be well out of your way by then."

"*Probably?* What do we do with the king if you're not finished by then?"

Nicky shrugged. "I don't know. Maybe you can take him to a movie or something."

The man looked at him in astonishment. "Take the King of Sweden to a movie? Are you *mad?*"

Nicky had a feeling that he would never again be offered any of this man's very special Brie.

Mr. Richardson allowed himself approximately another fifteen seconds of vexation before coming down to earth again in a very practical way.

He picked up the telephone. "Okay, I've got to get security in on this ... hello, Tony. Come into my office right away. We have an emergency."

"Are there Secret Service people here?" Nicky inquired. "We'd better notify them, too."

The man sighed piteously, but dialed a special Secret Service hot line.

Meanwhile, in the lobby outside, a new breed of guest began to enter the hotel: men with gruff, determined faces, wearing inexpensive trousers and tennis shoes. All of them had jackets and windbreakers that were slightly oversized, concealing an arsenal of pistols and tear-gas canisters, gas masks, and bulletproof vests. They fanned out through the lobby, waiting for further instructions, while Captain Molinari and Sergeant Katz were shown in to Mr. Richardson's private office, now transformed into a small war room.

Nicky was not surprised to see Captain Molinari and the hotel manager greet each other by first names. Beverly Hills, basically, was a small town. Charlie Cat winked in his direction and managed to gibe: "So *this* is where you hang out while I'm working my ass off back at the station."

The head of the hotel's security—an ex-cop named Tony Darnell—came in with two of his agents, as well as several Secret Service men, so that the office was becoming very crowded. Nicky found he did not like the feeling of being part of a pack of hounds about to descend on the hare. However, when everyone was gathered, he explained his plan, such as it was.

A very simple plan: He was going to dress up as a waiter, knock on the door to room 345, and ask to collect the breakfast cart. That was all. Nicky believed it shouldn't be much of a problem to take Lawrence Ferguson, once he was inside the room. He tried to impress upon this grim gathering that they were not exactly dealing with Al Capone, but with a rather sickly and pathetic office worker who had simply become unstuck.

In case there were any problems, several marksmen would be in the third-floor hall, as well as concealed in the bushes outside the room's window. As a further precaution, CHP units were standing by out of sight of the hotel, ready to cut off all traffic along Sunset, as well as the smaller streets to the rear of the hotel grounds.

Meanwhile, plainclothes policemen were strolling about the various public rooms, the bars and dining rooms, as well as the pool area and tennis courts—just in case Lawrence Ferguson was in any of these places rather than in his room as they supposed.

It was hard to imagine how the Car Killer might get away.

Mr. Richardson, however, was far from happy. "My main concern," he said, "has to be the safety of my guests. What I want to know is what happens if someone in room 343 across the hall opens his door at just the wrong moment and gets caught in a cross fire? I'm sorry, but I can't allow even the slightest risk of anything happening to a single one of my guests. What I'd like is to evacuate the entire third floor before you gentlemen begin your assault."

"Jesus, if we do that, we'll lose the element of surprise," Nicky objected. "Then we really could have a problem. We have no idea what kind of arsenal Lawrence has inside that room. If he suspects we're about to hit and decides to barricade himself, we could have a hell of a time getting him out. Then somebody really could get killed . . . besides that, of course, if he's not in his room, but somewhere on the hotel grounds, evacuating the third floor would alert him and give him a chance to do something really disastrous. Like take a hostage."

"How about a compromise," Captain Molinari suggested smoothly. Nicky had a feeling the captain had been learning to make a lot of compromises over the years. "What if we telephone the rooms immediately surrounding 345 and get the people out of there somehow or other? We could bring them right down to an office, or one of the dining rooms perhaps, and make sure they don't alarm any of the other guests. As for the rest of the hallway, we can put an officer in front of every door. Christ, we have enough men. If someone tries to come out of his room at the wrong time, we'll just push him back inside."

Nicky listened as his originally simple idea became more and more complex. Eventually, Captain Molinari's compromise was adopted with just a few additions. Six rooms would be totally evacuated, there would be police officers on the fire stairs, and the elevators would be stopped just before the raid began so that no unsuspecting person came upon the third floor from these various access points as well.

This would all require split-second timing and communication by walkie-talkie among various teams of police on different floors. Nicky had a feeling that Lawrence would appreciate all the attention that was being directed his way. But he was beginning to regret that he hadn't simply knocked on the door to room 345 and arrested Lawrence when he first arrived an hour earlier, avoiding all this fuss. It was so much easier to do things by yourself.

At last, with everything arranged, one of the security men led Nicky down a hall and through a doorway behind the glamorous facade, back into the inner workings of the hotel. The decor changed once again to functional institutionalism. Nicky and the security man hurried through a maze of hallways, passing waiters and maids, maintenance men and maître d's, all in their various costumes. Nicky felt as if he were backstage at a play.

He was led through swinging double doors into the enormous hotel kitchen. This was a quite fascinating world of stainless-steel counters and dozens of men and women dressed in their impeccable whites.

The dinner hour was already well under way, and there was a great bustle of activity, aromas, and confusion in several languages. Waiters who smiled so graciously in the charming world on the other side of the double doors showed quite another face here.

"Where's my goddamn baked potato . . . can't you read, you asshole?"

"*Chinga tu madre!*"

"The bitch at table twelve says her steak is overdone."

"Well, you tell her where she can stick it, Mario."

Nicky was led through the kitchen to a locker room that opened up off one of the many back pantries. Here he was given a white shirt, red jacket, black pants, and bow tie. Captain Molinari had already supplied him with a bullet-resistant vest that he was to put on underneath the entire outfit. As long as he was not shot above the neck or below the waist, he might survive this encounter with the Car Killer.

Still, Nicky found he was sweating. His forehead was hot; his hands were clammy cold. He thought of himself as an utter coward. One of the main reasons he had worked so hard to become a detective was to get off the streets and work in a more protected situation. He really didn't like the idea of bullets flying around. Sometimes he lay awake at night imagining how one of them would feel entering his body. All these late-night imaginings ended with an image of his father lying in a pool of blood.

He turned into a waiter as quickly as possible, trying to chase away the bad images. When he was ready, he regarded himself in the mirror. The brown loafers he had on were all wrong, but by the time Lawrence noticed his shoes, it would be too late. More worrisome was the bulge his revolver made in the tight red jacket. Nicky decided that he would simply hold it behind his back.

At last, he was shown up the service elevator to the third floor. Here, he passed through a door that returned him once again to the world of luxury and ease, except that now the hallway was full of policemen who were trying to be very quiet. Nicky walked down the corridor. His heart was beating quickly. Captain Molinari, standing near the elevator, with his own pistol drawn, handed him a key.

"This is the passkey to the room," he whispered. "Good luck, Nick."

On both sides of room 345, two SWAT marksmen knelt with rifles pointed to the closed door. Nicky walked up to the room. Ten feet away, the captain, holding a walkie-talkie to his ear, nodded that everything was go. Nicky held his revolver behind his back.

It was at this moment he suddenly realized how desperately he wanted to take a pee. . . . Why hadn't he done this earlier? He looked from one side to another, to see the marksmen and Charlie and Captain Molinari, all with their guns drawn, waiting for him to make his move.

And, Lord, his bladder was full. *Hey, guys, hold on a moment, okay? Just gotta go to the bathroom.*

No, it was absurd. He couldn't say that! Already, the captain was giving him a funny look: *Come on, come on! What are you waiting for?*

Oh, well.

He thought suddenly of his father, at the very moment he knocked on the door. *Boy, Dad, if you could see me now!*

"Room service!" he called out loudly. His voice had broken. The first part of "room" came out nearly an octave higher than the last part of "service."

There was no answer from inside. Nicky knocked again.

222

"Room Service!" he called out once more. His voice did not break this time. "I've come to take your breakfast cart, please."

Still no answer.

Nicky glanced over to the captain, who had his pistol held with both hands stretched out before him: classic firing-range position. The captain nodded grimly.

He put the passkey in the lock. The cops and the two marksmen inched closer. Nicky brought his own gun from behind his back, crouched, pushed open the door, and rushed into the room, ready to fire.

# 11

The captain, Charlie Cat, and the marksmen flooded into the room behind him, breaking into the bathroom, pulling open the closet door, poking their revolvers under the bed.

It was only when it was quite clear that the room was empty that the group adrenaline subsided. Someone laughed nervously. There was a smell of fear in the small hotel room. Someone could have been dead by now.

Nicky put his revolver back in his holster. "I would like everybody except Captain Molinari and Sergeant Katz to clear out, please. Don't touch anything . . . *please!*"

The men went into the hallway as Nicky began tentatively exploring the room. Clothes were still hanging in the closet; underwear, socks, and shirts lay in the drawers.

Charlie was searching through the bathroom. "Well, his toothbrush is still here. I'd say he's coming back, what do you think?"

Nicky spotted three $100 bills weighted down beneath an ashtray. "I don't know. Look at that . . . if it's a tip for the maid, I'd say Lawrence has split."

"Do you think he would just leave all his clothes here, and his car?" the captain asked.

"Maybe. If he was spooked enough . . . *shit!* I really thought we had him!"

"Well, he might still be in the hotel," the captain suggested. "There's a thousand places you could hide in a big building like this. Or maybe a friend came and picked him up for the day."

"Lawrence Ferguson doesn't have any friends, Captain. The man is a complete loner."

"Hmm . . . I tell you what. I'm going downstairs to organize a thorough search of the hotel. If that doesn't flush him out, we'll have to assume he's gone, but may come back. We'll place guards on all the ways in and out of this place. . . . I think the King of Sweden is going to have to stay somewhere else tonight."

"Poor Mr. Richardson ain't going to like that too much," Charlie put in.

"He'll like it a lot better than if the king gets his royal ass shot by the Car Killer. . . . That's about the only thing this case needs to become a bigger disaster than it already is!" With this bleak assessment, the captain smiled wearily and left the room.

Charlie sat down on the bed. "Well, what do you think, Rock Man?"

"Shit, he's gone. That's what I think. We were close, but not close enough."

"That's a tough break. He might be hard to find again."

"I don't know. He's sure leaving a fairly bloody trail behind."

Charlie stretched out comfortably on the bed. "You know, this is a pretty nice hotel. I've never been inside any of the rooms before. I think I would like to bring a girl here sometime. I can see it now. A little champagne supper in the room . . ."

Nicky wasn't listening. He continued to meander about the room, looking in the garbage, at the backs of drawers, and in the medicine chest. The clothes seemed newer and more expensive than those Nicky had found in the studio in Santa Monica. They were also more impersonal and told him less about the strange person who was Lawrence Ferguson.

The only object of interest he came upon, after twenty minutes in the room, was a blue spiral notebook that had been tucked away inside one of the two matching suitcases left behind in the luggage rack in the closet. The notebook contained long and disorganized ramblings on the subject of cancer. Nicky glanced through the handwritten pages, reading sections at random.

"Listen to this, Charlie: 'Waiting in line at the bank is death . . . Stoplights are death . . . Waiting in line at a crowded supermarket is death.' "

224

"Jesus, the guy sounds pretty sane to me."

Downstairs, several reporters and photographers had arrived, sensing that something quite unusual was happening at the Beverly Hills Hotel, but not knowing exactly what. Policemen lounged on the chairs in the lobby, awaiting orders, while the guests that passed in and out seemed irritated that their world was amiss. Several burly detectives stood by the front door, carefully looking at each person who went in and out of the hotel. It wasn't exactly the sort of greeting the residents of this hotel were used to.

The captain came hurrying up the entranceway from the carport. "Nick, I was just talking to one of the parking attendants. He says that Ferguson left in a taxi around eleven o'clock this morning to go to the airport."

"Which attendant told you this, Captain?"

"His name is Joey . . . the blond kid over there."

Joey was just stepping into a Rolls-Royce, to drive it down to the garage.

"I think I want to ask him a few questions."

"Okay. I'm heading for a phone. I want to get on this airport angle right away."

Nicky walked down the ramp while the captain rushed off in the opposite direction toward a telephone inside. He had to wait a few minutes for Joey to return from parking the Rolls. The blond attendant bounced up from the garage full of energy. Nicky intercepted him before he could return to his spot beneath the awning.

"Your name Joey?"

"Yeah, man. Who are *you?*" he asked, looking over the ill-fitting waiter's outfit Nicky still had on.

Nicky brought out his shield. The young man nodded, not too pleased to be confronted once again by the police.

"You just told Captain Molinari that Lawrence Ferguson took a cab to the airport around eleven this morning?"

"Yeah. That's right. I put him in the cab myself. I'm working a double shift today to cover for a friend."

"Why didn't he take his own car, the Corvette in the garage?"

"He said something about not liking to drive on the freeways anymore. I don't know. My job isn't to argue with the guests about what they want or don't want. Is the guy in some kind of trouble or something?"

"Did you get the impression that he was coming back?"

"Well, I thought so at the time. He didn't have any luggage with him or anything. Just a briefcase. But he gave me $200 as a tip, and I thought that was kind of strange. It was kind of like a farewell present, if you know what I mean. . . . Look, what has the guy done? He was pretty weird, you know, but really innocuous."

"Would it surprise you to know that Lawrence Ferguson is the Car Killer?"

Joey just looked at him blankly and then laughed. "You're fucking with my head, right? Just a joke?"

"No, I'm serious. He's the Car Killer."

"*That* little guy's the Car Killer, the one who's been terrorizing Beverly Hills?"

"That's right."

"*Jesus Fucking Christ!*" He laughed and made several strange noises. But suddenly he stopped laughing. "You know, the funny thing is, I *do* believe it."

"Why's that?"

"Well, last Thursday night he went out for a couple of hours in his Corvette, you know, and it was *real* strange. When he got back, the guy looked even more weirded-out than usual, and when I got in the car to park it, it just reeked of gunpowder. I mean, I used to go shooting as a kid, and the smell was unmistakable."

"He had just murdered four people."

Joey shook his head and looked far off. "Man, like this is going to take a little while to sink in. You know what I mean? Like my brain is going crazy. Totally weird! *I* parked the Car Killer's car . . . *mondo bizarre!*"

At this moment, a large black police car screeched up to the curb. One of the burly detectives standing guard at the front of the hotel rushed forward to open the car door. Out stepped Police Chief McWilliams, looking red in the face and more unpleasant than usual.

"Where's that cocksucking Lieutenant Rachmaninoff!" he muttered and charged like a bull toward the hotel lobby.

Nicky decided it was time to leave. He left Joey, who was still shaking his head and muttering *"mondo bizarre,"* and walked down to the garage to collect his Austin-Healey.

He drove away from the hotel and traveled the few blocks to Julie's house.

In this manner, he arrived at her doorstep two hours late for dinner, dressed as a waiter and sporting a bullet-resistant vest.

As usual, he had a lot of explaining to do before she would even let him in the front door.

# 12

They lay naked on top of the king-size bed in Julie's bedroom, their bodies lit by two flickering candles. She was on her back, sprawled out languorously on tangled sheets. Nicky lay on his side, propping himself up on one elbow.

They had already made love, eaten dinner naked, and made love again. Right now, he was busy tracing a line with his finger, from her left foot slowly up her ankle and long left leg. She seemed to him so perfectly sculptured; he felt absurdly happy and at peace just to run his finger up her shin, over the delicate kneecap, to the softer areas of the upper leg. Her skin was golden in the candlelight. He particularly liked the few little blond hairs—peach fuzz, really—that began above her kneecap. He stroked the little hairs with his index finger and moved slowly up her thigh.

"Nicholas?" she said at last. "I want you to talk to me."

"Mmmm ..." He was totally beyond words, exhausted by words. His finger outlined the triangle of pubic hair and moved up her flat stomach, stopping to explore the mysteries of her belly button.

"It's important," she insisted. "I'm trying to understand you, and really ... I don't."

"What's there to understand?" he replied absently, examining the nice way her stomach swooped up to her rib cage.

"Well, I always thought that being a cop was important to you. But in the last couple of days, from what you told me, you've been risking your entire career. After all, you knew about this Lawrence Ferguson person for almost a day and a half before you told anyone. Aren't you going to get into trouble for that?"

He sighed. He really did not want to think about it right now. Julie's breasts were much more interesting. He put his face down near her side, so he could see them in silhouette against the candlelight. They were wonderful little mountains, soft and mysterious, rising and falling as she talked. His roving finger moved slowly up the left mountain to the nipple on top. He explored the darkened aureole around the nipple and the little circle of goose-bump hairs.

The nipple itself was growing very hard.

He took it between his fingers and gave it a squeeze.

"Ah!" she screamed. "You're driving me *nuts!* What am I going to do with you, Nicholas?"

She jumped on top of him and pinned him down.

He put his arms around her. "Oh, I can think of lots of things."

"Me, too. But I want you to talk to me now. I have my reasons. Okay?"

"Okay . . . what do you want to talk about?"

She got off him, and their positions were reversed from what they had been moments before: Nicky lay on his back, while Julie—propped up on one elbow—regarded him curiously.

"I want to know why you're not obeying orders. Don't you want to be a cop anymore?"

Nicky groaned. "For chrissake, Julie! This is the very last thing I want to think about right now. I thought you didn't like me talking shop."

"This isn't talking shop," she insisted. "This is talking about *you.* I want to know why you are acting like you are."

"Okay." He rolled over to face her. "It's really very simple. I was pissed off last Saturday when the mayor took my case away from me and gave it to that fucking jerk McWilliams. On Monday, when I got a chance to solve it anyway, I thought what the hell, screw those ass-holes. I'll find the Car Killer on my own."

"Can you really afford to take that attitude toward the mayor of Los Angeles and the chief of police?"

He was beginning to feel decidedly defensive and irritated by this conversation. "Shit! What the fuck are you asking me all this for? What do you want me to say, Julie?"

Julie sat up and put her arms around her legs. "I want you to say that you're tired of being a cop, fed up with all the bullshit," she cried out passionately. "I want you to say that you're ready to quit."

Nicky could only look at her, baffled. Then he laughed. He could hardly believe the turn of this conversation. But Julie had always been full of surprises. "So *that's* what this is all about. You know, being with you is never dull. Not for a second."

"Do you want to be with me?" she asked, looking at him in a most challenging way.

"You know I do," he answered immediately.

"Listen to me, Nicholas. I put my house up for sale last week, and today I got an offer. It's not what I was asking, but I'm thinking of taking it."

He stared at her. She turned away from him painfully.

"Nicholas, look . . . we've never really talked about Gerald. Not since the beginning. I mean, what I feel about his death, and living in this house just a couple of blocks away from where he was murdered. I just can't, that's all. *I can't stay here.* This is his house, his city. I never wanted to be here in the first place. I don't even like Los Angeles. There's nothing to keep me here . . . except you."

He continued to look at her; she continued to look away.

"Where are you going?" he asked finally.

"I don't know. Spain. Greece. Nepal . . . I just want to travel for a while. I just want to *go.*"

"I don't blame you. It sounds . . . nice."

When she turned to him, at last, there were tears in her eyes. "Nicholas, I want you to come with me."

He laughed.

"Look, you don't belong in Los Angeles either. You don't belong in the police force. Christ, you're too eccentric to be a cop . . . you belong with me."

He laughed again and shook his head in true amazement. "I really don't know what to say. But, Julie, I've got to work, and being a cop is the only job I know how to do. And you're wrong about me being too eccentric for this job. Some of the weirdest dudes I know are cops."

"Okay, listen to me. I have this all figured out," she said earnestly. "First of all, you *don't* have to work, Nicholas. I'm rich—I didn't even realize how rich, until after Gerald was killed. I'm worth over ten million dollars *cash,* which is not even counting this house and interests in various films that are going to be coming in forever . . . and that sure as hell is not *my* money. I don't have any more right to that money than you do. Most of it is from *The Enchanter,* and I didn't even like the goddamn film. So why don't you help me spend it, Nicholas? You're not going to be a prude about this, are you? The money is just waiting there for us to fly away on."

Nicky lay back on his pillow and stared at the ceiling.

"Oh boy!" This was turning out to be quite a day.

He tried to imagine himself as a millionaire, cruising the shores of the Mediterranean. Exploring ancient temples in Greece and Nepal. Riding a camel across the Sahara . . .

She was watching him closely. "You're so stubborn," she said. "You're not going to let me support you, are you?"

"Now hold on, hold on. Let's not reject the idea too quickly. Do gigolos have any retirement benefits? How about Blue Cross?"

She laughed. "God! What am I going to do with you?"

He reached for her. "Listen, as I was saying earlier, I have some pretty good ideas."

She pushed him away. "Okay, I have another idea, since you're too proud to live off a woman. Here's Plan B: You can rent out your house. With your location, if you cleaned it up a bit, you could get $1,800, maybe $2,000 a month for it. Can you imagine how well you could live on $2,000 a month in Tangiers, or a Greek island? You've got it made, Nicholas. You don't need my ten million at all."

"You're incredible, you know that?"

"Will you think about it, at least?"

"Okay . . . let me think about it." He closed his eyes and spoke in a deep, travelogue sort of voice. "I see myself living in Tangiers. The sun and wind have turned my face brown and leathery. It's Tuesday afternoon, time for my monthly check to arrive, care of poste restante. We walk together down sun-drenched streets, stopping in a small café along the way for a cold beer . . ."

"Come on, be serious."

"I'm serious . . . we're in Tangiers. We have no worries, no responsibilities. On this Tuesday afternoon, the only pressing business we have is to get to the post office before it closes. Even that's a little hard. Maybe we stop at a few more cafés along the way, so we make it to the post office just in time. But the check is there, after all, so why worry? Two thousand dollars from faraway, polluted Los Angeles . . . Jesus, we don't have to do another fucking thing for an entire month. On the way back from the post office, we buy a gram or two of hashish. Shit . . . the good life. I don't know, Julie. Somehow it scares me to death."

"Well, what are you going to do with yourself when they fire you from the police force because you are pathologically incapable of obeying orders?" she asked angrily. "How much fun are you going to have standing in the unemployment line?"

"Now that's a low blow," he argued. "Just because I've been a little independent recently doesn't mean I'm going to get fired. I've still come closer to solving this damn case than anyone else."

She looked at him and sighed. "I know . . . it's useless. You're going to stay here in this horrible town."

"Hey, come on," he objected. "This is glamorous Beverly Hills. Lots of people would give their right arm to be here."

"*Glamorous?*" she sputtered, hardly able to speak. "Beverly Hills is about as glamorous as Forest Lawn cemetery. It's *dead* here, Nicholas. Body and soul. I want to go someplace where there are people laughing and talking and walking in the streets. . . . If you tried to take a walk here, you'd get arrested, for chrissake, by some asshole cop. Right?"

"Well, this *is* California, you know. And it *is* pretty suspicious to walk when you could be in an automobile."

She ignored his strange humor. "And clean air, Nicholas! Can you imagine breathing air that isn't brown with car exhaust? God! My only problem is that I want you, too. Won't you come with me? Please?"

"Well . . ." He started to sit up, but she got on top of him and pinned him down. "Say you will, Nicholas, *just say you will.* We'll be so good together. I'll love you so much. . . ."

She lay, at last, quietly on top of him, while he stroked the small of her back. He never even had to answer her. She knew as clearly as he did that he could not, would not go. L.A. was his town, crummy as it might be.

Julie raised herself just enough so she could look down at him with her intense hazel eyes.

"I know what really keeps you here. You're still trying to prove something to your father."

He smiled grimly. "You know me too well, Julie."

"I *should* know you, damn it! I think about you all the time."

He pulled her back down to him and kissed her on the lips. This time she did not resist but responded eagerly, and let him roll over until he was on top of her.

They made love, and it was as deliciously erotic as before. But the energy mysteriously had changed. Every other time, when they made love, it had seemed like two people saying hello. This time, it was like saying goodbye.

# 13

In the morning they made love again, ate breakfast, talked—carried on as usual. They did not mention Julie's plan to leave Los Angeles. It was as if they had all the time in the world. Nicky thought, Maybe it's best not to get too involved. This is what Charlie Cat would tell him—get it while you can, and don't worry too much about the future.

At breakfast, while he was sipping his coffee, his thoughts were more with Lawrence Ferguson than the woman at his side. Specifically, he was wondering again about Lawrence's annual trip to the desert. Maybe *this* is where he had gone.

"Do you know anyplace you can go fishing in the desert?" he asked Julie suddenly—out of nowhere, as far as she was concerned.

"Fishing in the desert? That's a strange thought . . . the Colorado River?" she said tentatively.

"I think I'm looking for someplace closer to Los Angeles."

"Well, there's always the Salton Sea," she said. "But I think all the fish died out there."

"What do you mean, the fish died out there?" Nicky asked tensely. "How could that happen?"

"The Salton Sea is evaporating. Actually, it's not a real sea at all, just an overflow from the Colorado River. There was an earthquake, I believe, in the early part of the century. By the time they got the river back on course, an enormous lake had been formed in the desert. But it's shrinking every year, because there's no source to it. I spent a few days down there with Gerald, when they were filming some of the off-planet stuff for *The Enchanter*. It's a very strange place."

"But what about the fish?"

Julie looked at him strangely. "They just died, that's all. Some developers tried to turn the place into a resort. They built a yacht club and stocked the water with fish. But the salt content was too great, so the fish died. And the yacht club is getting farther from the sea every year. . . . Why are you so interested, Nicholas? Are you thinking of leaving glamorous Beverly Hills to become a monk in the desert?"

"It's just something that came up," he said distractedly. "Part of the case."

"Ah," she said. "Part of the case."

Their eyes met, but the gulf between them seemed suddenly insurmountable. Nicky hurriedly finished his coffee, dressed once more in the waiter's costume he had arrived in, and got on his way. They did not make a definite date to meet again; he said he would call her when he got a chance.

Outside, the morning was warm and very still. It was November, but fall had not yet arrived in Southern California. Even this early in the morning, there was a static and exhausted feeling to the day that seemed to sap Nicky of all enthusiasm and energy.

Probably it wasn't the weather. He had to admit that, while he sat in his car, letting the engine warm up.

The house next to Julie's had a sort of Hollywood Greek-Modern facade, with fake Corinthian columns, surrounded by bright green plastic grass: Astroturf. Nicky had to smile: The house *did* look amazingly like a Forest Lawn mausoleum. Julie was quite right about Beverly Hills. He had lived in West L.A. most of his life and remembered Rodeo Drive when it still had a gravel bridle path down its center for horses to ride on, but even then, Beverly Hills had seemed strangely dead and dull. As if the canopy of wealth, combined with the smog and the Southern California weather, robbed the place of any vitality and motion.

So why the hell didn't he just go with her and help her spend her $10 million? They could fuck their brains out from Tangiers to Tokyo, Marrakech to Moscow, and still be in Pamplona in time for the running of the bulls.

The only answer Nicky could come up with, this Wednesday morning, was that he would be lost without his shroud of alienation and all those things he could be ironic about. Being a policeman, of course, was the perfect profession for an aging cynic. It constantly refed itself with new sources of irony and human weakness. What else did he need?

With these bleak thoughts to guide him, he drove back to his house above Laurel Canyon to change clothes and take a shower. He turned on his car radio for a while, but all the songs seemed to be about eternal undying love forever.

"Bullshit!" he swore savagely, turning off the radio. He drove home in silence, and then back to the Beverly Hills station. He had thought he might stop at the Beverly Hills Hotel to pick up the clothes he had left there yesterday, but decided to put it off. After the fiasco of the pointless raid on room 345, he doubted if anyone there would be happy to see him.

It was almost nine o'clock when he drove down into the bowels of City Hall, into the special parking area reserved for the police. He knew he would have some kind of confrontation with Captain Molinari today, but he was not prepared for it to happen so quickly. The captain, unfortunately, was just parking his large American station wagon as Nicky pulled into his numbered stall, three spaces over. Nicky pretended not to see him, but it was too late. As soon as he got out of his car, he heard the captain's booming voice calling to him.

"Nick! Come here a moment, will you? I want to talk to you."

Nicky sighed and walked over to where the captain was still seated in his station wagon.

"Get in," he ordered.

Nicky opened the door and sat down in the passenger's seat. The captain shook his head and studied him sadly. "My boy, I've known you all your life. Your father was my best friend. So let me talk with you for a moment as a friend, and not as your captain. Okay?"

Nicky nodded and felt about nine years old.

"The last couple of days, you have done some amazingly stupid things. The mayor himself took the Car Killer case away from you and put you under the direct orders of Chief McWilliams. But you disobeyed his orders, you didn't do what he asked you to do. You just kept on with your own investigation."

Nicky started to speak, but the captain interrupted him. "Lieutenant Hotchkiss from Santa Monica called me last night, pissed off that he wasn't involved in the raid on the hotel. You knew about Lawrence for at least twenty-four hours, didn't you? You should have passed on the information immediately to McWilliams. We might have gotten the Car Killer by now if you had not acted like some kind of adolescent Lone Ranger. Do you know that?"

"I wasn't sure about Lawrence."

The captain regarded him coldly. "You were sure. And it was mighty stupid to keep it to yourself. And then there was the disappearing act last night from the Beverly Hills Hotel. Jesus! No one knew where the hell you had gone. McWilliams is furious with you. He wants you brought up on charges."

Nicky slunk lower in the car seat, wishing he could disappear again.

"So tell me, as a friend, just what the hell you think you're doing? I promise you, I'll try to understand. Maybe you have some reason for destroying your career that I don't know about."

The fact that Nicky had just gone through all this with Julie did not make it any easier. Really, as far as he was concerned, it was all transparently simple, and he wished people would stop asking him about it. "Okay," he said at last, "I guess I thought I could go faster on my own. If I had had to report every move to the mayor and the chief and some fucking shrink from U.C.L.A., I never would have gotten anywhere on this case. That kind of task force the mayor put together . . . it's just not the way I work."

"Look, Nick, first of all it isn't your job to question the mayor. Second of all, you are sidestepping the issue. All you really had to do on Monday was to make a phone call downtown and tell the chief what you had on Lawrence Ferguson. *That* would have put you in the clear."

"All right, Captain. I'll admit I was pissed off at the way the case was taken from me. My ego was ruffled. I thought I could wrap up the case by myself. All right? I came pretty damn close."

"Damn you, Nick! Don't you know you can't act alone, like some born-again Wyatt Earp? Police work is a goddamn sensitive business, with all kinds of political and social repercussions. I shouldn't have to tell you that. The only way to play it is completely by the rules. It's just too fucking dangerous to have some immature guy with a gun running about the streets of Los Angeles, not subject to any discipline except his own. We simply can't afford it—no matter how good a detective you may be."

"Look, Captain, I *did* call you immediately, the moment I actually thought I had Lawrence located."

"Thank God for that," the captain muttered. "If you had tried to storm the Beverly Hills Hotel by yourself, we would have had to send the SWAT team after *you.*"

"Jesus!" Nicky moaned, and shook his head. This was turning into a terrible day, and it wasn't even ten o'clock yet. "Well, I did break this case wide open, didn't I? I should get some credit for that. Now that we know who the Car Killer is, it's just a matter of time until we find him."

"That's not the way the chief sees it."

"No?"

"*No!* He's blaming you for Lawrence getting away. If you had called Monday with your information, we would have put his picture on the

TV news *that night.* Lawrence would not have been able to walk out of the hotel on Tuesday."

"That's pretty theoretical, don't you think?"

"It doesn't matter what I think. That's what the chief thinks, and *he* wants your blood. He called me early this morning and ordered me to keep you off the case until he's had a chance to talk with you later this afternoon. Do you understand me, Lieutenant? *You are completely off the case.* You can go upstairs and work on whatever's on your desk, but you are to be downtown in McWilliams's office at three o'clock sharp. He would see you earlier, but he's spending the morning at the airport, personally supervising the operation there."

"What operation there?"

"That's where Lawrence went when he left the hotel. We're checking out all the flights that went out of L.A. yesterday, showing his picture around to all the flight attendants and reservation clerks. We may have a break, as a matter of fact. Someone thinks they saw Lawrence on an afternoon flight to Honolulu."

Nicky digested this information for a second. "Hmm . . . I don't see Lawrence going to Honolulu."

"Jesus, Nick, you don't give up, do you? First of all I shouldn't have even told you about this—you are *off* the case. Second, you're wrong. Hawaii is just the sort of place Lawrence would go. Dr. Anglund agrees completely. A man like that . . . he's probably wanted to go there all his life. But you are not supposed to think about this. Go up to your office, behave yourself, see the chief at three o'clock, and maybe—just maybe—I'll be able to keep your job for you. But you got to promise me, Nick, no more stunts. I want to help you, if I can, not only for your sake, but for your father's sake, too. But you got to behave yourself. Promise?"

He nodded miserably. The two men got out of the car and walked to the elevator without any further discussion.

Despite his promise, Nicky was thinking about Lawrence, trying to imagine him in Honolulu . . . but it didn't work. He could not imagine Lawrence in Honolulu. That was the problem. The man was tied to his drama in Los Angeles, caught in his own web. Just like himself.

Suddenly, he was talking in his mind to Julie. *That's* why he couldn't go to Greece and Nepal, lovely as they beckoned. Couldn't she understand? When you're in the middle of your own personal drama, you can't just pick up and fly away.

Can't you see that, Julie? I love you, but I'm stuck here. Me and Lawrence Ferguson. We just can't leave.

# 14

When Nicky shuffled into his office five minutes later, Charlie looked up from his desk in a sympathetic way.

"Hey, buddy, I'm sorry about you being taken off the case and all that."

Nicky slumped down in his chair. "You know about it, huh?"

"Sure. The entire Beverly Hills Hotel knows about it. When McWilliams couldn't find you last night, he threw a fit in the lobby that was like a soliloquy from *Hamlet*. For about five minutes, I thought he was going to put out an all points bulletin for you. However, Captain Molinari talked him out of it."

Nicky sighed and stared out the window at the post office across the street. It, too, looked like a tomb in the static morning sunshine. Charlie left his chair and came over to sit on the edge of his desk.

"Look, Rock Man, we've been friends for a long time. You've got to listen to me."

Nicky clenched his teeth. Dear God, not another heart-to-heart talk from a friend!

"You're simply taking this whole Car Killer thing too seriously. It's clouding your judgment, man. I mean, you got to *get down* to the nitty-gritty and remember what you're really doing on this planet. Ya know what I'm saying?"

"Please, Charlie. I know you mean well . . ."

"Every now and then, you got to put it all in proportion and ask yourself: *What is the point of all this?*"

"Charlie, please! I would be desperately afraid to get an answer."

"The point of all this," Charlie went on ruthlessly, "is to eat as much good food as you can, without getting fat. And to get laid as often as possible. . . . Now, being a cop is a good ticket to achieving both of these noble aspirations. Right? Play your cards, and you can get free food in all kinds of fine restaurants. And the girls just love a guy with a big rod. You follow? So don't blow it, my friend. Don't get too involved with nonessentials."

Nicky couldn't stand it any longer. He fled from the room with his hands over his ears.

Charlie shouted after him: "By the way, I made reservations at Le Coq d'Or for seven-thirty. We're going to have a dinner that will blow your mind. I also have two beautiful young dancers on call for later on. Charlie Cat's gonna show you how to live, boy. . . ."

Nicky walked quickly down the hallway. Some officers from the robbery division were looking at him in a peculiar manner. To make himself less noticeable, he ducked into the central computer room, which had become one of his favorite haunts in the station.

Like many of Nicky's generation, he had had a strong initial resistance to computers. Afraid, in fact, that they would eventually turn the planet into a world of zombie robots. He had been, himself, a liberal arts student in college. A humanist. He had liked to think that the human mind was nobler than any machine.

However, after fifteen years of being a policeman, his point of view had undergone a giant flipflop. He suspected now that the human mind, far from being noble, was a veritable cesspool of lust and greed and ego—with culture (like the law) a very thin layer on top, that tried to keep people from killing each other and eating their victims for breakfast.

Probably it was machines that were noble, for they had no ulterior motives. Machines rarely took advantage of other machines. They did not lie or cheat or steal; their innocence contained no original sin.

Anyway: Computers were more fun than dictionaries, more informative than the largest encyclopedia. Nicky had been seduced.

He sat down at a vacant terminal and played a game of Donkey Kong—programmed into the system by some enterprising soul—just to kill some time. And relax. And try to avoid thinking about his life. However, such was his state of mind this morning that he could only find reflections of himself. It even occurred to him that life was exactly like this video game, in which you tried to climb an endless stairway, while some gorilla at the top kept throwing barrels down on your head.

Nicky cleared the screen. He typed out an access code that allowed him entrance into a deeper part of the system. He requested gun registration information for Lawrence Ferguson. *This is what he was supposed to be doing, damn it!* For the first time this morning, he almost felt at peace.

Within seconds, the information began to appear on the screen. Lawrence had registered two handguns, a .22 target pistol and a .38 automatic. The .22 had been bought two years back, but the .38 had been purchased on Friday, October 18th, the same fateful day Lawrence bought his red Corvette, murdered Paul Hovarth, and moved to Beverly Hills. Both guns came from the same sporting goods store on Santa Monica Boulevard. The shotgun was not mentioned, since that did not need to be registered like a hand gun.

Nicky jotted down the name and address of the store, and then cleared the computer screen.

He walked back to his office, deep in thought, and sat down once again at his desk. Charlie, mercifully, was occupied on the telephone, talking to someone about the death of a sixteen-year-old girl—an accidental drug overdose. The girl was the daughter of a well-known film producer and had grown up with every material advantage. The whole thing was quite tragic. Nicky had become so obsessed with his one case that he had lost track of all the little bread-and-butter cases that his department was supposed to deal with. It was fortunate that Sergeant Katz was till functioning in his blissfully normal manner.

Nicky opened a folder to find the name and address of Molly Young, the typist Lawrence had been dating seven years ago. He dialed the number in Culver City that had been remembered by the computer at the Southern California Life Insurance Corporation.

A woman with a wheezy voice answered on the third ring.

"Hello? Is this Molly Young?"

"No, this is Molly's mother. May I help you, young man?"

"Yes, my name is Lieutenant Rachmaninoff, of the Beverly Hills Police Department. I was wondering if I could have a word with your daughter."

"Oh, dear me. Is there any sort of trouble?"

"No, ma'am. I just wanted to ask your daughter a few questions about a person named Lawrence Ferguson that she knew seven years ago."

Charlie sprang up from his chair, bounded across the room, and pressed down the button on Nicky's telephone, cutting off the call.

"Goddamn it, why did you do that?"

"Are you out of your mind? You're not supposed to be working on this case. Look, good buddy, give me a break. I'm *used* to you. You may not be a complete gourmet, but what if your replacement likes hot dogs?"

"Charlie, you asshole, get the hell away from my phone," he snarled. "I know what I'm doing."

The sergeant shook his head. "The man's Flip City," he mumbled. But he went back to his own desk.

Nicky dialed the Culver City number once more.

"Hello, ma'am? This is Lieutenant Rachmaninoff again. I'm sorry, we were cut off."

"Yes . . . well, I do remember Lawrence Ferguson, of course. Such a nice young man. Molly brought him home for dinner several times. I was rather hoping they would get married at one time. But Molly never did marry, you know." Her voice trailed off, ebbing away.

"Is Molly there now, by any chance? I would like to speak with her."

"My daughter has become a registered nurse," the old lady said, with some pride in her voice. "She is working in the pediatrics department at the U.C.L.A. Medical Center. She's always terribly busy, but you might be able to catch her at her lunch hour. She gets off at twelve-thirty."

"Thank you very much, ma'am. I'll do that."

He hung up the phone and looked at his watch. It was almost quarter to eleven. He would have time to zip down to the sporting goods shop on Santa Monica, then up to the Medical Center in Westwood. If he hurried, he would still be able to keep his appointment with the chief downtown at three.

Nicky stood up to leave.

"So what do I tell the captain if he comes looking for you?" Charlie asked from the next desk, without looking up from a report he was reading.

"Just say that I went home to change clothes and get a close shave for my meeting with McWilliams this afternoon."

"Close shave, indeed!" he muttered.

Nicky laughed. He knew he shouldn't be doing this. But he liked the feeling of being on the move again.

# 15

icky hurried down to Santa Monica, where he spent fifteen minutes with the head of the gun department at Goody's Sports and Surplus store, before rushing over to Westwood to meet with Molly Young at twelve-thirty.

The gun salesman managed to infuriate him, without giving any new information whatsoever. With some prodding, the man found the sales receipt, and yes, he had a vague memory of a bizarre-looking individual coming into the store a few weeks earlier, buying a Smith and Wesson .38 automatic, a 12-gauge Remington double-barreled shotgun, a hundred rounds of ammunition in various sizes, a bayonet, and a pair of sunglasses.

He remembered that the man was in a hurry, and bought everything without asking the price. He did, however, have a gun permit and proper identification. The clerk smiled brightly, clearly pleased with himself for being so helpful. "Everything's all right, isn't it, Lieutenant?"

Nicky gave the man a withering look. He was almost too angry to speak. He managed to say: "*How* could it be all right? A strange-looking guy comes in here and buys enough weapons and ammunition to blow away half the neighborhood, without even asking the prices. Now you tell *me,* under what conceivable circumstances could that be all right?"

The clerk's answer: "Hey, he had all the legal documents necessary to buy firearms. I don't make the laws. I'm just a salesman."

Nicky wanted to bust the guy, figuratively and physically—punch him right in the face. But he was running behind schedule and did not have the time. He drove to the U.C.L.A. Medical Center, writing virulent letters in his head to the National Rifle Association.

Molly Young turned out to be a big-boned woman with a square, plain face and dark hair on her upper lip. Her brown eyes had some intelligence and kindness in them. Nicky found her in the pediatrics department, just as she was getting off for lunch. He walked with her to the cafeteria. When he mentioned his visit had to do with Lawrence Ferguson, she seemed to wince.

"Is Lawrence all right? Is he in some kind of trouble?"

"He's not in trouble," he lied. "But he's not all right either. Lawrence has cancer, I'm afraid, and he simply disappeared from his job and his home about three weeks ago. We're only trying to find him."

"Poor dear," she said. "He was really very sweet to me. I thought he was a very intelligent and sensitive man. It's just that he was so . . . cut off from everyone else. I never got very close to him really. He was polite, but he never opened himself up. I never knew what was going on inside of him."

A good thing, too, Nicky thought. But he only said, "Did Lawrence ever mention going to the desert or the Salton Sea?"

She raised her eyebrows. "You know about that? Yes, he loved the desert, and particularly the Salton Sea. He used to go there every year on his vacation."

Nicky was curious. "Why the desert?" he asked.

"Oh, he used to go on and on about how beautiful it was. He always took his vacation in the spring, when the desert flowers were in bloom. He said they were very subtle, and that most people wouldn't notice them. A bit like Lawrence, really. People didn't notice *him* very much. Anyway, I always felt the thing he really liked about the desert was that there were hardly any people there." She laughed and shook her head. "Lawrence could be pretty negative about the human race."

Nicky studied the woman. She had not touched a bite of her food.

"Tell me, Molly, how did your relationship end?" he asked. "I don't mean to be too personal, of course . . ."

She looked away from him nervously. "Well, as a matter of fact, it had to do with his yearly trip to the Salton Sea. He wanted me to come along with him that spring and take our vacations together . . . but I didn't feel it was right to go off together, when we weren't married. I know I must sound old-fashioned." Molly seemed to be struggling with herself, just talking about this. Nicky waited.

"Sex was an area of disagreement between Lawrence and me, Lieutenant," she announced abruptly. Nicky only nodded. "Lawrence wanted us to be . . . lovers, but I was never really interested in him that way. I felt that if I went to the desert with him, the whole issue would become too . . . pressing. So I declined his offer. And he became terribly agitated. He began yelling at me, using all sorts of obscenities. It was quite a different Lawrence than I had ever seen before. I was actually afraid he was going to strike me. After that, I refused to see him, though he sent me letters for quite a while, trying to apologize. I was

242

terribly upset by the whole thing, and I even quit my job at Southern Cal Life just so I wouldn't have to see him anymore. And that's the end of it, Lieutenant. It's all quite ancient history now."

She looked up at him brightly, though her eyes glistened with distant tears. Nicky had a sense that Molly spent a lot of her life going over ancient history.

He shook hands and walked away, but the image of Molly Young stayed with him for some time. She was not an attractive woman. Like Lawrence, she would pass unnoticed in a city where youth and money, power and pleasure reigned supreme.

Nicky had a strong feeling that a great deal more attention should be paid to the lonely people of this world.


# 16

Outside, the day had become even more hot and still, so that Nicky actually put up the roof of his car, to provide some protection from the beating rays of the sun. He drove eastward on Sunset, from Westwood toward Beverly Hills.

If he were still on the Car Killer case, he knew he would not be looking for Lawrence Ferguson in Honolulu, but at the Salton Sea.

So what should he do with what he knew? This is what he asked himself, as he followed the curves of Sunset Boulevard, past the expensive houses that lay concealed behind great walls in the static sunlight. How could he steer the investigation from faraway Honolulu and direct it where it belonged—to the much closer and less glamorous Salton Sea? Without, of course, revealing what he had been up to this morning, so he could still keep his job.

One thought: He could give all his information to Charlie Cat and let the sergeant bring up the idea of looking in the desert. This might be a viable option.

Probably the task force would eventually start sniffing around the Southern California Life Insurance Corporation and get on the same trail Nicky had taken, which led quite clearly to the Salton Sea. He was simply a week or so ahead of everyone else, which was a very lonely position.

He was considering his options and trying to concoct an attitude and explanations that would guide him through his three o'clock meeting with the police chief. Nicky just had time to stop off at his house on Sunshine Terrace and put on a suit. He planned to be well dressed and penitent, with only a slight hint in his manner of *Well, I know I've been naughty, but, gee, I've been getting results, haven't I?*

He was driving on the expensive stretch of road between Bel Air and Beverly Hills when he noticed the fat lady who always sat beneath an umbrella with a large sign facing the boulevard: MAPS OF THE HOMES OF THE STARS. The fat lady had been selling her maps for years on this same corner of Sunset Boulevard. Nicky only noticed her now because, with her colorful umbrella in the deep green shade, she looked rather poetic today, like something from Renoir.

MAPS OF THE HOMES OF THE STARS. How ridiculous, he thought. Then the connection went through. It was like a telephone ringing in an empty house—at last the owner came home and picked up the phone. The message had been there all the time, trying to get through.

*Lawrence Ferguson had been in the tour van, outside of Susan and Frank's Bel Air mansion!*

His were the deep-set eyes that had been so strangely disturbing; the face that had peered longingly out the window, as the van drove away.

Nicky was so pleased with himself for finally making the right connection that he drove blithely for another block before the full significance sank in.

"Oh, *shit!*" he cried, and pulled over so suddenly into the nearest driveway that the car behind him nearly collided with his rear end. With trembling fingers, he opened up the glove compartment, brought out the plastic red light, and clamped it to the roof of his car. A switch beneath the dashboard made the light revolve and shine out its emergency message.

Nicky executed a fast U-turn on Sunset, cutting dangerously close to an oncoming car. He did not have a siren in his car, but used his horn instead, honking insistently until the traffic ahead of him saw the red light and cleared out of his way. He drove recklessly, faster than he should, accelerating on the roller-coaster curves of Sunset, until he reached the proud white arch that led to Bel Air. He continued up the narrow roads, holding down his horn so that everyone ahead of him would get out of his way, shattering the gentle peace in his hurry.

From Nicky's point of view, it seemed to take forever to reach the great iron gates in front of Frank and Susan's home. Impatiently, he pushed the button of the squawk box several times.

"Yes, may I help you?" came the voice of the maid.

"Anna, this is Nicky. Let me in."

The iron gates immediately began to swing open. Nicky was through them as soon as there was a space large enough for the Austin-Healey to pass. He rushed up the long driveway, squealing to a stop in front of the house.

Anna was standing on the front steps, holding her hands together in a gesture of prayer.

Nicky took one look at her, and he knew he was too late.

He rushed into the house, leaving his car door ajar, and telephoned Paramount to confirm what he already knew in his heart.

His ex-wife had not arrived at work that morning. On soundstage 5 they were all frantically trying to find the star of their show. Nicky talked with a semihysterical assistant director, who had telephoned all over town: to her agent, to Frank, even to various hospitals and the morgue.

But no one knew where she was. Susan Merril had completely disappeared.

# PART
# NINE

*The Dying Sea*

# 1

Early Wednesday morning, Lawrence waited, hidden in the shrubbery outside the electronic gate in front of Susan's Bel Air mansion. He had arrived before dawn and had concealed himself within a small cavity inside the bushes. Everything was slightly damp, and there was an unyielding root that pressed against the base of his spine. But what did he care? It was going to be a beautiful day. The sky slowly turned gray-white and finally a fragile blue as the sun edged up over the trees. For early November, this was clearly going to be an unseasonably hot day. From the beginning, he felt a certain transparency in the air that is usually present only on the first lovely days of summer.

He knew, from his previous spying on Susan, that she left for work at seven-fifteen. At least, he had watched her do this two mornings in a row. Today, as he waited, he was neither excited nor afraid. If she did not show up this morning, he could come back tomorrow or the next day or the day after that. What did it matter? Lawrence waited with the calm assurance of someone who was following the commands of fate.

And fate had been guiding him with remarkable success so far.

He had left the Beverly Hills Hotel late Tuesday morning, less than six hours before the police had raided his room. He simply knew it was time to leave. Monday afternoon, when he had sat in his room making his plans, it occurred to him that he had used up all his luck in Beverly Hills. He loved the wonderful pink hotel and his red Corvette—but when the time came to depart, he did it effortlessly, like a caterpillar shedding its skin. Perhaps it was because the future beckoned more enticingly than the past. He was a man with a lot to look forward to.

And so on Tuesday morning, he took only his briefcase, which contained a little less than $20,000 after the extravagance of the past three weeks, and his .38 automatic and five boxes of shells. Money and a gun: What else did a man really need?

He left the hotel surreptitiously, his final bill unpaid. There could be no question of checking out in the proper way. But it was important to him that those in the hotel think well of him after he was gone. For this reason, he left three $100 bills weighted down beneath an ashtray as a tip for the maid, and he slipped Joey $200 as he stepped into a taxi.

He had been clever to make certain Joey thought he knew where he was going and why he was not taking his own car. It was all quite plausible, and in this very simple way he managed not only to get out of Beverly Hills but also to leave a false trail behind him.

The taxi took him from the Beverly Hills Hotel to the United terminal at L.A. International. He went inside long enough to have an ice cream sundae at a restaurant, and then returned to the street, where he had another taxi take him to a small car rental company in Santa Monica, where he had already arranged to rent a van.

The van was a dull orange and had "U-Rent" and a telephone number painted in large black letters on the side. The vehicle was of the commercial sort and had few windows. This was exactly what Lawrence wanted.

From Santa Monica, he had driven to Bel Air, for a last reconnaissance of the area. He discovered a driveway several hundred yards past the entrance to the mansion. The driveway curved off the main road behind a tall hedge, before coming to a great padlocked gate, through which one could just see a neglected old house, with broken windows and shutters hanging at crazy angles. Finding this spot was a lucky break. It would be a perfect place to hide the orange van.

He spent the rest of Tuesday at an army surplus store and a supermarket, buying various supplies and last-minute items. Then he checked into a large, anonymous motel near the airport, where he slept dreamlessly from early evening until his alarm clock woke him at four the following morning.

And so at last, on Wednesday, he hid the van in the driveway up the road and took up his spot in the bushes in front of Frank and Susan's house. He waited for more than an hour, listening to the morning birds chirp noisily in the trees, watching the birth of a new day.

At seven-fifteen exactly, there was a sound not far away of a car door and then an expensive engine purring to life. Lawrence stood up from his cramped position and peered through the greenery up the driveway. Susan's Bentley was gliding down the slight rise, almost without a sound. As the car came closer, he could just make out Susan in the driver's seat, wearing a hat and dark glasses. The window on her side was down so the fresh morning air could flow into the car.

The electronic gate began to open, with its smooth whirring sound. Lawrence took the .38 automatic from his raincoat pocket, held it slightly behind his back, and stepped out from the bushes.

The Bentley passed through the main gate.

"Susan!" he called out loudly, like an old friend. "Hi!"

She had stopped where the driveway met the main road and was about to make her turn, when she heard her name called out in such a familiar way. She looked out her window, puzzled, to see a man walk out of the shadows wearing a ridiculously oversized raincoat and a peaked baseball hat that had "Beverly Hills, California" written across the front.

Her first reaction: panic. Her breath caught in her chest. After Nicky's visit to the set yesterday, it didn't take much to scare her. Her foot was about to jab down on the accelerator, when he called again, so insistently familiar.

"Hey, Susan! It's *me!*"

He took off his hat and performed a silly little bow.

She recognized him then. *It was the funny little man.* After her moment of terror, her relief was so great that she burst out laughing.

"Oh, God, it's *you,*" she called back to him. "You always scare me, the way you appear like that. Don't tell me you've run out of gas again?"

Lawrence joined her laughter. "Oh, no. Not today," he said, ambling closer to the open window. "Just taking a little morning stroll."

"Well, it's a good morning for it. I was just thinking, it's like spring today. I wish I didn't have to go to work."

"You don't," he said, and brought his gun up swiftly from behind his back, and pressed it through the open window to the side of her head.

"Don't move," he hissed. "Or I'll kill you."

Susan gasped. The muzzle of the gun was digging into her temple, so hard, so cold. She couldn't quite comprehend what was happening.

"I'll kill you if you move an inch. Do you understand?"

She nodded slightly, hardly daring to move even that much. Her mouth was open, and the whites of her eyes showed very wide.

*He had her!* How he wanted to shout for joy! But the next ten minutes would be very delicate. He had thought this over at great length and knew that the maximum risk of this entire enterprise was *right now.* He must keep her terrorized and intimidated—that was the key— so she would not have time to realize that she actually had the advantage: that she was stronger than he, was inside a car, and that actually the very last thing he wanted to do was shoot her.

He pressed the gun farther into her temple.

"Ow . . . *please* don't."

"Shut up!"

Yes. She was almost paralyzed with fear.

"Put on the emergency brake," he ordered. "Do exactly as I tell you. Do it! *Now.*"

The emergency brake was on the left-hand side. Susan had to slide down in the seat a little to reach it, but Lawrence kept the pistol firmly against the side of her head, as he watched her crank the brake into place.

"Now, put the car into neutral."

She hesitated, clearly trying to think for a moment of some way to escape.

"Do it!" he screamed, his voice rising several octaves.

She did as she was told.

"Now listen to me, Cassie. If you do exactly what I tell you, you may survive this. Otherwise, I am going to kill you. Do you hear me?"

She nodded.

"All right . . . now climb into the passenger seat. Don't do anything sudden. I'm very nervous, and this is a hair trigger."

"Please . . . don't kill me," she managed to say. Her mouth was dry as cotton; she could hardly speak. Slowly, trying not to make any sudden movements, she slipped from one bucket seat to the other. Lawrence quickly got into the car and sat in the driver's seat. From his raincoat pocket, he produced a pair of handcuffs he had purchased yesterday at the army surplus store. The pistol had left the side of her head for just a few seconds as he opened the door and stepped into the car. But now he pushed the gun underneath her chin, forcing her head upward into an uncomfortable position. She could only look at the ceiling of the car. She moaned.

"Hold your hands together," he ordered.

"Yes."

Lawrence closed one handcuff around her right wrist. It was a little more awkward to get the left one closed, using only his one free hand. But he could do no wrong this morning. The left cuff clicked into position, and she was his prisoner.

He kept the gun pressed into the soft folds beneath her chin, while he let out the emergency brake with his left hand and reached around the steering column to put the car into gear.

No one was coming. The road was still deserted.

Lawrence made a left turn and drove quickly toward the driveway a hundred yards away where he had left the van. It was only when he pulled up next to the van and turned off the Bentley's engine that he removed the gun muzzle from her chin.

He opened the door on his side and stepped halfway out of the car, not taking his eyes off her.

"I want you to get out this side," he said, aiming the gun at her. "Come on, quickly!"

He backed away from the door as she crawled over awkwardly, the handcuffs restricting free movement.

"Come on, come on!" he cried impatiently. They were mostly hidden from the road now, but still not entirely safe. "Nothing sudden now . . . all right, good . . . good."

She was out of the car, standing in the driveway in front of the orange van, panting a little with her teeth clenched and her lips slightly parted. She reminded Lawrence of a frightened thoroughbred horse. Even now, under these extreme conditions, he found her beautiful, with her clear skin and finely sculptured features. He had to force himself to be cruel, when really all he wanted was to hold her in his arms.

*Oh, how the two of them would laugh about this one day! She would tell their friends, He was so wild about me, you know what that crazy devil did? He abducted me at gunpoint! Larry was always such a terrible romantic!*

He jammed the gun harshly against her head once more as he opened the back of the van. "Inside," he told her. "I want you to lie on your back. Yes, that's right. Now put your arms above you. Yes . . . yes . . ."

Lawrence took a second pair of handcuffs from his raincoat pocket. He snapped one end around the center of the first pair of cuffs, which held her wrists. The other end, he attached to a metal bar that ran along the length of the van, halfway to the ceiling.

Only then did he put the .38 automatic back into his raincoat pocket. Finally, he took a length of clothesline and tied her ankles. They were such pretty ankles; he did not tie them too tightly. Still, she would not be going anyplace, unless he allowed it.

He looked down at her. Gloatingly. Lovingly.

Cassie was completely his!

"Open your mouth," he insisted.

She hesitated, so that Lawrence swiftly brought out his gun once again and pressed it into her forehead. *"Open your mouth."*

She opened. He shoved a clean, wadded washrag into her mouth and then wrapped a length of silver super tape around her head to keep the gag in place.

When she was completely gagged and bound and handcuffed to the back of the van, Lawrence allowed himself a little smile. She continued to regard him with the whites of her eyes showing very wide.

"I know this is starting off a little rough for you," he said. "But you're going to be glad I did this, Cassie. I promise you. We're really going to have fun."

She continued to stare at him with mute terror. But now a new element entered her expression, of sheer incredulity.

He patted her affectionately on the leg and crawled over to the driver's seat.

*It was going to be all right,* he thought smugly. *Women like knowing who's boss. You got to give them lots of love. But, God knows! With a beautiful woman like Cassie, you had to be very . . . very firm.*

# 2

The freeway cut across the city from the northwest diagonally southeast; past fifty miles of shopping malls, gas stations, miniature golf, pizza parlors, cemeteries, and still more gas stations, still more shopping malls.

Lawrence drove this long diagonal in his rented orange van, across the dusty basin, surrounded by the mountains that contained the city of Los Angeles. The day grew warmer as he traveled southeast. He felt quite happy and carefree, with his arm resting in the open window and the radio tuned to his favorite light rock station, which played only love songs.

Lawrence sang along, in a high falsetto:

"I'm gonna love you, girl, tonight,
 yeah, yeah
 It's all gonna be all right . . ."

Every now and then, he stole a glance into the rear of the van, where Cassie was bound and gagged. He had to remind himself that this was real; that he had indeed carried off the greatest prize of all—a beautiful actress who had once been on the cover of *TV Guide*.

"Woo-ee!" he shouted out the window, into the wind. *"Ya-hoo!"*

He chortled and shook his head, laughed and sang and drove through the endless suburban sprawl.

Cassie had been moaning for a while, but now she was quiet. After a while, he called back to her cheerfully, "You all right there? Not too much longer."

She did not, of course, answer.

Lawrence continued driving toward the mountains at the edge of the basin. Near the town of Riverside, the freeway passed through the mountains, out of the Los Angeles basin and into the vast and barren desert that lay to the south and to the east of the city.

The air changed. A hot, dry wind blew into the van. Lawrence greedily inhaled the scent of the desert. The smog was trapped on the other side of the mountains and did not penetrate here. Past Riverside, the road descended gradually to the desert floor. Even with his dark glasses on, Lawrence squinted from the intense light. The sun shone unobstructed upon the brown earth and the brown mountains. Above, the sky was a sheer dark blue. In the desert, Lawrence often had a sensation of being on a planet spinning in outer space.

"Gee, Cassie, isn't it grand? We should have come down here together a long time ago," he said. "Los Angeles is such a wasteland, don't you think? The desert is subtle—you have to be sensitive to see all the miraculous things that are going on."

He turned around to look at her fondly. "You're just going to love it, Cassie," he said.

Her eyes were open, staring back at him with mute horror and fear. And hatred.

Lawrence sighed and looked back toward the road. For just a moment, he had a brief but violent misgiving about this entire affair.

It was quite strange: In his imagination, he had already had countless conversations with Cassie O'Day. They had been through good times, bad times. They even had had a few friendly arguments. But she had never, ever looked at him like this.

# 3

**I**t had been another beautiful day: early summer, north of Morro Bay, the coastal hills still green with long grass. Golden sunlight. A long and dusty road that led up into a canyon to a spot where there had once been a logging camp.

*The two men drank beer, smoked weed, and took all the time they wanted. Garlic Breath and the One with the Tattoo: That was how she thought of them after all these years. There had never been a time since That Time, when she couldn't close her eyes and see them and feel their hands on her body. It was a memory that ricocheted down the canyon of years. Always fresh. Always there waiting in the dark.*

"Woo-ee . . . Ya-hoo!"

*They had tied her hands, just like today. But not her legs.*

Susan floated in and out of a time warp. It seemed to her that several eternities had passed since she had been kidnapped this morning.

At first, there was only blind terror, with the gun pressed to her head, believing she could die any millisecond. It had been difficult to breathe, impossible to think or move. And then, not even knowing how it had all happened, she found herself handcuffed and chained inside the van, her ankles tied together. She realized the gun was no longer pressing against her head. When the van started to move, she thought, I'm still alive. She was flooded with relief and fell into a numb exhaustion that was almost like being asleep.

Gradually the numbness turned to discomfort; discomfort changed to pain. First she became aware of her arms, held uncomfortably above her head. Then she felt the metal handcuffs chafing against her wrists, holding her shoulder blades so awkwardly against the vibrating metal floor. Occasionally, the van would lurch or jolt and throw her against the floor, grinding the base of her spine against the van. The rope around her ankles hurt for a time, but after a while she lost all sensation in her feet.

The worst part was the gag in her mouth. It was difficult to breathe and hard to swallow. Beyond that, the gag was stifling, claustrophobic. She was afraid she might vomit and choke to death; even the pistol at her head seemed preferable to that.

All these various pains and fears emerged gradually out of the numbness and grew over an eternity, a slow crescendo to unbearable, claustrophobic agony.

Susan could not see where the van was going. This was a horror of its own. The trip had no plausible beginning, no logical end. It became unrelenting torture, with every bone and muscle of her body throbbing with hurt.

How could she stand this another second? She must change position or die. . . . Tears came to her eyes. She struggled against the handcuffs and ropes. She wanted to scream and scream. . . . Then this phase, too, came to a climax and began to subside.

She stopped struggling against her bonds and was overcome by a new sort of numbness. As her body seemed to disappear, her mind became clear and detached. For the first time since her capture, Susan was able to think clearly about her predicament and wonder where she was and what the strange little man wanted from her.

She looked to the front of the van, where she could see the back of his head. The radio was on quite loudly, tuned to one of those pop stations that Nicky always made fun of. In the driver's seat, the man looked very small and insubstantial. She realized she could take him, if she ever got a chance. She was bigger, stronger, and clearly in much better physical shape. Perhaps, if she had had her wits about her, she might not have been captured at all. Except it had all happened so fast . . . and the gun and the terror she felt had kept her from taking action.

It was growing very hot inside the van. She realized she was soaked in sweat, but it wasn't the good, athletic sweat that came after she worked out. This sweat was sour and stank of fear. She was very thirsty and wondered if the man would stop and give her water.

The man . . . she did not remember if he had told her his name. She closed her eyes and relived her first encounter with him, from finding him outside her driveway, to letting him off at the gas station on Sunset Boulevard. She had found it quite amusing at the time and had told her friend the makeup woman all about the incident when she had arrived that morning at Paramount. What had he talked about? The imminence of death!

Jesus! It did not seem amusing now. How could she have treated it so lightly? A woman in her position should have been more careful . . . and in the end, she had blithely given the man her autograph and (she shuddered) kissed him on the cheek.

Oh, God. How could I have been so innocent? she thought. Just like the first time: hitchhiking up the coast to some absurd love-in at Big

Sur, in long-ago 1967. *When would she learn?* What was his name? *Larry.* It came to her. That was the name she had written on the autograph.

As if responding to an invisible call, the man turned and looked at her. Their eyes met. Susan shuddered and felt the wave of numb fear pass once more over her body. Larry looked to her like death incarnate, the way Death might be presented onstage for one of the interminable medieval passion plays she had been forced to study in drama school . . . only Larry looked the part, more than any of the actors at U.C.L.A.

The man looked back at the road and began talking to himself. No, he was talking to her. She distinctly heard the name Cassie . . . and his calling her by her TV character's name scared her more than anything else.

God, she was late on the set! At Paramount they would be going crazy, pacing the floor, wondering where she was. She actually felt a momentary stab of guilt, her indoctrination so firmly ingrained never to be late on the set.

At least Paramount would be sending out a hue and cry, looking for her. It cost approximately $10,000 an hour to keep a film crew waiting.

The man turned and spoke very distinctly: "Gee, Cassie, isn't it grand?"

God! It was like a line from an old movie—something Jimmy Stewart might say to Jean Arthur, gazing together at some perfect Hollywood sunset. It was the way the man smiled, so innocently pleased with himself, believing that *she was enjoying herself, too,* that was so terrifying.

What had Nicky said to her when he came on the set last week? She remembered his words: *There's a nut out there somewhere and he seems to be a fan of yours.*

But that wasn't last week. Nicky had talked with her yesterday . . . time had become unreal. She *was* going crazy. How could she endure this dreadful claustrophobia another moment? Susan found that her heart was pounding. She pulled at her bonds, until her wrists felt wet with blood, and she could hardly breathe.

Careful now. Relax. It won't help to panic.

The van drove on and on, while the air inside grew steadily more unbearably hot. Susan was terribly thirsty. She tried to swallow and recycle her own saliva, but the washcloth stuffed in her mouth seemed to absorb all the moisture . . . perhaps she would die of thirst. Death, at times, seemed preferable to the torture of riding another moment on the floor of the van.

In clear moments she thought about Nicky. He had tried to warn her; clearly, he must have known something. Nicky would save her, she knew he would. Nicky would not let this happen.

She also considered how her legs—although tied together at the ankles—were not chained to the van as her hands were. Her legs were free . . . and when the little man came for her, she might kick him with both feet so hard she would squash him like a bug.

For many miles, Susan fantasized this one killing blow. She brought her legs up closer to her body, so she would have more room to uncoil. In her imagination, she kicked him again and again. In the crotch, in the chest, in the throat, crushing his windpipe. If she could, she would kill him and revel in his death. . . .

But gradually the heat and the pain and the endless motion of the van were simply too much to take. Susan slipped away into darkness, far, far away into a blessed place of unconsciousness.

# 4

**W**ater ran down her mouth. She opened her eyes, sputtering for breath.

The van was stopped. Her hands were still chained above her head, but the gag had been removed. The man was bending over her, trying to pour water into her mouth from a small plastic canteen. Most of the water ran down her chin.

It took a moment to take all this in, to remember where she was. The man looked down at her with a worried expression. His eyes were very bright and intense.

Susan spoke, though her voice was hoarse and thin. "Why . . . why are you doing this to me?" she asked.

He looked startled, as if the reason were too obvious to merit consideration. "Because you're my favorite woman in the entire world, Cassie. You know that."

"No," she moaned, shaking her head.

The man screwed the top back onto the canteen. He was staring with great fascination at her bare stomach, where her jersey top had ridden up from her blue jeans. Tentatively, he put his hand down on her flesh. Susan tensed every muscle in her body at the violation.

"Don't touch me!" she screamed, with a violence that went back clear to 1967.

Lawrence jerked his hand away, as though he had touched a hot iron. He had not been prepared for the vehemence of her reaction.

"It's just that you are so beautiful, Cassie."

"I'm *not* Cassie," she said fervently. "My name is Susan. Cassie does not exist. She's just a television character, for chrissake! There are six different writers who make her up every week. . . . Why don't you pick on them and leave me alone!"

The man looked puzzled and hurt by this outburst of information. Then a sly smile came to his lips. "It's all right. I think I know you better than you know yourself."

Susan tried a new course. "Listen, if you care for me, as you say, please untie me. My hands hurt, I almost died with that gag in my mouth. If you let me go, we can be friends."

He shook his head. "If I let you go, you'll run away. You can't trust women. Everyone knows that."

"*Please,*" she said, "I was nice to you once, do you remember? When you ran out of gas, I gave you a ride."

He smiled smugly. "Oh, I wasn't out of gas, Cassie. That was just a way to get to know you."

Tears ran down her cheeks. "My daughter is waiting for me at home, and my husband. . . . Please, you've got to let me go. I've never hurt you . . . I don't know why you're doing this."

Her words came out chokingly, in sobs. The man listened sympathetically. "Shh!" he said. "It's going to be all right. We're almost there, you see, and we'll have a new life together. You'll like it, really you will."

She turned her face away from him and cried. The agony of the last few hours came pouring out.

Lawrence watched her and waited patiently for the tears to subside. "Shh!" he kept saying. "It's going to be all right." With fascination, he stroked her fine blond hair.

The sobs gradually ceased. "Are you hungry?" he asked. "I made some tuna salad sandwiches to bring along. You see, I really have thought of everything."

She turned to face him. "Okay. Will you untie my hands so I can eat?"

260

He laughed. "Oh, Cassie, what a sly one you are. No, I think I'd better keep your hands where they are. I'll feed you though . . . that'll be fun."

He crawled forward in the van to a small ice chest that lay on the passenger's seat, took out a sandwich and returned.

Susan had brought her legs up closer to her body, as though curling into a fetal position. Lawrence seemed not to notice. He unwrapped the sandwich and held it to her mouth. She was not at all hungry, but forced herself to take several bites. The tuna seemed to stick in the dryness of her throat. "May I have some water, please. I don't think I can eat any more, but I'm terribly thirsty."

The canteen was by his side. Lawrence opened the container and brought it to her lips. She took a long swallow.

"Thank you," she said. She smiled innocently. In just a moment, if all went well, she was going to kill him. She brought her legs even closer to her stomach.

"Would you like another sip?"

"Oh, yes, please," she murmured. The bottle was brought once more to her lips, but when she opened her mouth for another drink, instead of water, the gag was pushed back rudely into her mouth.

She tried to scream, but could make no noise. Lawrence put a new strip of super tape around her head to keep the washcloth in place.

"I'm sorry I have to do this, my love," he said with regret. "But I can't have you screaming at the wrong moment. Can I?"

Susan stopped fighting against the gag. It didn't matter; her legs were still in position, ready to strike. Patience, she said to herself. Not too soon.

Lawrence smiled at her lovingly and then began to move back to the driver's seat.

When he was just a few feet away, at the moment she judged right, Susan suddenly unleashed her legs, furiously aiming toward the side of his stomach. But her legs had been asleep too long. Without sensation in her feet, she misjudged her reach, kicking him harmlessly on his hip, not very hard.

Still, Lawrence was thrown against the side of the van. He cried out and fell in a heap, gathering himself up slowly, careful to stay out of reach of her legs. He rubbed his hip with his hand and stared at Susan with a hurt expression.

"Why did you do that?" he demanded. He really did not know.

She glared at him with pure hatred.

# 5

**L**awrence shook his head, unable to comprehend the mysterious ways of women. And she had smiled at him so sweetly just a moment before!

He crawled back into the driver's seat. The van was parked in a desolate rest stop off the freeway. A hundred yards ahead there was one other car, an aging station wagon with a black family inside, eating sandwiches and studying a map.

Lawrence started the engine and rejoined the main road that ran straight ahead, shimmering in the midday heat.

His side throbbed painfully where she had kicked him. But more painful than that was the look she had flashed.

"Women! What a mystery! Oh, Cassie, I wish I could understand . . ." Cassie, who had lived so long inside his head, who was his oldest friend—*she* would tell him what to do.

But daydreams obey their own hidden laws. They are like the unfixed images on photographic paper in a darkroom. They exist only in a perilous way. Let in any real light from the outside, and they are gone.

And so it was with Lawrence. He tried to summon his beautiful and imaginary Cassie to keep him company on this long desert ride. But she would not come. She was no longer there.

No. There was only the girl in the back, bound and gagged, who would not, could not talk. Who didn't even smell too good. And who would kill him, without hesitation, the second she got a chance.

The freeway skirted the elegant desert places: Palm Springs and Palm Desert, where the mountains rose from the desert floor like a piece of movie scenery, and even the cactus appeared well groomed.

He had no desire for this rich desert playground of hotels and swimming pools and gold. From the freeway, Palm Springs appeared briefly to Lawrence like some old prospector's hallucination, an improbable fantasy in the sun, and then was left behind. Indio was the last real town before the desert opened up in its true magnitude—stretching southward deep into Sonora, and eastward, under different names, clear through New Mexico, the panhandle of Texas, almost to Oklahoma. This vast stretch of arid wasteland had once challenged and exhausted the energies of the early pioneers. But when Lawrence saw it today, he was glad. This was the true place of his heart. It was like coming home.

Not far past Indio, he saw his first mirage. The road—which was just two lanes now, no longer a freeway—seemed to run straight into a large blue lake of shimmering water. Lawrence smiled; he knew the ways of the desert. The imaginary lake grew closer, closer—and then simply disappeared. The road kept going, straight as a ruler on a map, with sand blowing carelessly on both sides.

Before long, the highway made a gradual ascent to a barren rise. Great brown boulders were scattered carelessly by some giant hand. On one of the boulders, someone had painted: I LOVE PUSSY. A little farther, on another boulder, by a different hand: JESUS SAVES! These words, as well as broken beer bottles on the side of the road, were the only indication of the passage of man in an otherwise inhuman landscape.

At the top of the long rise, Lawrence looked down and saw a large body of blue water, sparkling and reflecting the intense sun. This was no mirage; this was the Salton Sea. In places it was no more than a few feet deep, but it stretched lengthwise farther than the eye could see.

The heat grew more intense as the van descended once more to the desert floor. Lawrence knew it might be over 100 degrees Fahrenheit. He loved it; he had been here once before when the temperature had soared to 125, and he had loved that even more. At 125 degrees, in the desert, time and reality seemed to stop, and open up like a hole in the wall of eternity.

For Lawrence, there was a perfect symmetry in coming to this spot with Cassie. Years ago, he had tried to bring another woman here— Molly, who had worked in his office. He had even made the reservations for their lodging and had planned it in his mind for months, the walks they would take together, the meals they would cook, their lovemaking at night. Everything. Except three days before their vacation was supposed to begin, Molly had decided not to go. That year was the only time Lawrence had ever felt lonely in the desert. What a sad vacation it had been, moping through the days by himself, doing alone what he had planned to do with Molly.

But now, what sweet revenge to come here with a beautiful and famous actress, whose picture (he reminded himself again) had once been on the cover of *TV Guide!* There was no comparison. Lawrence sniffed contemptuously, remembering Molly's shapeless body and thick legs. He had to glance behind to the rear of the van (yes, she was still there!) just to remind himself once more that this was real—that Cassie was with him, with her delicate features and soft skin and girlish good looks.

Lawrence smiled happily, forgetting how she had kicked out at him and looked at him with hatred. The difference between Molly Young and Cassie O'Day was like the difference between his old studio apartment in Santa Monica and the Beverly Hills Hotel!

He had certainly moved up in the world.

# 6

Nicky sat in the great baronial living room in Bel Air, with his head in his hands. It was easy enough to make decisions of life and death when it concerned people you did not know. But with Susan, he had to be entirely certain he was doing the right thing.

Yet how could he be certain of anything? He was disgusted with himself. Little Lawrence Ferguson, ex-accountant, dying of cancer, had managed to outwit him at every turn.

Anna brought him around. "Would you like a cup of coffee, Lieutenant?"

He looked up, remembering her presence. "Yeah, thanks. Give me a shot of brandy in it, too."

He picked up the phone and dialed the private phone in Captain Molinari's office.

"Captain? This is Nicky. I'm in Bel Air, at Frank and Susan's house . . ."

"Bel Air?" the captain exploded. "Goddamn it, it's almost three o'clock! You should be on your way downtown to see the chief."

"Let me explain, Captain. I'm pretty sure Lawrence has kidnapped Susan and taken her to the Salton Sea. I'm headed down there right now."

"Wait, wait, wait! Either one of us has gone crazy, or you're ten steps ahead of me."

"Captain . . . Dave, please trust me. I know this is all kind of abrupt, but I'm not really crazy. Listen to me. I've known for a couple of days

264

that Lawrence has been taking his yearly vacations down in the desert somewhere. He's something of a nut about the desert, as a matter of fact. He decorated the walls of his apartment with two things: pictures of the desert and photographs of Susan. Okay? Remember, that's how I got a line on Lawrence in the first place, when Dave Hotchkiss called me wanting me to check if Susan had got any unusual fan mail recently."

"Okay, I'm listening," the captain said. "Go on."

"All right. This morning I went to see Molly Young, who used to be a typist in Lawrence's office. They dated, about seven years ago. As far as we know, Molly is the only woman he ever went out with."

"Damn you, Nick! I gave you an order to stay in your office and keep away from this case!"

"Well, I didn't listen to you, Captain. . . . Shall I go on?"

"Go on, Lieutenant." The captain's voice was cold and very distant.

"Molly told me about the Salton Sea. *That's* where he's been going all these years on his vacations. It's his favorite place. Now everything I've learned about Lawrence Ferguson tells me that he is a creature of habit. Except for breaking out and killing a few people now and then, of course. So when he figures that Beverly Hills is too hot, he goes down to the Salton Sea. Not only is it his favorite spot, but the desert is a natural hideout. You follow me so far?"

"Yeah. It's all very iffy. Anyway, we're almost certain someone spotted him on the plane to Honolulu. But tell me about Susan."

"Well . . . she's gone. That's all. She didn't arrive at work this morning, and Paramount's going crazy."

"That's *all?* There's no ransom note or anything?"

"No, except I rushed over to Bel Air knowing she would be gone. You see, I remembered I had actually got a glimpse of Lawrence in a tour van outside here a few weeks ago."

"Nick, I think you've really gone off the deep end here. There are lots of reasons people don't show up at work other than being kidnapped."

"Not if you're in a TV series," he insisted.

"What if she was in an automobile accident or something?"

"All right. I'll let you check that out while I go down to the Salton Sea."

"Nick! Now you listen to me. I want you to come into the station right now, and we'll go downtown together and lay this all out for the chief. If he agrees you've got something here, we'll hop in a helicopter and get our asses down to the desert and do this job the proper way. Do you understand me, boy?"

"Jesus, Dave. I just don't have the time to convince McWilliams and the mayor and some fucking psychologist from U.C.L.A. I'm sorry. I'm gone."

"Lieutenant! This is an order! I want you to get your ass into the station right now."

" 'Bye, Captain."

Nicky gently let the phone fall back onto the cradle. He stared at it a moment, hoping to God he was making the right decision. Anna put his cup of coffee on a table in front of him. He took a few quick swallows and got on his way. His call to Captain Molinari had delayed him more than he intended.

# 7

Nicky cut across the giant city in a southeast diagonal, into the dense brown cloud of smog, and then out the other side, through the mountain pass and into the desert beyond. He cruised at seventy-five, weaving in and out of the heavy L.A. traffic, and then opened up to ninety when the road straightened past Riverside.

As he drove, he thought about Susan, not as she was today, but the Susan of long ago, at sixteen. He remembered the first time he had ever noticed her, in the hallway between classes at Hollywood High, wearing a blue sweater that accented the color of her eyes. Driving into the desert, into the rising afternoon heat, Nicky relived a kaleidoscope of images from his past: Susan on the beach at Malibu, in the skimpy green bikini she had worn for years . . . Susan and himself making love the first time in his car . . . the fight they had junior year about smoking dope . . . then, speeding up the reels, he saw them as a young married couple, taking themselves rather seriously, imitating what they imagined to be the behavior of adults.

He had a wonderful image in his mind of Susan pregnant, plump and very round.

He had a not so wonderful image of Susan packing her bags and leaving him to find her fame and fortune as an actress.

Undoubtedly, his affair with Julie had already changed his image of his ex-wife. Julie was definitely the woman for him today. She was a woman for a cynical cop who was almost forty years old. But Susan would remain the girl of his youth, in his mind forever young. The thought of losing her was like a scalpel cutting away at some of the basic memories that composed his life.

Grimly, he pressed down the accelerator of his Austin-Healey until the speedometer inched over one hundred miles per hour. Losing Susan would be to lose such a large part of himself that he could not imagine how he could survive.

The desert rushed by in a shimmering haze of yellow heat.

Behind him, a siren began to wail. Nicky looked in his rearview mirror to see a black-and-white highway patrol car right on his tail, having no trouble at all keeping up to his speed. He reached into his glove compartment and pulled out his radio microphone, punching over to the CHP frequency.

"This is Lieutenant Rachmaninoff of the Beverly Hills Police Department, to the CHP vehicle behind me. I'm on official business," he said hopefully. "Do you read me?"

"We read you, Lieutenant. Do you require any assistance?"

"Negative. Thank you anyway."

The patrol car dropped back another twenty feet and kept in place behind him, matching exactly his speed. He knew they were checking him out. Nicky wasn't certain of his status. For all he knew there could be an APB out for him. Nicky Rachmaninoff, the renegade cop. He waited for them to run his license through the computer, wondering what he was going to do if they tried to stop him.

Fuck it! There was no way they were going to stop him. . . .

Nicky put the accelerator pedal all the way to the floor. The road was straight and flat, and the old sports car drifted to 110. The CHP car on his tail matched his speed in an apparently leisurely manner. The desert landscape was so unchanging that it was difficult to imagine they were going this fast, except for the occasional cars in the right lane that he zipped past in a blur.

"Okay, Lieutenant, you're clear," came the disembodied voice on the radio. "Watch your speed, huh? I don't know about that old crate of yours doing 110. I'd hate to have to scrape you up off the road."

Nicky didn't answer. He seemed to shoot ahead, as the CHP car fell back into a more conventional speed.

Ahead, the sky and brown earth met at the far horizon. Nicky drove toward that point and prayed he would not be too late.

# 8

In the early afternoon, the orange van came to a sign at the side of the old two-lane highway, which proclaimed grandly: ALADDIN'S MAGIC CARPET RESORT CABINS. There was a painting of Aladdin himself, on a magic carpet, being pulled by a speedboat driven by a beautiful blonde in a bathing suit, across the glamorous Salton Sea.

They were obviously having the time of their life. Only, the sign was faded with age, and the blonde had a hairstyle that was thirty years out of date. Beyond that, there was nothing but brown sand: no indication whatsoever of either this world-famous resort or of the glamorous Salton Sea.

Undaunted, Lawrence turned off the highway onto a dirt road and traveled over a tortured landscape of dry gulches and thirsty hills, toward some unseen point nearly a half mile away. This was a homecoming, his thirteenth visit to the Salton Sea. All except one time, he had stayed at Aladdin's Magic Carpet Resort Cabins. One year, as an experiment, he had tried the Yacht Club, but had found the place not only garish and impersonal but also lacking in that one essential ingredient he sought most in the desert: privacy.

Privacy was Aladdin's main appeal. The resort consisted of a string of old wooden cabins stretched out along the water's edge. Cabin number 10—which he was able to reserve each year, as an old and valued guest—was at the very end of the dirt road, out of sight of the other cabins and the office, completely on its own.

Everything was fairly dilapidated here, and cabin 10 was no exception: just an old, wooden-frame building, bleached by the sun, fifteen feet long by seventeen feet wide, with a narrow porch at the front and two canvas chairs facing the sea. Inside were two narrow cots, a small kitchen with an ancient gas stove, and a black-and-white TV that received only two channels, one from Palm Springs, the other from Tijuana.

There was also a miniature bathroom, which contained a sink with rusty water marks and a metal shower stall with plastic curtains. The water pressure inside the shower was not very great, and the entire cabin was too old to ever get completely clean. Above the two narrow beds was a painting of a dancing Arab girl with bare stomach and large brown eyes peering out seductively above her veil. It was not a very good painting, but Lawrence had always found it quite sexy.

He knew, of course, that this cabin was shabby. It cost only $15 a night. But it was situated ten feet from the Salton Sea, and from the porch and front windows you could not see another building, or a road, or another person. Only the strange white-blue water and the brown mountains in the distance. And the sky. To Lawrence, this was Paradise.

He stopped first at the office, which was a cabin like the others, only larger, standing in the dusty shade of a weeping willow tree. He locked the van, careful to leave the windows open just a few inches for air, and went inside to register with Mrs. Gotch, the owner of this aging resort.

Mrs. Gotch was a large old woman with several teeth missing in the front of her mouth, giving her a ghoulish appearance. Some years back, there had been a Mr. Gotch, who had been as small as his wife was large. But he had died, and now she ran the cabins by herself, with the help of a Mexican couple who were in the country illegally.

When she saw Lawrence arriving, she came to the screen door to greet him like an old friend. She had grown so fat she could only waddle slowly, panting for breath in the afternoon heat.

"Mr. Ferguson! How nice to see you again!"

"The pleasure is mutual, Mrs. Gotch."

"Come in, come in."

Lawrence entered a world of clutter and dust. Old trinkets and souvenirs lay on every possible surface, as well as several sleeping cats. They exchanged pleasantries while the old lady with a great sigh sat down at a crowded desk and filled out the registration card.

Lawrence paid for three weeks in advance, peeling off the bills from his large wad. He mentioned that there would be no need for the Mexican couple to make up his room each day; he would bring the dirty sheets and towels up to the office himself, whenever he was in need of a change. Mrs. Gotch said, "Of course, whatever you want." She was well aware of Lawrence's inclination for solitude.

Last of all, he handed the old lady an extra $300.

"Here's just a little something for you," he said.

"Mr. Ferguson! Why, you don't have to do that."

"No, I insist, I insist . . . it's simply a little thank-you in advance, for your understanding of my need to be left alone. I hope I don't seem horribly antisocial, Mrs. Gotch. But you know, after a year in the city—all that hustle and bustle—I really positively *pine* for the solitude of the desert, to recharge my batteries, so to speak."

"Now, Mr. Ferguson, that's perfectly all right. Not many people really know how to be alone nowadays, do they? We won't bother you a bit. I'll tell Maria and Carlos to stay away completely from number ten. Why, you are one of the last real gentlemen, Mr. Ferguson. I'm always so pleased to have you here."

Lawrence smiled humbly, well pleased with himself, and walked outside back to the van.

Susan glared at him as he opened the door and started up the engine. "We have arrived," he announced pompously. She moaned.

Lawrence drove down the dirt road past the office to the water's edge, where he turned left and followed the road to the very end. Cabin 10 looked exactly as he had last seen it. This was another thing he liked about Aladdin's: Nothing ever changed.

He backed the van up to the porch, as closely as possible, just in case there were prying eyes. Actually, the resort was more deserted than he had even hoped for. As far as he could tell, he and Cassie were the only guests.

He opened the double doors at the back of the van. She lay on her back, looking very helpless and vulnerable. But Lawrence knew he must be careful, especially after she had kicked out at him like that.

He studied her for a moment, and then walked to the front of the van, where he had a half-dozen lengths of rope in various sizes. He brought back three pieces. The first, he tied around her wrists, near the handcuffs. With the second, he made a loop around her waist. She grunted as he slipped the rope beneath her, but he paid no attention. Last of all, with the third rope, he made a slipknot at one end and quickly placed it around her ankles, pulling the knot tight before she had a chance to resist.

"It's all right, my dear . . . just a little longer."

Finally, he pulled up the slack of all three lengths of rope. He was convinced he would be able to control her at a distance, puppetlike. He whistled happily, walked up the steps to the cabin, and opened the front door. The place smelled musty, but everything was as he remembered it.

Above the two beds, the dancing Arab girl still looked out upon the room seductively.

Everything was ready. Lawrence stuck the .38 in the belt of his pants, feeling like a pirate. Only then did he take out the key to the handcuffs that held her to the side of the van. He reached over and unlocked her quickly, just in case she tried to make a jump for him. He moved back, out of her reach, holding the three lead lines. He needn't have been so cautious. Susan, after being chained and cramped for three hours in the back of the van, was incapable of moving quickly.

He tugged on the ropes, urging her out of the van.

"Come on, Cassie. We're here. Once you get inside, I'll take the gag off. You'll be more comfortable. Come on now."

He tugged more insistently.

Susan groaned through the gag. Painfully, pulled by the ropes, she sat up, but showed no signs of wanting to move from the van.

Lawrence looked at her. She glared back defiantly.

"You want some water?" he asked.

She did not move.

"Well, do you?"

She nodded.

"Okay, I'm going to take off your gag, and I'm going to give you water, just as soon as we get inside the cabin. Are you going to do what I tell you, or are you going to make me think of something that will be more painful? For both of us."

Susan nodded again, after a moment's hesitation.

"All right, Cassie. The first thing is to slide your feet out the back. Come on, you can do it."

He tugged on the third rope encouragingly. She struggled, swinging her legs out the back. Lawrence, puppet-master, now tugged on the two upper ropes, trying to get her out of the van.

She managed to set her hobbled feet on solid ground, but collapsed in a heap the moment she put her entire weight on them. She cried out into the gag, as the gravel bit her legs and arms. Tears swam in her eyes.

Lawrence hurriedly tied off rope number two around a wooden post that held up the roof to the porch. He was nervous that someone might come by at this critical point. With the rope that went to her wrists, he helped her up, careful not to get too close. As soon as she was on her feet, Susan charged forward at him, with murder in her eyes. But the rope around her waist pulled her back with a jerk. She fell down again on the gravel, crying and panting for breath. It wasn't only the pain, but the humiliation and frustration of being so helpless.

"Cassie, this isn't getting us anywhere!" Lawrence told her petulantly. "I want you to behave yourself now. Come on, get up!"

She was too exhausted to resist any further. For the next ten minutes, Lawrence pulled Susan into the cabin with his ropes, as if she were a grand piano being hauled into place. There were three wooden steps that led up to the porch, and she fell half a dozen times trying to negotiate this obstacle with hobbled feet. Finally, Lawrence threw one of the ropes around an exposed rafter and hauled her halfway up the stairs. Susan groaned with pain, and Lawrence, too, was panting from his exertions. Patiently, he negotiated her inside the cabin and eventually managed to tie her to one of the narrow beds.

Once she was restrained, he turned on the TV to a bullfight that was being broadcast in Spanish from Tijuana. He turned the volume way up. Only then did he return to the bed and take off the tape and the gag that was stuffed into her mouth.

Susan tasted blood; her teeth had cut into her lips. She breathed heavily. Every part of her body throbbed and hurt, except for her feet, which still had no sensation in them at all.

Lawrence filled a bathroom glass with water, propped her head up with his hand, and poured the water into her waiting lips. Most of it ran down her chin onto the bed. He filled the glass again, and she got more down this time.

"Boy, I'm pooped!" he said. "I don't know about you, but I'm ready for a little nap. I'll unload the food from the van first. I bet you're hungry."

He made several trips from the van back and forth to the kitchen. Yesterday he had bought several cases of canned food in Los Angeles, enough to last for weeks. There were dozens of cans of Dinty Moore Beef Stew, Franco-American Spaghetti, tuna fish, soup, and sardines—as well as a case of Coca-Cola, several jars of peanut butter and jelly, a half-dozen loaves of Wonder Bread, and several boxes of cookies, for an occasional treat.

Lawrence was very hungry from his exertions and tore open a package of cookies. "Mmmm ... good," he said cheerfully. "You want an Oreo, Cassie?"

But Susan had her face turned as far from him as she could. She was crying steadily into the pillow.

# 9

The heat of the day reached an intense crescendo by two in the afternoon, and then waned gradually toward evening.

Lawrence took a short nap, and when he awoke he walked down to the marshy edge of the Salton Sea. He felt at peace with himself; content to be here, happy that he was not alone. He gazed out in all directions, across the sea to the distant mountains, to the dreaming blue sky and the outrageously shaped clouds that floated by on the far horizon.

Looking away from the sea, there was a ridge of hills rising up behind his cabin called the Chocolate Mountains. He had always liked this name.

*The Chocolate Mountains!* It was his favorite flavor. He thought heaven might be like this: a land of chocolate mountains and marshmallow clouds, waiting for you at the other side. The hills were dark brown, softly molded, barren as death. On the other side was an army reserve, where the empty land was used for artillery practice. Occasionally, from that direction, came the dull thud of distant explosions. Lawrence liked to think of this as the thunder of the gods. In the hot sun, the mountains sat, forbidding yet strangely beckoning. He had always thought, since the time he had first come here, that these mountains would be a most fitting place to die.

When the time came: to simply walk up into them and be absorbed into the stillness. . . .

Today, he greeted this familiar land as an old friend. He squatted by the edge of the sea and put his hand in the water. It was as warm as blood.

At last, having paid his homage, he walked back inside the cabin.

Cassie was still lying where he had tied her on the bed. He smiled at her.

"Feeling better?" he inquired.

"I have to go to the bathroom," she answered.

Lawrence looked at her in amazement. He had thought he had considered all the possibilities, but he had never once considered that she might have to go to the bathroom.

"Well, do you want me to shit in my pants?" she cried out. She laughed savagely. "I'd be glad to stink you out, you motherfucker!"

The amazement in his face turned to horror. "Don't speak like that!" he shouted. "You're not the kind of girl who swears!"

Susan had taken all she could take. After being kidnapped and chained and hauled into this cabin like a piece of furniture, this really was the last straw. *"Fuck you,"* she said slowly and very clearly. And then again: *"Fuck . . . you!"*

Lawrence paled. He stared at the girl on the bed, wondering if he had made a strange mistake and kidnapped the wrong person. This creature couldn't be his Cassie, his sweet and innocent girl of whom he had dreamed so long.

She seemed to enjoy the effect of her words.

"Asshole!" she muttered contemptuously.

*"Shut up!"* he screamed. The .38 was lying on the television set. Lawrence grabbed the gun furiously, rushed up to her, and pressed it against her cheek. For a moment, Susan felt certain he was going to kill her. Lawrence almost did pull the trigger. Only his lingering belief that this was no ordinary woman kept him from firing.

"You're not going to speak like that ever again!" he commanded. "Cassie doesn't swear, you understand that?"

"Yes," she said breathlessly. "I'm sorry."

"Never again!" he shouted.

"Yes . . . I won't. I promise."

He kept the gun against her cheek. The cold steel bit into her skin.

"Do you know who I am?" he asked, in a voice that was different, but even more terrifying.

"You . . . you said your name was Larry."

"Yes, but I'm more than that, Cassie. Much more. Can't you guess?"

"I can't . . . I don't know."

"I'm the Car Killer," he cried out proudly. "The Car Killer! I'm the guy who shot all those people in Beverly Hills. What do you think of that? Pretty amazing, huh? For a little guy like me that no one ever noticed before."

Susan opened her mouth but she could not speak.

"Do you believe me?" he demanded angrily.

"Yes," she whispered.

"So don't mess with me anymore! I want you to act nice, like you do on television. You understand?"

"Yes."

Lawrence held the gun into her cheek for just another moment. Then, satisfied at last, he smiled and relaxed, and became his usual, innocuous self. "Well then, I guess that's settled," he said, and let the gun fall limply to his side.

Tears streamed down her face. Her sobs came out in short gasps.

"Shh . . ." he said, stroking her hair. "Don't cry, my little sweetie. It's going to be all right now. As long as we have our little understanding. We're going to have a wonderful vacation together."

"You can kill me," she sobbed, "but I still . . . I still . . . I have to go to the bathroom. I can't help it . . . I'm only human." Her tears made it hard for her to speak. Her last phrase came out pitifully, like a little girl. Lawrence looked down at her and sighed. This was not going at all the way he had imagined it.

"All right," he said wearily, and began to untie her feet.

"I won't try anything. I promise," she said.

Lawrence believed her. It was clear to both of them that her resistance was over. When her feet were free, he undid the ropes that tied her to the metal frame of the bed, leaving only the handcuffs around her wrists.

When she was free, he stood back, covering her with his gun. "All right, you can go to the bathroom."

She rose tentatively from the bed and limped across the cabin.

"Leave the door open," he ordered. "I'll . . . I'll try not to look."

So many times he had fantasized approximately this: seeing her unfasten her belt, pull down the zipper, lower her pants. Yet this was like a parody of what he had imagined. He could hardly stand it. Lawrence looked away as she sat down on the toilet.

A horrible, animal noise of escaping stomach gas filled the cabin. Lawrence gritted his teeth. He wanted to cover his ears.

The stench that came a few seconds later was even worse. Cassie was experiencing a severely upset stomach.

"I'm sorry," she said meekly through the open bathroom door. "I just can't help it."

Lawrence felt dizzy and suddenly weak. He had to sit down on the edge of the bed while he waited for her to finish. She stayed on the toilet for the next ten minutes. The sounds he heard in these ten minutes destroyed her glamour forever. But he refused to look at her, trying to hold onto some last shred of his fantasy.

Movement caught his eye. He looked now, thinking she was finished. But he looked just a little too soon. Cassie was trying to wipe herself with toilet paper: a simple act that had become obscenely difficult with handcuffs on. She was half crouching in the bathroom, her pants at her feet, bent over like a contortionist.

"Stop that!" he cried. "You're doing this on purpose!"

She looked amazed. "I'm not! Really . . . I can't help it. If you would just take the handcuffs off me and let me close the door . . ."

"Pull your pants up!" he roared.

She tried to obey him. But with the handcuffs on, even this was difficult.

Lawrence looked away. "Oh, Cassie," he moaned, "Cassie, beautiful Cassie . . ."

The toilet flushed. She walked back into the bedroom. Roughly, he ordered her to lie down, and he tied her securely once more to the bed.

"Please don't tie my feet again," she pleaded. "I'm going to be good."

He did not answer, but simply bound her feet even more tightly than before.

When she was secure, he rushed out of the cabin back into the dry desert air. It was late afternoon, and Lawrence sat by the edge of the water and stared for a long time moodily into the shallow and dying sea.

# 10

Nicky drove down the long, gradual descent to the Salton Sea. The land here looked like a moonscape from an old movie. It was all strangely familiar. Most of the science-fiction movies he had seen as a kid had been filmed in this particular desert outside Los Angeles. He half expected some thirty-foot insect to come lumbering up from behind one of the great boulders.

He could pull out his ray gun and shoot the monster dead, but today, he was looking for a different kind of monster, one that came not from outer space, but from the nearby metropolis beneath the smog.

And where should he look?

The desert was so vast that Nicky wondered if he had made the right decision to come here by himself. It seemed almost impossible to find two people in an area this size. He soon arrived at his first choice: whether to take the road down the west shore or the one to the east.

Nicky decided to try the west shore first. The two-lane highway did not run directly next to the sea. In some places, it was as much as a half mile away from the edge of the water. Dirt roads ran off the main highway every hundred yards or so and traveled over the desert to the shore. Some of these roads were marked by signs with grandiose names: Golden Shores Trailer Park, Sunny Acres Retirement Community, Paradise Beach Camping and Recreation. Nicky followed them all, through the dust and heat to their disappointing end. It soon became obvious to him that the Salton Sea was no mecca for the rich and the beautiful. The trailer parks and cabins generally turned out to be a sad collection of aging structures inhabited by a breed of leathery old folk living out an inexpensive retirement in the sun. There were a surprising number of churches—mostly of a fundamentalist sort—erected next to the odd trailer parks. A static aura of complete nonmotion enveloped everything here. This was a place where the universe had come to a halt: the people, the buildings, even the sea, which was not disturbed by so much as a ripple of wind.

Nicky had arrived here just after four-thirty in the afternoon. The sun was falling low above the mountains to the west, but it was still incredibly hot. He had long since shed his jacket, but he kept up the canvas top on his car as a slight protection against sun and dust.

Methodically, he traveled up and down each dirt road, stepping out with his shirt-sleeves rolled up, to show his drawing of Lawrence Ferguson to old and incurious eyes.

"Excuse me, I'm from the Los Angeles police. Could you tell me if you've seen this man today?"

Old hands would take the drawing, look at it slowly. "No-ope, I don't believe so. . . . Martha, lookee here. You seen this fellow today? . . . No, nobody come here at all. Sorry, mister."

And he would be on his way.

Some of the dirt roads went nowhere, simply ambling through the desert, without apparent rhyme or reason. Or if they had a destination, it was long forgotten. Nicky wasted precious time, winding up and down these old tracks. He spent more than a half-hour at one point trying to find his way back to the main highway, afraid he was hopelessly lost.

Darkness began to fall by six o'clock. It came swiftly, as the sun sank behind the mountains. Halfway down the western shore, Nicky stopped at a gas station to fill his tank. He showed his drawing to an ancient Chinese man who pumped the gas. "No-o, don't look familiar to me."

He bought two cold sodas from an antique machine, the likes of which he had not seen since he was a boy. He gulped them down, one after the other, then rolled back the convertible top of his car. Now that the sun was no longer beating down upon him, he preferred the greater visibility of having no roof above him. Lt. Nicholas Rachmaninoff kept on looking.


# 11

Lawrence and Susan were seated at the small Formica table next to the kitchen window. Lawrence left the curtains open so he could watch the last part of the sunset in the far western sky. The Salton Sea reflected the brief orgasm of bright colors and then subsided into night.

"Would you pass the green beans, please?"

Cassie pushed them rudely in his direction, but he pretended not to notice. He remembered seeing a lady on a TV talk show saying that relationships were difficult and required work. So okay, he would try. This was, after all, a chance in a lifetime. He would show her how understanding he could be; that he could forgive and forget. Perhaps then she would care for him the way he cared for her.

To celebrate their first night together, he fixed up what he considered to be quite a gourmet treat: an entire chicken, precooked and packed in broth in a large can, as well as green beans and new potatoes, also from cans.

Everything had been heated on the ancient gas stove and now lay in various containers on the table. He couldn't find anything more elegant than a frying pan to serve up the chicken, but he had two candles on the table, and—for improvising in a motel—he thought it all looked quite nice.

They sat at opposite ends of the table, each with a Coca-Cola and a bathroom glass full of ice. Lawrence thought that Cassie looked absolutely lovely, though a bit subdued. He had handcuffed her ankles to the kitchen chair, but left her completely free from the ankles up. Cassie was going to behave herself now; she had promised. Just in case, he had his .38 tucked into his belt. But that was also out of sight, like the handcuffs. Lawrence didn't like to think of these things. Above the table, at least, they looked like a perfectly happy couple. If someone walked past the window, he might believe they were on their honeymoon. Perhaps.

"Well, it's not exactly the Polo Lounge," he said pleasantly, trying to make conversation. "But not a bad meal, don't you think? Have you ever stayed at the Beverly Hills Hotel?"

She grunted.

"I'm sorry? What was that?"

"No."

"Oh, you really must sometime. What a nice hotel that is! Truly elegant. I, uh, was there for three weeks just recently, and I must say, whenever I'm in Beverly Hills again, I'll certainly stay there."

She poked at her chicken, thinking she must keep her strength up. But she was not hungry. She was still feeling sick to her stomach, and the chicken looked remarkably like a stillborn fetus. The meat fell off the bone in greasy chunks.

"But, of course, you must go to wonderful hotels and restaurants," the man was saying, a strange animation lighting up his unhealthy face. Cassie seemed to be avoiding his eyes. "I can hardly imagine your wonderful life," he said. "The places you go to, the people you know. Tell me . . . what's it like to be a famous television star?"

She shook her head and groaned. "Oh, God! I just can't believe this is happening."

"*Tell me!*" he cried petulantly, with just a little threat in his voice.

"Okay," she agreed wearily. "It's a job you do, just like any other, except you get up very early and you have incredible amounts of pressure on you all the time, and you work very long hours, under very hot lights, and at the end of the day you are so tired you are usually in bed by nine o'clock. Is that what you want to hear?"

"I realize it must be hard work," he agreed reluctantly, "but, golly, the rewards! The travel! The houses! The parties . . . tell me about the parties you go to. What's it *like* to be a famous star and go to a party where everybody else is rich and famous and good-looking? I mean, what do you all talk about?"

Susan looked at the ceiling in frustration. "Oh, Lord," she prayed, "why is this happening to me?"

*"Tell me!"* he demanded.

"You want to know about parties? Okay. First of all, in Hollywood, generally the only people who have time to go to parties are the ones who are out of work. Do you got that? If you are successful and working, especially in television, you've got to be such a workaholic that you wouldn't be able to relax at a party anyway, even if you *did* have time. And let me tell you, if you make your living, like I do, by looking good, you sure as hell better not show up on the set in the morning hung over, with bags under your eyes. Or it's adiós, Charley. Are you getting a picture of the glamorous life? Shall I go on?"

Lawrence shook his head and laughed. "I don't believe you," he said, "I've seen the way you people look at the Academy Awards and the Emmys. Gosh, do you remember the year you sat in the same row with Robert Wagner and Farrah Fawcett *and* Mr. T? Why, it's like a dream come true. I think that maybe . . . maybe you have forgotten what it's like for the rest of us who aren't stars and don't have money, and don't live in nice houses. We can only *look* at your houses and cars and beautiful faces."

Susan quietly studied the hollow-faced man who had kidnapped her.

"Look, why don't you let me go," she said. "I'm not the person you want to be having dinner with. You want some fantasy that doesn't exist. Someone who doesn't ever have to go to the bathroom."

"Don't remind me of that," he said sternly.

"You see what I mean? You don't want someone who's real. The best thing for you is to keep your fantasies and just let me go. Believe me, fantasies are best when they are just in your head."

Lawrence gazed at her seriously. Suddenly he leaned back, clapped his hands together, and laughed. "Oh, Cassie, what an actress you are! You almost had me going there for a second!"

"Oh, shit!" she complained wearily.

"Cassie!" he shouted. "You don't swear! Remember that. I don't want to have to warn you again."

She nodded. He smiled, and his voice became very pleasant again.

280

"Now tell me about the time you caught that tennis star," he asked eagerly. "How did you know the heroin was in the tennis racket?"

"Oh, Lord! Gimme a break!"

*"Cassie!"* He brought the gun up from his lap and pointed it at her. "All right, I'll tell you . . ."

After dinner, he tied her once more to the bed, both hands and feet. He tried to make her as comfortable as she could be under the circumstances, propping up her head with a pillow so she could watch television while he did the dishes.

The only English-speaking station, from Palm Springs, was showing a made-for-TV movie about a one-legged athlete who won the Special Olympics. It was not a genre that Lawrence was particularly fond of, but he kept the show on, since there wasn't anything else.

"I feel just like an old married couple," he said, scrubbing out the frying pan in which he had heated up the chicken. She did not answer, which was just as well. Lawrence found that he could drift along for five or ten minutes at a time, and then she would generally say something to spoil it. Really, he was just as glad for her to remain quiet.

"You certainly didn't eat very much, my dear. No wonder you keep that wonderful figure of yours. Maybe I'll make chicken salad sandwiches for lunch tomorrow. Would you like that?"

"What I'd like," she responded savagely, "is for you to let me go."

"Ah . . . methinks the girl protests too much! You know who said that? That's Shakespeare, a true judge of human character."

"Crap!" she muttered softly. Lawrence heard her, but decided to let it pass. He was feeling too good to want anything unpleasant to come between them. When he finished the dishes, he came back to the bedroom and sat down on the other bed. He did not look at television, however, but at her. Even in jeans and an old jersey, and none too clean from the passage of the day, Cassie was stunningly beautiful. Touchingly vulnerable, he thought, as she lay tied on the bed.

Susan felt his eyes upon her in a different way from before. Her body tensed with a new apprehension. Hours earlier, she had considered the possibility that he might want to have sex with her, but had rejected it—thinking he most likely wasn't even capable. Now she was not so sure.

"You are so-oh beautiful," he said softly. "Do you know how long I've dreamed of being alone with a woman like you? I . . . I can't put into words what it means to me to have you here with me."

She turned away from him, as far as her bonds would allow. This talk was making her very nervous.

"Cassie? I love you," he whispered. He reached out and let his hand rest on her upper leg. She jerked as he touched her, but the hand remained firmly upon her.

"Don't touch me!" she said through clenched teeth. "Please take your hand off of me."

"Would you like to take a shower?" he asked. His hand wandered slowly up the side of her thigh to her stomach, slipping under the jersey to bare flesh. "Wouldn't you like to freshen up a bit?"

"Only if I can lock the bathroom door," she said angrily. "Otherwise I prefer lying in my own filth."

"Now, Cassie, I feel there is a special connection between us. You don't have to be afraid of me. You can show me your real self, as you really are. That's why you can take off your clothes for me."

He reached for the button at the top of her jeans.

"No!" she screamed and jerked around so roughly that he pulled back. "Get away from me. I hate you!"

"You don't mean that," he cried. "You are everything to me . . . please, Cassie. I know you'll feel differently about me after a while."

"Just don't touch me. I'll try to be friends with you, only if you *don't touch me!*"

He stood over her, looking down. "Listen to me, I'm forty-seven years old and I've never made love to a beautiful woman. Don't you think that's a terrible thing?"

She tried to reason with him. "You can't force a woman to make love with you," she protested. "Love has to be given."

"Then give it to me," he demanded. "I've waited too long for this, don't you see? There's no turning back. All I want is just once in my life to make love to a beautiful woman. *Just once.* After that, I really don't care if I die."

"Not me," she said firmly, glaring at him.

"Oh, I think you are wrong, my dear. I've decided that life is definitely too short not to take what you want. And I very much want *you.*"

He reached once more to the button on her jeans. She squirmed frantically and screamed, but he was able to open the button and pull the zipper down. Still, Susan was much stronger than he was. She pressed her ass hard against the bed and kept her legs rigidly together, so that try as he might, he could not get her pants more than halfway down her hips.

He struggled for a long time, until he was exhausted and panting for breath. He was able to get her jeans just low enough to see the top of her golden triangle, but no more.

It seemed that most of his life was like that: to see enough to be tempted, but never be able to obtain the goal. At last, he stopped struggling and staggered into the kitchen where he had left his gun.

He returned to her, brandishing the .38.

"If you don't let me take your clothes off, I'm going to kill you," he shouted. The gun was trembling in his hand.

"Then go ahead!" she shouted back. "You still won't get me. I'm tired of you waving that fucking gun in my face."

He brought the pistol up to her head.

Susan stared at him, never taking her eyes off him for a second. *She would not allow herself to be raped again.* Once was quite enough for any lifetime. Now that she had taken her stand, she felt very calm and unafraid.

Lawrence held the gun against her forehead for what seemed a very long time. Susan met his eyes, staring back into his cadaverous face, not certain if this was her last moment on earth. However, she was a woman who was used to getting her own way. She was haughty and proud and angry. Susan stared him down.

Lawrence did his best to meet her indignant eyes, but at last, he sighed piteously and let the gun fall limply to his side.

He just couldn't do it.

Wearily, he shuffled out of the cabin to the front porch, sat down in one of the canvas chairs.

And cried.

# PART
# TEN

*The Chocolate Mountains*

# 1

It was after nine o'clock when Nicholas Rachmaninoff rounded the southern tip of the Salton Sea and headed up the western shore. He continued to explore each dirt road and bone-grinding trail, discovering churches and trailer camps and old motels, but not a middle-aged ex-accountant with his captive prize. After the burning heat of the day, the desert at night seemed as cold and impersonal as the billions of bright stars that shone down upon him. The vastness of the landscape seemed mocking of his efforts. But Nicky did not allow himself the luxury of getting discouraged. He just kept on.

It was nearly eleven when he came to the faded sign announcing Aladdin's Magic Carpet Resort Cabins. The sign was unlit, and he passed it before the wood frame caught his eye.

Wearily, he backed up on the highway and swung into the dirt road. His twin headlights shot off in crazy directions as he made his way over the twisted landscape. Something was knocking in his engine, banged loose by the abuse of too many roads just like this one. When he arrived at the office, he parked and walked to the front door. Aladdin's Magic Carpet Resort Cabins looked pretty much like all the other places he had seen on the Salton Sea. The office was dark, but an outside porch light was switched on as he closed his car door. Mrs. Gotch, clutching onto her bathrobe, peered out from the screen door.

"Hello there," she called. "We're closed for the night, but I guess I can give you a cabin anyway. I wasn't asleep yet."

"Good evening, ma'am. Actually, I'm from the Los Angeles police. I was wondering if you could help me," he began, as he had so many times since his arrival here. "We're looking for a man named Lawrence Ferguson. Would you take a look at this drawing and tell me if you've seen him today?"

She blinked at the name and took the drawing. Nicky was instantly alert, feeling something in her manner that had been absent in the dozens of other motel owners and managers he had talked with.

"Well, let's see now." She studied the drawing carefully. "My eyes ain't so good anymore. I'm not quite certain. Why are you looking for this fellow, anyway? He break the law?"

"Oh, nothing like that." Nicky laughed pleasantly. "His friends are just worried about him. You see, a doctor told him he had cancer three weeks ago, and he simply disappeared, left his job and everything. We're just hoping to find him and convince him to get medical attention."

She handed him back the drawing. "You ain't a very good liar, son. Ain't no cop from Los Angeles going to be nosing around the desert this time of night for an innocent reason like that. I may be a hick, mister, but I ain't no fool."

Nicky smiled. "I can see that's true, ma'am. Now why don't you just tell me which cabin he's in. I'm not exactly a fool either, and you'd just as soon not get yourself in trouble with the law."

"Well, I just don't like to have my guests disturbed, that's all. And I don't like to be threatened. But if you've got to know, you've got to know. He's in cabin number ten."

The hairs on the back of his neck prickled and stood on end. Nicky turned his back to the old lady and looked out to the desert night, alert to any hostile sound.

"Where is cabin ten?"

"You go down the road there to the water and turn left. All my cabins are right on the sea. Number ten is the last one."

Nicky started off in the direction she indicated.

"You can drive down there if you want, mister," she called after him.

"Thanks, but I think I'll walk."

Nicky hurried off down the dirt road, opening his jacket and pulling out his revolver. As he moved away from the light of the office, the desert seemed to open up and engulf him, like a living thing.

Mrs. Gotch watched him walk away. "You be gentle with him now," she called out. "Mr. Ferguson is a nice man. Just a little bit lonely, that's all."

Nicky was already too far away to hear her.

She shook her head. Mrs. Gotch knew all about being lonely. The desert was the right place for lonely people to be. She was tempted to take the shortcut and warn Lawrence of his unexpected company. But she was no fool. It didn't pay to get involved; that was the number-one rule of loneliness. She went back into her cabin, locked her door, and minded her own business.

# 2

**N**icky passed the line of dark cabins, walking as quietly as he could in the soft sand, just off the gravel of the road. Number 10 was off by itself, around a bend in the road, with an orange van in front. He saw there was a dim light inside the cabin, masked by cheap yellow curtains. A television set was on loudly. Voices of a disembodied love scene, underscored by swelling strings, drifted out into the desert night.

Nicky crouched and stood very still. He listened and watched for movement. With the thumb of his left hand, he removed the safety catch on his revolver and took several careful steps toward the van.

He stopped. On the porch, someone had sighed and shifted position on a chair. Nicky stared in the direction of the sound, until he was able to make out, in the deep shadows, the denser shape of a human being.

A breeze came up from nowhere and moved restlessly between himself and the cabin. Nicky stood like a statue. He hardly breathed. The shape on the porch abruptly stood up, sighed once again, and leaned over the railing. The new position brought the person in profile against the light of the window.

It was Lawrence. He was perhaps twenty feet from where Nicky stood. He could see no sign of Susan. Was she inside the cabin? He raised his gun and decided to creep a little closer. But the slight movement made Lawrence turn his head and look directly his way.

For just a second, Lawrence did not seem to see him. Then his eyes opened wide with recognition.

"Don't move," Nicky said softly. "I have a gun."

Lawrence's own pistol was resting on the porch railing. In the darkness, Nicky did not see his hand reach for the gun until it was too late.

The first shot was deafening, bursting through the intimate stillness of the tableau. Nicky heard the bullet go by horribly close to his right ear.

He fired back immediately, but missed by a half-dozen feet. He had always been a terrible shot. Lawrence ducked below the porch railing and crawled toward the cabin door. Nicky aimed carefully, fired, and missed once again.

"Damn!"

Lawrence shot once more in his direction. Nicky heard the electric *zing* as the bullet passed close to his side. Instinctively, he dove down into the gravel, rolled to his left, and came up crouched and ready to fire. A good move—but Lawrence was already inside the cabin.

"Don't shoot!" came a voice from inside. "I've got Cassie with me. I'll kill her if you come any closer!"

"All right! Don't hurt her," Nicky shouted back immediately.

"Get away from the cabin!" came the hysterical, high voice from inside. "Get away from here and leave us alone!"

"Lawrence, listen to me! All I want is Cassie . . . give me Cassie and you're a free man."

There was no answer. Nicky waited a minute, with his gun covering the front door. What was happening in there? He called out again. "Lawrence! Let her go. I'll help you get out of here safely. But you've got to let Cassie go."

Nicky moved closer to the door, at an angle he hoped would give him a glimpse inside. He tried to keep the van between himself and the cabin, so he would have some cover when Lawrence finally emerged.

He heard something, a strange laugh from inside. He wasn't sure, but it sounded like Lawrence said "Boy! This is just like a scene from 'Cassie and the Cop.' "

# 3

Lawrence fumbled with the ropes that held Susan to the bed. His hands had trouble obeying the commands of his brain. Eventually, he managed to set her legs free, and her arms, but he kept the cuffs around her wrists.

"Now you listen to me, young lady. I don't want any more trouble from you," he told her. "You do exactly what I tell you to do, or I'm going to shoot you. I don't have a thing to lose. You understand? I'm a desperate man." He liked saying that. He said it once again. "A desperate man!"

She nodded. The man was smiling so strangely that it frightened her more than his gun. Hearing Nicky's voice shouting from outside had filled her with temporary elation, which deflated quickly. There was still an immense distance between them.

Lawrence led her to the front door, while he stood behind her, the gun at the back of her head.

"We're coming out!" he shouted through the open door. "I'll kill her if you do anything foolish. Where *are* you?"

"I'm over here, Lawrence," Nicky said in a soothing tone, from where he stood near the van. "No one wants to hurt you. Let's just relax . . . I'll do whatever you say."

Lawrence pushed Susan out on the porch, keeping her between himself and the policeman. She stared at Nicky with great, pleading eyes. Nicky forced himself to look not at her but at the man behind her. He saw the gun at her head. He had his own revolver held out ahead of him, in the classic firing-range position, ready to pull the trigger the second he had a clear shot.

"Put your gun down," Lawrence demanded.

"No way," Nicky responded pleasantly. "If I do that, you'll just shoot me."

Lawrence could not fault this logic; it was exactly what he had intended to do. The policeman was a mere fifteen feet away. He was tempted to shoot anyway, but in the dark there was no telling how it would turn out.

"All right. Your gun doesn't scare me. Step backward. Slowly now, no sudden moves. I want you all the way down by the edge of the water."

Nicky did as he was told, but he kept his gun raised and pointed at Lawrence, maintaining the stalemate between them. He stepped backward slowly, letting the distance between them increase. All the time, he talked soothingly. "I had lunch with Molly Young today, Lawrence. She is very worried about you. No one blames you for what you've done. We're all very worried about you and want to get you into a hospital so we can make you well. You know, cancer really can be treated today."

"Shut up! Keep going backward, all the way into the water."

"Good idea. Hey, I've been dying for a swim! It sure has been a hot day."

Nicky was not being quite as flippant as he knew he must sound. He was following clear police procedure in dealing with a hostage situation of this kind. The theory was that talk of any kind tended to defuse the situation. Nicky hoped this was true. He could feel Lawrence's tension: coiled, dangerous, unpredictable.

"Hmm, the water's great. You know, I think I could get to like the desert, though I'm really an ocean person myself. Know what I mean?"

"*Shut up!*"

He eased into the blood-warm water, until it was up to his chest. He was careful to keep his gun dry. Lawrence, well out of effective pistol range, moved with Susan to the back of the van. He opened the rear door and ordered her to get inside. The second pair of handcuffs was still hanging on the metal bar. He was about to attach her to this dreaded bar once again, but the thought of being chained again in this hideous fashion was too much to bear.

Susan rebelled. She lashed out with her arms. But Lawrence had seen it coming, telegraphed in her eyes a fraction before she actually moved. He already had the pistol above her. He simply brought the butt of the gun down hard on her head. As far as Susan was concerned, one moment she was there; the next she was not. Her legs dangled out the back door. Lawrence hurriedly pushed her all the way inside and climbed in himself, shutting the door and climbing over her unconscious body to the driver's seat.

Nicky, from his position in the water, knew something had happened, but he was not certain what. The van's engine started up like a sleeping monster; the headlights flicked on, illuminating the desert, catching a jackrabbit, which froze in the sudden glare. Lawrence raced away, back up the dirt road to the office and the highway beyond. He gave one last wild shot in Nicky's general direction, and then disappeared over a rise.

Nicky pulled himself out of the water and ran, dripping wet, up the road toward the disappearing headlights. His car was waiting a few hundred yards away, by the office. Panting for breath, Nicky jumped in and fired up the engine. In the distance, the van's headlights were in and out of the terrain. Nicky decided to leave his own lights off, hoping he wouldn't be spotted. He followed as quickly as he could, half standing over the windshield to get a better view of the dirt road. But the van had a substantial head start and made it to the paved highway at least five minutes before he did. On the main road, Lawrence accelerated sharply. Nicky watched the headlights moving away at a great speed, afraid he would lose them entirely. He sped up, until he was half flying down the last stretch of the bumpy road. He turned on his lights now, to go faster; the van was too far away to see him anyway. At the main road, he turned north and raced through the gears, straining the engine, until he was up to ninety-five. His only chance lay in the fact that the Austin-Healey was much faster on pavement than the bulky van. In the distance, the headlights followed the gradual curve of the road, until they disappeared behind a low hill.

Nicky let out a string of four-letter expletives that did him no good. He sped up as much as he dared, with a terrible feeling that if he lost Lawrence this time, he might never see Susan alive again.

In less than a minute, he reached the curve where he had last seen the orange van. Nicky followed the road around the base of a small, squat hill. Around the bend, the highway stretched out in a straight line over many desert miles, disappearing finally into the night.

But there was no van. No headlights. No Lawrence. No Susan. As far as the eye could see.

"Damn fucking hell!" he shouted, and slammed down his foot on the brake, so that the car skidded and swerved to a stop.

Where could they possibly be?

Nicky turned off his engine and headlights, stood up on the seat of his car and scanned the rocks behind him. As far as he could tell, there was no place by the foot of the rocks where a van could pull off the road.

The desert had apparently swallowed them.

Gradually, his ear became accustomed to the stillness around him. He heard a car engine not too far away, but he could see nothing. Slowly, he turned in a semicircle, peering out into the night, until he was facing the highway once again.

There was still nothing to see.

Yet he heard the engine quite plainly now, laboring in a low gear. The van had simply become invisible.

At last he saw a cloud of dust moving away from the highway across the desert toward the mountains. The dust seemed to run parallel to a row of high-tension electric towers; perhaps there was some kind of service road there.

Nicky sat back down in his car, turned on the ignition and drove without headlights to the spot, a half mile away, where the high-tension wires intersected the highway.

The dirt road wasn't much, hardly more than tire tracks through the desert. Under ordinary circumstances, Nicky would have been very doubtful of even attempting such a road without four-wheel drive. But tonight he did not hesitate. He just did it, turning off the highway and hoping for the best. He raced along at a high rpm in second gear, hoping if he went fast enough, his car wouldn't have time to settle in the soft sand. For a half mile this tactic seemed to work. Most of the road passed over a fairly thick gravel crust, with just a few spots where his rear wheels spun helplessly in the sand before getting a grip on firm ground. But the road got worse rather than better, until he was simply driving through the sand; without his headlights, he wasn't even certain there *was* a road anymore. By some act of mental levitation, he was able to maneuver his Austin-Healey over another quarter mile of desert, before the car sank inevitably into deep sand up to its fender. The engine coughed and died.

"Damn!" His frustration was so great he was bereft even of his usual swear words. The cloud of dust in the distance kept moving toward the mountains—by what magic, Nicky could not imagine. Perhaps it was a simple matter of wider tires and a higher wheel base. Whatever: He himself was stuck, while Lawrence continued on. Nicky was able to start up his engine again, and he tried to rock his way out of the sand trap, rolling back and forth. But it was useless. All his efforts only succeeded in getting himself more completely buried.

He watched the van drive away, knowing he had really fucked up this time: made the wrong decisions all the way down the line. If he had only gone to Chief McWilliams as he was supposed to do, he would have had three or four helicopters at his disposal, as well as dozens of armed men. Instead of which, he was alone in the desert, stuck in the sand, and Susan was in greater danger than ever.

He hit the steering wheel disgustedly with the palms of his hands. If ever he needed help, the time was now. At least he still had a radio in his glove compartment, though he was a long way from Los Angeles, and he was not certain whom he could raise from here.

He took the mike in hand and pressed the send button. "This is Lieutenant Rachmaninoff, officer in distress. Can anybody hear me? I need assistance. Come in, please."

A crackle of static was the only response.

He tried again.

"This is an officer in distress. Can anyone hear me?"

A voice, very loud, came through suddenly on the speaker.

"This is Gilroy to officer in distress. Give me your name and location. Over."

294

"Gilroy, this is Lieutenant Rachmaninoff. I'm a few miles west of the Salton Sea, on a service road going up toward the mountains. I'm in pursuit of an armed suspect with hostage, and I need urgent assistance. Over."

There was a slight pause from the other end. Then: "Please repeat your location. Over."

Nicky, unfortunately, had no idea where he was, but he tried to describe the service road more carefully, with reference to where he had left the sea.

There was another pause. A new voice came over the speaker. "Lieutenant, where exactly are you calling from? Over."

"The Salton Sea, for God's sake!" he shouted in frustration. "South of Palm Springs. Over."

"That's Palm Springs, as in California? Over."

"Yeah. Where else would Palm Springs be? Over."

"Well, this is Gilroy, Oklahoma. Holy smoke, boy, how'd you get all the way here? Over."

Nicky held on to the microphone and stared out into the bizarre science-fiction landscape of the desert at night. He felt as if he had just entered the Twilight Zone.

He pushed the send button once more. "Can you record this transmission? Over."

"Affirmative. Tape has been rolling since first signal of distress. Over."

"Okay. Please telephone Captain David Molinari at the Beverly Hills police station." He supplied the number and area code. "Tell him that Nicholas Rachmaninoff needs urgent helicopter assistance, at given location. I am in pursuit of the Car Killer after an exchange of gunfire. He is in an orange Chevy van, holding Susan Merril hostage. My car is stuck in the sand, but I'm about to continue pursuit on foot. Thanks, and over and out."

Nicky stuffed the microphone back into his glove compartment and jumped out of the car. He went around to the rear and opened up the trunk. He had a spare box of ammunition hidden away beneath the tire jack. He took out his revolver, reloaded the two bullets he had fired, and then stuffed the remainder of the shells into his jacket pocket.

Not knowing what else to do, Nicky began to run across the desert, after the retreating cloud of dust.

# 4

**L**awrence also found the desert road tough going, but he managed to get almost a mile farther than Nicky had, before the wheels of the van sank once and for all into the shifting desert sand. Ahead of him, the Chocolate Mountains lay perhaps another half mile away. The moon, almost full, was trying to rise up from behind these hills, illuminating their smooth contours in a silvery silhouette.

To Lawrence, it looked like an enchanted landscape. He was neither happy nor sad to reach the end of the road. Unlike Nicky, he did not try to rock his vehicle backward and forward to free himself from the sand. He simply turned off the engine and let it be.

On the floor in the back, Susan groaned and shifted position. He had not been certain she was still alive. Lawrence stepped outside, and walked around the van and opened the rear doors to look in on her. He was greeted by a sour body smell that made him wince. There was a clot of blood on the top of her head, where he had hit her with the butt of his gun. She stirred uneasily, at the verge of consciousness. The girl did not look very glamorous this evening, but Lawrence did not imagine she had suffered any great harm.

He fetched the plastic jug from the front seat and came back to pour water over her head. Susan returned to consciousness, sputtering for breath. "Oh, my head!" she moaned. She sat up and looked around uncertainly, not knowing where she was.

Lawrence enjoyed the girl's confusion. Her eyes, at last, came to rest on him. They grew very wide, as memory came flooding back.

"Where's Nicky?" she asked, after a moment.

"I killed him," he lied. "There's only you and me now."

She winced at his words and looked away. A single loud sob came from deep inside. Tears fell down her cheeks.

"Come on, out of the van," he ordered. "We've got some walking to do."

She didn't move.

*"Get out of the van!"* he shouted, furious that she was crying about the policeman. He grabbed her handcuffed wrists and gave a tug so that Susan fell out of the back door onto the sand. Lawrence pressed

the muzzle of his gun into the back of her neck. "I'm getting really tired of this, Cassie. I've been very nice to you so far. But I'm not going to take any more of your sass. Do you understand?"

Susan was kneeling in the sand, sobbing.

Lawrence slapped her hard across the face, with the back of his free hand. She fell over on her side, crying louder than before.

"Get up," he told her. When she didn't move, he screamed at her: *"Get up!"* Susan struggled awkwardly and slowly to her feet. Her tears gradually subsided, and she gazed at Lawrence with a dismal hatred and resignation.

"Okay. Let's start walking."

"Where to?" she asked wearily.

"Well, my dear," he said with a smile, "we are going to visit the Chocolate Mountains. Doesn't that sound like fun?"

He made a broad gesture to the dark shape of the nearby hills. Susan sighed, but she turned and began the arduous hike across the sand. Lawrence followed behind her, pressing the .38 harshly into the back of her spine whenever she tried to slow down.

Before long, the moon rose above the soft hills and shone for them the way.

# 5

Nicky ran through the desert, as fast as he could go. He was not in great shape. The best he could say about his body was that its natural strength had not been completely depleted by the general high level of abuse he heaped on it. He eased himself into a regular rhythm. After some time, a needle of pain shot through his right side. He kept running anyway, and it gradually subsided. His feet sank into the sand, which made it more difficult, but he ran and ran, and never slackened his pace.

When the moon rose above the hills, the entire landscape changed, bathed in a surreal silver light. Ahead, not more than a quarter mile away, he could see the van now quite clearly. It had stopped moving, and two figures were walking away from it, heading directly toward the moon and the mountains.

Nicky quickened his pace. He ran until he thought his heart would burst; and he still kept running. In the expanse of desert, everything was farther away than it appeared. At last, he passed over a small rise and then raced down toward the open doors at the rear of the van.

It was empty, as he had already surmised. He collapsed on the sand near the back door, gasping for breath. His heartbeat and breathing gradually returned to normal.

A pistol shot cracked the air like thunder. It came from no clear direction, echoed against the mountains, and subsided very slowly, until there was just a whisper in his ears. Nicky jumped to his feet and looked desperately toward the hills. He could not see a thing.

Just one shot, but it frightened him more than anything else had this evening.

He took a deep breath. His legs felt like rubber, but he began running once more into the moonlight, up the long valley toward the spot where he had seen the figures disappear. He was torn between his desire for haste and his absolute horror of what he might find.

A few hundred yards from the van, Nicky came across a sign nailed to a post. He soon saw there were many signs, just like this one, spread out across the desert floor. They all said the same thing:

WARNING

YOU ARE ENTERING A U.S. MILITARY RESERVATION

DANGER

ARTILLERY TEST RANGE

Nicky jogged on by. He had never been a great believer in road signs and other warnings. This one he did not even consider.

# 6

The moon turned the desert into a soft carpet of light. Not far past the signs that warned against entry, the land began to tilt upward at a gradual but significant angle. Nicky felt like someone caught in a dream: he ran, but seemed to make no progress. Eventually, he slowed down to a fast walk. The hills ahead of him were absolutely devoid of vegetation—simply mounds of rock molded by the winds. As Nicky continued, the ground beneath him changed from sand to gravel, so that at last the going became a little easier.

Ahead, a small piece of metal lay on the gravel, reflecting the moonlight. It shone like a small star. Nicky pulled out his revolver and approached cautiously. He was at the base of the hills, among a rubble of giant boulders. Behind any of these boulders there could be death. He stopped and listened for any sound, however slight.

There was nothing. This was the most desolate and empty landscape he had ever seen. A few feet away, the piece of metal glittered in the gravel. Nicky crept toward it on his hands and knees. It was the empty casing of a .38 shell, still reeking of gunpowder. He held it, while his eyes scanned the rocks above.

What had happened here? For the next twenty minutes, Nicky crept about the area until he gradually realized he was alone. He found a few footprints, but not many. Mostly, he was encouraged by what he didn't find, for there was no body, and no sign of blood.

He decided to continue up into the hills. Near where he found the shell, a crevice made a natural trail upward. He kept his revolver ready in his left hand and began to climb, alert for any sound. He followed the course of least resistance into the mountains. Nature had conveniently provided a series of switchbacks that took him swiftly a thousand feet above the desert floor. From here it was a matter of scrambling up over the boulders. He climbed for more than half an hour in this manner, until his face and arms glistened with sweat.

About three quarters of the way to the top, Nicky stopped to rest on a giant boulder. The view from this height was astonishing. The desert stretched out in the moonlight to the Salton Sea, which was jet-black, shimmering with pieces of broken silver. The dry air filled his nostrils. A slight breeze had come up, moving through the rocks like uneasy spirits.

Inexplicably, the hairs on the back of his neck stood up. Nicky realized he was not alone.

# 7

**L**awrence walked toward the Chocolate Mountains with Susan a few feet ahead of him.

She was not Cassie O'Day; he knew this now. The girl had told him the truth. Playing Cassie had been only a job. Susan Merril was not much more than a kind of glorified head accountant. She was young, she was pretty, she even had a lot of money. But basically, she was not so different from him.

This was a hard truth to come by. Lawrence's own life may have been lonely, repetitive, and dull. But he had always been a believer.

Somewhere, somehow, he believed there must be glamour in this world, beauty and adventure. A place where bold people did exactly as they pleased. But glamour was like a desert mirage: As you approached, there was a point where the illusion suddenly dissolved, leaving nothing in its place. Lawrence had a strange feeling, walking toward the mountains with a gun in his waistband. *He* was the bold one, doing as he pleased. *He* was the stuff of which he had always dreamed.

It was all quite different from what he had imagined. And soon it would all be over.

Occasionally, Susan would stumble or try to stall, and he had to urge her on. Lawrence wasn't certain what he wanted from her now. But he was not quite ready to give her up. When they reached the base of the mountains, she stopped and turned to face him.

"That's it," she said. "I'm not going a step farther. You're going to kill me anyway. It might as well be now."

Lawrence pulled the .38 from his waistband and pointed it in her direction. She glared at him defiantly.

He fired, aiming a few feet to her right. The explosion was deafening against the stillness of the night. Susan screamed and brought her hands to her mouth. He pointed the gun directly at her, but she did not need any more encouragement. She turned and began to climb up the crevice into the rocks. Lawrence smiled contemptuously. Susan had not been hard to manipulate.

They followed the crevice for as long as it went, zigzagging up the face of the mountain. From there, they moved in and out of the boulders, finding footholds where they could. It was tiring work. Lawrence felt himself possessed of an uncanny strength, but eventually they reached a point where he agreed to stop. Susan stretched out wearily on top of a flat, smooth boulder. He took a position a few feet above her, at a spot where he could keep an eye on her and also enjoy the spectacular view of the desert and the far-off Salton Sea.

He loved it up here. For thirteen years he had gazed up at the Chocolate Mountains from the desert floor; now at last he was up in their heights, looking down. It was where he had always wanted to be.

Lawrence felt at peace. In the stillness of these mountains was a hint of the eternity to come, an intimation of the vast indifference of the physical world toward man.

Below him, the girl was breathing rhythmically. She seemed to be asleep. Lawrence himself was beyond exhaustion. He felt at some plateau of time and space where ordinary concerns no longer applied.

A sound, far below, disturbed his meditation. He stretched forward, peering over the edge of his boulder, and saw Nicky climbing up the crevice. He thought he had lost the policeman long ago, when he had turned off his headlights and left the highway for the service road into the hills. His first reaction was anger. This was really too much, to be followed here into the cathedral sanctity of these rocks! Why couldn't people just leave him alone?

Then he smiled and brought out his gun. He had been wise enough to carry along a box of shells in his pants pocket. Careful not to make any sound, he pulled out the spring clip from the butt of the gun and reloaded. Susan still appeared to be asleep; she lay on her side, in a fetal position, her cheek against the smooth rock. Lawrence turned over on his belly, leaning just a bit over the edge of his boulder, so he could see what was happening below. Adrenaline flowed through his body and made every sensation sharp. This was an unexpected final treat—to hunt, as he had in the streets of Beverly Hills, and experience this dangerous exhilaration one final time.

For the next fifteen minutes, he watched Nicky climbing slowly up the boulders, moving in his direction. The policeman climbed without much grace, and he seemed to be unaware of any danger for him in these rocks. At one point, Lawrence heard him swear very distinctly, as he hit his knee against a rock: "Fuck sucking hell!"

Whatever that meant! Lawrence did not have much sympathy with people who used that kind of language.

He waited patiently, until the policeman eventually stopped and stretched out to rest on a boulder that was a dozen feet below him, and at a slight angle to his right. Lawrence, from his prone position, held the .38 in front of him with both hands and aimed along the sights of the barrel. This was not the best shot he could imagine, but he knew he would be at a great disadvantage if Susan woke up right now.

He decided he would chance it. He held his breath.

"Nicky! Look out!" Susan screamed.

Lawrence fired. It would have been a fatal shot, but Nicky had a fraction of a second to react to Susan's warning, and rolled out of the way. Lawrence fired quickly, two more times. The bullets ricocheted among the rocks. Susan continued to scream hysterically, but her ex-husband had managed to roll off the boulder unharmed. He was now safely under cover.

A movement at the periphery of his vision made Lawrence turn. Susan was about to throw herself on him. She looked wild, crazed with anger. Her fists, still in handcuffs, were raised to smash down upon him.

But Lawrence had the higher ground. He kicked out with his feet, and Susan was sent sprawling backward, off the boulder to the hard ground several feet below. She landed with a thud and a sharp cry. He slipped off the rock and came down next to her. Susan was on her back, breathing hard. He brought the gun up next to her temple. This was a moment he had been dreading. He had to kill Susan now. There was no way he could handle her and the policeman at the same time.

She looked up at him. *She knew.*

"I'm sorry," he said softly. "Look at the moon. It'll be easier."

But she only looked at him, into the eyes of her death.

He kissed the palm of his hand and then placed it over her eyes. He didn't want her to see what he was about to do. Her skin was warm and soft; she felt as vulnerable as a child. She was trembling.

That's when he knew he couldn't do it. Not now, not ever. He took his hand from her eyes and stroked her blond hair one last time. Susan was watching him with a dread curiosity, her mouth a little open with surprise.

Without another word, Lawrence turned and left her, and began to climb up into the higher rocks.

## 8

icky? Where *are* you?"

"I'm here," he called back softly. "Are you all right?"

"I think so . . . I feel terrible."

They were out of sight of each other, hidden behind different rocks. Nicky had heard Lawrence climbing away into the higher ground, but had not wanted to shoot, afraid he might hit Susan. At this point, he had no idea where Lawrence might be.

"Nicky?" she called out again, from the rocks somewhere above him. "He told me he killed you." She started to cry.

"Shhh . . ."

"Nicky, where *are* you?"

"Susan, for God's sake, *shut up!*"

She was crying and babbling, nearly hysterical. "Here I've had this absolutely *horrible* day, with this *horrible* man sticking his gun in my face all the time, and now you're telling me to shut up. I just don't know if I can take it anymore, I really don't."

Her coherency ended; heavy sobbing took over. Nicky crawled out from behind his boulder and began to make his way toward the sound of her voice. He stayed mostly on his hands and knees, and kept very close to the rocks. He had good cover most of the way, but even when he was forced to move through the open, there was no sign of Lawrence in the rocks above. Within a few minutes, he crawled around a boulder and found Susan lying on the ground, curled up in a ball, still crying, though more softly than before.

Nicky took her in his arms. Her tears were refueled by the relief of seeing him. Nicky held her for a long time, though he kept looking about for any sign of life in the upper rocks. It was impossible to relax, with Lawrence still on the loose.

"What happened just now?" he asked, when her tears had died away a bit. "Why did he let you go?"

"I don't know. I thought he was going to kill me. He had the gun against the side of my head . . . then he just walked away." The memory of this brought on fresh tears. Nicky was becoming decidedly nervous, sitting on the ground holding a sobbing woman while there was a killer somewhere not far away.

"Look, Susan, we're still in danger here. I know you've been through a lot, but you've got to get a grip on yourself. You hear me?"

"Okay," she said. "I'm going to be all right."

"Do you think you can walk?"

"I don't know ... I guess so. Everything hurts like hell, but it all seems to be there. Can you get these handcuffs off me?"

He studied her wrists. "It's going to have to wait. I don't have anything to spring the lock. Now listen to me, Susan. In a moment, I'm going to start shooting up at those rocks above us, to give you some protective cover. When I do that, I want you to scramble on down out of here and go for help. Okay? You've been knocked around a lot, but I know you can do it."

She looked up into his eyes suspiciously. "What are you going to be doing?"

"I'm going to get that fucker," he said. "If it's the last thing I do."

She shook her head emphatically. "Let him go, Nicky. You and I are safe—what else is important, for God's sake? Just *let him go!*"

He gave her one last hug, and then gently—but firmly—disentangled himself. "Look, Susan, I have to do this. Anyway, I've radioed for help," he said, not mentioning the circuitous route his call for help was taking. "There'll be police helicopters out here before long. What you've got to do is go back to the van, and when the helicopters come, show 'em the way."

He smiled optimistically, but she only shook her head. "Damn it, Nicky! Can't we both just get the hell out of here?"

"Look, I haven't come this far just to let Lawrence Ferguson get away now. Okay?" He brought out his revolver and spun the cylinder. "Are you ready?"

"I guess so," she said with resignation "You always were the most stubborn person I ever knew."

Nicky aimed at the higher rocks and began to fire, methodically, six shots in a row. When he stopped to reload, he glanced down to check Susan's progress. She was making good time and had arrived at the top of the trail-like crevice. He was very glad to see she was well out of the range of fire.

# 9

Alone once more in the desolate hills, Nicky had to face the fact that he did not know what to do next. He didn't even know exactly where Lawrence was.

The only real chance he had was somehow to get on higher ground. He looked about for any possible route up to the higher rocks. There was, of course, the way Lawence had gone, from boulder to boulder. But it didn't seem wise to follow in the killer's footsteps. He soon saw another possibility. Not far from where he crouched, a steep crevice went straight up the side of the mountain, like a chimney, for forty or fifty feet to what appeared to be a ledge. Could he climb this? he wondered. Not only was it steep, but he would be exposed to gunfire, if Lawrence was anywhere nearby.

It was a hard choice. Also, although Nicky wasn't frightened of heights, he wasn't wild about them either. All in all, his field of expertise did not lie in scrambling about rocks and shooting at people with his gun. He was much more effective sitting in people's living rooms and prying their secrets apart.

Probably the wisest thing he could do would be to edge his way down the mountain and scurry off to safety, waiting with Susan for the reinforcements to arrive. Perhaps with a few helicopters and several squads of men, they might be able to dislodge this middle-aged accountant from these rocks.

It was all rather embarrassing.

A man like Lawrence Ferguson should not have been able to take them for such a ride. But somehow—by some unlikely miracle—he had held the high ground all along.

It was probably Nicky's ego that led him finally to take a chance. He took one more look at the chimneylike crevice, shook his head in dismay that he was actually going to attempt this, then went for it.

The climb was straight up. Nicky didn't dare look down or think too much about what he was doing. He used his hands and feet, like a spider. Most of the time he had no real footholds, but simply wedged himself between the crevice walls and just kept going up.

At least Lawrence did not take any shots at him. His only adversary here was Mother Nature. Halfway up, he stopped to rest, wedging

As it had been from the beginning, Lawrence was just one step ahead of him. Nicky had only enough time to think: *Damn! He got here first!*

Then a gun was fired that was not his gun. He felt as if a freight train had hit him in the stomach. The force of the bullet lifted him off his feet and threw him onto his back.

Lawrence was a few feet away, walking toward him slowly, with a strange, twisted smile on his lips. He raised his gun for the final shot.

Nicky watched it all in slow motion; he had all the time in the world. He smiled when he realized that being left-handed was finally going to have some earthly use, other than playing blues piano. It might even save his life.

Lawrence was no fool. He was approaching Nicky very cautiously. *But he was looking at the wrong hand.*

Nicky raised the gun in his left hand and fired six times until it was empty.

Despite the fact that he was no great shot, two of the bullets actually found their mark: the first shot, fortunately, which hit Lawrence directly in the heart and immediately put an end to his forward progress. And the last shot, which grazed the dead man's ankle. The other four shots flew off in the general direction of the moon.

Nicky kept squeezing the trigger, spasmodically, hearing a dry clicking sound as the hammer fell on the empty chamber. With his right hand, he clutched his stomach and felt the blood ooze between his fingers.

Strangely, it didn't hurt. He simply felt cold and far away. The moon, he noticed, was many times brighter than he had ever seen it before. A few feet away, Lawrence also lay on his back. But Lawrence's eyes did not blink, and his free hand did not bother to clutch at the blood that was escaping from his body.

"Well ... well ... well," he said softly. Or thought he said, because no words actually emerged from his lips. "Who would have thought it would be like this?"

Nicky was very glad he was on his back.

The view of the universe was magnificent. A shooting star streaked across the heavens. Just like an astral orgasm, he thought.

He liked that. It made him smile.

An astral orgasm ... oh, yes, we are all little pollywogs of spermal desire, shooting forth to our end. What does it mean, oh, what does it mean?

The pain began gradually, emerging from the shock. Lt. Nicholas Rachmaninoff clutched his stomach, gazed at the stars, and waited to die.

# 10

Artillery practice began promptly at dawn. The first shell came whistling out of the southeast and landed on the ledge a half mile from where he lay. The explosion shook the ground.

Nicky opened his eyes. He must have been dozing. He had been having a wonderful dream that he was playing an enormous white piano. A beautiful melody had come effortlessly to his fingers, as they flew across the ivories with a virtuosity that he had never before possessed. It was all so easy.

He didn't know what woke him, but he closed his eyes and tried to return immediately to the pure land of music. The melody still lingered in his ears. *Next time around, I'm going to be a musician,* he thought. *Fuck this policeman bullshit!*

Another shell came screaming through the air and landed much closer than the first. The explosion was overwhelming, sending up a plume of dust and smoke far into the sky. In rapid succession, five more shells rained down through the air and shook the earth. Nicky lay on the gravel, waiting to be blown apart. Then, as suddenly as it began, the barrage of artillery fire was over. Smoke drifted away across the far valley, the sky cleared, and there was utter silence.

Nicky smiled in some amazement. It looked pretty silly, bombing a dead landscape. He was glad he didn't have to do this sort of thing himself anymore. Lying on his back in the desert, with a bullet in his gut, was providing him with many new and interesting thoughts.

That is when he noticed, for the first time, the dozens of large birds that were flying in lazy circles not far above his ledge. He thought they were rather nice to look at, until he realized the significance of their presence.

It made him remember, suddenly, that he had missed his dinner date with Charlie Cat last night at Le Coq d'Or ... poor Charlie! He must have been pissed as hell.

Nicky had a fond image of Charlie, with his round, hedonistic face, those twinkly eyes, sitting down at a great table with nice linen and silver, crystal glasses, and a great plate of duck à l'orange set before him. . . . Oh, yes, Charlie, you were really very close to understanding the meaning of life. But you just got it backward. The point of life is not to eat but to be eaten.

Nicky looked up at the vultures above him, and he had a strange perspective that all his life was simply a direct route to this moment; all that pizza and beer, just to fatten him up to become bird food.

So what do you think about that, Lawrence Ferguson, you old son of a bitch! You and I know that life is for the birds.

Nicky turned his head, with some difficulty, to get a look at his comrade in death.

Ah! he said, with a sudden new understanding.

A busy highway of ants was flowing across the desert, up Lawrence's cheek, and disappearing down his half-open mouth to the goodies inside.

Life was not only for the birds, but the ants as well.

How strange it was! Some things you always knew, deep inside: like the fact that one day someone was going to shoot you in the stomach. Other things came as a surprise, like the final knowledge that you were just the main course of someone else's dinner.

None of it mattered very much at all. At the last moment, Nicholas Rachmaninoff looked up to see a shadow fall upon him. There was a rush of air and a beating of wings, as a great bird, larger than the others, descended from the sky to carry him away.

# Epilogue

The helicopter that swooped down from the sky saved not only Nicholas Rachmaninoff's life but his career. For in the helicopter—besides the pilot, Captain Molinari, and Susan Merril—was an enterprising photographer from the *Los Angeles Times* who had managed to come along. The photographs he took appeared the next day on the front page of every large newspaper in the nation.

The first picture, which later won many prizes for photojournalism, was shot from the air as the helicopter descended. It showed the policeman, still clutching his revolver, lying only a few feet away from the Car Killer. The angle was such—and the two men positioned in such a way—that it was considered by many to be a classic portrait of cat and mouse, pursuer and pursued, frozen in eternal mortal combat.

The second photograph, not nearly so arty, was the one all the newspapers used. This was taken after the helicopter landed, and had Susan in the foreground, prostrate by Nicky's side, in apparent grief for the uncertain fate of her savior and ex-husband.

Actually, Susan had just noticed the road of ants flowing in and out of Lawrence's open mouth, and she was retching violently on the gravel—giving the photograph its vivid air of gut-wrenching despair. The truth of the matter was carefully omitted from the newspaper accounts. The highway of ants likewise disappeared through a little darkroom magic. In its edited form—suitable for family viewing—the photographs made Lieutenant Rachmaninoff an instant media star.

The rescue of a nationally known television personality by her ex-husband cop was more than news—it put less interesting matters such as the budget deficit and disarmament talks on the second page. Police Chief McWilliams was no fool. The L.A.P.D. had few heroes and needed all the good press it could get. The mechanisms of departmental discipline, which had been primed and ready to come down hard on Lieutenant Rachmaninoff, were hurriedly reversed and revised for commendation instead. The mayor would present Nicky with a medal in a high-visibility ceremony as soon as he was well enough to stand in front of the television cameras.

As for the object of all this attention: Nicky lay oblivious, near death in an intensive care unit for two days, before being transferred to a private hospital room when his life was judged out of danger. He lay in a pleasant morphine mist, in a land where vast birds soared effortlessly upon gentle breezes and the sky was soft with a strange white light. It was not a bad place to be, and he was not particularly anxious to return to the less paradisiacal world of L.A.

One afternoon he decided it was probably time to open his eyes. He found Susan above his bed, looking down on him. He closed his eyes quickly, but it was too late.

"Oh, Nicky, darling! How do you feel?"

He smiled vaguely, and she kissed him softly on his lips. "You don't have to talk, darling. You're going to be all right. I've been so frightened, but it's all right now. You're going to get well and then we'll be together, Nicky. I'm not going to let you go again. I've talked with Frank, and he's been awfully understanding. I'm going to move into a bungalow at the Beverly Hills Hotel just until we can figure out what's happening. Maybe we can get married again, don't you think? We can live at the beach and have a whole new start . . . Nicky? Sweetheart?"

He had closed his eyes and was drifting back into the sky, far away. For quite some time he glided in and out of the clouds, performing gentle acrobatics. Gradually, after a long time, he became aware of a new presence in the room. He recognized her scent.

"Julie," he said, his eyes still closed. He felt her smooth hand holding his own.

"How are you, Nicholas?"

He opened his eyes to look at her. Julie was dressed conservatively in a dark skirt and jacket, with a strand of pearls around her neck. Her hazel eyes shone down on him.

"I brought you a newspaper," she said. "I thought you might enjoy seeing your picture on the front page. You know, you're quite a hero now, Lieutenant Rachmaninoff."

Julie placed the newspaper on his bedside table, but Nicky looked only at her. She was more beautiful than ever.

"It's crazy outside in the hallway," she told him. "You'd hate it. With all the cops and reporters and your ex-wife looking at me like she wanted to claw my eyes out, I wasn't even certain I was going to get in to see you. Luckily, Frank Fee came to my rescue and helped me get in. He's a nice guy for a movie star, but he sure comes on fast. After about thirty seconds, he tried to invite me for lunch at some hideaway in the valley."

"Are you going?" he attempted, though he had trouble speaking and it came out simply "Goin'?"

She laughed slyly. "I think I'll pass on it. It did occur to me, though, that if I could steal Frank from Susan, then *he* would be the ex-husband and Susan could get all nostalgic about him and leave you alone. Does all that make sense? We would make a perfect Hollywood foursome, don't you think?"

Nicky grunted unintelligibly; this was way beyond his present powers of comprehension.

She took his hand again. "Seriously, Nicholas, I can see that Susan has you staked out as her own property, and I don't really blame her. I know you two go way back, and if you could make a go of it again, Christ, Tanya would be in heaven. I wouldn't want to be the one to stand in the way. Anyway, I've got a better idea. Susan can be your wife, but I'll be your mistress. Okay? I think I'm more the other woman than the wife anyway."

Nicky tried to speak, but the words were inaudible. Julie had to put her ear close to his lips. He tried again.

"Who gets my liver?" he asked.

She looked incredulous for a moment, but laughed, kissed him one last time, and then was gone. Nicky tried to return to the pleasant land of soft mist, but it was no longer there. He lay restlessly before remembering the newspaper Julie had brought. Dimly curious, he managed to reach to his bedside table and unfold it; not an easy task with an IV needle in his arm.

The photograph he saw on the front page had a dreamlike quality and raised goose bumps on the back of his neck: Lawrence in the background, lying on his back, and Susan kneeling by his own wounded body, in an attitude of devout prayer. He stared at the picture for some time, fascinated, before his eyes moved down the page to the caption underneath.

"Holy shit!" he cried aloud. "I don't fucking believe it!"

When the nurse came into the room a few minutes later, she found her patient laughing wildly—small giggly bursts that would cease, only to rise again, in an ever-greater crescendo of laughter. She knew that people who have just been shot in the stomach do not generally lie in bed laughing, so she immediately summoned a doctor. Together, they gave Nicky an injection that for another twelve hours returned him to the land of gliding birds.

The nurse was an older woman, with a kindly face; her children were grown and gone, her husband was dead. She was a little lonely, and when the policeman was completely asleep, she took a few minutes to tidy up his room. She saw the newspaper on the floor, picked it up, and smiled. The photograph on the front page was quite powerful, she decided, and the caption underneath was really very cute.

She read it again and sighed: "CASSIE AND HER COP."

Her favorite show.